"You're seducing me again," Suisan said, but heard no complaint in her words.

****

He grinned and raised his eyebrows. "You've tickled me, right enough, lassie." He twirled the quill pen and tickled her with the feather. "What do you intend to do about it?"

A sigh of longing lodged in her throat.

He leaned closer. The quill fell to the table. Then his lips touched hers, and the world seemed to drift away. He tilted his head to the side and brushed his mouth across hers, his tongue tracing the sensitive edge of her lips. Suisan pulled him closer and opened her mouth wide, wantonly hoping his mouth would cover hers again.

It did. And suddenly she was out of control. Excitement robbed her breath, and desire stole a forbidden path from her whirling mind to the aching core of her womanhood.

He pulled back and said, "Come to my room tonight."

****

Threads of Destiny

Arnette Lamb

POPULAR LIBRARY

An Imprint of Warner Books, Inc.

A Warner Communications Company

POPULAR LIBRARY EDITION

Copyright © 1990 by Arnette Lamb
Popular Library® and the fanciful P design are registered trademarks
of Warner Books, Inc.

Cover illustration by Lisa Falkenstern
Hand lettering by Carl Dellacroce

Popular Library books are published by
Warner Books, Inc.
666 Fifth Avenue
New York, N.Y. 10103

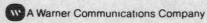 A Warner Communications Company

Printed in the United States of America

First Printing: August, 1990

10 9 8 7 6 5 4 3

To Marcella Lamb

For all those times you said,
"Keep writing, Arnette,
and you'll get published."

Thanks, Mom, for believing in me.

Many thanks to my literary best friends and Thursday night pals: Barbara Dawson Smith, Susan Wiggs, Joyce Bell, and Alice Borchardt.

To Elaine Kimberley, a bonny, bonny lassie, who answered hundreds of questions about her homeland and taught me about things Scottish.

Threads of Destiny

·~ *Chapter 1* ~·

London, 1760

"Nelly?"

"I'm here, Lady Suisan," the maid said softly, her familiar voice cutting through the London night.

"You mustn't call me that!" Suisan hissed, both hands gripping the high sill of the cellar window, fear and anxiety evident in her voice.

The maid spat an expletive in Gaelic.

"Nelly!"

"Oh, very well." The servant girl squatted on the pavement above her mistress. Nelly's blonde braids brushed the damp windowsill. When their faces were on a level, she said, "Maura." The name seemed to be pulled from her. "But I don't see why we have to pretend when no one else is about—except the rats, the cats, and the gin-soakers."

Suisan's hands began to shake. "We'll be pretending in Newgate gaol awaiting the hangman if we're not about our business carefully."

At once serious, Nelly asked, "Did ye find them, then?"

"Aye, they were hidden in a rickety old box beneath a case of brandy."

"Where?"

"'Neath the basement stairs."

"The accursed, thievin' lout," Nelly spat.

"So he is," Suisan agreed, then lowered her voice. "Put your hand out and I'll pass one up, but have a care now, and don't be scratchin' it on the bricks! 'Twill ruin the sett.'"

"Yes, milady."

"Nelly . . ." Suisan warned.

The maid did as she was told, but even in the faint glow of the nearby lamppost, her fingers looked too small for the task. Suisan felt the weight of the wood leave her trembling hands.

"This one's a bit unwieldy," Nelly grunted, breathing hard.

"Like the Lochiel Camerons themselves."

Nelly giggled, the sound a nervous whisper of her usual jollity.

"Shush!"

"I've got it, an' by the saints, 'tis a gift from God to touch it again," Nelly said. "Will ye pass me another?"

"Could you be managing more than one?" Suisan asked, doubtful.

"Well, no, but goin' slow as this, 'twill take months to rescue all of them."

"Then so be it. We'll not return to Scotland without each and every one."

"Did Himself arrive?"

"Not yet, and the staff's in a dither over his absence."

Nelly's sigh of relief was audible. "Saints be with us and mayhap we'll get all of them out of here before the greedy bugger comes home."

"My thoughts precisely."

"But, then again," Nelly said thoughtfully, "I'd trade away my dream of a lusty night with Lachlan Mackenzie to be a mouse in yer pocket the first time you see that scurvy rat, Myles Cunningham."

"Let's hope he's not as bad as Uncle Rabby says," Suisan whispered.

"You'll be careful, milady? He knows your face from that portrait your uncle sent him."

"Of course I will. Truth be told, I've had an easy time of it so far. He hasn't bothered to hang the portrait. No one suspects me to be more than a servant, but *you* must watch your words."

"What about our cloth? Did you learn why we're paid such a paltry price?" Nelly asked.

Anger welled up in Suisan again. "I found Myles's ledgers. Seems he pays Uncle Rabby more for the cloth from Strathclyde than he does for ours."

"That dog-faced nitwit. 'Tis a wonder he came to the wealth he's got, bein' as how he can't tell fine cloth from privy rags. Those scunners from Strath got no right to call themselves weavers. We see that well enough every spring at Glasgow Fair."

"I'll worry over finding a new market for the cloth later. We've more important business to see to now."

Nelly groaned, then darted a glance down the London street. "Oh, no!"

"What is it?" Suisan balanced on tip toes and strained to see beyond the cellar window.

"Someone's coming," Nelly hissed.

"I suspect it's Mrs. Mackie. Off with you then, and come back in two days' time."

"Yes, milady."

"Go . . . and Godspeed, my friend."

"Aye, Maura," the maid said, with too much emphasis on the false name. "St. Ninian's blessing on us both."

When Nelly was safely away, Suisan stilled her shaking hands. The old metal hinges creaked as she swung the window closed. The latch clicked shut. Her heart beat like a drum in her chest but she willed herself to be calm. Caution and patience were necessary if she were to complete her dangerous mission here in London and return to Scotland.

Gingerly, she stepped off the wooden box she had used to reach the high window. After brushing her footprints from its dusty surface, she walked across the dark cellar to the small table between the wine racks. She picked up the lamp and moved toward the narrow steps. Eerie shadows danced on the stone walls and ceiling.

By the time she stood in the elegant upstairs hallway,

Suisan had once again assumed the servile demeanor of the maid she was pretending to be. The familiar chiming of the great case clock in the parlor soothed her. Gone was the apprehension, gone the fear of being discovered. Both were replaced by determination and more anger than she wanted to feel. She hated acting the thief in order to regain her mother's precious legacy, but what other choice did she have? The danger she and Nelly faced was secondary to their will to succeed. They had already managed to move one of the treasures to safety.

Suisan thought of Nelly, alone, picking a dangerous path through the darkened, smelly mews as she made her way back to Beacon Row. She prayed Nelly would be safe.

Suddenly, the front doors crashed open, thudding against the silk covered walls. Suisan gasped and stepped back. The glass chimney of the lamp she held rattled against its pewter base. Without thinking, she stilled the fragile glass with her free hand, burning her fingers. The stinging of her skin seemed a distant pain as she stared, transfixed, at the man who stood in the doorway.

His greatcoat swirling in the night wind and his arms burdened with the weight of an unconscious man, Myles Cunningham stepped into the foyer of his London house.

"Mackie! Will'am!" he bellowed, his deep voice echoing through the sprawling mansion. Then, moving easily despite his burden, he headed for the great mahogany staircase.

Suisan's feet moved but her voice refused to co-operate. Stunned, she stared at the man Myles carried. His name was Ollie Cookson. He, too, was from her past.

"You there!" Myles called to her. "Light the way upstairs."

Not a flicker of recognition shone in his dark brown eyes. And why should there be? Her distinctive red hair was dyed black; she was no longer the reed-thin little girl who had pestered her adopted brother each time he returned home from the sea with her father. Momentarily bolstered by the effectiveness of her added years, her womanly figure, and her dark hair, she held the lamp high, picked up the hem of her homespun skirt and started up the stairs.

"Where's Mackie?"

"Visiting her daughter, sir," Suisan answered as they rounded the landing.

"Damn!"

"She said she'd be back tonight," Suisan offered.

He continued up the stairs. Seemingly unaffected by Cookson's weight, Myles took the steps two at a time. Suisan had to hurry to stay ahead of him.

"In here," he said, stopping before a closed door.

Suisan opened the door and stood aside. Myles strode with the unconscious man to the bed.

Cookson's bed, Cookson's room, Suisan thought. Too many years had passed since she had last seen Ollie Cookson and the image she remembered of the bearded man was influenced by the child she had been. Ollie seemed smaller and older now. He lay deathly still, his eyes closed and his mouth opened.

"Did you hear me, girl?"

She jumped at the sound of Myles's voice. "No, sir," she stammered.

"Bring the light," he repeated. With an economy of movement he drew the greatcoat from his shoulders and tossed it onto a nearby chair. Then carefully he began to remove Cookson's boots.

She stepped closer to the bed, but her eyes remained on Myles's face. He was not the man she thought he'd be after all these years. She'd expected him to be weak; he was strong. She'd expected dissipation; he was dashingly handsome. She'd prepared herself for cold indifference; his brow was furrowed with concern. She'd anticipated cruelty; his large hands were gentle on the injured man.

She stared in confusion while strong emotions warred within her. Familiarity tugged at her heart and stole her breath, and the pain of Myles's betrayal of her—of all Scotland, settled rock-like in her breast. She hated Myles Cunningham, and yet the little girl she had once been still saw him as her conquering hero. Pushing aside her childish notions, she reminded herself she was a grown woman, one well-acquainted with the treacherous deeds Myles Cunningham had committed.

Cookson groaned, drawing her thoughts away from Myles

and their past. Moaning, the white-haired man tossed his head back and forth. Myles swore under his breath, then pulled a wicked looking knife from his boot and cut away the leg of Cookson's trousers.

"Easy, friend," Myles soothed. "We're home now, and soon Mackie'll fix you all up."

Suisan studied the two men. Ollie Cookson was Myles's steward, just as he had been her father's steward. The last time she'd seen Ollie had been at her mother's deathbed in Aberdeen. Suisan had been ten years old then. The day of the funeral had been the last time she had seen Myles Cunningham.

The knife clattered to the floor. Over his shoulder, Myles said, "Send Will'am for the doctor and fetch a bottle of brandy."

Anxious to be away, she set the lamp on the bedside table and rushed from the room. She found the boy Will'am in the stable.

"Mr. Cookson's been hurt and you're to bring the doctor straight away."

The boy's eyes widened in shock. "The master brung him?"

"Aye."

"Bet Himself's fit to be tied," he said with authority. "Thinks of Mr. Cookson as kin, he does."

The comment angered Suisan. Her father had been the one to raise Myles Cunningham, not Ollie Cookson! Defensively, she said, "Cookson'll be no one's kin if you don't go for the doctor!"

Will'am nodded and scurried off.

Her thoughts were spinning in confusion as she went for the brandy. Her first meeting in ten years with Myles Cunningham was not going as she'd imagined, but perhaps some good would come of the situation. Myles was preoccupied and that was in her favor; the less he looked at her, the safer she was.

When she re-entered the room, Myles was examining Cookson's leg, which was turned at an odd angle.

"Here's the brandy, sir."

He didn't answer but took the bottle. When he had coaxed Cookson into swallowing a generous portion, Myles put the bottle to his own lips and tilted his head back.

His thick, golden hair had come loose from the leather tie that bound it and hung in boyish waves about his face. In profile, his face seemed sterner than she'd originally thought. His nose was slender and blade-like, and his high brow was smooth. The skinny orphaned lad she'd known as a child in Aberdeen had become a dangerously attractive man. Against her will she smiled, remembering Myles tagging after her father and hanging on his every word. Those worshipful brown eyes were now worldly, and the gangly youth was now a fine figure of a man. Oh, yes, she thought bitterly, Myles Cunningham would turn the lassies' heads in any port he visited, and he visited many—thanks to the fortune her father had entrusted to him.

"Who are you?" Myles addressed her, but his eyes were trained on Ollie Cookson.

Even though he wasn't looking, Suisan made a proper curtsy and said, "Maura, sir. The new maid."

"What happened to the other one?"

Suisan had paid the girl handsomely to quit her post. "She returned to Leeds a fortnight ago. I've been here a week now."

He still did not look at Suisan when he said, "You're not from Leeds."

Apprehension raced up Suisan's spine. "No, from Scotland." She held her breath.

Quietly, he said, "My stepsister lives in Scotland. In Perwickshire. Know you of Roward Castle?"

Suisan thought she detected a sentimental note in his voice, but she had no time to ponder it. The topic of Scotland was dangerous ground. She must be very careful. "I hail from Roward, sir," she had to confess.

The admission got his attention. He turned to face her. She prepared herself for more questions and, possibly, recognition. He looked her up and down, then grinned. "Good. You can tell me how my sister Suisan Harper fares. She was away from the castle when I visited there last fall."

Relief, sweet and welcome, washed over Suisan; Myles hadn't an inkling—yet—as to her true identity.

He continued to stare at her, but she was saved a reply to his statement when Will'am ushered the doctor into the room. It was just as well. Now Suisan knew Myles Cunningham was more than a thief. He was also a liar. He had certainly visited Roward Castle; he had also stolen her most prized possessions.

The doctor began his examination of Ollie's leg. Shaking his head, he spoke softly to Myles, who continued to hover near the bed. Myles nodded, then turned to Suisan.

His braw face seemed pulled and his square jaw tightened. ''Fetch hot water and something to bind his leg,'' he barked. ''And I want Mackie up here the minute she gets back.''

His intense gaze was disconcerting, and his commanding tone rumbled in Suisan's ears. With great effort she turned away. Quietly, she eased out the door and hurried to the kitchen.

She filled the water kettle and hung it over the hearth fire to boil. Then she went in search of clean linen for bandages. The pantry was neatly organized, reflecting Mackie's fastidiousness. But unlike the well-stocked storeroom at Roward Castle, this pantry contained only a few medicinal aids.

Roward Castle. At the thought of her home, Suisan felt tears pool in her eyes. Were it not for Myles Cunningham's treachery she would be in her Highland stronghold, safe and sound. She promised herself that as soon as she found out the truth about the small price she was paid for her cloth and once the patterns were out of Myles's basement, she would return home and find a new market for her fabrics. And this time she would hide the patterns well.

She wondered why Myles had risked offending the English crown by stealing and harboring the ancient and outlawed sticks. She didn't understand why he would want them.

She gathered the medical supplies and returned to the kitchen. She looked up when she heard a noise from the back door. Mrs. Mackie, the housekeeper, hummed a tune as she let herself into the house.

''Good evening, dearie-do,'' Mackie cooed, her round face

tinted pink from the cool London night and most likely a buttered rum or two.

Unable to summon dislike for the woman, Suisan replied, "Evenin', Mrs. Mackie." as she helped the woman off with her cloak. "Master Cunningham's home." Suisan added, hanging the damp garment on a peg.

Mackie beamed. "'Tis a fine night for his return, too. And I wish you'd take to callin' me plain *Mackie*, like everyone else does."

Suisan sighed. Though she harbored no ill will toward the woman, she didn't plan to be in London long enough to develop a friendship with her. "The day's not been too bonny, Mackie; Mr. Cookson's broken his leg, I fear."

Mackie's hands flew to her cheeks. "No!"

"Aye, but the doctor's with him now, and Master Cunningham's calling for you."

Flustered, the housekeeper grabbed her apron and slipped it over her head. When the sashes were tied she said, "We'll be needin' boiled water, bandages and such."

"I've seen to it." Suisan walked to the table and began putting the rolled bandages onto a tray.

"Bring those along then," Mackie said. Wrapping a thick towel around the handle, she lifted the steaming kettle from its hook over the fire.

"I knew something like this would happen—yes, I did," Mackie huffed as they climbed the stairs. "That Cookson's been courtin' trouble in every grog shop from Londontown to Araby, and old age ain't slowed him down—"

A loud, agonized groan came from Cookson's room. Suisan winced and looked at Mackie. Her lips were pursed, her eyes alarmed.

"Mackie?" Suisan queried.

The housekeeper took a deep breath and began walking again. "Ain't no way to live, if you ask me," she went on, faster than before. "Cookson's too old to be keepin' up with the young master—yes, he is. Should've dry-docked his weathered bones years ago. But would he?" The corners of her mouth turned down and she shook her head. "Not for all the tea in China, he says. Says he's bound for the wanderin' life, he does. But this time won't be like their last visit home. Why, they'd hardly washed off the ocean's salt, and what does they do? They ups and goes off to visit that ungrateful chit in Scotland. And her not even havin' the good manners to be there to receive them after all these years.''

Mackie cast Suisan a knowing look. "You might think it proper to be loyal to Lady Suisan, comin' straight from her employ and all, but she's got a selfish streak in her, just like that odd Uncle Robert of hers in Aberdeen.''

Another groan, weaker than before, halted Mackie's diatribe. Suisan's first thought was to challenge the housekeeper's derogatory outburst, but she did not. Somehow Mackie had heard a twisted tale. Suisan guessed it had come from that thieving blackguard, Myles Cunningham.

"Mark my words, Maura girl, Cookson won't be doin' no wanderin' now, I'll wager." Her tone became light. "If his leg's busted, he'll be beached 'til harvest time. Yes, he will . . . and the master'll stay here with him.''

The housekeeper might be pleased at having Ollie Cookson home; Suisan was not. If anyone could ferret out her disguise and her purpose, Ollie Cookson might be the one. If that happened she would be at the mercy of Myles Cunningham.

Yet Suisan couldn't understand why Mackie would think Uncle Rabby an odd man, and why she believed Suisan ungrateful for being absent from the castle when Myles had finally deigned to visit. He had sent no word of his coming. She had responsibilities in Perwickshire and responsibilities to her uncle. In a fit of temper, Myles had left before a messenger could be sent to her in Aberdeen. She had been insulted beyond belief.

Her own temper flared. Myles had all but ignored her since her mother's death ten years ago. He had inherited her father's wealth and moved to London to live the decadent life of the rich. Thanks to Uncle Rabby's generosity, Suisan had been returned to her mother's ancestral home. Roward might be a crumbling castle and Perwickshire a district of poor bonnet farmers, but they were all she had. Since the Battle of Culloden, many clans were still estranged from their homeland, unlike the Lochiel Camerons.

Suisan vowed to tread lightly around the injured steward and Mackie. She could only hope to avoid Myles. Resolutely, she followed the housekeeper into the sickroom.

Cookson's face was twisted in a grimace of pain and his skin was as pale as the rumpled bed linens. Myles paced the floor, his hands clasped behind his back. His long fingers were knotted, his white knuckles jutting out as he clenched and unclenched his fists. The physician was still bent over Ollie's leg.

"Welcome home, sir," Mackie said.

"Hello, Mackie," he answered on a sigh and raked a hand through his hair. Casting a glance to the bed, he added, "Ollie's met with an accident."

Her florid face twisted into a crooked smile. "Seems more like fate to me, sir."

Myles emitted a half laugh.

"Ah, Myles," Cookson said, groaning. "Would you double my pain by giving me the devil's own nursemaid? Have you no pity, man?"

Myles chuckled and shook his head.

Mackie huffed up and declared, "You should know of the devil, Ollie Cookson. You've been courtin' his wrath since I was in nappies, and that's the God's own truth, yes, it is!"

"You in nappies?" Ollie countered weakly. "That'd be a picture to send any man running to the church, broke leg or straight."

"Enough, both of you," Myles commanded. "We've only just arrived after months at sea, and already you two are yammering like fishwives. I insist that you postpone this verbal battle at least until the doctor's set the leg."

Suisan, obviously forgotten in the heated reunion, tried unsuccessfully to stifle a giggle. The sound drew Myles's attention. He shot her a reproving glare.

"Find your bed, girl," he ordered. "We've enough hands here to put Mr. Cookson to rights."

She bristled under the command and very nearly challenged him; she was accustomed to giving orders, not receiving them. Cookson groaned again, and she came back to her senses. She was a servant here, nothing more.

Suddenly feeling the outsider, she put down the tray and went to her own room on the third floor. She didn't bother to light the lamp as she undressed in the dark and climbed into bed. Her mind was a confusing jumble of questions. Nothing about Myles's household was as she'd expected. She was curious as to why, but she was more concerned with achieving her dangerous goal and returning home to Scotland.

Pulling the covers up to her chin, she shivered, but not from the cold. She was afraid. Far from the home she loved and without the people she cherished, she felt vulnerable and lonely. Her imagination conjured the ultimate forfeit for her illegal mission—King George's soldiers dragging her, on charges she could ill understand, to the gallows like so many other Scots before her. Thoughts of her brave countrymen bolstered her courage. She would not scream, she would not cower. She was Lady Suisan Harper, by God! She was not some sniveling ninny ready to quail before the English; she was a descendant of the Lochiel Camerons, and she would succeed! Comforted by the thought, she closed her eyes.

After a fitful night of intermittent sleep and ghastly dreams of the hangman, Suisan dragged herself from the bed just before dawn and trudged downstairs.

The kitchen was cold, but the hearth was still warm. She added coal to the embers, put water on to boil and gathered the makings for scones, her only contribution to the fare at Roward. She sliced a ham and cut wedges of cheese, and nearly hacked off a finger in the doing. She gathered honey, butter and an assortment of jams. Just as she finished the preparations, she heard footsteps.

Himself.

Casually dressed in a gathered white shirt, tight fitting doeskin breeches, and bucket-top boots, Myles Cunningham strolled into the kitchen. Oddly, he seemed at home in the domestic room.

"Morning, miss," he said with a smile in his voice. Wrinkling his perfect nose and raising his tawny eyebrows, he asked, "Do I smell scones?"

She looked at him warily, wondering why the sight of him set her heart to racing. "Aye, sir," was all she could manage.

His brown eyes danced with pleasure. "That's a good Scottish lass. I haven't had scones since I was a lad of—" he paused, rubbing his freshly shaven chin with a thumb and forefinger, "perhaps . . . fifteen."

Suisan remembered those times, too. She'd been a clumsy but well-meaning five-year-old, trying desperately to recreate the scones her mother so effortlessly made, and Myles had been a slim and earnest youth of fifteen, equally determined to imitate her fat' r in every way. Discomfited, she said, "Take your seat i.. the dining room, sir, and I'll be bringing them in."

"I'll eat in here," he declared, seating himself at the oaken table. He wasted no time in slathering one of the hot, crusty scones with butter and honey. When it was gone, he reached for another. Uncomfortable in his presence, she headed for the pantry.

"Stay," he said, the sound muffled through a mouthful of scone.

Pretending she hadn't heard and twisting her shaking hands in the folds of her gray skirt, she kept walking.

"I asked you to stay, miss . . ."

She stiffened at his commanding tone. Then, remembering her charade, she forced herself to turn back meekly. "Yes, sir?"

He cocked a golden eyebrow again and said, "Miss . . . What's your name?"

"Maura," she murmured.

He frowned. "An ordinary name for such a pretty lass." When she flushed, he chuckled. "Don't be coy. Surely the braw lads in Perwickshire have said as much to you . . . among other things."

She felt an absurd pleasure at the compliment. Annoyed with herself and with him, she asked in a servile tone, "Would you like more tea?"

He chuckled again. "No, I'd like you to tell me about my sister, Suisan Harper. Now sit down and do so."

He spoke her name in the old, familiar way, the way any

Scot would. The pursing of his handsome mouth as he rounded the first syllable made Suisan go warm inside. She felt her animosity lessening. Why did this rogue, this thief, make her feel so fluttery inside? And how could he, in good conscience, call her his sister?

He made an event of laying his napkin aside and leaning back in his chair. "I do not tolerate disobedience. Not here." He waved an arm to include the house. "Nor on my ships nor in my warehouses. Put your shyness aside, lass, and speak to me of Suisan Harper."

Angered by his demanding tone and his constant references to his 'sister', Suisan decided to play her own game. With aplomb, she sat down and said, "Lady Suisan is the most beautiful woman in Perwickshire."

He roared with laughter and reached for another scone. Resting his elbows on the table, he said, "The truth, if you please."

Puzzled by his disrespect, and angered that her pulse raced at his nearness, she searched for something to say, anything to satisfy Lord Rodent, as she was beginning to think of him. "Lady Suisan is quite busy, most times, what with the weaving, and the people, and all. She's well-respected and dearly loved by all in Perwickshire."

"Were you her maid?"

"No, sir. Nelly's her personal maid."

"Nelly, Nelly, Nelly," he mused. "Is she fair and buxom and about my age?"

"Aye, sir."

He smiled. "Does her vocabulary rival a sailor's?"

It was Suisan's turn to laugh; Myles was correct.

"There was a time," he began conversationally, "in Aberdeen, when Nelly fair singed my ears with curses, and I was not inexperienced at the time, in spite of my youth." He shook his head slowly and his eyes softened, as if the memories were fond ones. "Half the words from her mouth were blue as a barmaid's. As I remember, Suisan's mother, Lady Sibeal, despaired of ever teaching Nelly manners, or proper English."

All of what he said was true. Against her will, Suisan

warmed to the subject. "Before his death, even the monk, Father Sebastian, threw up his hands at Nelly's language. Most people at Roward just ignore her and go on, but some say having a child dulled her sharp tongue." Suisan stopped, fighting back a wave of homesickness.

"And what does Suisan say?"

"She says she'd be right lost without Nelly."

"And what does she say about me? Does she ever mention coming to London?"

Suisan was taken aback. What was this blather? Why, after all these years, would he expect a visit from Lady Suisan Harper? Why, suddenly, did he care? She was assaulted by painful memories—memories of a lonely little girl, prowling the castle battlements and praying for his return.

She looked deeply into his eyes. His expression was so open and honest she was certain he expected to hear pleasant things about himself.

She could challenge him now, she could pound the table, she could demand to know why he'd treated her so unfairly, so cruelly, over the years.

"Lass, you shouldn't stare so boldly at a man."

The reproof brought her back to her senses. *Damn Myles Cunningham. Damn him to bloody hell.* "I've forgotten the question."

He chuckled. "I'm flattered, lass." Holding out his empty cup, he added, "We were speaking of my sister."

She took his cup and walked to the stove. Now that she wasn't staring into those enticing brown eyes she could think again. As she filled his cup, she asked, "What did you wish to know about Lady Suisan?"

"Most anything, I suppose. The monk taught her well?"

The tense moment had passed. "Oh, aye, sir," she boasted with good cause. Setting the cup before him, she added, "She speaks and writes French and Latin and English—Scottish, of course. She tallies the castle ledgers, oversees the looms and midwifes all of the—" She gasped, embarrassed at discussing such a topic with a man.

Myles's eyes crinkled with mirth. "And does she have suitors?"

"Nay, sir."

He didn't seem surprised. Suisan wondered if he knew the reason she could never marry. Surely not, for the secret had been well kept.

"'Tis time the lass married, in spite of—" He stopped and turned at the sound of footsteps. Suisan was more than relieved at the interruption. The topic of marriage and children was too painful, too personal.

Mackie entered the room. She looked tired and stiff. One hand cupped the back of her neck, and she rolled her head in slow circles.

"How is Ollie?" Myles asked.

"As bitter as a spinster on May Day," she grumbled.

"Is he in pain then?"

"He was, 'til I stuffed a measure of that tonic down his gullet." Suddenly her eyes twinkled. "When I left him he was sleepin' like a babe and snorin' loud enough to wake the froggies across the channel."

Suisan stifled a laugh.

"Good," Myles said. "Rest is what he needs. Have some tea, Mackie, and fresh scones."

"Scones?" She glanced at Suisan.

"Our Scottish lass has made a fine batch." He reached for yet another. "She's also been telling me of Suisan."

"Disrespectful baggage," Mackie spat, pouring herself a cup of tea. "And after all you've done for her!"

"Mackie . . ." he quietly warned.

Unaffected by his rebuke, Mackie went on, "The only good thing Lady Suisan's ever done is give our Maura here a recommendation, and a fine one it was. Bless King George, she managed to pick up a quill to do that." The spoon rattled against the cup as Mackie stirred the tea with vigor. "'Tis always the same with Lady Suisan. She acts your devoted sister when she's wantin' something, yes, she does, but other times—"

"That's enough! I'll hear no more criticism of her," Myles commanded, rising from the table. "I'll be at the docks; we're unloading the *Dream*."

Puzzled by their exchange, Suisan lowered her eyes just

as Myles left the room. She ached to find out why the house-keeper thought so little of Suisan Harper, but she wasn't given the chance to ask.

"I'm off to market," Mackie announced. "While I'm gone, you're to make the master's bed and begin the laundry."

Suisan's heart skipped a beat at the prospect of being in Myles's private chamber. Hiding her discomfiture, she asked, "The laundry?"

Mackie nodded. "The first mate brung their sea chests last night after you was asleep. And if we don't get to it quick, everything'll be mouldy."

"What shall I do?" Suisan asked in complete honesty; Nelly and Flora MacIver did the laundry, Rowena and the younger lassies did the cleaning.

Mackie adjusted her cap, picked up her basket and opened the back door. "Same as you do on any wash day—any-where, dearie. Have Will'am build a fire out back, then you bring the dirty things downstairs. I'll help you sort them out."

The door closed but opened again quickly. "And be sure to look in on Mr. Cookson."

"Yes, Mackie," Suisan replied evenly, though her mind was racing. Myles's bedchamber was the last place she wanted to go. She had sought a position in his household only as a means of getting her treasures back. Now she re-alized just what that involved. How could she avoid Myles and his curious stares if she had to make his bed, wash his clothes, and heaven only knew what else? How was she to manage the task of pretending to be a servant?

"Lassie?"

She jumped at the sound of his voice. He stood in the doorway, hat and coat in hand. His head was tilted to the side and a puzzled frown marred his handsome brow. Un-willingly, her gaze was drawn to his eyes, which were study-ing her intently. Anticipation, animosity, and no small measure of fear gripped her. She held tightly to the edge of the table.

Then Myles seemed to shake himself. Smiling brightly, he walked toward her. With their gazes still locked, he leaned over the table. She was surrounded by the scent of his shaving soap, an aroma reminiscent of her father. She held her breath and her fingers stiffened painfully as she tightened her hold on the table.

His face was only inches away and Suisan's heart pounded so loud she was afraid he'd hear it.

She felt herself flush under his scrutiny, and when he began a lazy examination of her shoulders and her breasts, Suisan thought she might slither to the floor.

"You've a certain look about you, lass," he said softly, his warm breath tickling her cheek. "Have a care with it, or you'll charm the wrong man with those blue eyes."

Her mind went blank. She was helpless to move away from him.

Finally, he straightened. "The scones were delightful," he said, as if the tense moment had not happened. He winked rakishly, tossed the last pastry into the air and deftly caught it. "I'll expect them every morning."

Then he was gone.

Suisan wilted into a chair and her breath came out in a rush. Her heart still beat like thunder. She was frightened by Myles Cunningham—oh, yes, she was. How could she ever hope to succeed in her mission if he continued to make her jump like a puppet on a string?

～ *Chapter 2* ～

Clutching Mackie's well-worn shopping basket, Suisan threaded her way through the crowd at Shepherd's Market. All around her fishwives and piemen loudly hawked their wares from gaily decorated booths and wagons. In contrast to the musical brogue of the Highlands, the hard-edged Cockney grated on Suisan's nerves.

An aproned maid offered crusty kidney pies and pints of bitter beer. The stench of offal, pigs and rotting fruit assaulted Suisan's nose. Compared to the crisp air and tidy paths of Perwickshire, London was a dung heap.

A little girl, smiling a toothless grin, sold daisies and tulips. Suisan's heart ached as she envisioned the Highlands as they would look now—blanketed with wildflowers and fragrant heather. The rich purple fields had been her playground and the elusive white heather a good luck charm she forever sought.

Homesick, and unable to resist the allure of spring, Suisan purchased a daisy and tucked it into her bodice.

The little girl smiled. "Thanks, mum."

Suisan wondered where the girl's mother was, and what kind of woman would turn her child out to work on the streets? Suisan would never be so neglectful a parent, but then she would never be a parent at all. A fierce, hurtful yearning burned in her breast. She willed it away.

A glance at the noontide sun told her she was late for her meeting with Nelly. Not until she had passed several stalls did Suisan spy the maid.

With her hands on her hips and a determined set to her chin, Nelly stood nose to nose with a dollmaker. Like her invincible Viking ancestors, Nelly was fearless. Her slender nose was dotted with childlike freckles; her pale blue eyes flashed with familiar defiance. Obviously unhappy with the dollmaker's price and unwilling to strike a bargain, she shook her head, sending her thick blonde braids swaying energetically.

"Do ye think me blind?" she railed, waving a doll, which resembled Sorcha, her yellow-haired daughter. "You'd skin me of my pension, you bloody Sassenach!"

Suisan tapped Nelly on the shoulder. The maid swung around and snapped, "Keep yer filthy hands to yerself or you'll wish you had! I was here first." Then her mouth dropped open as she realized her mistake. "Lady Sui—?"

Quickly Suisan pulled Nelly close and hissed, "Guard your tongue!"

Rebuked, Nelly glanced around to see if her indiscretion had been overheard.

"Never you mind," Suisan insisted, seeing the worry on Nelly's face. "Pay the man and let's be off."

Without further haggling, Nelly gave the merchant several coins. Gape-mouthed, he pocketed the money.

"Forgive me," Nelly said as they walked away. "My tongue'll be the death of me someday, but lor', I can't get used to your hair or you looking like that."

Suisan touched her hair. "The dye was a good idea."

Beaming, Nelly said, "Aye, 'twas. Who'd have thought you'd look so different with black hair—since your skin's so fair and all?" She chuckled, eyeing her handiwork. "Women all over London are wiggin' theirs up or tryin' for a true red like your own. We foxed 'em well enough."

Suisan smiled. "I should be used to the color by now, but every time I pass a mirror I have to look twice."

"We should be washin' and colorin' the roots today," Nelly said, still studying Suisan's hair.

"Please, yes." Suisan sighed with delight. "I've not had a real bath in over a week. Mackie doesn't approve of bathing, you know."

Nelly drew herself up. "She's not all bluff 'n go, then. You bathe too often to suit me—always have."

"Be that as it may, I intend to soak until the water's cold."

Nelly looked down at Suisan's basket. "Have you shoppin' to do?"

"A bit. Turnips and squabs for supper." She wrinkled her nose at the unsavory menu. "And I hoped to find a spyglass for Lachlan MacKenzie."

"I'll do your marketing, then meet you at Chipton's Retail. They've spyglasses there."

Suisan handed Nelly the shopping basket and turned toward Portugal Street. A troupe of actors paraded down the lane hawking their nightly production of a Wycherley bawdy and tossing wooden ducats and tin coins to the crowd.

When the troupe had passed she crossed the street and tried to pick her way through a cluster of gin-sodden street tramps. Disgusted at the sight of them and impatient to be on her way, she shot them an icy stare. Grumbling, they removed their caps and gave her the clean edge of the lane.

Chipton's Retail did indeed have spyglasses; the shop also had a skelly-eyed clerk who refused to show her the item she wanted unless she showed him her coin. She was about to demand he fetch the proprietor when a deep and familiar voice spoke from behind her.

"May I be of assistance?"

She whirled around. Myles Cunningham stood there, a curious gleam in his eyes, a heart-stopping smile on his lips.

"Uh . . . I was . . . Oh! Damn and dungeons!" she spat, exasperated with her tongue's refusal to work, and disgusted with her stomach's wild fluttering.

He tilted his head to the side and grinned insolently. "May I be of assistance?"

Her temper heated to a slow boil and she ached to dislodge that grin from his handsome face. When he crossed his arms over his chest and cocked his eyebrows, she had to ball her fists to keep from slapping him. Blessed St. Ninian, what was she doing? She was a servant. She should be grateful for his offer of assistance.

She relaxed her hands and smiled. "Why, thank you, milord," she said in the clipped English she'd been practicing for weeks. "I'd like to see that spyglass." She pointed to a velvet lined shelf. "The brass one—with the engraving of a stag."

Myles turned to the clerk. "You heard the lady." Leaning close to her Myles said, "And I'd be interested to know why the lady is shopping for a spyglass."

The woodsy aroma of his shaving soap was intoxicating. Suisan's mouth went dry. "'Tis for the MacKenzie," she croaked. Clearing her throat, she added, "Lady Suisan asked me to fetch it, you see."

Myles frowned, then blinked. "*The* MacKenzie?"

Suisan nodded and stared at his long eyelashes. Catching herself, she turned away and reached for the spyglass.

"I'll take it," she said and opened her purse.

Addressing Myles, the clerk said, "That'll be one pound, two, sir."

Suisan drew out the sum and placed the coins on the counter.

"Who is this MacKenzie person?" Myles asked.

Suisan was momentarily stunned. Hadn't Myles read her letters? "He's laird of Longmoor Castle. Surely you remember."

"And what," he challenged, "makes you think I should know of this MacKenzie? Lady Suisan and I lived in Aberdeen until her mother died. I've been to Perwickshire but twice in my life."

Oh, yes, she thought. *Once to take me there and once to steal my treasures*. She remembered the pain of being ten years old and lost by the death of her mother. Instead of promising to take care of her, Myles had insisted Uncle Rabby buy back Roward Castle. That done, Myles had sold her home in Aberdeen. Without Rabby, she would have been an orphan, too.

Through the bleak reverie she heard him say, "I asked you how I'm to know this Highlander who fancies spyglasses."

"Lady Suisan wrote to you of Lachlan MacKenzie. He's her neighbor—to the north."

"How do you know what Lady Suisan puts down in her letters? Do you read them?"

She knew he was angry, but couldn't understand why. He had deserted her. Confused, and anxious to be away, she blithely replied, "Of course I don't read her letters. She told me of it. Now, if you'll excuse me . . ." She darted around him.

"Wait." He took her arm. "I'll walk with you."

Suisan groaned inside, but allowed him to escort her from the store.

"I had no right to snap at you. But the topic of Lady Suisan is sometimes distressing. We were close until her mother died."

Surprised by his tone, Suisan looked up at him. The afternoon sun turned his hair to burnished gold and highlighted the rich brown color of his eyes. He smiled and said, "I feel as if you're looking at me through that spyglass. I've warned you about that."

Suisan gasped and looked away. Embarrassed, she searched for some quip. A phrase of Nelly's came to mind. "What's to keep me from looking at a comely man?"

"Naught," he drawled, "but the consequences."

Suisan went warm inside, and not from the sun. He turned her to face him. She clutched the spyglass so tightly she could feel the shape of the stag against her palm. Myles Cunningham was a charmer, a womanizer, she told herself. He obviously considered himself a prize.

Eager to put the conceited blackguard in his place, she boldly said, "I'm not afraid of your consequences."

It was the wrong thing to say, for his eyes began a slow, lustful perusal of her womanly curves. When he'd looked his fill, he lifted a hand to her breast. She couldn't move.

His warm fingers touched the exposed curve above her bodice; his heated gaze touched her in a more intimate place. Then he plucked the daisy from her cleavage and tossed the wilted flower aside.

"You should wear violets there, to match your eyes." His voice was soft, seductive and dangerous. Had he swooped her up in his arms at that moment and carried her away, Suisan could not have summoned the will to resist him.

He grinned that breath-stealing grin and called out to a street vendor. As if in a trance, she watched him purchase the flowers. Her skin began to tingle long before he touched her. Her breasts swelled when he slid his hand lower than he ought to place the violets. Her throat grew dry when he withdrew his hand sooner than she wanted.

"Perfect," he whispered, his clean breath fanning her heated face. "But if you continue to look at me that way, lass, I'll break my rule and kiss you."

"Kiss me?" she squeaked, powerless beneath his charm.

"Well." He grinned crookedly. "I'd start with a kiss, since that's obviously what you want. The rest I'll leave to my—consequences."

His words had the same effect as a plunge into icy Loch Eil.

"Close your mouth, lass," he chuckled, "people are staring."

Blood raced to her head and shame fueled her pride. She was acting the wanton . . . here in broad daylight . . . and with Myles Cunningham! Striving for composure, she glanced around the marketplace. They were indeed being watched. A foppish dandy in a sedan chair doffed his hat in salute. Suisan wished she could vanish. Then she spotted her maid, and the knowing look on Nelly's face told Suisan the servant had witnessed the entire scene.

Suisan swallowed her bruised pride, fixed her eyes on Myles's lacy cravat, and said, "You misunderstood me, milord. 'Twas only the excitement of London. Excuse me." She turned and walked away.

A deep chuckle followed her.

Suisan sailed past Nelly and into the mainstream of shoppers. Not until she was blocks away did Suisan look back. Nelly was on her heels but Myles was nowhere in sight.

"If you say one word of this to anyone, Nelly Burke, I'll tell the MacKenzie the things you dream about him." She meant it, too. She was not about to be harassed by her own maid.

"Who was he?"

"Myles Cunningham."

"Blessed St. Columba," Nelly shrieked. "I knew he'd turn out bonny. He was the brawest lad in Aberdeen, but I never thought he'd look so . . ." She rolled her eyes.

"Oh, stop it," Suisan scolded. "He's a thief and a bounder and a seducer of innocent women."

"Aye," Nelly said with vigor. "He can seduce me whenever the mood strikes him. And you can tell the MacKenzie whatever you like, because I've a new man to fill my dreams."

"Enough! You're a respectable widow with a daughter to think about."

Nelly smiled. "A woman don't always think respectable thoughts. Especially with the likes of him running loose."

"No more," Suisan spat, slashing her hand through the air. "You will not speak of him again."

"My lips are buttoned-up tight as Mrs. Peavy's corset."

"Fine. Because we have better things to do than discuss Myles Cunningham."

"Aye, milady."

"And do not address me so again."

Neither spoke for sometime. Suisan began to feel guilty

for the sharp reproof. Hoping to ease the tension, she glanced at the doll in Nelly's basket. "Sorcha will love that Pretty Poll."

"Aye, she will."

"You miss your daughter."

"That little heathen?" Nelly asked, her blue eyes round with mock surprise. "She's likely kickin' MacAdoo Dundas in the shins and callin' him ugly names."

Suisan relaxed; the rift between them was over. "She's a bonny lassie."

"If she was yours you'd think differently."

Suisan sighed. She'd given up the dream of having children years ago, but the yearning still tugged at her heart.

"Sometimes I think this whole adventure is all a dream," she commented, waving a hand in the air.

"Aye, I ken. Who'd've thought we'd ever come to Londontown—and for such a purpose?"

Their eyes met. "We'll get all of Scotland's treasures away from him. I know we will," Suisan vowed.

Nelly grinned. "Aye. What's one slimy Sassenach to do against two stout-hearted Scots lassies?"

"He'll lose, that's what Myles Cunningham'll do," Suisan said fiercely.

Nelly's eyes twinkled at the mention of Myles's name. "We've other gifts to buy before we leave London, you know." She stopped at a stall overflowing with flowers and seed packets. "Posies for Aunt Ailis's garden?"

"I suppose," Suisan said, despondent at the thought of her aunt.

"Lamenting won't help Ailis. She is what she is—a confused bairn in a woman's body." When Suisan didn't reply, Nelly said, "There's no bein' certain your bairns would turn out like her. Especially if you handfasted yourself to the MacKenzie. He's too braw to father an afflicted child."

A familiar ache thrummed in Suisan's breast. How often had she considered casting her fears to the wind and agreeing to a handfast marriage with Lachlan MacKenzie? Too often, but practicality always held her back, for nature could be cruel. "So long as there's a chance," she said with conviction, "that's gamble enough for me. Besides, I don't love the MacKenzie."

When Nelly started to protest, Suisan said, "The subject is closed, no matter what you say—or what Myles Cunningham says."

Nelly stopped. "An' just how did Himself come to speak of your marryin'?"

"He thinks 'tis time Suisan was wed."

Grasping Suisan's arm, Nelly said, "Are you sayin' he knows who you are?"

"Of course not."

Nelly relaxed. "What else did he say?"

"That was all of it," Suisan paused, "except for some reason he thinks Suisan is plain and simple."

"He's a bletherin loonie," Nelly swore vehemently. "Robert sent him your likeness last year, and a bonny one it was."

"Perhaps he favors blondes like you," Suisan teased.

Nelly preened. "There's something to be said for that! But he must have said more than you're tellin'."

Laughing, Suisan said, "Myles hasn't been home since the morning he mentioned my homeliness. He's busy unloading the *Highland Dream*."

"Himself weren't busy unloading no ship back there in front of Chipton's. He was unloading his lust on you."

"Nelly . . ." Suisan warned, wanting no reminder of her own wanton behavior.

Nelly frowned. "Well, then, why would he be unloadin' his prize ship himself?"

"Mr. Cookson's broken his leg."

"Cookson's here, too?" Nelly gasped.

Suisan patted Nelly's hand. "Don't fret. He doesn't suspect anything either."

"I thought the old curmudgeon'd be dead and buried by now."

Suisan laughed louder, thinking of Mackie and Cookson squabbling like children. "He's not that old."

"For the love of heaven, what else aren't you tellin' me?"

Suisan related her first meeting with Myles and described the rest of the staff.

"This Mackie sounds like she's got a right fine head on her shoulders." As an afterthought, Nelly added, "Even if she is a damned Englishwoman!"

But Suisan was only half-listening. Her attention was focused on the window of a dressmaker's shop.

"Oh, Nelly," she sighed. "Isn't that a bonny sight?"

The window featured a beautiful array of cloth from the looms of Roward Castle. A bolt of crisp muslin dyed a soft green and sprigged with delicate daisies formed the center of the display. Scattered tastefully around it were dozens of other bolts. Suisan's gaze was drawn to the berry red wool with neat black stripes. Beside it lay a length of nubby linen in bright indigo blue.

"Milady?" Nelly sounded distressed.

Through teary eyes, Suisan faced her and asked, "Why the frown?"

Nelly pointed to a small sign in the window. Suisan's breath caught in her throat. Neatly stated in flowing script were the words, *From the looms of Strathclyde.*

"Nay!" Suisan breathed as anger and disbelief surged through her. "That's Roward cloth. Someone's pulled a switch on us."

More practical, Nelly said, "Well, someone should hire a clerk who can read, but since they didn't, we'll just tell 'em their mistake."

Nelly headed toward the door, but Suisan stopped her. "Wait."

Through a veil of anger, Suisan pondered the situation. She had long suspected that her cloth should yield more than the pittance she received. Now she knew the reason. She just had to stop it. But whatever course she took, she could not call attention to herself.

"What is it, milady?"

"We can't just storm the place, Nelly. Who would believe us? I've a plan."

Nelly seemed to relax. "What do we do?"

"We do nothing, but *you* will try and get a position here.

Then you can find out who's behind this." Suisan pursed her lips and glanced at the window.

"Grubby thieves, is what they are. All these foosty Sassenachs!"

"*Haud yer wheesht!*" Suisan hissed. "At least until we get to the house on Beacon Row."

"Sorry," Nelly murmured. "My tongue's snappin' but I'm as curious as the Widow MacCormick."

"Just remember," Suisan warned, "if she wants you, you're not to quibble over the wage she offers you, no matter how paltry the sum."

But Nelly was still grumbling about the English when she opened the door to the house Suisan had secretly rented for their stay in London. The place was small, but neatly furnished. Only a few blocks from Myles's rambling residence, the little house was well suited to their purpose.

"What's all this?" Suisan asked as they entered the upstairs bedchamber.

"Just some clothes for you. I stitched two more skirts and blouses, a nice dress of saxony blue, and a pretty white pinafore. If you're to be a servant and dress as such, I'll not have you wearin' shoddy rags."

Suisan took her hand. "Thank you, Nelly. I'd be lost without you."

"Posh!"

Seeing Nelly's embarrassment, Suisan said, "We'd best wash my hair soon or it'll never dry. And just a little dye around my face."

Confidently, Nelly said, "I've found a new recipe. 'Tis smelly until it's dry, but the clerk at the apothecary store said the color won't come off until we want it off."

"Good," Suisan sighed, "my brush is a fair mess. I have to clean it every day."

Nelly smiled. "I'll be fetchin' the water and the dye then."

"The *Maide dalbh*," Suisan said reverently. "Where are they?"

Proudly, Nelly said, "In the chest," and pointed to the corner. Then she left the room.

Lifting the lid, Suisan reached into the large chest. She

picked up one of two bundles and stood it on the floor. She chuckled at the weight; in the light of day it didn't seem so heavy, so dangerous. Hugging the tall bundle to her breast, Suisan reveled in the feeling of accomplishment, of having her treasure once more. She longed for the day when all of the pattern sticks were safe at Roward again.

Tenderly, she traced the row of colored pegs running down each of the four sticks. These pegs had guided the weavers' threads for over a hundred years. She pictured the finished cloth this pattern would yield, the tartan of her mother's people. Like other Cameron clans, the Lochiels' tartan had a background of brightest red with narrow black plaids. But the Lochiels distinguished themselves with two wide black stripes down the center, each flanked with a smaller white one. It was a bold and glorious trademark, the tartan of the Camerons of Lochiel, and it was Suisan's proud legacy.

Sadly, she replaced the *Maide dalbh*. She had been born too late to see her tartan worn as it should be, but she could imagine a regiment of Highlanders, proudly wearing the Cameron colors and marching to the haunting skirl of the bagpipes.

Tears stung her eyes. She closed the chest. Men and their wars, kings and their stubborn pride had put an end to the Highlanders' culture. What harm could come from a beautifully woven cloth and a bag of musical pipes? Suisan knew the answer. The English seemed to consider them a national threat. Jacobites on Culloden Moor, Bonny Prince Charlie against the Duke of Cumberland, and a score of other factors had marked the end for Scotland.

Suisan knew she would hang for treason if she were caught with the outlawed pattern sticks. She'd carried the burden, the honor of protecting the illegal *Maide dalbh*, since her mother's death ten years before. Suisan considered the other patterns representing the outlawed clans that were hidden in Myles's basement. She also considered the danger she courted in transferring the *Maide dalbh* to Nelly, for Nelly would hang, too, if they were caught.

But I'm a simple woman, content to live in peace in the hills of Scotland, Suisan thought wretchedly. Her shoulders slumped and she was besieged with despair. What would happen to the weavers of Roward, to their children, to all the beloved people of Perwickshire, if she failed to return? Who would guide them? Who would care for them?

Later, as Nelly's nimble fingers worked the smelly dye solution into Suisan's hair, she tried unsuccessfully to clear her mind of troubling thoughts. Each time she closed her eyes she could feel Myles's hand on her breast, and imagine how his lips would feel against hers.

"Now will you tell me more about Himself?" Nelly asked.

Suisan jumped as if caught in some forbidden act. "What do you want to know?"

"Well, bein' as how he's braw as any man I've ever seen, I wonder if *you* thought he was handsome?"

"Aye," Suisan answered truthfully. "He's a handsome, thieving, miserable liar."

Nelly whistled. "Spoken like a true Highlander. Tell me more."

Suisan leaned back in the warm tub. Nelly knelt on the floor beside her. Ignoring the flutter in her stomach at the thought of him, Suisan said, "He's strong as an Aberdeen Angus stud. He carried Cookson with ease."

"I see him dressed like a fop of an evenin', wearing a wig this tall." Nelly held a dye-stained hand a foot over her head. "Like all the other London gentlemen do."

Suisan shook her head. "He wears his hair plain, without powder or bows, with just that simple leather tie."

Nelly tilted her head to the side. "He never acts the dandy?"

"Not that I've seen. But I wish he would. 'Twould make it easier to see him for the cheat he is." Lowering her voice, Suisan reminded her maid, "He's done us terrible harm, Nelly."

"What's one thing to do with the other? Nothin' wrong with appreciatin' a comely man, especially when he appreciates a comely woman like you, milady. He's got a good eye on him—even if he is a thievin' lout."

Grudgingly, Suisan said, "He seems kind and thoughtful,

at least to Mackie, Cookson and Will'am. He even winked at me.''

''He was doin' more than winkin' at you today. I say he'll be tryin' to up yer skirts before we're done.''

''He's in for a surprise then,'' Suisan said, ignoring the way her pulse raced at the thought.

Nelly clucked her tongue. ''And wouldn't he be surprised if he knew who you are? He don't remember yer Harper eyes.''

''I was only six when father took him to sea.''

''Your father loved him, there's no denyin' that. Took Myles off the streets of this slimy place and cared for him like his own. Taught him to be a sailor, and when your father drowned in that storm, Myles saw to it that the business prospered. He looked after you and your mother, even though he was only a lad at the time.'' Nelly's voice dropped. ''Lady Sibeal favored him.''

''I don't want to think about that, Nelly. No doubt he duped my parents, too.''

''Is the mansion fine?''

''Oh, yes. 'Tis filled with treasures from all over the world. Turkish carpets on the marble floors, a wonderful stained glass window in the upstairs hall, and great urns as tall as you. And my room has a regular bed, not a broken-down cot.''

Nelly looked impressed. ''What about his private quarters?''

Averting her eyes and skirting the truth, Suisan said, ''Odd place, his bedchamber. Oh, 'tis furnished royally, make no mistake, but you'll never guess what he stores his clothes in—my father's sea chest.''

''That old thing? Why would he do that, unless he's sentimental?''

''I don't know, Nelly. 'Tis a puzzle.''

''Does he have a mistress?''

Suisan shrugged, wondering why her heart constricted at the thought. ''He keeps a miniature of a woman in Papa's sea chest, but the painting of me is not in the mansion— anywhere. I asked Mackie if there was a special woman in his life, but she huffed up and said she's not allowed to speak of *her* again.''

"I knew it," Nelly declared. "He's the kind to growl like a bear and work his servants 'til they drop."

"Wrong again, Nelly. He seems to tolerate much from Mackie and Cookson. Will'am fair worships the man."

"An' how do you get on with them?"

"Better than I thought I would. Mackie's been busy seeing to Cookson most of the time. That's why I was able to get away today. And I'd best not be late returning. How's my hair?"

Nelly looked smug. "Black as Loch Eil on a moonless night."

"Good. Now I can take myself back to the devil's den."

"That's the spirit, milady. And I can take myself off to the dressmaker and get that position."

Nelly was so confident, so naive about their mission. Did she truly understand the danger they faced? "Nelly . . . I worry about you. The streets are dangerous at night. I think I was wrong in having Dundas and the soldiers wait for us in Aberdeen."

The maid's bravado vanished. "I've that pistol he gave you. And don't think I won't use it. Besides," her tone became lighter, "'tis a short walk from here to there. The soldiers are better off where they are. Imagine the stir those six rowdies would cause in London. Why, that hot-headed Dundas would most likely go after Myles before we could get the patterns back."

Suisan relaxed. "You're probably right. Come tonight, then, at nine o'clock. I'll be waiting at the cellar window."

"What if Himself's there?"

"If he is home, he'll be in Cookson's room on the second floor. Mackie says he's worried that Ollie might not walk again."

"Perhaps we're doing him a disservice?"

"Cookson?" Suisan asked.

Nelly's eyes narrowed. "You know I was meanin' Himself."

Suisan ducked her head to hide her smile.

"Laugh if you will," Nelly said, "but Myles Cunningham don't sound like such a bad sort to me."

Suisan looked up. "He's a thief and a liar, and I won't be taken in by his handsome looks and charming manners."

But as she made her way back to his house, her heart beat faster at the prospect of seeing him again.

∼ *Chapter 3* ∼

"Here's something toward your wages, Maura," Mackie said, taking several coins from her pocket. "You'll be gettin' the balance when Cookson's able to handle the books again."

"I couldn't take money from you, Mackie."

"'Tis from the housekeeping fund," Mackie said, obviously confused.

Suisan realized her mistake. Servants were expected to be anxious for their wages, no matter the source. Averting her eyes, she took the money. "Thank you, then. I didn't think it proper to ask."

Mackie smiled benevolently. "You've done a fine job, girl; caught on quicker than most, you have. Who could expect a weaver to learn a maid's chores overnight? Once you learn our ways, you'll be fine."

"That's kind of you to say." The housekeeper couldn't know just *how* much Suisan had learned.

"'Tis the master's opinion that counts," Mackie declared, lifting her chin. "And he's pleased with your work."

"Master Cunningham said that?" Suisan asked, wondering why Myles would bother to notice and compliment a servant. "He's had nothing but scones for breakfast for a week."

"He's takin' a likin' to your scones. Don't look so surprised at his kind words. He's a fine man. The finest I've ever served."

An argument with Mackie on the dubious virtues of Myles Cunningham was the last thing Suisan wanted. "Shall I do the marketing for you today?" she asked.

"No, dearie, 'tis best I see to it this time. There's much to buy, what with the Earl of Ainsbury, his snooty daughter, and those other hob-a-nobs comin' to dine tonight."

Suisan felt a flash of dismay. She had become accustomed to doing the everyday marketing, giving Mackie more time to care for Ollie Cookson, who was recovering slowly. This allowed Suisan to secretly visit Nelly, who was fast becoming disenchanted with London.

Out of desperation, Suisan said, "We could make a list, then."

Mackie looked startled. "You can read and write?"

Suisan had been reluctant to admit those skills; most English servants were uneducated. But she was tired of playing the maid and weary of feeling the thief. An afternoon at Cuper's Gardens would refresh her spirits. And surely Nelly would have the proof Suisan needed to charge Myles with counterfeiting their cloth.

"Yes, I can, and just as well as Lady Suisan," she couldn't help adding.

A delighted smile transformed Mackie's face and she clasped her hands together. "Sit down, then, and I'll fetch the writing things from the master's study," she said and left the room.

Suisan poured herself another cup of tea and sat down at the kitchen table. Since Myles's return she had tried to be diligent in her role, even when he was off tending to his business, enjoying the races at Newmarket, or taking in a play at Lincoln's Inn Fields.

Would he become suspicious of her when he found out she could read and write? Of a certainty, Mackie would tell him, but what would he say? The occasions when Suisan did see him were invariably unsettling. She was cautious, to be sure, but as each day passed she found herself revising her image of Myles Cunningham. Why did he continually question her about his 'stepsister,' Suisan Harper, and always with such fondness in his voice?

But there was something much more disconcerting about him. He had a way of looking at her—a direct and open perusal that made her extremely uncomfortable.

Hoping the tea would settle her jangled nerves and put Myles from her mind, she drank deeply. Her forays to the basement were becoming more frequent; she and Nelly had managed to smuggle to safety more than a dozen of the patterns.

At the sound of Mackie's footsteps, Suisan put aside the troubling thoughts and concentrated on acting the servant. The shopping list was indeed long and Mackie went into detail about every item. The parsley must be crisp, the quail picked clean, and the cherries free of blemishes. "And no brown mushrooms," Mackie called out from the pantry where she dictated the list. "I'll have the nice little white ones or none at all."

Suisan was well into the second page of the list when a strange, uneasy feeling assaulted her. The fine hair on the back of her neck rose. Mackie's voice became a distant noise; another presence was in the room.

She didn't need to look up to know Myles was nearby, but the knowledge drew her like bairns to a Highland fair. He stood in the kitchen entryway, his hands grasping the door frame overhead. The pose accentuated the leanness of his hips, the sleek lines of his flanks, and the breadth of his shoulders. Inexorably, her gaze was drawn to his face. His generous lips were parted the slightest bit, the set of his mouth something shy of a smile. His brown eyes, too sensitive and expressive for a man of his size and reputation, were examining her, picking her apart, much as always.

In the space of a heartbeat and completely against her will, Suisan prayed she would not be found wanting. It was all she could do to keep from rising, from going to him, from begging the verdict. Instead, she held her breath and his gaze.

Then he began to smile, and in the next heartbeat, she

came to her senses. She cleared her throat and put down the quill. Tilting her head to the side, she quietly asked, "May I get you something, sir?"

The smile reached his eyes and with the lazy grace she'd come to know, he strolled around behind her. Resting a large, sun-browned hand on the table, he leaned over her shoulder and looked at the list she'd been preparing.

"You've a lovely hand—easy to read." His voice was quiet; the whisper of his breath on her neck set her head to spinning. The familiar fragrance of his shaving soap permeated her senses and reminded her of other times—of times when they'd been friends.

"I'll be wantin' some new carrots, if the tops are fresh," Mackie called out.

Suisan managed to wield the quill, but even the scratching of the pen grated on her heightened senses. He scanned the list, then his eyes came back to hers.

"And a pair of cabbages for soup," Mackie called out. "Himself says the broth smells like bilge water, but he empties his bowl all the same."

Through a haze of wanton images, Suisan added the item to the list.

"You've misspelled cabbages."

She was dangling on the sound of his voice. She hardly noticed when he pulled the quill from her hand. Mackie yelled something; Suisan had no idea what the housekeeper had said, but Myles heard.

"I hate kidneys," he stated flatly, though his eyes were dancing. "Don't you?"

She nodded; at that moment she would have agreed to give up her bed to MacIver's sheepdog. But deep in her mind a question was forming—or was it a warning? Something was wrong.

She forced herself to add kidneys to the list.

"Your penmanship is much like Suisan's."

The words crashed through her mind. Her tongue grew thick at the searching, questioning look on his face. Dear God, she had at last exposed herself! Myles surely recognized her writing from the letters they had exchanged. Now she would hang for an impostor and a traitor . . . unless she could brazen her way out. To that end she replied, ''And why not? We had the same tutor.''

''Why are you frowning? I thought you liked Suisan.''

Her mind worked feverishly. She managed to say, ''I was still thinking of kidneys.''

The curious expression on his face eased. He placed his elbow on the table, then rested his chin in his palm. He was close, too close, and his warm, minty breath now fanned her cheeks. His expressive eyes held no suspicion; she was relieved for that, but something new was there, something exciting, something dangerous . . .

''I was speaking,'' he murmured suggestively, ''of likes and dislikes.'' His eyes boldly raked her face and settled on her mouth. ''Particularly . . . likes.''

At that moment Suisan was more frightened than she had ever been in her life. Even the hangman's noose, grisly and terrifying, might be preferable to Myles's heated gaze. Still, she couldn't turn away.

''And a good supply of flour, Maura,'' Mackie said, laughing. ''You've tickled the master's palate with that Scottish fare.''

He grinned and raised his eyebrows. ''You've tickled me, right enough, lassie.'' He twirled the quill and tickled her with the feather. ''What do you intend to do about it?''

A sigh of longing lodged in her throat. She ached to have his lips on hers, to explore the exciting new feelings budding within her.

The quill touched her lips, then made a slow and agonizing journey over each cheek, the bridge of her nose and her brows. Her lips went dry; her palms went damp. ''You're seducing me again,'' she said, but heard no complaint in her words.

His eyes grew dark. His lips parted. ''You've a way about you lass . . . that makes a man want to wrap you in his arms . . . build a house in the country . . . see his sons suckling at your breasts . . . bounce his daughters on his knee.''

''Don't be forgettin' a round of that smelly, foreign cheese, the one with the tiny holes,'' Mackie grumbled. ''Good English cheese don't suit his palate, he says.''

He leaned closer. The quill fell to the table. "My palate," he whispered, "has an unmanageable hunger for your lips."

Then his lips touched hers, and the world drifted away. But the floating, swirling sensation soon gave way to some deeper need. Her hand found his cheek; then her fingers threaded through his hair. She found it silky and thick to the touch and wondered if his chest were covered with a mat of the same. He tilted his head to the side and slanted his mouth across hers, his tongue tracing the sensitive edge of her lips. When his tongue stabbed deeper then retreated, Suisan pulled him closer and opened her mouth wide, wantonly hoping he'd come into her again.

He did.

And suddenly she was out of control. She was trapped in a runaway cart drawn by a thousand straining Clydesdales, and careening wildly over endless braes and glens. Excitement robbed her of breath, and desire stole a forbidden path from her whirling mind to the aching core of her womanhood. A measure of relief came when his hand slid into her cleavage then splayed, a thumb caressing one aching nipple, a finger soothing the other.

He pulled back and his labored breathing wafted across her face. "Come to my room tonight," he said quietly.

Drawing up the last thread of her resistance and ignoring the inner voice damning her for a fool, Suisan opened her mouth to voice a denial.

His expression silenced her. His eyes were a deep shade of brown and alive with the promise of wondrous things. "Or will you leave me to sleep alone—" he placed her hand on the fine bulge in his breeches, "—with naught but this?"

Fire raced up her arm; her fingers instinctively curved to grasp the shape of him. He quickened, and Suisan closed her eyes, only to hear bells ringing in her ears. Dear God, how she wanted him . . .

"Lassie?"

With an effort, she dragged her eyes from his. And gasped, seeing the reality of her hand caressing the formidable swell of his manhood. Jerking her hand away, and dislodging his hand from her blouse, she felt her sanity return, and reached for the quill. With a flourish, she scratched the offending kidneys from the list.

Her voice was once again level, as was the gaze she cast him, when she said, "We'll botch the list and the meal if you don't leave us to it."

Myles chuckled, a sound Suisan was fast coming to fear, because the enticing sound disarmed her. "By all means," he allowed condescendingly, and pushed away from the table.

At his arrogant tone, her patience snapped. "I will not come to your room, Myles Cunningham!" she hissed, "Or your bed! You're a rakehell of the worst sort—to seduce a servant."

"What was that, Maura?" Mackie called out.

"I may have kissed a servant," he said anger showing in his eyes, "but she was willing, I'm certain."

She opened her mouth to protest, but before she could speak, he stalked from the room. She berated herself for a naive fool. How could she hope to succeed in her mission if she kept letting her memories rule her actions? She must forget those happy childhood years in Aberdeen. And yet, if she relaxed her guard she could picture herself and Mama, standing on the Harper quay waiting for Papa and Myles to return from the sea. She'd learned geography by tracing the lines from Aberdeen to Cadiz, Aberdeen to Calais—lines on a map drawn by Myles's own hand. She'd learned about calendars then, too, and marked off the days during their short voyages.

The once sweet memories, embittered by years of estrangement and reticence, now seemed like bad dreams.

"A codfish for Friday's meal," Mackie said.

Suisan welcomed the respite.

"But don't buy it if the eyes are cloudy."

"Certainly not," Suisan whispered.

She certainly had been willing, Myles thought, but the knowledge was not pleasing—not one bloody bit! Angry at his growing attraction to the servant and angrier at the wrenching desire clawing at his loins, he made his way to the study.

But something else was bothering him: a longing for something softer, sweeter than mere physical release. Since the night he'd first seen the comely lass he'd been distracted by her. Thinking her to be no more than a naive, country maid experiencing London for the first time, he'd been indulgent of her wide-eyed scrutiny. Today, however, Myles knew he'd been wrong.

Once again he'd caught her staring boldly at him, once again he'd been intoxicated by her fresh-faced beauty, and only through sheer determination had he avoided whisking her upstairs and spending the better portion of the day showing her precisely what those inviting stares and that lush loveliness could yield. When he thought of the evening to come, desire surged anew. Desire and something else. He longed to hear her laugh, to while away the hours listening to her speak in that musical brogue. She had a way of making him forget the troubles in his life and concentrate on his dream. She made him believe he could quit the sea someday and sink his roots in a plot of fertile ground that was his own. She made him think of keeping bees and hearing the cock's crow.

Annoyed with himself, Myles stalked into the study and jerked open the glass-fronted cabinet. Ollie had pegged the girl's purpose weeks ago, and if Myles didn't compose himself before he faced Ollie, there'd be hell to pay. For weeks, Myles had steadfastly denied the possibility that she was interested in more than making scones and seeing London. But that was in the past; tonight he would see if that delectable body was as willing and tasty as it looked.

As he yanked the necessary ledgers from the case, he was still troubled at the prospect of seducing one of his maids. Other men in his position considered the women in their employ fair game; Myles did not. He had a mistress to dally with, an elegant and experienced woman without pretense of sentiment or expectations of the future. But Barbara's charms and beauty paled when compared to the Scottish lassie. He shouldn't take advantage of his position; he'd been taught that by a very special man.

Thinking of that man, Myles headed out of the study. He

held the heavy ledgers easily in one arm as he slowly mounted the stairs to Cookson's bedchamber.

Born of the streets and nurtured on little more than the will to survive, Myles had fought and scraped his way through fifteen years of loneliness and poverty. Kindness and love were unknown to him, until one blessed day when Edward Harper came along. Each time Myles thought of Suisan's father, tears stung his eyes and an empty ache drummed in his chest. A kind man, a loving man, Edward had pulled Myles from the gutter that had been his existence and introduced him to the world that was now his life. In a giant sweep of love and good will, Edward Harper had taken Myles under his wing and given him a family. Sibeal Harper became his mother and Suisan his younger sister.

"Don't be afraid to love these Harper women," Edward had teased many years ago when he'd first taken Myles home to Aberdeen. "Though my Sibeal will always think of herself as a Lochiel Cameron, she's a good wife to me." Those Harper-blue eyes had twinkled when he added, "But, bless St. Margaret, the lassie has my eyes."

Myles paused at the top of the stairs. The moment of reverie brought to mind another pair of Scottish eyes. But Maura was much too familiar and free with her quippy tongue. She seemed to feel she had the right to speak up to him as she chose, to look him in the eyes and to dare him to venture closer. Against his will and in spite of his vow, Myles intended to take up her challenge and discover what was behind those daring indigo eyes.

Walking down the hall to Cookson's room, Myles stilled his wayward thoughts. With the steward incapacitated, Myles's work had trebled. Two of his six ships were in port; one from France and the other from the American Colonies. He must assign each a cargo, for every day their holds were empty, Myles lost money. He hadn't even instructed Will'am to move the cases of wine from the warehouse to the basement, damn it! He needed that brandy and Madeira to bribe the stuffy English lords who awarded him the tobacco, indigo and cotton contracts that were his livelihood, his very profitable livelihood.

A guilty notion occurred to him then. Ollie's illness prevented them from returning to the sea.

Myles opened the bedchamber door to find Cookson propped up in the bed, a mirror in one hand and a brush in the other. He was practicing his greatest vanity, grooming his beard. Thick and white and perfectly trimmed, the beard swept up toward his ears and gave his face a perpetual smile.

"You've a bit out of place," Myles teased and pointed, "there, by your left ear."

Taking the bait, Ollie studied the spot, then plied his brush carefully.

Myles laughed aloud.

Ollie frowned. "And you've a streak of the devil, my boy. You never was one to respect your elders."

Myles pulled up a chair and laid the ledgers on the bed. "*Moi*?" he asked, feigning bewilderment.

"And your sap's up, too—higher'n the maples in the Colonies. Must be that spicy little Maura got your blood afire again, eh?"

Myles looked away; Ollie was too astute for his own good.

"I thought as much. Why don't you just take what she's offering and be done with it?"

"Laudanum has addled your brain," Myles countered. "She feels comfortable with me only because Suisan Harper is my stepsister."

"You're foolin' yourself." Ollie's tone was kind. "Since Suisan's father took you in you've had a soft spot in your wicked heart for her."

Grinning, Myles said, "Wicked?"

"Yes, wicked," Ollie declared crossly. "Why else would you taunt a man facing life's worst fate?"

"Your leg will heal; you know it will."

"But I may be permanently maimed by that doting Mackie!"

They both laughed, much as they always had. Myles knew Ollie was sweet on Mackie; Ollie knew it too, but neither would voice the thought.

"What have you there?" Ollie asked.

"The *Prize* is docking this morning; the *Highland Wind*, yesterday."

"Good God!" Ollie swore and looked disgustedly at his injured leg. "Our work's certainly cut out for us." He held out his hand. "Give me the books and you call out the cargo. Nobody's ever read your scrawl."

When all the figures were reckoned and the cargo assigned to warehouses, Ollie put down the quill. "The *Highland Wind's* brought a king's ransom in brandy from France. Will fifty cases be enough . . . persuasion?"

Myles laughed. "Aye, and the Earl of Ainsbury's coming to dinner tonight. Perhaps he can be persuaded to award us the tobacco contracts for next year."

"What about the indigo and cotton contracts?"

"I've seen to both of them."

"Good going, my boy," Ollie said exuberantly. "You've got a way with those bluebloods."

Ruefully, Myles said, "I believe it's the persuasion, not my sterling personality."

Ollie laughed. "Thank God the earl's got a weakness for brandy." He looked at the ledger. "Is there room in the basement for all this persuasion?"

Myles straightened in the chair. "I don't, as you well know, frequent the basement."

"Then you'd best have Will'am move that cognac to the cellar," Ollie said, then added sarcastically, "that way your sensibilities won't be disturbed." With a grunt of distaste, he turned a page. "As I see it, we can load the *Wind* by Tuesday and have her headed to the Chesapeake on the tide. The *Prize*'ll be tomorrow's worry."

Myles nodded. "I'll have the lass tally the inventory once the persuasion's in the basement, then Will'am can deliver it to my noble . . . friends."

Wrinkling his brow in surprise, Ollie said, "The lass?"

"Aye, she reads and writes—Suisan saw to it."

Ollie crossed his arms over his chest. Smugly he said, "'Tis a pretty sight, a soft spot in a hard man like you."

Myles's eyes narrowed dangerously. "You're pushing your luck, old friend, broken leg or not."

Ollie laughed and reached for his pipe. When it was lit, he said, "Why are you so touchy about the girl?"

"I'm not touchy!" Was he feeling guilty about the night to come?

"Oh," Ollie blew a perfect ring of smoke into the air. "Mayhap then, your mistress is neglecting you."

Myles rose and picked up the ledgers.

"Or could it be," Ollie continued, "you've a craving for a saucy one with dark blue eyes and black hair?"

"Stow it! I'm not a green boy in need of your limited, if slanted advice."

"She's comely," Ollie offered lightly. "Got a way of looking with those big blue eyes. And the way she looks at you has nothing to do with being a serving girl. Well, not the kind of serving she was hired for."

Myles shook his head and tried to stave off a new wave of guilt. "Suisan would have taught her better."

"Suisan, Suisan, Suisan," Ollie sing-songed. "There's your big soft spot."

"She's the sister I never had."

Ollie seemed to consider the statement. "I'll give you that excuse," he said magnanimously. "And if she's grown up to be as homely as that miniature dear Robert sent, she needs more than your kind words."

"She's not homely."

"All I'm saying," Ollie went on, "is if Suisan cared she could've troubled herself to be in that mouldy castle to meet us after we trudged halfway across Scotland to pay her a visit. I tried to talk you out of buying that place after Sibeal died, but would you listen?" He shook his white head. "No. You were bound and determined to keep Roward Castle for the Camerons even after the Duke of Cumberland executed most of the family and confiscated the estate back in '46. You even let Robert take credit for convincing the Crown to sell the castle."

Myles felt the familiar tug of loyalty to Sibeal and Suisan. "I think it's sad that a proud family becomes tenants in their own home. Suisan's the last Lochiel Cameron. I promised her mother I'd buy Roward back, and Edward left me the means to do it. Why should I care if Robert took the credit? He has little enough as it is.''

Ollie leaned forward. ''To hell with Robert. You've increased your inheritance tenfold. And done it by your own wits and cunning.''

''But I started with Edward's money.''

''That doesn't mean you have to dabble in Scottish politics and make Robert Harper a hero!'' Ollie seemed exasperated. ''I always wondered what happened to those damned tartan patterns—not to mention the King wantin' to know their whereabouts. Old George'd love to get his hands on 'em, especially the pattern for the Royal Stewart plaid.''

''Robert Harper said he destroyed them—swore to it at Sibeal's funeral.''

''And you believe that miserable sod—''

''Enough!'' Myles roared. ''I don't like him either, but you needn't stoop to name calling.''

''Then why do you cater to him and give him leave to stay here when you're away?''

''Because he's my only link to Suisan.''

''He doesn't have to be,'' Ollie argued. ''If you hadn't lost that infernal temper of yours and stormed out we could have stayed at the castle until she returned.''

Myles stilled the urge to throw the ledgers across the room. How many times had he regretted his angry departure from Roward? Too many. He felt guilty still. ''I've allotted extra funds for Suisan's allowance. I want the castle repaired.''

Ollie looked shocked. ''You've sent her enough money over the years to make Roward a palace. The least she can do is come here and get it, since you're determined to shovel more money into the damned mausoleum.''

''I've tried. In every letter I've asked her to come to London.''

''And what's her excuse?''

''She never gives one, but according to Maura, Suisan's busy with the weaving.''

Ollie frowned. ''Something's amiss with those letters, Myles. Seems to me you write to her in sixes and she answers you in sevens. Are you sure Robert delivers them?''

"Of course he does." Myles fought to keep the hurt from his voice. "She always writes back, but never mentions coming to London." *Or anything remotely personal*, Myles added to himself.

"Ungrateful chit," Ollie muttered.

Myles's patience snapped. Without another word to Ollie, he stormed from the room. And came face to face with the serving maid.

Her blue eyes were wide with shock; dishes rattled loudly on the tray she carried. She might not be the best of serving maids, but Myles didn't care. He put down the ledgers, took the tray and set it on the floor.

She took a step back; he took a step forward.

"Nay," she breathed, holding up her hands as if to ward him off.

She was being coy again, but he knew how to deal with her reticence. He took her in his arms and kissed her.

But she didn't yield—not as before. Her defiance made him more determined. He kissed her slowly, and as the fire in his loins rekindled, the resolve to take her grew stronger. She smelled of wildflowers, and her lips tasted like a sweet confection fit for a king. She reminded him of his dream again.

Reluctantly, he ended the kiss. Leaning back, he studied her lovely face, now flushed with passion. She was wavering, fighting some inner battle. But agreement was what he wanted, agreement was what he'd get. "You've slipped inside my heart, lassie, 'til I think of naught but you—your smile, your lovely eyes, and the way you say my name. I intend to make you mine. Tonight, lassie."

She swallowed visibly. "Nay, 'tis wrong."

"'Tis right," he insisted, and moved a hand to her breast.

When she sucked in her breath and closed her teeth over that lush bottom lip, Myles almost carried her upstairs right then. But he had business to tend this afternoon, and when he took this lassie he wanted hours in which to play. He wanted time to learn every curve and hollow of her body, time to hear every passionate response. Time to become a dreamer again.

"Tonight," he repeated firmly.

She shook her head, dislodging the mobcap.

"And don't wear that cap." Smiling, he snatched it and added, "'Tis one less thing for me to remove."

She grabbed the cap and drew herself up. "I won't come to you. I won't be your whore."

He was challenged by that familiar defiance, yet he was troubled by her choice of words. "You're no whore, lassie. And you'll come to me. If not tonight, then tomorrow night or the next."

~ *Chapter 4* ~

Suisan tied the ribbon into a pert bow at the crown of her head, then plucked at the ruffled edges of the mobcap until it evenly framed her face. She picked up the crisply starched pinafore, gently laid it over her arm, and with one last glance in the small mirror, left her room and headed down the front stairs. As she rounded the landing at the second floor, she saw Myles coming out of Ollie Cookson's room, a dinner tray in his hands.

Candlelight from the wall sconces shone on his neatly groomed hair, turning it to burnished gold. The dark brown, scissor-cut coat might have seemed ordinary on another man and the off white waistcoat lost in the flashy colors and fabrics dictated by the mode of the day, but not so on Myles; for he was no ordinary man. The subtle male hues and finely woven satin complemented his deeply tanned skin and accentuated the trim, yet powerful lines of his tall frame. Instead of trousers, he wore jaunty knee pants which hinted at his male attributes but did not overtly showcase that part of him, as was the current fashion. White hose, unadorned with clocks or bows, molded his shapely calves, and the soft light twinkled off the elegant gold buckles on his highly polished, square-toed shoes. At a time when most men dressed like peacocks, Myles Cunningham seemed the epitome of understated male grace.

He steadied the tray he carried, shifted it to one hand and used the other to close Cookson's door. When the latch clicked he raised his head and spied Suisan. His brown eyes raked her from head to toe, then settled on her face, which she knew was flushed.

"Turn around," he quietly commanded, but with a smile in his voice.

Her hand refused to leave the wooden rail and her palm suddenly felt damp on the smoothly polished mahogany. The force of his speculative gaze held her captive. She had to will herself to breathe. Only when he arched a flaring brow and ran his eyes up and down her form once more, did she regain her composure. His imperious expression and dominating countenance fired her stubborn pride.

If she must humor him on occasion, it was a small price to pay, for in the end she would have the upper hand. Gracefully, and with the demeanor of one accustomed to being obeyed, not ordered, Suisan twirled around. The soft fabric of her saxony blue dress whispered in the tense silence. "Very nice," he drawled approvingly. "But don't wear the apron. I like the dress as it is."

So he thought her an object to be displayed for his pleasure! Her pride was now tweaked beyond the point of good sense. She curtly replied, "Yes, milord." Then she pasted on a smile.

Reaction was immediate; his forehead smoothed, his sensuous mouth tucked at the corners. "You've a sharp tongue, lass. I'll warn you again to curb it."

Fear and anger jostled for position within her. Anger won. "Again?" she asked, stiffening her back and her resolve. "Perhaps your memory has tricked you, for I remember no such previous warning." The instant the words were out she wished them back. He was suddenly as rigid as a statue and his eyes were now piercing. Surely he would dismiss her on the spot for her insolence. Then she would never be able to retrieve the rest of the *Maide dalbh*.

He didn't. Instead, he did the unexpected. He threw back his leonine head and laughed. Dishes rattled on the tray and sounded a tinkling to his booming melodious voice.

Oh, she seethed inside to be taken so lightly. Afraid that her next words would settle her fate, she clamped her jaw tightly shut. When the urge to tell him to go to the devil had passed, she turned toward the stairs. His voice stopped her.

"And take off that silly cap," he said, coming to stand beside her. "I'm sick to death of the things women do to their hair, and damn me if I can remember the last time I saw a female without a mobcap, a frilly bonnet, or a towering powdered wig harboring boats and birds and God only knows what else." His voice dropped. "I'll not have it in my house, nor on my girls."

In spite of herself and ignoring his possessive remark, Suisan laughed at his description of current styles. He responded with that deep and familiar chuckle that discomfited her so. Shaking her head to ward off the humor, she began walking down the stairs. He did the same but his long strides quickly put him in front of her.

Before they reached the landing between floors he glanced up at her. "Will you please step lively and walk at my side or must I take the stairs at a bridal gait?" He moved the tray slightly to the left and looked down the length of his long legs. "I'm hardly suited to the step," he added ruefully.

Suisan forced back a giggle at the picture he made. Dressed in evening finery and groomed to absolute perfection—yet his handsome face was pulled into a silly grin. And the unlikely sight of his large hands holding a tray of dirty dishes caused laughter to bubble up inside her.

Sheepishly, he eyed his burden. "No doubt, if the Earl could see me now, I'd be the laughingstock of London tomorrow."

Unable to summon a suitable rejoinder, Suisan held out her hands and said, "Then give it to me, for I've naught to lose in the balance . . . and we can't have you offending the gentry, can we, sir?"

He started to comply but held back the tray and said, "First the cap, lass, if you please."

His tone was so gentle, that Suisan untied the bow and stuffed the offending cap into her pocket. He smiled and yielded the tray.

They descended the remaining steps in companionable silence until he said, "I've not seen you wear that dress before."

"I've been saving it for best."

"Tonight's certainly that, I suppose. Did you perchance sew it?"

"No, sir. 'Twas the head seamstress at Roward who stitched it for me."

"Silver-tongued Nelly?"

"Aye," Suisan said, smiling.

He was quiet once more as they walked through the parlor toward the kitchen. Then he said, "I've wondered why I didn't see you when I came to the castle."

Prepared for the question, she confidently said, "I was away with Lady Suisan."

He turned so their eyes met. "Collecting roots and urchins and dye stuffs, I was told." His gaze moved to her hair.

"Lichens," she corrected, wondering if her chignon was askew. "We must gather them before winter, if we're to have enough dye for the cloth."

"And was that your work—dyeing the cloth?"

Comfortable with the subject, she said, "On some days, but we all share the work. 'Tis more pleasant that way."

He seemed to muse aloud when he said, "Perhaps herein lies the problem with Roward cloth."

They passed through the butler's pantry.

"The problem?" she asked, instantly alert to the criticism.

"'Tis nothing," he said with a slight shake of his head. Before she could question him further, he added, "You sound like you miss Scotland."

Homesickness struck her a low blow but she fought it back, put on a smile and lied. "With all there is to see and do here? No, I don't miss Perwickshire, not while I've things to do in London."

He stopped just outside the kitchen door and indicated she

should precede him. "Then you'll go back there someday—to Perwickshire?"

Their eyes met and she could not speak the lie on her tongue. "Yes," came her quiet reply.

The answer seemed to please him; his beguiling eyes danced with merry lights. "I'd like to visit again myself, but . . ." He stopped and his happy expression quickly faded.

Suisan started to ask him to explain but caught herself. Pleasant conversation was not what she wanted of Myles, and yet somehow their exchanges always wound up that way. Thinking her constant caution was the reason for their amiable moments, she kept silent as they walked into the kitchen. Myles's volatile temper was the reason he'd left the castle so quickly—and taken her treasures with him.

Mackie, wearing an apron over a black dress with an intricately crocheted collar, was cutting a rich cherry cake into thick slices. Will'am, dressed in new livery, fidgeted nearby.

Mackie looked up, glanced at the tray and said, "Cookson's back on his feed, I see." Then to Suisan, "Put those away and baste the quail with that drawn butter."

Without reply, Suisan did as she was bid.

Myles chuckled. "His appetite's back, but he's unhappy about missing our fancy doings and important guests tonight."

Mackie made a distasteful noise. "That's because he always lightens the Earl's purse at the chessboard."

Among his other duties Ollie served as Myles's interim butler when the 'gentry' were entertained for pleasure or profit—especially when Ollie got some of the profit.

"Not tonight," Myles said. His eyes twinkling mischievously, he turned to Will'am. "Well, lad, will you challenge the Earl in Ollie's stead?"

Will'am looked like he would choke. "Me, sir?" he pointed a shaking hand to his chest.

"You mustn't be afraid of these highbrows, boy," Myles said, his voice kind. "Do as Ollie instructed and we've naught to worry about."

"I'll try my best, sir. Mr. Cookson said if I blundered he'd skin me for parchment—like the Indians in the Colonies do."

Myles shook his head. "I'll deal with Mr. Cookson."

Will'am stood a little straighter, cleared his throat and said, "I'll be takin' my post in the foyer then." He exited the kitchen, his new shoes squeaking loudly as he crossed the tiled floor.

"Here, Maura," Mackie said, holding out the tray of cake. "Put this on the dessert server." She stopped and eyeing Suisan carefully, asked, "Where's your cap, girl?"

"She won't be wearing it—nor the apron," Myles stated.

Mackie frowned. "Whoever heard of a maid servin' bareheaded and without a proper apron?"

"*Moi.*"

Mackie obviously disapproved, but said, "You'll have to speak the King's English if you want her to understand you."

"She understands well enough," Myles said, and Suisan thought the statement involved more than mobcaps and a knowledge of French.

"Well," Mackie continued, "perhaps they won't notice and gossip 'round about it. Lord knows they look for any slip-up when they come here—especially the Earl's snooty wife."

"Lady Ainsbury won't be coming tonight," Myles said and reached for a slice of cake. "Just the Earl and his daughter."

Hands on her hips, Mackie glared, watching him eat. When he hummed his approval, she beamed. "You always did favor my cherry cake."

Myles, having finished the cake, brushed his hands against each other. "And everything else from your kitchen."

Noise from the front of the house drew Myles's attention. He straightened his back and clicked his heels in military fashion. "'Twould seem my noble guests have arrived. Shall we do it up proper?"

Suisan nodded, but Mackie said, "We'll do our best and pray they ain't lookin' for tales to tell." Then she turned to Suisan, "Keep your distance from the Earl when servin' him; that pretty frock you're wearin' will draw more than his eye, to be sure, and his hands move faster than the plague through Whitechapel."

Myles chuckled and approvingly said, "Lady Suisan's seamstress stitched it for her."

Suisan watched Mackie closely but the housekeeper's expression revealed nothing of her earlier disapproval of Suisan Harper.

Mackie had not exaggerated the Earl's lecherous behavior. The overdressed, overperfumed and overbearing nobleman plied his searching hands with the skill of a cutpurse. He leaned much too close to Suisan at every opportunity and by the time the main course was served her dark dress was dusted with chalk from his enormous wig and splotched with grease from his groping hands.

His daughter, whom Myles addressed as Miss Phoebe, was decorated much like her father—and smelled like him, too. As was proper in mixed company, Phoebe ate little. She took great care in selecting each morsel and at one point pondered a carrot round for so long a time Suisan wanted to scream. At last, the decision made, Phoebe moued her little rosebud mouth to accept the chosen bit.

When Phoebe spoke of herself, which was often, she had the ridiculous habit of using collective terms.

"We must order a new wig," she declared, patting the towering configuration on her head and sending a shower of pomatum onto the beautifully set table and the remaining food on her plate. "Our birthday is very soon and Papa has promised us a ball."

Disgusted, Suisan slipped back to the kitchen.

Mackie was standing near the back door, a bleak expression on her face. Wringing her hands, the housekeeper listened intently to a young man Suisan had never seen before.

"Mackie?"

When she turned, Suisan saw tears in the housekeeper's eyes.

"What is it?" Suisan rushed toward them.

"It's my Peg," Mackie said on a sob. "Her time's come and I promised I'd be with her, but—" She waved her arms and rolled her eyes which were streaming with tears. "With all this, I can't leave now! Tonight's too important to the master."

Suisan looked to the young man who seemed equally shaken. His desolate expression offered no explanation. Childbirth was an everyday occurrence. Why were they so upset? Knowing Mackie visited her daughter often, and thinking the expected child was merely coming early, Suisan said, "You go along Mackie, I'll see the dinner through."

Relief shone in the housekeeper's eyes. "Bless your heart. But I must tell the master before I go."

"I'll fetch him." Suisan said and returned to the dining room. Catching Myles's eye, she tipped her head toward the kitchen. He frowned, but made his excuses and joined her in the butler's pantry.

"Is something amiss?" he asked, leaning close and placing his hand at the small of her back.

Ignoring how pleasant the touch felt, Suisan said, "Mackie's daughter's having a baby and she—"

"God in heaven, help us!" he swore as he tightened his grip around her waist and began walking, almost dragging her along.

Assuming the remark was pure selfishness on his part, Suisan grew angry and defensive. "I'm perfectly capable of carrying on without her. And keep your hands to yourself!" She tried to pull away but he held her fast.

"What did you say?"

"I've been pawed and ogled all evening by that worthless English lord, and I'll not be insulted by an insensitive brute like you! Mackie's very upset."

"Of course she's upset," he said. He cast Suisan a chilling look but did not release her. "And if you continue to wag that disrespectful tongue, I'll send you back to Scotland on the first packet."

Frightened by his angry look and convinced he would carry out the threat, Suisan said no more. When they entered the kitchen he released her and sped to Mackie, his arms outstretched.

The housekeeper flew into his embrace and sobbed against his chest. "My Peg's time's come, and oh, sweet God, it'll be just like before. I know it will."

"Now, now, Mackie," Myles soothed, his voice kind, his large hands stroking her back. "No, it won't. I promised you, didn't I?"

When she continued to cry Myles grasped her upper arms

and set her away from him. His eyes drilled into hers. "Did you hear me?" The sobbing continued and he shook her slightly. Louder he said, "Mackie! It will not be like before."

She blinked and seemed to collect herself. The sobs became hiccoughs.

As he continued the reassuring words, Suisan stood frozen. The worried expression on his face, the kindness of his words completely baffled her.

Then he turned to Suisan and said, "Fetch Will'am."

His commanding tone set her in motion. When she returned with the boy, Myles was putting Mackie's cloak around her shoulders.

Addressing Will'am, Myles said, "Ready the carriage and take Mackie to her daughter. Then you're to fetch the doctor straightaway, take him there, and wait until the babe comes." Myles's eyes became cold, same as his voice. "And if you dally, boy, I'll have your head on a pike!"

"Aye, sir." In a rush of squeaking shoes, Will'am dashed out the back door; the other lad, who had been standing by, followed close on his heels.

Myles returned his attention to Mackie. "You're not to fret. Do you understand?"

She nodded, the unsecured hat bobbing on her head.

Then Myles smiled. "If you continue to cry, you'll surely scare the babe to death." Using his napkin, he gently dabbed at Mackie's tears. "We mustn't have him seeing you so troubled, not on his first night into the world. He'll think something's amiss with his new grandmother, now won't he?"

Mackie smiled gratefully up at him and the tears began to flow again. "Thank you, sir. You're a blessing."

"I'm no such thing." He leaned close and kissed her reddened cheek. "But you, on the other hand, will be the grandest grandmother of all."

Will'am stuck his head in the door. Myles gave Mackie a gentle push. "Off with you now." He glanced at Will'am and added, "And take good care, boy."

When the door closed behind them, Myles turned to face Suisan. His expression was again a worried frown.

Ashamed of her behavior toward him, Suisan swallowed the lump in her throat and waited, watching him.

"Mackie had only two children, both daughters. The elder died last Michaelmas while giving birth to a stillborn son."

Shame turned to remorse and Suisan lowered her eyes.

"I thought she might have told you, but—" He stopped, sighing heavily.

"I didn't know," Suisan whispered thickly. Raising her head, she added, "I'm dreadfully sorry."

"So are we all," he said flatly.

His hurt expression was devastating to Suisan and she ached inside. Desperate to change it, she said, "Please don't be sad. All will be well with Mackie's daughter. The doctor's skilled—you've seen him work."

Myles studied her closely, his gaze boring into her. After what seemed an eternity, he nodded and blew out his breath. The smile that came next was a godsend to Suisan. She returned it and her heart fluttered wildly in her breast.

"You can manage then?" he asked and she knew he meant the meal.

Standing taller, she said, "If not, you can put *my* head on a pike."

He chuckled, but the sound was a faint echo of the one she had come to know.

"They expect you to fail, you know." He tipped his head toward the front of the house.

"The Earl and Miss Phoebe?"

"Yes."

Bewildered, she asked, "Whyever would they?"

Crossing his arms over his chest, he said, "Because *your* grandmother did not serve *my* grandmother."

Understanding dawned; the gentry took pride in their staffs—generation after generation after generation, and Myles was not of the gentry.

Before she could reply, he said, "But since I've yet to meet either your ancestors or mine, I couldn't give a fig." He lowered his voice. "Do you ken, lassie?"

Loyalty and sympathy for Myles Cunningham swelled within her. Putting on her brightest, sauciest smile, Suisan said, "If the Earl's grandsire had hands as fast as his, my grandmother would have slapped his painted face and quit! But I won't, and you can count on that."

The real chuckle came. "Are you afraid of the pike? I really do have one, you know."

At that moment Suisan thought Myles had everything in the world. "Then put it away, sir. You'll not need it this night."

"Very well, but I will need a fresh napkin."

Without thinking, she said, "They're in the laundry room."

His eyebrows shot up and his chin went down. "I *know* where the napkins are," he said regally, still grinning.

Suisan could but stare at him.

"Close your mouth, lassie, and fetch your master a napkin."

She did both, and quickly.

In painful slowness, the meal continued but Myles's thoughts were not on the fare. The pretty lass was as good as her word and better than he'd expected. Even when the Earl plied his pitiful charms, which was often, she never flinched, never protested.

Seeing her, graceful as a gazelle, skirting the table and the Earl, Myles was struck by the differences between Maura and Phoebe. Not in several lifetimes, nor with the finest instruction to be found, could Phoebe attain such grace as his serving maid from Scotland.

Maura carried herself with an innate confidence and sureness of step that was sheer beauty to behold . . . as was her form. The perfectly tailored dress molded the high, round curves of her breasts, then dipped to shape her tiny waist. The soft fabric whispered in Myles's ears each time she moved and he came to anticipate his turn at being served.

But it was the color of her dress, dark and rich, that continually drew his attention to her eyes. Fringed with lacy dark lashes, her eyes were the deepest indigo he'd ever seen. Neither sloed nor slanted, her eyes were round and perfectly suited to her heart-shaped face. Her pert chin was no longer stubbornly set, as he'd seen it on many occasions, but now served as a fitting frame for her mouth. Her mouth was trouble, though, and Myles did his best to avoid staring at it. He continually failed.

When she leaned over the table the candlelight illuminated the swan-like curve of her neck and the elegant line of jaw and chin. In profile, she was lovelier than any woman he'd ever seen. Every now and then he would catch a sparkle of red in her black hair—or was it perhaps a trick of the candles? He didn't know, didn't particularly care.

Too soon, he again fell victim to her mouth. Her lips formed a perfect bow when a smile lifted the corners, but when she concentrated, the lower lip pouted out, just enough—and too damn much. Myles ached to see just how well her mouth would fit against his own tonight.

Then she was staring at him, a curious frown on her sculptured brow. He couldn't have stopped the smile, nor stifled the appreciative chuckle, not for all the tobacco contracts in the world. He was rewarded with a maidenly blush that brought a glow to her creamy complexion and an ache to Myles's loins.

With tremendous effort, Myles mentally backtracked until his mind clung to the word *tobacco*, and he returned his attention to his guests.

Over brandy, which the earl loved, Myles would broach the subject that was the evening's purpose. To gain the earl's favor, which Myles required, he would mention the generous amount of cognac in his basement, which the earl could not refuse. Then Myles would suggest handing the matter of the tobacco contract over to their solicitors, to which the earl would agree.

Boringly so, the evening went according to plan. Myles's only diversion seemed to be the Scottish lassie and she was a pleasant distraction, to say the least. He no longer cared that she was a servant; he intended to have her.

By the time the earl and Miss Phoebe rose to leave, Will'am had still not returned with news of Mackie's daughter. In his absence, Myles showed his guests to the door. He'd sent the lass to the kitchen long before, and now he headed that way.

He found her fast asleep at the oaken table which was

spotlessly clean, like the rest of the room. Resting her cheek on folded arms, she slept silently. Myles studied her as was his wont all evening, only now he looked his fill. When the familiar heat rose within, he moved toward her.

Unable to resist touching her, he traced the delicate line of her jaw and called her name. When she did not respond, he touched her lips.

Her soft breath flowed over his finger; the desire in his loins flared. Clamping his jaw tight, he momentarily stifled that desire and swept her into his arms.

"What?" she gasped, her eyes fluttering open.

He'd expected blue, and blue they were.

"Why are you looking at me that way?" she asked.

Soft words, soft lips. Like an eagle swooping down on its prey, Myles covered her lips with his own. She protested at first and he'd expected that, but tonight he was prepared to counter any objection.

He did, and admirably so. Only when she yielded to him and returned the kiss, did he pull back.

"I want you lass," he declared tightly and carried her to the stairs. "I've waited long enough."

"No," she gasped. "'Tis not what I want."

" 'Tis," he insisted and held her gaze.

" 'Tis not. I swear it."

"Then I swear I'll prove you wrong."

She looked frightened for an instant, but in the next she made a fatal error; she dared him with her eyes.

He kissed her again—kissed her until she moaned his name, until her breathing became labored.

"Lass?"

"Set me down," she declared, even though her eyes were dark with desire.

"Nay," he breathed. "Not even if I could."

He felt her stiffen. "Look at me," he commanded softly.

An eternity seemed to pass before she faced him.

"Put your arms about my neck now," he instructed softly. "We're going upstairs—to my bed."

She opened her mouth and he knew the word on her lips was "no." He smothered the denial the only way he could, the best way he could. As his mouth moved on hers, he felt the renewed battle she waged against him.

She lost.

The feel of her arms twining about his neck and the absolute harmony of her lips moving against his own made Myles want to shout out loud, but it made him want to do something else more. Again he moved toward the stairs.

In his mind he saw her naked beneath him, heard her voice, touched with the Highlander's gentle brogue, whispering his name.

"It's a boy, sir! A fine and healthy—"

Will'am's voice exploded through Myles's mind and shattered the lusty image he'd begun to conjure. He looked over to see the lad standing in the doorway.

She stiffened. "Set me down!" No gentle brogue, a direct command.

Myles complied, and she ran from the room.

Will'am turned white as a corpse.

Myles considered making him one.

·~· *Chapter 5* ·~·

Dismayed by the latest scene with Myles and cross after a sleepless night, Suisan attacked the defenseless mound of dough with a vengeance. She reached for more oats, then fiercely kneaded them into the lump of flour, water and fat.

"Buzzards and bailiwicks!" she spat, slamming the lifeless wad onto the table.

"You're a thief and a liar and the lord of all rodents," she cursed at the empty corner of the kitchen. "You wanted scones?" she jeered, her eyes still molded to the spot. "Then it's bannocks you'll get!"

I want you, lass. His voice echoed in her mind.

As if awaiting his summons, a part of Suisan struggled to answer him in kind. Now yielding and weak, she relaxed the night-long vigil and his image swam within her mind. He was tempting, he was desirable, but he was out of reach. She was not meant to have a man, nor a family of her own. Yet she thought of a make-believe world of tomorrows—a world she had always ached for, a world she would always be denied. It was a world she might never have missed had it not been for his kiss.

Steeling herself against the memory she tried to concentrate on the motion of her hands, but even as she placed the bannocks on the griddle, Myles's lustful declaration crept into her thoughts.

I want you, lass.

Once again, she fought the aching loneliness she had always held at bay—until now. Her life's path was laid and she had but to follow it. A narrow course, a lonely existence. She dared not stray from it.

I want you, lass.

Again, his voice seemed to call out into the darkness, and for a brief, shining moment someone was there to meet him.

Her name was Maura, and she was free to love, free to wed, and able to breed a castle full of healthy, normal children. Hope, however futile and destructive, flowered within her breast.

She was overcome by a dreamy lethargy as she recalled every detail of last night's romantic encounter with Myles. She saw again the naked hunger in his eyes, a hunger she ached to appease. She heard the rumble of his husky voice calling her name and she relived the floating sensation of being held in his powerful arms. Her heart had stumbled when he'd cradled her against his chest; her heart was stumbling now. The erotic feel of his lips on hers, coaxing and intimate, had at last awakened her long dormant passion, and in those thrilling moments of ecstasy when she'd yielded and returned his passion, she'd glimpsed the sweet fulfillment of her secret, forbidden dreams.

"Miss Maura?"

Yes, that's me, she thought and smiled a private, lover's smile.

A sliding, scraping noise intruded into the dream.

"They're burning, don't ye see!" It was Will'am's voice . . . and reality.

Suisan stared as he raked the flat and blackened oat cakes from the griddle. Not only had she burned them, she'd forgotten the leavening!

"Take them outside!" she ordered crossly, fanning the acrid smoke toward the back door.

The boy obeyed and Suisan began to collect herself. She reached again for the oats but the bin was empty.

"Damn!"

"Just as well," Will'am declared from behind her. "You bein' out of oats and all, 'cause Himself don't like bannocks."

Whirling around, Suisan shouted, "Then Himself can break his fast elsewhere!"

Will'am's mouth dropped open and his eyes grew round in surprise.

Sobered by his expression, Suisan gathered her wits and said, "See to Mr. Cookson."

The boy relaxed and hopefully asked, "Then you'll be makin' scones?"

"Aye," she said, resigned.

Will'am scurried off and Suisan, gritting her teeth, made the dreaded pastries.

By the time she'd prepared the meal and headed upstairs to Cookson's room, she had banished Myles from her mind. Ollie smiled warmly when she entered.

"Morning, Mr. Cookson," she said, placing the tray on his lap.

"You pegged it proper, my girl," he replied enthusiastically. "And a day to celebrate it is, since our Mackie's a grandmother at last."

Lost in her own fantasy, Suisan had forgotten Mackie's plight. A boy, that's what Will'am had said last night.

Ollie stared at her, a curious gleam in his eyes. Then he glanced at the tray, and finally back to her. "You've a talent to rival Sibeal Harper's when it comes to scones."

Suisan pretended to smile. "So I'm told."

Still he didn't touch the food. "By Lady Suisan?"

"Aye . . . and others."

The gleam in his eyes became a twinkle. "By 'others' you mean Myles?" he queried knowingly.

Fond memories of Ollie hung on the edge of her mind; she pushed them back. The crafty steward had teased her as a child, but she wouldn't fall prey to him now. "He favors them well enough," Suisan said, imitating Mackie.

Thankfully Ollie began to eat, but for some unknown reason. Suisan stayed. "You leg's healing quite well," she said, unable to think of anything else to say, yet somehow unable to leave.

"Hmm." He smiled over the rim of the teacup. "I'm up to one hundred paces a day, with the help of my fancy new cane." Setting the cup down, he added. "And by the time Mackie comes home I'll be getting up and down the stairs."

"Today?"

He took great care and an inordinate amount of time to wipe his moustache and beard with a napkin. "Myles is giving Mackie a holiday," he said at last.

"How long?"

"A fortnight or so, I suspect."

Relief surged through Suisan; with Mackie gone, she had one less person to worry about, one less person who might uncover her disguise.

"I see you're happy for her, too. That's good, lass; Mackie's due a blessing."

"Aye." Suisan turned to leave but at the sound of a door opening down the hall, she stopped.

"Maura, where are you!" Myles bellowed.

Holding her breath, she waited for him to come. He didn't. Instead she heard footsteps taking him upstairs—to her room, directly above Ollie's. In her mind she could picture Myles's every movement. The door to her room crashed open.

She stole a glance at Ollie. The hand holding a buttered scone was stalled between the plate and his open mouth. His head was tilted to the side and his eyes were focused on the ceiling. When the door to her chamber slammed shut Ollie turned his gaze to her.

Holding up his free hand, he splayed his fingers. "I give him to five."

When Ollie began to count Suisan moved away from the door. As if preordained, on the count of five the door swung open.

Wearing only doeskin breeches and the look of a wild, stalking animal, Myles rushed into the room.

His disheveled appearance and naked chest were so startling to Suisan she took a step back. Her mouth went dry at the hungry expression in his eyes—eyes that were trained on her. She'd seen that look last night and the power of it made her weak. The ensuing silence grew thick with tension.

"Won't you join us?" Ollie said at last, his voice mockingly humorous.

Slowly, and with what she perceived as reluctance, Myles turned toward the bed. Suisan thanked God for the reprieve.

"Have a scone, my boy; they couldn't be better . . . unless we had some maple syrup." Ollie paused to glance at Suisan before adding, "Nothing like sweet syrup after the sap's been harvested." He smiled in a silly way. "Don't you agree, Myles—about the sap?"

Anger flared so quickly in Myles's eyes Suisan thought she'd imagined it. The notion brought to mind her father's long forgotten warning: *Our Myles is a good boy, lassie, but that temper'll be his undoing—and yours, too, if you don't respect it.*

Myles was now holding that notorious temper by a slender thread. As rigid as a statue, as imposing as a gladiator, he glared at Ollie, who seemed unaffected. Suisan, however, was held spellbound.

Then he seemed to shake himself, and raking a hand through his tousled hair, he relaxed and smiled as he looked from Ollie to her. "Bring me a tray, lass," he commanded. "I've a yen for Ollie's company while I take my scones this morning."

Suisan wasted no time in fleeing the room. After preparing the tray, she ordered Will'am to take it upstairs. Then she picked up the shopping basket and made a cowardly retreat onto the streets of London.

The empty house on Beacon Row offered a quiet comfort she desperately neéded. After drawing her bath, she languished in the warm soothing water. Nelly was working in the dress shop and would be home soon. Perhaps she had learned why Madame LeBlanc sold Roward cloth under the Strathclyde name. At the thought of the awful deception, Suisan felt the heat of anger race through her veins. Her people labored long and hard to produce such fine cloth; they deserved the revenue and praise for their work. She thought of the roofs that needed mending, the bridges and roads that needed repair. All in due time, she vowed. And if Myles Cunningham had played a role in the fraud she would expose him. The profit for him and the obscurity for the weavers of Roward was a cowardly ruse she despised.

Disappointment assaulted her. How could the young man she had once respected and adored have become such a deceiving, miserable lout? And why did the change cause such an aching in her woman's heart?

Safe and secure and momentarily out of his reach, she dozed. At the feel of a soft, familiar hand on her arm, she opened her eyes.

"Good day, milady," Nelly said, smiling.

Suisan stretched and yawned. "Oh, Nelly—I was hoping you'd come."

Nelly's cheerful expression faded. "'Tis a lucky chance an' nothin' more. That Madame LeBlanc's in a right tizzy over a big, new commission."

"What time is it?"

Handing Suisan an orange from the shopping basket, Nelly sat down on the floor, a smug look on her face. "'Tis noon-tide, and I've a bit of gossip."

Suisan raised her eyebrows.

Choosing an apple for herself, Nelly took great pains to polish it and twist out the stem. Familiar with the delaying tactic, Suisan waited.

As if she were speaking of mundane things, Nelly said, "Himself's turned out his mistress."

"Truly?" Suisan gasped, at once elated and puzzled.

"*Oui, oui,*" Nelly said with a flair as she warmed to her favorite pastime. "Her name's Barbara and her new protector's the one who ordered the big commission. Not that Himself didn't settle on her nice and proper—and generous, too. Some say men were standing in line, waiting for him to tire of her."

Elation raced through Suisan. "Did you see her?"

"Of course, and a right bonny thing she is, with dark hair, green eyes and skin as fair as my little Sorcha's. Has the look of the Irish, if you ask me." Pausing to screw up her face, Nelly distastefully declared, "In spite of her being a high-paid whore and all."

Suddenly Suisan did not want to hear more of Myles's mistress, former or not. "What else have you learned?"

Nelly frowned, obviously disappointed. "I ain't learned who switched our cloth if that's what yer referrin' to."

"You will," Suisan said as she began to peel the orange. The pungent fragrance filled the room.

"That be the truth," she declared, determination sparkling in her eyes. "I'm sick to bletherin death of Madame and her goonies ravin' on about how fine Strathclyde cloth is." Nelly lowered her voice conspiratorially. "I've a plan, though."

"What will you do?"

"I've offered to stay late tonight, and when everyone's gone I'll slip myself into Madame's office and have a look at the account books. Then we'll see who switched our cloth."

"Please be careful. If you're caught we may never learn who's behind it."

"Don't you be fretting over Nelly," she huffed. "I'm too smart for the likes of them that works for her." Nelly shifted, getting comfortable. "Now tell me about Himself and the earl and last night."

"Wouldn't you rather hear what Myles said about you?" Suisan taunted.

Nelly's eyes flashed. "Me? He remembers me?"

"Aye, he does."

Doubtfully, Nelly said, "He speaks of me?"

Chuckling, Suisan said, "Often, and he calls you 'Silver-tongued Nelly' when he does."

Nelly chortled. "Didn't I say he was bright? When your parents were alive, Myles was the perfect son, always goin' out of his way to please them. And Flora thought him bonny, too; said Myles planned to modern up the castle and the weavin' room." The smile faded, and shaking the apple, she added, "Don't seem right, you know, the stories your uncle tells about him."

"Rabby knows him better than we do. If Myles Cunningham is so 'bonny' why'd he storm away from the castle before we could return from Aberdeen?"

Nelly looked thoughtful. "Your uncle *says* he knows Myles but what would make a good man change so much in ten bloody years?"

"My father's money, that's what changed Myles Cunningham," Suisan stated bitterly.

Nelly didn't argue but scooted closer to the tub. "We can speculate 'til the bagpipes play again but it won't change nothin' or no one."

Ruefully, Suisan said, "I'm glad you're full of wisdom again. I was beginning to worry about you."

Nelly tossed the apple core into the cold fireplace. "Tell me about last night."

Suisan relayed the happenings of last evening but did not mention the romantic interlude with Myles.

"Will Mackie be visitin' her daughter for a time?" Nelly asked.

"Aye, Ollie says she'll be gone at least a fortnight, and while she's away, we'll meet every night. We've few more than a dozen patterns left."

Nelly's shoulders slumped. "Can't be too soon for me—when all of them's out and we're on our way back to Perwickshire."

"There's still the cloth to deal with," Suisan reminded her.

Confidently, Nelly said, "We'll find the root of that, too."

Suisan finished the orange; Nelly held out her hand for the

peelings. When she was again dressed, Suisan said, ''Nine o'clock tonight.''

''I'll be there, milady.''

At a leisurely pace, Suisan strolled through the market-place. Here and there young men courted their sweethearts. Playfully, and with universal coyness, the lassies accepted or rejected the amorous attentions. Occasionally, she saw couples holding hands and casting familiar glances at each other. One couple openly embraced. Suisan sighed wistfully, an ancient ache constricting her chest.

Taking a deep, shaking breath, she continued, her eyes open, her expression closed.

Was it London or merely the freshness of spring that seemed to coat the very air with love? Or had she accepted her lonely fate so long ago that she had ceased to notice the ritual of courtship? She was noticing now and grudgingly she knew the cause. Myles Cunningham. He had given her a glimpse of a world she wasn't supposed to see. And it was lovely.

Giving her imagination free rein, she pictured herself and Myles, strolling across Comyn's Moor, knee deep in a field of rare white heather. He was her laird, she his lady fair, and together they governed the peaceful kingdom of Perwickshire. Without warning, nor cause, save his love for her, Myles would grasp her about the waist, lift her up and swing her 'round and 'round. Then his beseeching brown eyes would begin to smolder with passion and he would pull her to his chest. Long and deeply, he would kiss her, and when they were both breathless he would pull back and allow her to slide down the length of his body, and all the while those eyes would speak of love and desire.

Biting her lip to hold back the tears, Suisan willed the enchanting picture away. In its place she saw the world and her life as they truly were. She mustn't have children. She couldn't take the risk of bearing a child like Aunt Ailis. Despair and loneliness overwhelmed her. Calling up the cour-age she'd put away years ago and thought never to use again,

Suisan closed her mind to the image and returned to Myles's home.

Much later in the day and long after she'd exhausted the mental list of excuses, Suisan climbed the stairs to clean Myles's room. As she stood in the upstairs hall her spirit faltered; his room was the last place she wanted to be. She searched the quiet corridor, hoping as she often did that her portrait would materialize. But the wish was foolish; Myles didn't care enough to display a likeness of Suisan Harper. His interest in his stepsister was most likely a ploy, a ploy to get closer to Maura Forbes.

As the sun's waning rays poured through the large stained glass window at the end of the hall, pools of colored light dappled the walls and carpeted floor. She must remember to sweep the hall and clean the glass, but she hadn't the slightest idea of what to clean the glass with. Soap? Wax? She'd have to ask Nelly.

The rattling of harnesses and the creaking of wheels drew her attention. Walking to the stained glass window, Suisan looked out and saw Will'am driving a heavily-laden dray around the corner of the house. Time was wasting. Out of habit, she reached for a lamp before entering Myles's room.

Dark and cool and cocoon-like, the room bore no resemblance to the chamber she'd described to Nelly. Oddly, Suisan felt no remorse at the lie. She suspected the room itself and the contradictory images it presented were the cause.

For a man who spent the greater portion of his life on a merchantman sailing the open seas and visiting exotic lands, Myles Cunningham's room was surprisingly sedate and unexpectedly inviting. Each time she entered it she was assailed by her own misconceptions of Myles.

The bed, so large as to be made in sections, was covered with the soft fur of an enormous black bear. Draping the four posters was a canopy of dark blue velvet tied back with golden cords. Curtains of the same fabric blanketed the windows and effectively shielded the room from the outside world.

Two chairs and an ottoman of brass-studded Cordovan leather sat before the huge marble fireplace. On the mantel was a collection of hourglasses—some ornate, some ordinary. The largest and most impressive was cast in sterling silver and housed a pitted glass with sparkling white sand. The smallest was of delicately carved ivory, offset with dark green sand. The most unusual featured massive handles of solid gold shaped like fishes; one tail up, the other tail down. Between the sapphire-eyed carp rested a glass tinted a lighter shade of blue. Unable to resist, Suisan grasped the carp and, twisting her wrists, set the exotic timepiece in motion. Hypnotically, the sand trickled and pooled. Now and then, a jewel-like sparkle of dark blue caught the light and flickered as it fell. As the sand mounded in the lower glass, Suisan was struck by what it represented. Time. Why would Myles Cunningham be so obsessed with time?

She scanned the odd collection again as if the hourglasses held the answer. She knew so little of Myles, and yet he stirred deep emotions and triggered endless memories. Their early lives had been tangled, but ten long years had passed with nothing more than an occasional letter. And now her life was entwined with his again, only Suisan was no longer the gullible little sister. She was a woman and her heart had become involved in the struggle.

Her father's sea chest, crafted of indestructible ironwood at least a hundred years before her birth, sat on a bench at the foot of Myles's bed. She ached to open it again, to touch the things inside, the things Myles chose to accompany him on his long voyages. But she did not; it would only bring her closer to him.

As she went about tidying the room, she continually avoided the one possession she could not tolerate: the miniature painting of Myles's love. But like a siren, the woman in the ornately framed oval called out to Suisan, and as the sand continued to fall her resolve weakened. When she could no longer stifle her curiosity she walked to the writing desk and picked up the miniature.

Plain. The wench was as plain as neeps 'n tatties and homely to the point of pity. Thin hair of a shade that could have been dark blonde to brown was piled on the woman's small head. Her face, captured in a three-quarter pose, was so ordinary Suisan wondered if the artist were at fault. A simple and common necklace of pearls served as her only ornament. Since the artist chose to halt the likeness at the shoulders, even the woman's style of clothing was obscure.

What would attract Myles Cunningham to such a dull-looking woman? What secrets and occasions had they shared? What emotions linked her so steadfastly to Myles that he would keep her likeness in such a prominent place in his private chamber and take it with him when he traveled?

Jealousy, new and uncomfortable, assaulted Suisan. She disliked, nay, despised a woman she had never met—a woman she might never know. Of a certainty, the likeness was not Barbara; Nelly's description of the dark-haired Irish mistress was an ocean away from the pitiful woman in the oval.

Sighing, Suisan replaced the oval and scanned the other items on the desk. She gasped when she spied a note addressed to Maura.

In what she deemed an angry scrawl, since the penmanship was unlike the style of Myles's letters to her, he'd penned a list of instructions.

Take the small, blue ledger. . . . Which was on the desk. *Inventory the brandy Will'am has put in the.* . . . Squinting, Suisan struggled to make out the last word in the sentence. As if impatient, Myles had not re-inked the quill before finishing the thought and the word faded off. At last she defined the words as "basement." Before beginning the next sentence he'd dipped the quill into the ink. The next words were clear and shocking.

Do not disobey me by wearing the . . .

Again, he'd lazily ignored the necessity of re-inking the quill. After some guesswork, she deciphered the faint word and as she did so, her temper flared. *Mobcap.*

"Damn your domineering hide!" she spat aloud. "I'll wear what I please!"

Then she caught herself. She was a servant, an underling expected to obey, and she must play the part for now, but once she had recovered her treasures she would be free of Myles Cunningham and her life would be her own again.

And lonely as a Lowlander's lute, her woman's heart cried out.

"Be silent," she commanded the traitorous voice within.

She folded the note, when in truth she wanted to crumble it, and put it in her pocket. Defiantly, she left the mobcap in place.

Considering the task ahead, Suisan realized what the note had said. The *basement*. Will'am was in the basement at this moment unloading the dray she'd seen him driving!

Apprehension flooded through her; what if he opened the rickety old box tucked beneath the basement stairs? But she discounted that possibility; surely Will'am had no idea of what the box contained. Myles was too clever to involve the boy in something so dangerous as harboring the *Maide dalbh*, the collective tartan patterns that could give him the gallows for a necklace.

That brought to mind another recurring question. To her knowledge, not once since his return had Myles ventured into the basement—nor had anyone else. She'd lightly sprinkled flour on the narrow stairs and it had yet to be disturbed. But why not? Why would Myles go to the trouble to steal the Highland patterns and then ignore their presence in his basement? What were his plans for the *Maide dalbh*? No rational answer came to mind, because only one person wanted the patterns, and his name was George and he was King of all England.

"I'm taking them back to Scotland where they belong!" she vowed, and quickly set about the task of cleaning Myles's room. When she was done, she gathered the ledger, the quill, and the bottle of ink, then headed for the basement.

With practiced ease and the confidence of one who senses victory, she made her way to the open basement door. Will'am's footprints were mapped in the white powder and she easily followed the faint path. A slight breeze from the windows he'd opened mingled with and diluted the musty air.

As she descended, she searched the room, but Will'am was nowhere about. She breathed a sigh of relief. The old box containing the *Maide dalbh* was literally beneath her feet—under the basement stairs.

When her shoes touched the hard-packed earthen floor, she became aware of another difference in the room: the smell of wood and liquor. Had Will'am broken a bottle of the precious brandy? Still piqued by Myles's domineering note, she hoped the whole damned cargo had been spilt.

Bolstered by the thought, she smiled as she pivoted to face the room. The smile died on her lips and she froze in place. The ledger and the quill tumbled to the floor. She grasped the ink bottle and fought the urge to throw it as far as she could.

Towering before her was a mountain of crates, stacked to the ceiling. It was impossible, it was unbelievable, but it was undeniably true. Myles Cunningham had effectively put the Highland patterns out of her reach again. They might as well be in the Tower of London, for the result would be the same. She could never move the boxes that hid them, nor could she climb over them.

Failure! She had trudged across Scotland and faced a challenge even her wildest dreams could not have imagined. She groaned in despair. Robbing that hated English Tower would be easier than reaching the patterns.

⌁ *Chapter 6* ⌁

Myles tugged gently on the reins and his horse slowed. Blowing softly, the Arabian stallion shook his head and stamped his feet restlessly. The hollow sound of iron hooves on the pavement echoed in the darkened street. After stroking the animal's neck to further soothe him, Myles settled back in the saddle and studied his London home.

From his vantage point across the street, the grey stone mansion seemed to dwarf the other residences. Myles knew he should be proud to call such an address home, but that had never been the case. Although elegant and costly and envied by many, the house was no more than a stopping place between voyages, a place to linger when he could find the time. Myles was growing weary of voyages and wearier still of having so little time to himself. He longed to flee London and all the city represented, and someday he would.

The horse quieted and only the distant pealing of a clock's bell broke the stillness of the damp night. Myles counted the hammer's strokes. Nine o'clock. He had accomplished much this day, albeit slowly. He knew the reason for his frustration—a raven-haired beauty with eyes as blue as the Indian Ocean and a stubborn will that begged to be conquered.

Many times during the long day his thoughts had strayed to her lips and the way they'd felt pressed against his own. He was certain she had wanted him last night. And if London didn't fall to the Turks by sunup, he'd have her!

Lust, of the kind to spawn legends and busy the bards, urged Myles on.

He chuckled, the sound partly sinister and wholly confident. He closed his eyes and thought of something singularly pleasant: the way she would feel beneath him, the way her eyes would darken with passion and the way she would whisper his name.

When his body reacted, as was its wont all day, he diverted his lusty thoughts again to his London home.

He'd liked the place on first sight, only the location had troubled him. It troubled him still. For a moment he pictured the stately mansion sitting atop a windy bluff in Cornwall or nestled in the rolling hills of Scotland. The second image brought a wistful smile to his lips and a long discarded dream to his mind. A sadness now hung over that dream.

The horse whinnied. Myles glanced about to see a shadowed figure coming toward him. He leaned forward to view the pedestrian more closely.

With her head down and covered by a shawl, Myles could not discern her features. Determined and angry steps brought her closer. In a moment she, too, would be in the circle of lamplight. What was she doing on the streets alone at this time of night?

"Thievin', miserable Sassenach!" she grumbled through tightly clenched teeth. "Buggerin' son of a carrion-eatin'—"

Spying Myles, she stopped an arm's length away and gasped, "Oh!"

"What were you doing back there?" He jerked his head toward the alley behind his house.

She took a step back into the darkness but not before he caught sight of a golden braid peeking out from her shawl. He urged the stallion forward but stopped when she pulled a pistol.

"Takin' meself home." She aimed the gun at his chest and added, "without no trouble. Do ye ken?" The threat in her voice was obvious and the steady hand on the pistol was convincing enough for Myles.

Thinking she was, with good cause, merely protecting herself, Myles doffed his cocked hat and replied, "You'll get no trouble from me, ma'am."

She stood a little straighter, and still facing him, cautiously backed away. He watched her until she reached the next corner. Standing in the pool of yellow light she turned to face him. Or was she studying him? Myles was struck by a feeling of familiarity, but at that moment she disappeared into the night.

Ah, London, he lamented, as he guided the horse across the street and to the stable, *just when I think you've shown me all of life's oddities, you toss another in my face.*

He smiled, but not at the oddity. Through the open basement window he spied Maura sitting at a small table, her head dutifully bent over the blue ledger. Her elegant profile was beautifully etched in the lamplight and seeing her, so pensively at ease, Myles felt the same familiar pull he'd held at bay for too long.

God's breath, she was lovely.

Myles shifted in the saddle to ease the fullness building in his loins. The low and twisting ache was again grinding away at him but tonight that ache would be soothed. The lass had put it there with her curiously bold eyes and her saucy ways. He had a hunger for her, a ravenous craving to know her most secret thoughts, to touch her everywhere and to make her his own. No other woman would do, of that he was painfully certain.

And, by damn, he would have her!

She turned away then and fixed her gaze on some point across the cellar. Suddenly she went rigid, then her small fist banged on the table. The lantern wavered, the inkwell toppled. She scooped up the ledger and flew out of the chair. That's when Myles noticed the cap.

Perched defiantly on her head was that frilly mobcap! The obstinate gesture fired him anew. He'd yank that cap off himself and burn it to blazing cinders—just as soon as he dismissed Will'am for the evening.

By the time Myles stood at the top of the cellar stairs he was outwardly calm but inside his emotions were churning like a Caribbean storm. The lass was leaning over the table, her back to him. He took the small steps four at a time and with each stride begged her to turn around.

She did, but her expression surprised him. He'd expected apprehension or defiance but what he saw was anger.

Thinking she was upset at herself for spilling the ink, Myles hurried to her side and said, "'Tis nothing to fret over. I've barrels of the stuff."

"I'm sure you do," she indignantly replied.

Myles frowned and considered reprimanding her for the tart words, but he did not. Instead he watched her as, flustered and tensed with ire, she continued to clean up the oozing ink. Then, with lightning quick fingers he pulled the offensive cap from her head and tossed it onto the spill.

She gasped, one ink-stained hand flying to her uncovered head. "How dare you?"

Masking his shock and holding back an equally sarcastic reply, he allowed one eyebrow to rise, slowly and imperiously. The intimidating gesture succeeded, for she stepped back.

"You were," he began smoothly, "instructed to dispense with the cap."

"Instructed?" she challenged, her blue eyes wide with defiance. "Nay, I was commanded."

Fighting back the urge to throttle her, Myles said, "And am I not master of this house?"

"And master of all you survey, I suppose?" she taunted, sweeping the air with the ink-stained mobcap.

Cold droplets of ink splattered his face; her mouth fell open in surprise and her white teeth contrasted against the ripe red color of her lips. Myles's control snapped, but before he could reach for her, her expression changed. Her eyes twinkled with laughter and she covered a smile with the back of one hand. When she stifled a chuckle, Myles too saw the humor of the situation—even if he was the brunt of the joke.

In a calm yet superior voice, he said, "Clean up your mess, girl."

Her eyes grew wide and the smile faded. She swallowed slowly and with difficulty but did not move to obey; she was battling herself and the fight was obvious. So was the outcome. "Do it now," he further encouraged.

Surrender, both sweet and welcome to Myles, was written on her face but her words startled him. "Then sit down," she urbanely said, motioning toward the chair, "you're too big for me to reach."

In a pig's eye, he thought, *we suit each other in every way!*

He ached to take her in his arms but suspected she would bolt. Deciding to go slowly, Myles shrugged his shoulders and sat.

Deciding he was harmless. Suisan did as she was bid. What harm could come from touching him? she blithely thought. Much, she soon discovered, for Myles Cunningham exuded a masculine power she had assumed was the stuff of romantic legend. But now the legend was real, and like a helpless beggar tossed into a web of riches, she gave up the fight.

Smiling a crooked, rueful smile, she said, "You'll have a time, you know, explaining these spots on your face." Leaning closer, she truthfully added, "I'm sorry."

A deep dimple dotted his cheek and softened the fine lines of his face. "No harm done, lassie, but will they pass for freckles, do you suppose?" he asked, his dark brown eyes gleaming with golden lights.

Tendrils of desire wrapped around Suisan and she shivered at his husky tone. Recovering somewhat, she rejoined, "Only if you had freckles as a boy."

"I had little else in my youth," he stated flatly, but his expression did not change.

Knowing the truth behind the cryptic remark, her heart melted, but not with pity; she was beyond that. Other, deeper emotions were rising to the fore and she was frightened by them.

His boyish smile vanished. "What are you thinking?" he asked, obviously concerned.

She looked away. "Naught . . . of consequence."

He smiled. "Pardon me if I argue the point."

She faced him again. "And how would you know?" she queried, warmed by his intense gaze.

"Perhaps," he drawled, rubbing his leg against hers, "the same way I know where to look for a rainbow after a storm." Even though his gaze remained blithely innocent, his hand crept to her waist.

Suisan saw an old memory, still vivid after the years of separation. Myles was holding her securely on his hip and with their faces side by side, he pointed toward a colorful rainbow in the sky. She pushed the memory away but a feeling of kinship remained. Playfully, she said, "I doubt you have the time to search for rainbows."

His hand moved higher. "And how would you know?"

Her eyes locked with his. "The carp told me so."

His lips puckered at the corners; she wished he would go on and smile.

"What else did they tell you?" His voice was soft and suggestive, like the expression in his eyes. The feel of his hand drawing lazy circles below the sensitive curve of her breast chipped away at her resolve.

"They told me," she began, fighting to keep her voice even, "that I've work to finish before I find my bed."

She regretted the words the instant they were out; she should have anticipated his response. Even so, when that arching brow cocked high in cavalier fashion, she could barely hold back the grin.

"I'll help you find a bed," he offered magnanimously, rising from the chair.

Pretending not to understand the suggestive remark, Suisan moved out of his reach. "So kind of you to offer. But best we get to work. Perhaps you would call out the numbers like Mackie does her shopping list?"

He looked as if he would protest but then he chuckled knowingly and walked toward the stack of crates. *He has the most graceful stride*, she thought, as she admired his slim, tight buttocks and long, muscled legs. Her chest grew tight and perspiration heated her skin. What would he say if he turned now and caught her staring? She shivered at the consequences, and prayed he would not.

He didn't.

Breathing a sigh of relief, she dabbed at her brow. She seated herself in the chair, still warm from his body, and opened the ledger.

When Myles spoke his tone was mockingly like Mackie's. "Four cases of Madeira for that wretched wastrel, Lord Argyle! And not a smidgen more."

Suisan laughed aloud as she sought the correct column and entered the number.

"And for the lecher Lord Ainsbury, twelve cases. 'Tis more than he deserves, but little enough to keep his hands busy."

Again, old familiar memories assaulted Suisan. Though grown to manhood when she was barely out of the nursery, Myles had forever played the child to please her. He was pleasing her now and as they worked she basked in the glow that had been their youth. He had enriched her childhood and somehow, over the years, she had forgotten that. She felt a little ashamed of herself; she felt a little sad.

Through her reverie, she heard, ". . . cases for Robert Harper." Myles's voice was more effeminate than before. Suisan's head shot up. Myles was leaning against a stack of crates, one hand on his hip, the other limp-wristed and holding an imaginary handkerchief. She frowned, confused, but did not question him. He shrugged, tossed the make-believe handkerchief in the air and returned to the task at hand.

The jesting continued until the last of the liquor was consigned to its proper person. Suisan put down the quill and recapped the ink.

Myles walked to her chair and, standing behind her, his hands sought the curve of her shoulders. When she tried to rise he held her fast. She tipped her head back and in doing so brushed intimately against him. The familiar blue eyes that had been haunting him were now wide and glistening with apprehension. Bending from the waist he leaned forward and quietly said, "Come with me, lass."

She shook her head but he was unmoved by her refusal. He was, however, extremely moved by the feel of her head brushing across his manhood. He quickened, yet held himself perfectly still, content to enjoy the way his body was responding. Highly sensitive and highly aroused, he reveled in her touch while gazing down into her eyes.

He leaned closer, hot blood pounding through his head, unabated desire thundering to his loins. She stilled, and lacy, long lashes fluttered down. Grasping her shoulders tighter, Myles lifted her from the chair and turned her to face him. Small hands pressed against his chest.

"Open your eyes and look at me."

When their eyes met, she said, "Nay, Myles, 'tis not meant to be."

"We're not speaking of prophecies," he murmured, loving the way she said his name, "we are speaking of you and we are speaking of me—but most of all, lassie," his voice dropped to a husky whisper, "we are speaking of *us*."

Lifting her stubborn chin, she shook her head. "I do not —do not want you. Not in that way."

The waver in her voice was answer enough but the challenge in her eyes spurred Myles on. One arm snaked about her slender waist and the other grasped her hair.

"Strange words," he insisted, staring deeply into her eyes, "when your body speaks a different tongue."

In the next instant his lips were on hers. When she tried to turn away he tightened his grasp to hold her still, and still she was, even though he could sense the battle waging within her and the desire she tried to stifle. Why was she fighting him?

"Put your denial aside, lass," he breathed against her lips.

Her fists pushed against his chest but Myles's concentration was on the feel of her lips and the sweet taste of her breath. Endless moments later, when his mind was awash with dizzying passion, she yielded, and it was a moment neither would ever forget.

Desire tugged at his soul and Myles swayed, suddenly afraid this woman would be the one to expose him for what he was, for what he'd been. What would her reaction be if she saw what he had hidden so well—a lonely and frightened little boy, rejected by the ones who, in an instant of animal lust, had created him then carelessly tossed him aside?

Somehow he knew she would see the man he really was in that way, in all ways, and the knowledge was much like a promise of some great gift or a brush with glory. He felt sunny inside, clean and fresh and pure, for the first time in his life. He wanted to trust this woman like no other before her.

He deepened the kiss and following his lead she threaded her fingers into his hair. When his tongue dallied with her lips, tracing, mapping their shape, she sighed a lover's sigh. Caught in the throes of unparalleled desire, he dove into her sweetness. Again she became the willing pupil, and sooner than he'd expected, her tongue circled his. Angling his mouth across hers he drew her tongue deeply into his mouth. With the slightest pressure he held it there and savored the taste of her. When she retreated he plunged his tongue into her mouth and began a rhythm no amount of artifice could disguise. Without command his hips joined in the beat and as his fervor mounted, he struggled as never before to contain his passion.

He wanted her upstairs, he wanted her in his bed, and he wanted both—now. Knowing he couldn't hold back much longer, he broke the kiss. Imagining what her eyes would look like, he waited for her to open them. The wait was worth his time; when her long lashes fluttered up, he knew he'd been right on the mark. Her eyes were lustrously blue, a shade to rival a king's robe, and they bespoke desire. He smiled and when she smiled back Myles felt his tormented soul slip free of its dreary moorings.

His gaze slid down to her mouth and his immediate reaction was pride, for he was responsible for its budding fullness. He leaned close and pressed soft, tender kisses across the bow of her mouth, her face and her eyes.

"'Tis time, sweet lassie," he murmured.

At the low rumble of his voice Suisan felt her heart leap

into her throat. Then she was lifted by strong arms and pulled against the solid wall of his chest. Effortlessly, he mounted the stairs, his lips pressed lovingly to her temple. The warm cadence of his breath, not altered in the least by her weight, drifted over her face. This was the dreamy world she had always imagined and even if it was wrong, she did not care. This was where she wanted to be and no matter the consequences, here she would stay.

"Open the door, love," he said, bringing her back to reality. When his shoulder dipped down she reached for the handle and pushed the barrier open.

Gently he stood her on the floor of his chamber. Languidly alive and hopelessly charmed, Suisan leaned toward him.

He groaned, then his mouth again sought hers. Aching to discover all the ways he desired her and eager to master each one, Suisan returned his passion and gave her own free rein. He coaxed with tongue and lips, drawing back now and then so she could take the lead. With growing confidence and a need that was reaching unmanageable proportions, Suisan moaned into his mouth.

The feel of his hands loosening the laces of her jerkin brought momentary relief to the pressure building inside her. Following suit, she unbuttoned his shirt and wove her fingers into the golden silk covering his chest. Beneath the soft down was muscle, hard and strong, and the insistent drumming of his heart. Pleasure beyond her wildest dreams ran a race with expectation and desire.

Then his lips caressed her cheek, her temple and the sensitive shell of her ear. His raspy breath and warm wet tongue introduced her to sensations she had never imagined. He kissed her bare shoulder and then the rise of her breast. In his path lay a trail of tingling senses and cool yet heated skin. Around and around he worked, brushing tender kisses over the globe of her breast, yet never touching the nipple. Thinking she might die if he didn't kiss her there and soon, Suisan raised herself in unmistakable need. Without delay he pulled the aching, hardened bud into his mouth.

Suisan gasped at the rough-sweet texture of his tongue. "Oh, dear God," she breathed as the ache was assuaged. Just when she felt herself hovering on the fringe of a swoon, he moved to the other breast. With the straight edge of his teeth he tantalized the tender peak, then soothed and suckled with his mouth and tongue. Helpless under his expert movements and awash in an uncharted sea of longing, Suisan was only vaguely aware of his hands sliding over the rounded curves of her bottom. When he grasped her there and drew her closer reality spun away.

"I need you, lass," he rasped against her breast while his hands held her against the stiffly swollen ridge of his desire. "And you need me."

She moved against him, saying, "Aye," over and over.

With infinite care he began to peel her clothes away and as each garment floated to the floor, he whispered some heady endearment, some lusty lover's phrase hinting at what was to come. Excited to the point of screaming and desperate to have him carry out his promises, Suisan reached for the closure of his doeskin breeches. His sharp indrawn breath was incentive enough and she boldly slipped the garment past his hips.

A spike of warm steel, heavy with need and insistent in purpose, lay against her. An ache formed in her belly, then clutched and coiled until she cried out for him. He seemed to sense her need and pulling her up on tiptoes he insinuated the proud shaft of his desire to the exact point of her greatest need.

Her head lolled to the side and she clutched him closer lest she fall, aching and unfulfilled, into a pit of black despair.

Then she felt the cool fur of the bearskin beneath her and the warmth of Myles above. When he pulled away she opened her eyes, prepared to plead with him to return to her, but he was sitting up and removing his boots.

She took the unguarded moment to study Myles Cunningham. Golden in the dim fireplace light, every muscle and sinew of his finely honed body seemed bronzed . . . and beautiful. Her gaze moved to his broad back which fanned out at the shoulders like a Viking's shield then tapered down to his slim waist. The soft hair covering his forearms and thighs glistened as he worked at the boots, his movements sure and insistent.

There was something so natural, so unassuming about the

moment; Myles Cunningham, her faithful mentor who'd once carried her on his shoulders, who'd taught her to snap her fingers, who'd brought her prizes from foreign lands, was now shedding his clothes and readying himself to be her lover. No longer the thief who'd stolen her treasure, he was now the same Myles Cunningham she remembered from her childhood. Suisan was momentarily taken aback by what her reverie represented but the moment he turned to face her all thoughts save those of the man himself were banished.

When he lowered himself beside her, Suisan was afforded an unobstructed view of him, and she was shocked; rising proudly from the pelt of spun gold was the proof of his desire.

"Don't be afraid," he whispered, as if sensing her anxiety.

When she remained silent, he said, "Lassie?"

Expelling her breath Suisan forced her gaze away from his engorged manhood and to his eyes. Kindness warmed the soft brown color and pleasure crinkled at the corners. Then he smiled gently. "I suspect you're a maiden, lassie," he said, rather than asked.

Suisan felt herself blush and the answer lodged in her throat.

Warm, strong fingers traced the line of her shoulder and up the column of her neck, then his lips followed the path. Against her neck, at the shivering hollow below her ear, he said, "Are you a maiden, sweet lassie? Is that what's troubling you so?"

"Aye," was all she could manage.

"You've naught to fear," he whispered, sending frissons of longing streaming down her naked limbs.

With infinite care he kissed a path to her neck, then across her shoulder. He grasped her hand, drew it away from her body, and that loving, warm mouth caressed the tender flesh under her arm. Gooseflesh followed in his wake. When at last his hand moved to the dark thatch between her legs Suisan thought the world was beginning anew. She was primed under his skillful hand, charmed by his tender care. Deep and well-tended desire curled in her belly, and when he touched the jewel of her womanhood, Suisan cried out her pleasure in the form of his name. He caught the sound with his mouth and in fevered phrases rife with lusty words he told her exactly how he would appease her.

When he settled himself between her parted thighs, Suisan was close to madness. When he pushed inside her ever so gently, she was nearing insanity. Anxious to have the desire fulfilled, she lifted her hips but the sudden pain sobered her.

"Not so fast," he rasped, shifting his weight to his elbows and withdrawing himself a little.

"Something's terribly wrong." Her voice was ragged with tears and clouded with pain.

"Shush," he soothed against her temple. "Nothing's amiss, I swear." Moving slowly, he spread kisses across her furrowed brow, over her nose and down to her mouth. "Just a little more, sweet lassie," he said in a tortured voice, "and then you'll be mine."

Gathering control he'd never before summoned, Myles harnessed the desire pounding at his brain. He coaxed and kissed her until she quieted beneath him once more. He knew he had a problem: not only was the lass a virgin, but her maidenhead was strictly opposed to the notion of being breached.

Resting his head beside hers, he slipped his hands around her waist. Holding her with gentle pressure, he clamped his jaw shut, put away his second thoughts, and in one swift movement, pushed passed the barrier of her innocence.

A strangled sound of pain lodged in her throat and her nails scored his upper arms. The soft hissing of her breath, labored and sporadic, tortured Myles. "Forgive me, love," he whispered, fighting his body's reaction to her warm sweetness, yet striving to hurt her no more. He shivered under the strain. She was heaven, pure and simple. She was an angel who had transformed a basic and carnal act into something magical, something memorable, and with the certainty of one familiar with life's oddities, Myles Cunningham knew he would never, never be the same.

Marshalling his strength, he beat back the desire hammering in his loins. Then he shifted his weight to his elbows again and stared into her face. The agonized expression marring her lovely features stabbed like a knife in his heart.

Desperate to soothe her and eager to see her eyes glistening with passion once more, he set about renewing her desire. Between tender kisses he alternately whispered apologies and vows of how wonderful he felt to be inside her, and how complete she made him feel. Success, when it came, was like a crisp ocean breeze cooling his heated senses. She sighed, purring a contented kitten's purr.

And what else could she possibly do? Suisan thought. Desire spiraled through her, gnawing low in her belly. Above her, Myles remained motionless for so long a time she thought she would be forced to beg him to continue—to go on and give her what she ached for. When he moved inside her, gently yet insistently, Suisan closed her eyes.

"Lass?"

She looked up to find him staring at her intently. "Is the pain gone, then?" he asked.

"Oh, aye, Myles," she said, laying her hand on his cheek and gazing deeply into his eyes.

He smiled and moved closer until his lips were almost touching hers. "Then hold tight, sweetheart; there's no going back from here—not ever," he breathed, opening his mouth wide over hers.

Then she was being swallowed up—tossed into a blissful world of pleasure and soaring to unimaginable heights. He withdrew slowly until she thought he would leave her. Despairing at the possibility, she clutched his buttocks to hold him near. Then he was lunging, driving deeper, filing her completely, and setting a pounding pace that made her want to scream out with the joy of it. "Oh, dear God, I'll surely die," she cried out.

"Nay, you won't, love," he pledged, "but I vow you'll be in heaven soon."

"I fear I've arrived," she said, bewildered at her confession and bewitched by the man himself.

He chuckled knowingly before his mouth renewed the kiss and his body resumed the fine art of making love. When they were both slick with a sheen of passion and her body was on the edge of something fine, she understood the meaning behind his confident chuckle. He had tutored her until she was consumed with naught but their pleasure, now he was honing and polishing to the point she was desperate to reach.

"Let me hear you, lass," he rasped, his own breathing labored, strained.

"Sweet St. Margaret, Myles," she crooned, "'tis too glorious to describe."

"Aye, 'tis that."

So saying, he quickened his strokes to a devilishly fast pace. No longer able to match the rhythm, Suisan let go and before she could catch her breath, the shuddering, quaking release began. It continued for an endless moment, first pounding at her conscious mind, then drumming in her belly and lower until she thought she would swoon. Only the sound of Myles's voice, repeating, *aye, sweet lassie*, over and over, kept her senses intact.

He groaned, then stiffened above her. Suisan opened her eyes. He was rigid, the corded muscles of his neck and arms taut with tension and something else she could not name. But name it she did, when he grew larger inside her, tossed back his head and thundered out his release.

He collapsed against her, and pride, greater than any she'd ever know, swelled within Suisan's breast. To see him replete from their loving, to feel him hugging her like a precious prize, was a gift tenfold greater than she could ever have desired.

Repercussions would come; she knew they would—and whatever penance resulted from this night would be hers alone to bear. The remembered joy she felt tonight would carry her through all of the lonely tomorrows.

Feeling the complete woman for the first time in her life, Suisan bravely asked, "Is it always so wonderful?"

Tunneling his arms under her, Myles rolled over. When they faced each other his expression was pensive and he did not answer.

"Myles?" she prompted.

A rakish grin transformed his face. "No," he said, kissing her quickly on the nose, "'tis not always so."

She smiled, contented. "You're very warm."

He chuckled and Suisan felt him quicken inside her.

"And getting much, much warmer, my dear," he murmured, pulling her down for his kiss and his passion once more.

~ *Chapter 7* ~

Suisan was dreaming. She was home again, safely wrapped in the loving arms of Scotland. She was surrounded by security, by a thousand years of Highland tradition and by the love of Myles.

According to her dream, Myles had designed and built a courtyard at Roward Castle. A fountain formed the center of the garden-like area. Imported Mediterranean tiles laid in a series of rainbows fanned out from the noisy fountain.

She was sitting on one of several stone benches placed on the periphery of the courtyard. In her lap was tartan of the Lochiel Camerons. She was mending a large tear in the center of the plaid. At her feet toddled their first child, his hair golden like his father's, his eyes deep blue like his mother's.

Her little one, considered by all to be the brightest child ever born in Perwickshire, was constructing his own castle of pieces of wood. Aunt Ailis and Father Sebastian sat nearby, exercising their favorite pastime, the discussion of theology and its effect on early civilizations.

Returning her attention to the torn tartan, Suisan threaded her needle with sturdy white thread. Then she began to count the rows from left to right; four black, thirteen red, six black, thirteen red . . . She stopped in mid-count; something was wrong with the tartan. Certain the problems lay with the pattern, she tucked the torn cloth under her arm and went in search of the chest containing the *Maide dalbh*. She would check the sett of the plaid against the colored pegs; then she would correct the mistake.

Once inside the cozy chamber she shared with Myles, Suisan walked to the Balticwood chest. She lifted the heavy lid, but the sight that met her eyes filled her heart with terror. Empty! The chest was empty! The *Maide dalbh* were gone!

As if diving into the icy waters of Loch Eil, Suisan jolted fully awake. And what she saw in the dim light of dawn was more alarming than the dream.

A golden blonde head was nestled between her breasts and doing disconcerting things to her already shaken senses. Myles's head, Myles's bed. London! She was just dreaming!

Myles raised his head and the smile on his lips caused Suisan's heart to flutter.

"I'm glad you're awake, lassie, unless," he paused, slipping his hand between her legs, "you were dreaming of me?"

She winced at his prophetic question, for the query was as earnest as the look in his warm brown eyes.

His hand stilled. "Are you sore, love?" He frowned and pursed his lips. "Did I use you ill? I truly meant to be gentle."

At his sincere expression, she felt the first twinge of guilt, but not at having been his lover; she felt remorse for having deceived him. Her guilty mind waged a war with her smitten heart. Her heart won.

"Nay, Myles, you were more than gentle." A blush crept up her cheeks. "'Twas waking in a strange bed that confused me so."

He smiled a blinding smile that sent shivers dancing down her spine. Aching to touch him, and powerless not to, she cupped his face in her hands.

He groaned and moved over her. When he was settled nicely and his lips were almost touching hers, he said, "This is where you belong, lassie—and this," he let her feel his desire, "is why."

Before she could form a reply, his mouth closed over hers. When his tongue slid past her lips, all thoughts save those of Myles and the moment fled on the wind. In unison, his sensuous mouth and agile hips began that now-familiar rhythm. Encouraged by his ardor and confident after their earlier loving, she returned his passion.

When they were both breathless with need and eager to be joined as one, Myles broke the kiss. Feeling his gaze, Suisan opened her eyes. His expression was tender yet expectant and his voice was rough and strained when he said, "And will you let me in, lassie?"

Thinking she might die if she didn't, Suisan opened her thighs. He wasted not a second and before she could take a breath, he slipped, hard and long and hungry, into her aching warmth. She groaned, jarred anew at the exquisite perfection of having him inside her.

When her eyes drifted shut, he rasped, "No! I want you to look at me when I make love to you."

Embarrassed, she did not obey. The thought of watching him as he again did such delicious things to her was unthinkable, but when his lips touched the sensitive spot below her ear all thoughts of denying him were quickly forgotten.

"Tell me what to do," she said softly.

He chuckled, low and lustfully. "With you, lass," he said confidently, raising his head, "'tis academic, but if you insist—" He paused and licked his lips. "Lock your ankles about my waist and keep your eyes to mine."

She did both and was soon overwhelmed by the double assault of his beseeching gaze and his hard driving thrusts. She was climbing a stairway of pure pleasure and with every step her passion mounted and her need rose.

"Tell me what your mind sees," he coaxed between labored breaths.

She could not possibly speak, could she?

"Tell me, lass."

Still she was unable to voice the delirious thoughts running pell mell through her mind.

Abruptly, he withdrew from her.

"Nay!" she gasped and flexed her legs to draw him back.

He complied, sinking deep into her. She sighed and grasped his buttocks to prevent him from leaving her again. When he raised one eyebrow and waited, unmoving, she knew he expected an answer.

Understanding full well that he would pull away again, she harnessed a wayward thought. "I know what every woman has always known . . . at last," she confessed, lost in the deep brown of his eyes, awash in the need to have him move forcefully inside her.

"You are much the woman," he breathed, "*my* woman."

So saying, he shifted, threading his arms beneath her and lifting her legs over his shoulders. Rising high above her, he filled her as never before, and when he ground his hips against hers, she felt him touch her aching womb.

"Dear God," she cried, perched on the edge of the chasm of fulfillment. He lunged again and she began to teeter, to lose her footing.

"Go ahead, love," he said, his voice entreating, his eyes piercing, "take your pleasure."

She did, and the experience surpassed everything they had shared earlier. The strain of keeping her eyes locked with his when she wanted to close them allowed her passion to soar like a wild thing, to grasp and ride the crest of each wave instead of being pounded and weakened under the tide that was her pleasure.

As the last ripple echoed through her, Suisan saw a change in Myles's expression. Within the depths of his eyes she saw him holding back, fighting against what she had just encountered. But why? Why didn't he seek the same reward? Before she could voice the question, he said, "Don't move. Not one bloody eyelash."

His piercing gaze and strong words held her motionless but he was not obeying his own command, for deep inside Suisan felt him straining, swelling as if ready to burst.

She blinked, but not with her eyes.

Myles groaned—an agonizing sound that began low in his body and gathered volume as it sped past his lips. His eyes narrowed. "You moved," he accused, breathing through flaring nostrils.

Confident now that she could control his passion as thoroughly as he controlled hers, she softly said, "'Twas you made me do it. Move with me."

He held himself rigid.

"Move with me now, Myles," she repeated, and lifted her hips.

His eyes smoldered but he did not speak. Instead, he drew back and thrust again. The cadence was set and the outcome inevitable; the unknown factor was his endurance . . . and hers.

As he continued the pounding, slapping rhythm, Suisan came to know the bounds of his strength and the vast extent of his willpower.

Strong and hard and lasting, he held himself back until she was again poised on the threshold of paradise. When she called his name in tortured rapture, his strained expression eased.

He smiled a wicked grin and taunted, "After you, my dear."

Aghast at his bold demand, Suisan's eyes grew wide but her protest ended there when he said, "I'll cease if you don't. I swear I will."

The thread of steel in his voice was real but so was the desire pounding in her loins. Crying out his name again, she sought her second release. Straining above her, the corded and taut muscles of his neck and shoulders quivering, Myles did the same.

With a satisfied groan, he tucked her securely to his side and kissed her sweetly. After a long contented silence, he said, "Tell me about yourself—about your life."

Suisan's mind reeled. She didn't want to face this now . . . or ever.

"We've talked of baking scones." He kissed her nose. "At which you excel. And of Scotland." He kissed her cheek. "From whence you hail." On a half-laugh, he fell upon her. "God, woman! I've become a bloody poet."

To hide the chuckle she turned her head into the pillow.

"Are you laughing?" he asked with mock gruffness.

"Nay," she lied happily, assailed with old memories.

His hands moved to her ribs. "Then perhaps you should. I've a yen to hear you laugh."

"Don't," she pleaded in vain, as the tickling began.

Then she was writhing and moaning under his playful assault.

"Will you grant a boon?"

"Oh, aye," she begged. "Anything."

"Hmm." His hands stilled. "'Tis a prize to my liking, but what shall I choose?" Close to her ear, he made a clucking sound. "'Tis a dilemma to be sure."

Casting reason and good common sense aside, she said, "Choose."

"I don't know your family's name," he said, a frown in his voice. "All we ever talk of is my sister—"

"Suisan Harper," she finished for him.

"But not now," he went on, unaware of course, that she had given him the answer. "'Tis time I learned about *you*."

She tensed, afraid he might see through her disguise, afraid she might let something slip. But when he hugged her, she relaxed and said, "Maura . . . Forbes."

"Maura Forbes." He seemed to be testing the way it sounded. "From Perwickshire."

"Aye," she breathed.

"Tell me of your family, and why you left Scotland."

That was the end for Suisan. Fleetingly she ached to tell him the truth, because she longed to believe he was not the one who'd stolen the treasures of Scotland and swindled her out of a fair price for her cloth. But he *had* stolen the *Maide dalbh* and even if she didn't know why, she could not ignore the truth—nor could she even trust him.

"I wanted to see a city full of Sassenachs."

"What?"

Thinking he hadn't heard, she repeated herself and saying the derogatory term seemed to bolster her nerve.

"That's twice tonight I've heard that word, only the other woman held a gun on me when she said it." He nuzzled her neck. "But she was plain compared to you."

Charming, Suisan thought. Charming and very bold. "Did you take the weapon from her?"

His lips moved to her breast. "No. I hurried home, sent Will'am away to his light o' love and came straight to mine."

Sweet, seductive words, designed to put her at ease. Grateful for the change of topics, she said, "And got ink tossed in your face." She touched a faint spot on his cheek.

"Not on purpose." His hand caressed her thigh.

"No," she agreed, stirring anew.

"But I've a purpose now," he said meaningfully, his mouth following his hand.

"Myles?" Her voice was breathless to her own ears.

"Yes?" he drawled, pulling her beneath him and burying himself in her again.

She gasped, completely aroused, yet completely baffled at his ardor. "'Tis nothing."

"We shall see about that, my dear," he chuckled. "We certainly shall see."

A long time later, when he again held her passion by a thread, Suisan said, "I do see, I swear I do."

"I thought you would."

And so it was, in the predawn splendor of a London morning in the Lord's year 1760, Suisan Harper, late of Perwickshire, unwillingly gave her heart to Myles Cunningham.

In Aberdeen Scotland, however, no such tranquility existed.

Tying the sash of his robe, woven from Roward's finest wool, Robert Harper stormed into his study. The exhausted messenger jumped back as he spied Robert's angry expression.

Dark blue Harper eyes narrowed dangerously. "This had better be important, Weeks, or I vow you'll be sorry."

Swallowing nervously, his eyes wide with fatigue and fright, the messenger said, "You, uh, told me I was to come back—and straightaway, if aught was amiss at the castle."

"Cease your stammering," Robert bellowed. "And out with it."

"Lady Suisan ain't at the Glasgow Fair!"

"Of course she's not," Robert scoffed. "The fair's closed by now."

Weeks drew himself up and said, "She never went to the fair."

"Impossible," Robert snorted. "She would have told me otherwise. Where did you come about such drivel?"

"Lady Ailis told me so."

Robert threw back his head and laughed. "And what else did the loonie tell you? That she's poor Toom Tabard come back to reclaim his kingdom?"

When the messenger failed to see the humor, Robert eyed him carefully. "Was she lucid when you saw her?"

"Lu . . . lucid?"

Robert cursed and paced the floor.

"Rabby . . . ?" The soft, almost feminine voice drifted from the bedchamber.

"Go back to sleep, Geoffrey," Robert said, then turned back to the messenger. "Did Ailis have her wits about her?"

Stuffing his hands into his pockets, Weeks said, "I—I believe she did, sir. She'd been at the weeds in her garden all day, and she didn't once cause no trouble."

Robert picked up a poker and stabbed at the coals in the hearth. "Did you look for Lady Suisan?"

"Aye, sir. She weren't about. Not even at the MacKenzie's castle."

"Did you ask anyone else . . ." Robert paused. "Any *normal* person where she was?"

Weeks seemed to relax. "Aye, sir. I asked Jenny, the lorimer's daughter."

Robert threaded a hand through his thinning hair. "And what," he asked impatiently, "did the good harness maker's daughter allow?"

"She . . . uh . . . she said she'd . . . uh . . . lead you to Lady Suisan, but weren't doin' nothin' until you sent her more gold."

"Why, that ungrateful little tramp!" Robert whirled on the man. He stepped back. Alert to the possibility that Weeks might be telling the truth, Robert asked, "Who else was missing from the castle?"

Frowning, the messenger's gaze darted here and there as he considered the question. Finally, he said, "Only the maid, Nelly, and Graeme Dundas and Lady Suisan's personal guard."

Robert spat another expletive as he walked to his desk. From a drawer he pulled out a small bag of coins and tossed it to the messenger. "Get back on that horse and ride to Perwickshire. Jenny will help you find out where Suisan is. You do remember how to get the truth from Ailis, do you not?"

"You mean like we did before?" Weeks looked aghast. "The way we found out where them old sticks was hidden?"

"Precisely."

"But she's scared to death of that mausoleum."

Bracing his palms on the desk, Robert leaned forward. "I'm leaving for London by the end of the month, and if you're not back here by then . . ." He let the threat trail off.

Eyes wide with fright, Weeks nodded and backed out the door.

Angrier than he'd been in years, Robert Harper yanked a bottle of brandy from the table. After taking a long pull, he wiped his lips on the sleeve of his robe and seated himself in a chair. Just before retiring he'd written a letter to Myles about visiting him in London. Robert was anxious to leave Scotland and put his plan in motion, but not until this trouble with Suisan was resolved.

The chit had better be in Perwickshire where she belonged. As soon as he'd conceived the thought, Robert put it aside. Why should he be concerned? Suisan was biddable to a fault; had been since Myles Cunningham had taken her to the remote castle ten years before. No doubt the trouble lay with half-wit Ailis.

"Rabby, come to bed."

Robert smiled at the seductive, pouting tone, and his groin grew tight in response. "Soon, dearie, soon," he said, "keep the bed warm."

Robert turned and gazed at the large portrait of Suisan Harper. Her flaming red hair marked her a Cameron, but those blue eyes spoke of her Harper ancestry, and if Robert had his way, he would be the last Harper. His stodgy, self-righteous ancestors deserved no better. And what sweeter revenge on the Camerons of Lochiel than to let their line die out with Suisan.

He smiled as he continued to stare at the striking likeness of his niece. A real beauty, no one could deny that. Well, no one except Myles Cunningham.

Feeling quite pleased with himself, Robert propped up his feet. Getting the upper hand with Myles had been the challenge, years ago. But now, getting his money was the ultimate goal, and it was in sight! The fortune would guarantee Robert the high-ranking post in the Exchange Ministry that he sought. Only now he would have to wait a while longer.

Still staring at the likeness of Suisan, Robert thought of Myles's expression the day he accepted the miniature. Oh, he'd been shocked at Suisan's appearance, just as Robert had intended. Tricking Myles into thinking his beloved little sister had turned out so homely by having the artist paint an uncomely face was a treat Robert had savored for months—was still savoring now.

"I see you're disappointed," Robert had said to Myles that day last year, and reached for the oval. "I'll have him touch it up here and there. I've already written on the back."

"No," Myles was adamant, holding the thing like a treasured keepsake.

Robert had sighed, "Pity she didn't look more like Sibeal; the Camerons are a handsome lot, wouldn't you say?"

But Myles was ever the businessman when Robert visited London. After carefully putting the miniature away, Myles said, "How much cloth have you brought from Roward and from Strathclyde?"

As Robert now recalled those lucrative, yet bothersome transactions, he felt renewed determination. Once Myles was out of the way there'd be no more peddling of cloth. Once Robert had achieved his rightful place in the Exchange Ministry, he could live the noble life Edward had promised and Myles had taken away. Robert took another pull on the brandy.

The fiery liquor warmed him, but not as much as his comfortable bed partner soon would.

Lounging in his favorite chair, he envisioned his bleak past and his bright future. Everything would be his, and rightfully so. Edward's wealth had been denied him, but patience would bring his reward. His brother's inheritance was a mere stipend compared to the fortune Myles had made of it, and Robert stood to collect every shilling, the shipping contracts, and those magnificent ships. He had but to whisper two words in the proper ear. Two Scottish words, and Myles Cunningham would hang for treason.

"*Maide dalbh*," Robert whispered.

Chuckling contentedly, he held the bottle high. "To you, Myles Cunningham," he toasted. "To your brief future and my long and wealthy one!'' His triumphant laugh echoed off the smooth marble walls of his Aberdeen home.

When the fit of laughter had subsided, he picked up the letter addressed to Myles. As a formality Robert always announced his arrival in London.

Chuckling again, he kissed the missive. ''But when I return to Aberdeen as Minister of Scottish Exchange,'' he declared, '''twill be aboard my newly acquired ship, the *Highland Dream*.''

∿ *Chapter 8* ∿

Myles stood on the torn and jagged planks that had been the deck of the *Highland Star*. An hour ago he'd been lounging in bed and listening to Maura as she told him of her life at Roward Castle. He's been at peace with the world.

But not now.

All around him, the crewmen, though bandaged and bruised, labored steadily to clear away the debris. They sang no bawdy songs; they spun no tales of adventure. Today they were simply men—men who'd faced the worst the sea had to offer and survived. Tempers would flare, but that would come later . . . and someday they would boisterously remember the occasion in prose and in rhyme. The wreck of the *Highland Star* would become another seaman's tale.

But not yet.

''Hell of a blow. Worst storm I've seen since the winter of fifty-five,'' Briggs McCord said.

Hearing the despair in Captain McCord's voice, Myles turned to face him. Sired by a swarthy Gypsy, and born to an Irish mother, Briggs was a mixture of both cultures. Fierce Irish pride was his only anchor, for at heart Briggs was a wanderer. At twenty-nine he was the youngest of Myles's officers. A serious sailor, a devoted rogue, Briggs prided himself on his ability to keep the wenches happy and the *Highland Star* to the wind.

But not today.

"She'll mend, Briggs. A good ship always does."

"I lost two men: Carter and Scoggins," Briggs offered, his tone flat, his mouth a hard line.

Myles blew out his breath and shook his head. "I'll tell the families and see to their welfare."

Briggs was staring up into the tangled mass of rigging, his eyes distant. A soft breeze ruffled his pitch black hair.

Hair like Maura's. A warm, contented feeling curled in Myles's belly.

"More than a score of men were taken to the infirmary," Briggs said tightly.

"It wasn't your fault," Myles said evenly, pulling his mind from the comely lass.

"No." Briggs looked up at the mainmast. "No, it wasn't my—Hold your footing up there, mate!" he yelled to a crewman in the rigging. He turned back to Myles, "What men are left are fair dead on their feet."

"Stop berating yourself," Myles said. "You're the finest sailor I've ever seen. Who else but you could have brought the *Star* to dock? My God, man. Will you look at her?" To emphasize the point he turned in a slow circle and surveyed the splintered railing and ragged canvas. "No one but you could have done it, Briggs, and that's the Lord's own truth."

Briggs shrugged and turned up a poorly bandaged hand. "I've a plucky crew and the luck of the Irish on my side."

"But you were at the helm. That's why the *Star's* here instead of at the bottom of the Atlantic Ocean." Myles wanted to ask about Brigg's injury, but knew he would make light of it. Instead, Myles slapped him on the back. "You've weathered a storm, and a bad one to be sure, but there will be others."

Frowning, Briggs said, "'Tis a depressing thought and we might not fare so well the next time."

Myles was doubtful; Briggs McCord had a way with the sea—what the poets would call a love affair. "Modesty doesn't become you," he said reprovingly. "The sea's your mistress and 'tis true she's done you a bad turn but it'll take more than a storm to drive *you* to land."

Raising his clear blue eyes, Briggs replied, "I'm truly humble at heart, you know."

"Spare me, friend." Myles feigned a wounded look. "And let's get started."

Briggs didn't move. "We lost better than half the cargo."

Completely unconcerned, Myles said, "Cookson'll be glad of that. It'll mean less work for him."

Briggs looked confused. "Why the grin? That doesn't sound like the Cookson I know."

"He had an accident while we were unloading the *Dream*. His leg's broken."

"Perhaps it's a bloody curse," Briggs spat. "First Cookson, then this."

"I think you've been at sea too long." When Briggs scowled Myles added, "Ollie was foxed, not cursed—and you are neither."

"I take it he's on the mend, having such good care and all."

Myles chuckled. "Better everyday. He's walking now, with the help of a cane."

"Oh, and doesn't that bring a picture to mind," Briggs began, sounding much like himself again. "Randy ol' Cookson thump-thumping down the hall hot to get under Mackie's skirts."

"Not to worry. He caught her years ago."

"You've seen them? Together?" Briggs looked incredulous.

Myles cleared his throat and scratched his unshaven cheek. "Let's just say I've seen Mackie sneaking out of his room before daybreak looking like she'd done considerably more than light the fire."

Briggs howled, pressing his injured hand to his side. "Damn me, I thought 'twas my lecherous mind, nothin more."

Happy the conversation had taken a lighter turn, Myles laughed too. "Your mind far exceeds merely lecherous; I can testify to that."

"If I weren't so bloody tired I'd defend myself."

He did look tired, and more. Again, Myles considered asking about the hand, but did not. "I'll hire a crew to unload her," Myles offered. "Your men need rest and I'll wager you've a hunger for a willing wench or two."

Much to Myles's surprise, Briggs looked affronted. "I'm still her captain."

Myles thought of the unwanted errand he still must perform—the visit to the families of the dead seamen. For the first time, he decided his solicitor would handle the task. Briggs was in need of company, and Myles wanted to be the one to supply it. "Then let's be about your ship, Captain McCord."

Through the long day they sweated and strained aboard the *Star*. The salvageable cargo was unloaded and moved to a nearby warehouse. Myles summoned the shipbuilder, who examined the vessel from stem to stern. Like a doting father defending his daughter's honor, Briggs dogged the man's footsteps and challenged his every opinion. Exasperated, the fellow finished his inspection in silence and requested a private meeting with Myles later in the week.

At sunset Myles and Briggs stood near the helm. Myles caught sight of the the blood encrusted rope hanging from the ship's wheel and knew immediately how Briggs had injured his hand. Respect for Briggs McCord increased tenfold.

From across the scarred deck the purser approached, a lantern swinging at his side.

"Here's the log, sir," he said.

"I'll take it." Myles held out a hand for the canvas bound ledger. "Ollie needs something else to keep himself busy." He winked at Briggs.

Laughing, Briggs said, "I see the *Dream's* ready to go." He motioned toward the ship docked nearby. "You've added more sail."

The *Highland Dream* was considered Myles's personal vessel. In answer, he nodded absently; he was deeply concerned that Briggs would continue to blame himself for the disaster, but no solution came to mind.

"She'll slide through the water like Goliath through a well-worn whore," Briggs remarked with a wistful note.

"Aye, she will, but the doctor says it's too soon for Ollie to sail."

"What's her cargo?" Briggs asked.

"Mercantile for the most part, and a good supply of Irish crystal."

Briggs looked like a man hopelessly coveting his best friend's wife. With the analogy came the solution Myles had been searching for. Watching Briggs closely, Myles kept his voice very businesslike when he said, "You'll sail her until Ollie's recovered."

Briggs grew still as a statue. "But I've just lost one of your ships."

"Nonsense. The *Star* will sail again."

"But the *Dream's* your command," Briggs protested although Myles knew he was excited.

In his most convincing fatherly voice, Myles said, "Oh, not this time."

Briggs stood a little taller and his eyes were alive with excitement. "Superstitious about sailing without Cookson, are you?"

Myles glanced at the *Dream*, a stately square-rigger that had been his home more often than not these last ten years. But the sea and the ship no longer pulled at him. God, he was tired of the sea. "It's more than that, Briggs," he admitted honestly.

"Sounds like a woman to me."

Myles said nothing.

Briggs whistled. "Damn, Myles, I never thought to see you caught in love's trap."

Myles wasn't sure how he felt about Maura but one thing was certain; he didn't intend to discuss the matter with Briggs McCord.

"The men are dog tired and the light's all but gone," Briggs said, pointing toward the city. "Let's have a drink and you can tell me about her."

"No."

Undaunted, Briggs asked, "Is that 'no' to the drink or 'no' to the telling?"

"I expect the *Dream* to sail on Tuesday. Pick as many men as you need from my crew to replace your injured."

"Oh, very well. I know when to keep my mouth shut," Briggs said. "But will you at least tell me what she looks like?"

Myles walked to the gangplank. Over his shoulder he said, "No."

Briggs's knowing laughter could still be heard when Myles stepped into his carriage.

As he guided the team away from the wharves and onto the street, Myles tried to sort out his jumbled feelings. He desired Maura; after last night he knew she desired him, too. Whenever he thought of her he felt inner contentment.

A virgin, he sighed, trying to remember the last time he'd taken a woman's innocence. No answer came to mind, and with the surety of one who'd learned to make important decisions early in life, Myles knew this Scottish lassie was different from any woman he'd ever known. And much to his surprise, he was glad.

"Eh, Gov'na!" a rusty voice yelled. "You're 'eaded for the ditch!"

Myles shook himself. The team had veered dangerously to the right. Deftly he reined them back onto the road. God, he was tired! And not from lack of sleep. He was tired of problems—like the damage to the *Star*. He was sick of the toll the sea could take—like the two women widowed from the wreck of the *Star*. He was weary of coat-tailing lords like the Earl of Ainsbury. Life seemed an endless line of loathsome duties and unwanted obligations stretching out for years to come—if he held to his present course.

He cursed out loud, but the sound was lost in the noisy London night. Hell, he couldn't even hear himself think. And he needed to think, needed to be alone.

Instead of going home, Myles went to the other house he owned in London. Larger than necessary, the house on Partridge Street was perfectly suited for the perfectly proper mistress of a perfectly upstanding businessman.

"Perfect, perfect, perfect," he grumbled as he climbed

down from the carriage. Glancing up, he noticed several windows gaping open on the second floor. "She could have closed the place at least," he spat angrily, remembering how furious Barbara had been when he had ended their arrangement. Recently he'd made a list of the unwanted things in his life, then systematically he'd begun to weed them out. Barbara had been the first to go, simply because she was the easiest to deal with.

His spirits lightened a little when he entered the house. Oh, he'd enjoyed this place and each of its lovely occupants, even though he'd felt pressured by society to keep a mistress. He paused at the foot of the stairs and rested his hand on the newel post. Carved of oak to resemble a pineapple, the cool wood felt good against his work-sore hand. He didn't know what to do next. Perhaps he would sell the warehouses. He wondered what to do about his six ships.

Five ships, the disillusioned portion of his mind corrected.

Myles flexed his hand then suddenly shouted, "One down, five to go!"

Elated, he sat down and rested his elbows on his knees. He could sell the *Star* as she was and give over permanent command of the *Highland Dream* to Briggs. The proceeds from the crippled ship would help buy a country place, in Sussex or perhaps on the rugged coast of Cornwall. The acquisition of horses would follow naturally. He pictured the English terrain but the vision did not satisfy. An old and sentimental dream tugged at his heart.

"Settle in Scotland—when you're ready," Edward Harper had said. "She's a place to call home and she'll always do right by you. I'll be there, with Sibeal and Suisan, and when you find that special woman, bring her to Scotland. What more could a mortal man ask?"

As if cleansed, he leaned back and breathed deeply of the cool night air that filled the house through the front door that had swung open. He felt giddy as a cabin boy who'd climbed up to the crow's nest for the first time. Getting to his feet, he walked through every room downstairs. Barbara had not taken all of the furniture as he'd expected, but by taking occasional pieces she'd effectively destroyed the continuity of the decor.

"*C'est la vie,*" he declared to the frilly wallpaper.

Lighthearted for the first time in years, he looked to his future. He could marry, but not immediately. And his bride would be selected very carefully. Most men in his position would look to the gentry, for even though his blood was as common as a carpenter's, his money would compensate for any lack of breeding.

Did he want a blue-blooded bride? A frown wrinkled his brow. What would he do with a noblewoman, pray tell, other than the obvious? She would give him children, of course, but what of the later years? He wanted a hand, nay, both hands, in the rearing of his offspring. Matronly nannies and pinched-faced tutors would never do, not for his little ones. He wanted a houseful of children; lads to brag and pull pranks, and adoring lassies to giggle and squeal.

He chuckled at the prospect. In a span of hours, he'd added a wife and family to his growing list of possibilities. He'd made the decision to reshape his life, and now he had but to put the changes in motion. Certain the trip home would be considerably more pleasant, and his welcome would be more enjoyable, he returned to the carriage.

The team of horses responded to his gentle commands as they always did. Staring at their broad backs, he wondered what breed of horses they were. With a self-deprecating chuckle he realized he couldn't tell one horse from another.

But that, too, would change. And soon.

When he walked into the stable, Will'am was asleep in one of the stalls. Myles called his name.

The lad got to his feet. "Sorry, sir. I must have dropped off." He paused to yawn. "But I ain't been sleepin' long, I swear. Miss Maura had me movin' crates all day in the cellar. My back feels fair broken."

"Why?"

"They was heavy."

"Why were you moving them again?"

"Ain't my place to question my betters, sir, but the cellar ain't such a mess now, that's for sure. Had me make a path through all that brandy, she did."

Myles wondered where she'd found the energy, but then he remembered she was young. But how young? How old was she? Then he realized how little he still knew of her. Just when she'd begun to confide in him this morning the message had come about the *Star*. Well, he'd correct that oversight, too.

Returning his attention to Will'am, Myles said, "You may have the evening to yourself but I've an errand for you first thing tomorrow."

"Oh, yes, sir. Anything, sir."

"I've just come from the house on Partridge Street. Several windows are open. You're to close them and lock up the house."

"First thing tomorrow, sir," Will'am said excitedly. "But what will Miss Barbara say?"

"The house is empty."

"But—"

"That will be all, lad."

"Sorry, sir." Will'am smiled apologetically and left the stable.

With determined steps, Myles went in search of Maura. The kitchen was dark, as was the parlor. Then he noticed a lighted lamp on the narrow table in the foyer. Leaning against the glass bowl was a letter. Myles picked it up. He recognized Robert Harper's flowery script and smelled the fop's cloying cologne. Impatiently, his nose twitching, Myles pulled at the seal. With the slightest pressure the flap popped open. Myles wondered if Ollie had read the missive or if Robert had failed to seal it properly. Probably, the latter, since Ollie bore no kind feelings for Suisan's uncle.

"You must press your seal harder, dear Robert," Myles mimicked the writer's lisping voice.

His carefree mood vanished as he read of Robert's upcoming visit to London. In looping and curling script, Robert went on to explain that his stay would merely be a stopover before continuing to France.

"And why should this year be any different?" Myles asked aloud. "You must have your holiday abroad, mustn't you, ducks?"

Disgusted by the man, whom he took lightly, and the message, which he regarded seriously, Myles tucked the letter into his coat. Robert would no doubt be delivering the cloth from Roward and from Strath. He would also expect payment . . . in gold.

"Damn!" Myles spat. As if he didn't have enough to do these days, soon he would have to either sell the cloth in London or store it until another of his ships docked. He could delay the *Dream's* departure, but what effect would the idle time have on her new captain? Remembering Briggs McCord's failing confidence, Myles discarded the notion. He would visit his banker and get Robert's gold and Suisan's allowance. The cloth he'd deal with later.

He climbed the stairs but did not stop at his room on the second floor. Neither did he knock on Maura's door, but let himself in.

She seemed lost in the bed—only her face and hands visible. Then he saw the mobcap and almost choked.

"Oh, you're a stubborn one to provoke me so," he whispered, desire kindling in his loins. "But you have much to learn about Myles Cunningham."

Suisan moved the slightest bit, trying to rouse herself from sleep. She was warm, ever so warm. And cozy.

Sighing softly, she pointed her feet, lifted her arms and stretched.

"Hmm," came the throaty groan from near her ear.

She froze. A strong arm girdled her waist, then pulled her back, against the warmth. Trepidation, like a cold north wind, seeped into every limb. To calm herself, she began to count.

At six, she started to shake and perspire.

At nine, she closed her eyes until her breathing slowed.

At fifteen, she felt the first twinge of regret.

At nineteen, she wanted to cry.

At twenty-one, she wanted to kill Myles Cunningham for what they'd done.

At twenty-six, she wanted to scream.

At twenty-eight, she remembered the letter from Uncle Rabby.

At thirty, she pictured herself and Nelly and the Highland patterns safely aboard a ship bound for Aberdeen.

At thirty-two, she eased from Myles's embrace and out of the bed.

At one hundred, she entered the kitchen and closed the bottom half of the dutch door leading to the servants' stairs. She made tea and settled herself at the table.

Since waking in Myles's bed yesterday morning, Suisan had been on edge, her nerves pulled tight as lute strings. Oh, she'd done all the regular things yesterday; the chores, the marketing, the meals, but her mind had never fully relinquished the vision of Myles and what they had shared. Nor had she forgotten how her heart had soared.

All her well-meant intentions, all her stony resolve, all the things that had brought her to London, were suddenly overshadowed. For one glorious, harmonious night she'd mingled, naked and aching, with the most dangerous of men. Myles Cunningham.

Her chest felt hollow. Her hands still quaked. And deep in her soul she knew she had committed the gravest of errors. Not only had she fallen in love with the one man she should hate, she had exposed herself to the one horror she could not face—the one evil ploy of nature she must not risk.

And yet a part of her longed for him; he was a light in the dark tunnel of loneliness that had been her solitary life. But what lay at the tunnel's end? Suddenly she was frightened by the light.

"What will I do now?" she whispered aloud.

"You'll stop badgering your feelings to death," he said plaintively from behind her, "and come give me a kiss."

She went hot, then cold. He expected her to be the same. "Are you unwell?"

How could he sound so concerned? He was a scoundrel, and a thief! "Nay," she admitted, not turning around. "Just a bit tuckered."

"Then do as I asked."

Suisan gathered her courage, but before she could rise, he said, "Can't you manage it?"

Suisan knew what he meant. He was asking if she could

accept what had happened between them. What choice did she have?

None.

Her eyes sought his and like a rabbit snared, she was powerless to look away. Slowly she rose and walked toward him.

He had assumed that indolent pose in the doorway. His hair was loose, framed by strong, bare arms grasping the facing overhead. She stared at his face, so familiar, so handsome. He was smiling, a lazy, confident grin that reached his eyes and held her captive. When she could, she allowed her gaze to move to the soft furring on his chest. He flexed his muscles in response to her perusal. A sharp retort, concerning his use of the servants' stairs, was on the tip of her tongue, but her mouth was too dry to voice the words. She looked lower, but the Dutch door concealed the rest of him. Lowering an arm, he swung the door open.

She gasped. He was naked, and he wanted her very, very much.

Blushing, her heart beating fast, she whirled around. His warm breath caressed her neck and the same moment his arms enveloped her. Sinking, floating feelings assaulted her, but she forced them back. He must have sensed her withdrawal, for he sighed a sigh of impatience.

"What are you afraid of? You can tell me, you know."

Her mind screamed, *I'm afraid of loving you. I'm terrified of having a child like Ailis*.

"This won't do, lass. This won't do at all."

She frowned. "What do you mean?"

He turned her around. When she did not raise her eyes, he lifted her chin. His gaze was as intense as she remembered, his voice too persuasive to ignore. "You can't pretend." He leaned closer. "Not any longer."

Their noses almost touched; the warm glow in his eyes caused Suisan to sway. Then he was tipping his head to the side and moving closer.

A river of anticipation flowed down her spine. She was weak; she was inspired. Her heart was drumming loudly against her ribs.

But it wasn't her heart, she soon acknowledged. It was a cane thumping on the stairs! It was Ollie, and he was on his way to the kitchen. And Myles was naked. And she was in his arms.

Pushing away from him, she said, "Ollie's coming. Please don't let him see you so."

Myles glanced toward the sound, then pulled her back. "Ollie's a man of the world. He'll not be shocked."

"He can't see us like this." She was desperate. "He can't! 'Tis wrong."

"I believe it might be inevitable," Myles insisted, his gaze solidly fixed on hers, "for my trousers are upstairs."

The knocking of wood on wood was louder, but Myles made no move to cover himself. Suisan's mind raced. The laundry, she thought, there were clothes in the laundry.

"I'll get your breeches." She twisted out of his arms.

"And if I choose not to put them on?" he drawled, leaning casually against the table.

"Say you will." She found herself pleading as she backed away.

"He'll find out sooner or later," Myles said much too reasonably.

"But you're naked!" Couldn't he understand?

He looked down at himself. Chuckling, he said, "And obviously quite moved."

"Oh!" she flustered, but suddenly the situation triggered her ire. "I insist that you cover yourself."

She should have expected the arching, imperious brow, but her mind was distracted by Cookson's steady progress.

"And what," Myles said crisply, "will you do if I refuse?"

She dashed into the laundry room and snatched up the first pair of trousers she saw. Holding them to her breast, she approached him. "Ask what you will, but I cannot bear to have him find you—"

"Bare?" he asked, his voice dripping innocence.

"Aye, bare," she hissed and thrust the trousers at him.

He smiled and took his time shaking out the legs. When he'd threaded one lean leg into the soft doeskin, he stopped. "I'm much more comfortable without them. Truly I am."

''You rakehell!'' she said through her teeth. ''You miserable, conniving—'' She stopped. The thumping was muffled; Ollie had reached the rug-covered parlor. Her eyes grew wide and her temper flared. Balling her fists, she said, ''Cover yourself.''

''In exchange for . . . ?'' he drawled, though his eyes were shining with mirth.

She shot a glance over her shoulder, but the hallway was blessedly empty. Turning back to Myles, who still had only one leg in the trousers, she said, ''Whatever you will.'' The words were wrenched from her.

''No more creeping from the bed without waking me?''

She wrung her hands and glanced over her shoulder again. ''Whose bed?''

''Either bed. Henceforth, you'll be sleeping with me.''

Ollie could pass through the doorway at any time. Taking a deep breath, she said, ''Agreed.''

Myles grinned a grin to light up the night, and like a hand slipping into a favorite glove, he slid his other leg into the trousers.

Suisan turned to the stove and poured him a cup of tea. She knew she was trapped now and that she would have to share his bed!

''Having second thoughts about the sleeping arrangements so soon?'' His voice was silky smooth.

She wanted to kill him. As her anger rose, her weak woman's heart grew silent. Suddenly her hands stilled and her emotions sought an even keel. All of her sentimental thoughts were replaced by sweet and inspiring revenge.

She smiled and picked up the cup. Let the rogue think he'd won. She had but to get the remaining patterns to Nelly. By the time Uncle Rabby arrived in London, she and Nelly and the patterns would be gone. Away from smelly London . . . and out of Myles's dangerous grasp. It was what she wanted, what had to be.

When she placed the tea before him he grabbed her wrist. ''Tonight,'' he murmured, pulling her hand to his lips, ''I choose my bed.''

Gooseflesh tickled her arm. ''Let me go.''

Much to her surprise, he did, but his next words were more shocking than their agreement.

"Later in the week, I'm taking you shopping. I've a fancy to see you in something," he paused, a mischievous gleam in his eyes, "something of my choosing."

Dumfounded, she merely stared at him. By the time she found her tongue, Ollie was strolling into the kitchen, a very perceptive look in his eyes.

~ *Chapter 9* ~

Any other woman would be tittering like a maiden aunt at the prospect of having Myles Cunningham escort her to Madame LeBlanc's exclusive dress salon, but not Suisan. She could think of little else during the carriage ride save her original glimpse of the salon. How long had that been? Two months, a little more. Too long.

What if Myles recognized Nelly? What if Nelly challenged him? No, Nelly would keep her wits; she was no one's fool. Suisan, on the other hand, felt destined to claim sole proprietorship of that title.

When they arrived at the shop, she had mixed emotions about the display window, even though Nelly had told her what to expect. Instead of the bolts of counterfeited Roward cloth, the window now featured a variety of laces from Mechlin, Ireland and Spain. She hoped the cloth from Roward had been so popular that all the bolts had been purchased. All except one. Thanks to Nelly, Suisan intended to expose Myles Cunningham and the dressmaker. What would he say when faced with the truth? He'd probably say Ollie entered the wrong figure in the ledgers.

"Shall we?" he asked.

Turning to face him, Suisan was struck anew at his handsomeness. In the bright light of day, his soft brown eyes danced with anticipation and what she immodestly thought was appreciation. But most outstanding about Myles Cunningham was the carefree way he smiled and the casual grace with which he helped her from the carriage. As if he'd performed the gesture a thousand times, he took her hand and tucked it securely in the crook of his arm.

Her courage faltered in the face of his charm and she suddenly prayed Ollie had been responsible for the mistake.

"And what, milady," he drawled, bending his head to hers, "is your favorite color?"

She tipped her head to the side and when their eyes met she came very close to giving herself away. Two long-forgotten words hung on the tip of her tongue. As a child she'd been unable to say the words to describe her favorite color, "saxony blue". Her best attempt came out, "sassy boo."

The sentimental reminder of her early life with Myles brought a pang of regret, but instead of letting the past mar the friendly ambience and foil her plans, she put on a saucy smile and said, "I shan't tell you. You must discover that for yourself."

Examining her face closely, he said, "Hum. Your anxious expression tells me one thing. My experience, however, tells me another. I think you secretly like red, but will not choose it." He stopped and with his free hand, reached for the door handle. "No, Maura Forbes, you would not be so bold as to pick red. I think you'll choose a blue to match your eyes or a dark green to complement your hair."

Suisan tingled inside at his seductive and familiar tone. A blush crept up her cheeks when he moved his hand to the small of her back. She looked away, hating herself for her weakness, hating him because he'd deceived her so.

"There it is, you see," he declared confidently as he ushered her through the door, "I've hit the mark again."

"Are you never wrong then," she queried defensively, "at your guessing games?"

"Never." His gaze was warm, his tone amiable. "And as you will soon discover, I am most certainly not wrong about *you*. We suit each other well."

Regret and second thoughts plagued her. He seemed so sincere, yet she knew him for the rogue he was.

"*Bienvenue*, Monsieur Cunningham." Madame LeBlanc said, sounding like a poor imitation of Nelly's imitation of her.

Myles doffed his hat in cavalier fashion. "Madame LeBlanc, 'tis a pleasure to see you again. May I present Mistress Forbes."

In French, and obviously for Myles's ears only, she replied, "Ah, she is most beautiful, but then she is with you . . . and one has everything to do with the other."

He winked in traitorous fashion. "I insist you speak English."

"But of course. Your preference is always our perference."

The cryptic statement irked Suisan, because anyone possessing a dew drop's worth of sense would see her as Myles's paid whore. She wasn't a whore! She was merely a weak woman, vulnerable to his considerable charms.

"Maura?"

She glanced up at him, but out of the corner of her eye, she saw Nelly, her face a mask of shock disappearing behind a draped doorway.

"What is it?" he asked, pulling her closer.

His solicitous manner was unnerving. She shook her head. "'Tis naught."

"Won't you follow me, please?" Madame said.

They passed through French doors stained a nutty brown, and down a panelled hall to a private sitting area. Dark leather chairs, a large couch and a marble smoking stand gave the room a decidedly masculine air. A wall of mirrors made the small room seem more spacious, and several brass lamps compensated for a lack of windows, making the purpose of the room more pronounced and the intimacy of the room unmistakable.

Clapping her hands rapidly, the proprietress summoned a

servant and ordered tea for Suisan, brandy for Myles. He declined the brandy and requested tea for himself.

Watching Madame speak caustically to the uniformed maid, Suisan wondered how Nelly was faring here. She never complained about the work, nor had she seriously fussed about Madame LeBlanc, who seemed a veritable tyrant.

In her youth, the Frenchwoman had most likely been considered petite, but the years had not been kind to her tiny frame. She wore her artificially darkened hair in a simple twist with only an ivory comb for decoration. A rather bulbous nose and small dark eyes distracted from her most striking feature: her complexion. Glowing, and as fine as porcelain, her skin seemed translucent.

Catching herself in a lengthy perusal of their hostess, who was now gathering pattern books, Suisan cast a glance at Myles and found him studying a hunting scene on the wall. How many women had showcased themselves and preened in this room, and for how many men? She took offense at the thought.

"Is it to your liking?" she asked.

He looked surprised at her question. "I wasn't admiring the artist, but rather the animals." He cleared his throat before adding, "I know little of the beasts."

Suisan examined the painting. "The small red one is the fox."

He tried, but failed, to muffle his laughter. "You're quite saucy this morning."

And why not? She would expose him for the cheat he was today. "And helpful?" she ventured boldly.

Draping his arm around her shoulders, he said, "Just so, but I wonder at the source. Could it perhaps be something *I* did, or *we* did that put such sauce on your tongue?"

The lustful look in his eyes was disconcerting, the pointed reminder of their lovemaking devastating. When he leaned closer, she drew back and said, "You mustn't kiss me—not here."

"Then here?" He touched a finger to her forehead. "Or here?" He touched her nose.

Her heart clamored in her chest. "Nay. Neither."

"Perhaps I had no intention of kissing you at all," he murmured.

"You did," she whispered, feeling suddenly warm. "I'm certain of it."

"And do you presume to know me so well?"

During moments like these she could forget their long separation. "Aye, better than you think."

He looked pensive. "Why do I believe you? Is it perhaps because you just spoke with a Scottish brogue? You let it slip out on occasion, you know. When you're angry or think no one is listening. 'Tis good you feel relaxed enough with me to be yourself. I had hoped for that."

Swallowing with difficulty and feeling anything but herself, she said, "I would speak of something else."

"Of foxes?" His mouth twitched at the corners.

"Nay, the fox always gets caught."

"And will you get caught, little vixen?"

She tore her eyes from his and glanced across the room. Having made her selections, Madame was stacking the books. Could she hear their conversation?

As if reading her mind, Myles said, "I would have your answer now, while no one else can hear."

She ignored him.

"Your answer?"

"And if I refuse?"

He shrugged. "'Tis early in the day and I'm a patient man."

If he didn't stop baiting her, she wouldn't be able to carry out her plan. "But I must return soon; Cookson will need—"

"Nothing from you today. I've declared today a holiday," he said magnanimously. "I'm to be your London guide."

"But I've seen everything in London."

"When?" He demanded, muscles tensing. "And with whom?"

"Please," she hissed at the sound of rustling skirts. Still, her heart leapt at the prospect that he might be jealous.

Tea was served under Madame's baleful eye.

"We'll speak of it again, you can be sure." His tone was deceptively pleasant.

Suisan considered dozens of designs. An endless array of fabrics was paraded before them, but not the fabric she sought. Not until Myles had made a third selection did she realize he intended to purchase her an entire wardrobe.

Madame held up a rosy pink satin. "Her coloring is deceptive and most difficult to judge," she said, suspiciously eyeing Suisan's hair.

Suisan hated pinks and with good cause; the color was abominable with her red hair. She also hated being discussed like a ewe before shearing.

"The blue silk," Myles finally said. "And something pastel and frilly, with little flowers."

Madame nodded regally. "I have one such fabric, and you'll be pleased to know it's from Strathclyde."

Myles looked impressed; Suisan tried to look casual. The moment was coming.

Madame excused herself, then returned with a bolt of cloth. Even from across the room Suisan recognized the batiste cotton, dyed a pale green and embroidered with delicate cabbage roses. Nelly had chosen the dye, Flora MacIver had woven the cloth, Suisan herself had drawn the flowers, and Nelly's daughter, Sorcha, had done the needlework.

Suisan fought back the urge to scream out the truth. Myles Cunningham had betrayed the clans of Scotland by stealing the *Maide dalbh*, but by counterfeiting the cloth of Roward, he had cheated the people who had accepted and cared for her when he was too busy to bother. She would get back all of the tartan patterns tonight, and now she would expose him for the despicable bounder he was.

Extending her hands, she accepted the bolt. Turning it on end she examined the wooden rod on which the cloth was rolled. Just as Nelly had predicted, Suisan found the proof she sought. Stamped into the wood was a sheaf of five arrows tied with a band, the coat of arms of the Camerons of Lochiel. The emblem would be repeated more than a dozen times down the length of the rod, the same as every bolt of cloth woven at Roward.

Victory, sweet and fine, welled up inside her. Glancing first at Myles, then at the Frenchwoman, Suisan declared, "This is not Strathclyde cloth. 'Tis from the looms of Roward Castle."

Madame gasped. Myles smiled sadly and patted Suisan's arm. "Nay, sweet, 'tis from Strath," he explained patiently. "Suisan's cloth is not nearly so fine."

Offended by his apologetic tone, she shot him an icy glare. "Oh?" Rising, she held the roll of cloth in the flat of her hands. As if shaking out bed linens, she flicked her wrists while grasping the cut edge of the fabric. The bolt unfurled, the rod clattered against the far wall. Reeling in the fabric as she went, she crossed the room and picked up the wooden rod.

Her head held high, triumph pounding in her veins, she marched to Myles and held out the stick. "See for yourself. 'Tis Lady Suisan's trademark, and no other."

Now frowning, Myles took the rod and examined it carefully. His mouth drew tight and his brown eyes went cold with fury. "What trick is this?"

Madame looked genuinely shocked. "Monsieur, I do not know."

Myles turned to Suisan. "When did Suisan devise this trademark?"

Suisan was amazed by his question. "'Twas her mother's mark, the arrows of the Camerons of Lochiel."

"A Scottish clan?" Madame asked, her eyes wide, all trace of the French accent gone. "I knew nothing of it, Monsieur. I beg you to believe me."

"I'm certain you had no part in it," he said, distracted.

He seemed to be searching his memory. But how could he have possibly forgotten? Suisan had a moment's doubt. Could someone else be responsible for the switch? Perhaps Cookson? She scolded herself for the weak thought; she had fallen under Myles Cunningham's spell, and like a lovesick fool, she wanted to believe the best of him.

With hands still blistered and bruised from his labor on the *Highland Star*, Myles traced the emblems. Then his eyes sought Suisan's. His gaze was level, determined. "You're certain, Maura?"

"Aye."

"So be it." He turned to Madame. "In exchange for keeping this quiet, I want an inventory of every bolt like this you bought from Robert Harper. I want to know how many bolts you've sold and the price you received." He gripped the rod. "I want the figures today, Madame."

"Of course, Monsieur."

Suisan's mind reeled with ambiguous thoughts; she was at once thrilled and disappointed. He was either an exceptional actor or he told the truth and had no part in the scheme. Then why was his first thought of money? Why was he concerned about the price paid for the cloth?

She began to shake. She might have decided to find another outlet for her cloth, but he must undo this wrong. "Will you do nothing in defense of Lady Suisan?"

"Tread lightly, Maura. I'll see this wrong righted."

Attentive to the warning in his voice, she retreated. But her heart soared at the possibility that Myles might not have been involved. "Have I your word?"

"On Sibeal Harper's grave," he swore, holding the rod like he intended to keep it. "You've done the proper thing. 'Tis my place to set it aright, and I will not let it spoil our day. Neither will you. Understood?"

It wasn't a question. And she had achieved her goal and more. Still she grew sad when she considered that Uncle Rabby might have been the one who cheated her.

"Put it from your mind, lass. I won't have you fretting over this." When she did not reply, he said, "Promise?"

"Aye, 'tis agreed."

He grinned broadly and tapped her nose with the rod. "Now let's see about that new frock."

She was dumfounded. She had not expected him to reward her for uncovering the deception. He was treating her like a servant.

She allowed herself to be led from the room. She didn't come to her senses until she saw Nelly seated on a stool in the dressing chamber.

"Help Mistress Forbes out of her dress," Madame said and quickly left the room.

"*Mistress*?" Nelly drawled meaningfully. "Don't take a scholar, nor a soothsayer to see *that*."

"Sarcasm doesn't suit you, Nelly." Suisan began unbuttoning her dress.

"Well," Nelly huffed, "it looks bad—if you ask me."

"I didn't ask you."

Nelly got up and helped Suisan out of the dress. "But not as bad as *that* looks."

She was staring at Suisan's shoulder. Suisan turned to the large mirror and blinked in disbelief. Just above her collar bone was a lover's bruise. Damn! Why hadn't she noticed it? Because she hadn't realized the delightful lovemaking they'd shared would leave such a mark. She sighed and allowed her eyes to meet Nelly's.

"Did the foosty bastard hurt you?"

Suisan fought back the tears. "No," she said thickly, "he did not hurt me."

Nelly relaxed, and much to Suisan's surprise, smiled. "'Tis past time you were made a woman. Did he please you well?"

Suisan could not stop the blush.

"I see he did," Nelly said ruefully. "He's a bonny man, just as I said, and I'll wager he's considerable where it counts, too."

"He's a scoundrel and a thief and—"

"Your lover."

Her stomach lurched. "I won't be dressed down by your vulgar mouth, Nelly Burke!"

"'Tis woman's talk and never vulgar," she said as if she were discussing when to beat the rugs.

"Everything about Myles Cunningham is vulgar."

"Good. That means he's a lusty lover, and not bothered by preacher's beliefs on how the marriage bed is only for begettin' bairns. Religious men got no place tellin' a person how often to raise their passions and how well to—"

"Nelly. . . ." Suisan warned.

Undaunted, she went on. "I don't see why you're frettin' so. It's not like we ain't discussed it before."

Suisan was getting more uncomfortable by the minute. "I was a child when you—when you told me about men and women."

"You were twelve, milady, to my twenty-two, when we talked about taking a lover—about what a man does when a woman sets his jack a twitchin' and about the pleasure a woman can—"

"I had no choice."

Nelly looked pensive. "No, I don't suppose you did, milady. Who could resist a braw devil like him?"

"You forget your place."

"And who wouldn't?" the maid challenged. "I've seen enough deceit and misery since we left home to last a lifetime. If I didn't work to keep my wits I'd be as confused as Ailis when the sickness comes over her."

Suisan was moved by the desperation in Nelly's voice. "I'm confused, too."

"I ain't never served a bloomin' tyrant before, nor lived in a city that smells of a dung heap." She stopped and blew out her breath. Then her voice was quiet. "*My* lady is, most times, sweet and caring."

Suisan hugged her fiercely.

When Nelly drew back, she looked contrite. "Forgive me, Lady Suisan, but working here has sharpened my tongue. I should be thinkin' more of you and your plight."

"No, you shouldn't," Suisan said, feeling on comfortable ground again. "You can quit now."

Nelly smiled. "Aye, I can. I heard you out there." She rolled her eyes. "Damn me for a fool, but I believe he's innocent in this."

Suisan had no desire to discuss the mixed emotions she was feeling toward Myles Cunningham. "'Twould seem so. But no one will ever cheat us again. I'll market the cloth myself and Myles Cunningham be damned."

"You've come to care for the rascal."

"Not so much," Suisan lied. "And we'll be leaving in a few—"

"Shush!" Nelly said, glancing at the door. "Cover where he marked you or 'twill be all over London tomorrow. 'Tis why these wretched Sassenachs live—to gossip."

Quickly Suisan put her hand to her shoulder.

Madame entered, a frothy white dress draped over her arm. Nelly curtsied and held out her hands.

"See that you make a proper bow, and do not take all afternoon." Turning her disdainful expression on Suisan, she added, "As I'm sure you know, Monsieur Cunningham does not like to be kept waiting."

"Aye, mum," Nelly replied in a tone so docile Suisan felt her anger rise anew.

How did Nelly manage to hold her tongue? She had witnessed their cloth being sold under another name, and she had submitted to Madame's stringent demands. Yet, still, Nelly played her part.

Upset that she had to endure such rudeness, Suisan said, "That will be all, Madame. The maid is quite capable."

In a haughty swirl of silk, Madame LeBlanc flounced out. When Nelly made a vulgar sign with her hand, Suisan had to smother her laughter.

"The old crow deserves a hot poker in her ass. And I'd give every copper she's paid me to be the one to wield it, but I'd have to wait in line. There's others beggin' to do it and they was here before me."

"You don't have to come back."

Nelly smiled. "Thank you, milady. I miss Scotland more and more. No wonder the Sassenachs covet our fair land; they've turned their own country into a stinkin' hell hole. But enough of that. Finish what you started to say before we was so rudely interrupted."

"Help me with the dress while we talk." Suisan bent from the waist and held out her arms.

"Careful so you don't muss your hair." Nelly slipped the dress over Suisan's head and fastened the buttons. "Now tell me."

"We must get the rest of the patterns out and quickly."

Nelly peered around Suisan. Their eyes met in the mirror. "I wasn't thinkin' of stayin' here 'til Hogmanay."

"Uncle Rabby's coming to visit Myles."

"Sweet St. Margaret!" Nelly's hands stilled. "Someone's told him and he's comin' to fetch us. When I find the louty traitor who told him—"

"No one knew, only the men in Aberdeen."

Nelly's face was red with anger. "I'll bet Dundas and those wags he calls soldiers told half of Aberdeen. He never could control 'em. Turn around.'' She began fluffing out the skirt. "Fine escort they turned out to be. 'Tis glad I am you didn't bring them here to London. Although it was hardly fair to threaten to dismiss Dundas if he didn't do as you said.''

Guilt twisted inside Suisan. She had been cruel to Dundas, but he left her no choice. She pretended to study the dress but her senses were attuned to Nelly. Hoping to soothe her, Suisan said, "And can't you see those Highlanders parading through Cuper's Gardens or marching down Fleet Street? Why, they'd probably storm Westminister Abbey and steal the crowning tablet right from under King George's nose."

"And return it to *Scone Abbey* where it belongs," Nelly hissed.

Eyeing her maid carefully, Suisan decided a change in topics was prudent. "'Tis a nice dress, but it won't do." She touched the bruise which was entirely revealed by the low neckline.

Nelly wasn't fooled. "If your uncle's not coming to fetch us home, will you tell me why he *is* coming?"

"He's probably stopping in before taking a holiday in France. Summer's almost over, you know."

"Better than most," Nelly grumbled.

"But we'll not spend the fall in London."

Nelly chuckled, fussing at some detail of the dress. Her anger had passed. "Aye, 'tis a lovely dress, and the finest weavin' Widow MacCormick's ever done. Will Himself be angry if you refuse to wear it?"

"Probably, but I don't care."

"Think on it this way," Nelly began, a twinkle in her eyes. "You'd be relievin' the buggerin' jackal of part of his purse 'cause Madame ain't had a charitable thought since Robert the Bruce was a bairn. And," Nelly drawled, "he'd be buying back the cloth. Serves him right, don't you think, considerin' the way he's cheated us? Unless you believe him innocent."

Banishing the memory of his shocked expression, Suisan said, "Of course he's guilty."

Nelly's eyes narrowed. "Then why not seek a bit of vengeance?"

Nelly's train of thought was appealing. What better way

for Suisan to keep her emotions under control when dealing with Myles than to know she'd gotten the upper hand? "I could pretend a little, I suppose."

"Of course you can."

Suisan flashed a brilliant smile. "Thank you, Nelly."

"'Twas nothin'. You'd have thought of it yourself in time."

Nelly stood back and examined Suisan from head to toe. Then she pulled a pair of shears from her apron and clipped a length of the yellow ribbon from the bow tied just under Suisan's breasts. From another pocket, Nelly produced a brush. "Sit here." She indicated the stool.

Nelly pulled the pins from Suisan's hair, brushed out the tangles and drew the long, black mass over Suisan's marked shoulder, effectively hiding the bruise. Then she tied the ribbon into a perfect bow around the swath of hair.

"I should have shot Myles while I had the chance the other night," Nelly offered, spooling a long strand into a curl.

"It was you!" Suisan exclaimed, then drew in her breath. "You called him a Sassenach."

"'Twern't time to tell him the whole of it, you ken. Be still," Nelly said gruffly, though her eyes were alight with laughter and pride. "I could have coshed him good, too, had you passed me one of the patterns that night. Bonny weapons, those."

"But he said you had the pistol."

Nelly looked thoughtful. "I wouldn't have truly shot him. Too messy."

"I'm glad to hear that. If you'd had one of the patterns, we'd most likely be rotting in jail now."

"A body can rot anywhere in this slop jar they call a city. Don't take a cell for that." She eyed Suisan carefully. "You look lovely."

Suisan glanced at the mirror. She looked predictably different, but lovely? She wasn't sure.

"Don't get missish," Nelly fussed. "You're a beauty, dark-haired or red. And I think you've kept Sir Rodent waitin' long enough."

"*Lord* Rodent."

"'Tis fittin'." Nelly wiggled her eyebrows. "Shall I come tonight?"

"Aye, and hire a carriage. You'll have to take them all. We've no time to spare."

"I can't manage a carriage, and I'd sooner trust Cumberland himself as a London hackie."

"A cart then. Could you manage a cart?"

Nelly looked affronted. "As well as you can doctor old Seamus's gout, milady."

"'Tis settled then. Nine o'clock." Suisan walked to the draped doorway. "Nelly . . ."

"Aye milady, what is it?"

Suisan turned. "I want no children from—" she faltered. "From Myles. I'll not risk having a child like Ailis, not even for the *Maide dalbh*."

"Makin' a bairn takes time," Nelly reasoned. "We'll be leaving too soon for that."

"Are you certain?"

Nelly grinned lecherously. "My Ian, rest his soul, worked for months before I conceived little Sorcha."

Suisan wasn't convinced. "But—"

"Don't worry," Nelly broke in. "No harm's yet done, and if you use your woman's wiles, you can have him where you choose."

Nelly was right; Suisan was not using her head. Bolstered by the prospect of playing Myles Cunningham for a fool, and encouraged by how quickly she'd be leaving London, Suisan said, "Wait at the back door tonight, not at the cellar window."

Nelly looked impressed. "That's the spirit, milady. Flirt with him a little, and make him think he's won you. Turn on the charm, milady, and you'll knock his twitchin' jack in the dirt. And when we're gone, the bugger'll wonder where he went wrong. Do him good, it will, to set his knobs down a notch."

Myles wondered what was taking her so long. Was she still upset about the cloth? By God, he intended to take

Robert Harper to task for what he'd done. Suisan would have to be told, and Robert would have to be watched. If that bloody oddlot tried to pull such a trick again, he'd be peddling cloth from the back of a mule instead of entertaining hopes of getting that post with the Exchange Ministry. Myles could deal with Robert. Didn't the lass know that? But then, perhaps Maura had woven that bolt herself and pride had fueled her anger. Well, he'd spend the day with her. That would sweeten her mood. His other women had always responded favorably to such attention. Before he could delve further into the subject, the lass appeared in the door.

He leaned back to study her as she approached. Blue might be her best color, considering her eyes, but the frilly white concoction she was wearing made her look like a new spring flower. Her skin seemed to glow, and the saucy way her hair was draped across her shoulder brought a smile to his lips. She was smiling, too, in a pert, confident way. And why shouldn't she be pleased with herself? She had uncovered Robert Harper's scam with Suisan's cloth. *Suisan*. What would her reaction be when she learned the truth about Robert Harper? Myles didn't relish hurting her. He only hoped she'd accept his comfort and protection.

"Don't you like it?" she asked.

"Stop there and turn about," he said, leaning forward and tapping the wooden rod on the floor.

She whirled, much the same as she'd done the night of Ainsbury's visit. The memory triggered hungry thoughts. Myles chuckled when she curtsied deeply, then walked toward him.

"You haven't answered, milord."

Myles smiled at the playfulness in her tone. If she continued to tease him, he'd forget his plans and give her a long, lusty view of his bedroom ceiling. Determined to make the most of her lighthearted mood, he stifled the thought. "The dress pleases me, too." He rose and held out his hand, which she took.

"I'm most relieved to know that," she purred as they exited the room. "And where will you take me?"

She was doing it to him again, and this time he didn't hold back. "To bed, if you don't cease your teasing."

"Oh!" Her cheeks turned pink and she scanned the room.

Thinking he'd put a stop to her coyness, Myles said, "Shall we bid Madame LeBlanc a good day?"

"If you insist."

"And if I don't insist?"

She looked surprised at the question and Myles wondered what she was thinking. Of all the women he'd known, this Scottish lassie was the most complex, the least predictable.

"Then we simply shan't bid her good day, Myles," she replied amiably.

Completely confused, Myles guided her out the door and to the carriage. When they were seated, he said, "Since you've seen your fill of London with someone else, I propose a ride in the country. I'm told John Stemmons has acquired some of Darley's Arabians. Would you like to see them with me?"

"If they're horses, yes; if they're foxes, no."

A passerby whistled loudly and she turned to the sound. The rake blew her a kiss then bowed regally. For the first time in his life, Myles experienced the cutting edge of jealousy. He didn't like the feeling: didn't like it at all. "Tell your friend you won't be accompanying him on any more outings."

"My friend?"

"Aye," Myles grumbled, "the other man you were seeing."

Her eyes sparkled and Myles fought back the urge to kiss her. "By all means, milord," she said meekly, "I'm sure my friend will understand."

Myles was relieved at her acquiescence, but something in her tone made him suspicious. "Are you flirting with me?"

For an instant she looked like an adorable child who'd learned a forbidden thing.

"*Moi*?" she asked, placing a delicate hand to her breast and batting her eyes.

Myles roared with laughter. Anxious to have her alone on

a deserted country road, he popped the reins and guided the team out of London.

~ *Chapter 10* ~

The hallway was dark except for a single shaft of yellow light spilling from the study. From where Suisan stood in the hall, she could hear Myles addressing Ollie but she did not concentrate on the words. She needed all her wits and strength, if she and Nelly were to succeed tonight.

What if something went wrong? What if Will'am came home early? What if she and Nelly were discovered by Myles or Ollie? Forcing the gruesome possibilities from her mind, she took a deep, settling breath. They must recover the rest of the pattern sticks, no matter how risky.

As she stopped at the threshold of the study, she was struck by the poignant familiarity of the scene before her. Ollie Cookson, a ledger in his lap, listened intently as Myles, lounging in a nearby chair, gave instructions. The natural progression of events, of Myles following in her father's footsteps with Ollie at his side, brought a sentimental pang to Suisan. Fighting back her tender response to the scene, she remained silent and unobserved by either of them.

"But do you think it's your place, Myles," Ollie was saying, "to reimburse Suisan for the money Robert gained in switching the cloth?"

Suisan felt her worst fears realized; had Uncle Rabby been behind the ruse after all?

"Of course, it's my place," Myles grumbled. "I should have kept closer watch on him but, Christ, I never thought he'd stoop to cheating Suisan."

"I still don't think it's your place."

Myles chuckled. "I'm not surprised, since you forgot your place years ago."

Ollie snorted derisively. "Well, if you intend to take on the responsibility of Suisan's cloth from here on out, my, uh, place will be something different altogether. You can't manage her business, and your business at the same time."

Myles cleared his throat. "I've made some decisions about that, too. Some sweeping decisions."

Suisan fought to keep her composure. Myles couldn't possibly take over Robert's role. If he ever came to the Highlands again . . . The thought was too devastating to consider. The thought was insulting, too. She had obviously erred in turning over the marketing of her cloth to another, but that was in the past. In the future, she would market her cloth in Glasgow. But still, the thought that Myles cared enough to involve himself in Suisan Harper's life was uplifting. And she knew the reason why.

She, who'd governed her own life and managed the commerce of an entire Highland district, had wanted for naught when at Myles's side. She had been free of the day-to-day decisions and burdens regarding Perwickshire since coming to London. How would she go back to being the mistress of Roward Castle after the soul-deep love she'd experienced in London? Remembering her goal brought Suisan to her senses. Feeling suddenly confident about the evening to come, she took a step forward.

Myles looked up, as if sensing her presence. His expression was warm, familiar; his eyes sensually alive. When he smiled and winked, excitement raced up her spine. Her palms went damp. She rubbed them on her apron.

". . . selling the *Star*'s good business," Ollie said. "But these other changes are radical indeed."

She heard Ollie's voice but was unable to tear her gaze from Myles. Lustful thoughts were mirrored in his eyes and, try as she would, she could not ignore the sensual message he was sending. He was remembering their lovemaking and anticipating their next encounter, and he was encouraging her to do the same.

"Are you listening?" Ollie asked, then followed Myles's

gaze to Suisan. A knowing glimmer in the steward's blue eyes set his bearded face to smiling. "No," he chuckled, "I don't suppose you are."

Reluctantly Myles turned his attention to his steward. "Let's get on with it or we'll be here all night."

"Aye, we will," Ollie replied. "You've yet to decide about the warehouses."

Myles scanned the books scattered about the room.

"You won't find it here," Ollie said. "The wharf ledger's still in my room."

"I'll fetch it," Suisan offered. "I only came in to say that dinner's ready. 'Twill keep, but," she paused, saying a silent prayer her plan would work. "I wondered, since Mr. Cookson's better and all, if he wouldn't join you at the table tonight?"

Myles folded his arms across his chest. Still looking at her, he said, "The lass has a point. What say you, Ollie? Are you fit enough to dine downstairs tonight?"

"Of course I'm fit enough," Ollie declared crossly. "But if we don't get done here, we won't be eatin' 'til midnight."

Grinning, Myles said, "You're sure you don't mind getting the ledger?"

Warmed by his sincere tone, Suisan said, "Of course not."

Ollie rolled his eyes and sighed dramatically. Myles shot him a scathing look, but Ollie didn't seem to notice. When Myles frowned and narrowed his eyes, she rushed to say, "I'll just get the ledger, then."

As she made her way to Ollie's room, Suisan thought of other times, of times when her father, Ollie and Myles had sat in the parlor of the Harper home in Aberdeen years before. She'd been six when Papa brought Myles home for the first time. Until Papa's death three years later, he and Myles had been inseparable. They had been a family. At what moment, she wondered, had Myles taken complete control of the business? A year after her father's death? Two years? Myles had been only nineteen when Papa died, Suisan had been nine. She remembered little of the funeral, except mind-numbing sadness and loss. But when her mother died a scant year later and Myles had deposited her at Roward Castle, Suisan came to know the true meaning of utter loneliness.

The Cameron family plot in Perwickshire had been the site of much sorrow for Suisan. The only comfort for her as they laid her mother to rest had been the warmth of Myles's hand holding her smaller one. He had grieved, too, as they buried Sibeal Harper; he had grieved and he had cried. And he had shared his handkerchief with her. She'd kept the square of linen, for it became her link to Myles, until he announced she would stay in the Highlands and live at Roward Castle and he would return to the sea. At the thought of being separated from him, she had responded in a fit of childish rage, she had cast the handkerchief aside, and with it her fondness for Myles Cunningham.

She remembered her hurtful parting words to him. "I'm glad you're too young to be my guardian. You're not fit to govern a snake."

In the ensuing years, her animosity toward him had continued to grow, and each time Uncle Rabby visited the castle she came to expect his derogatory news of Myles. But more than the stories of Myles's decadent behavior, Myles's disappointingly curt letters had wounded Suisan deeply. With adulthood had come tolerance toward Myles. She no longer expected love and affection from him. He was what he was, a selfish man uninterested in nurturing the slender thread that had once bound them together. Too many disappointments had cured her of expecting more than Myles was willing to give. She accepted the small allowance he sent via Rabby because she assumed Myles recovered the funds through the sale of her cloth.

She stopped at the door to Ollie's room. Myles had not profited from the sale of Roward Cloth. To the contrary, he now willingly assumed a loss, because Uncle Rabby had cheated her.

She gripped the cold enamel surface of the doorknob, as cold reality gripped her heart. Myles was innocent; Uncle Rabby was to blame. And yet, Myles was guilty of a greater crime than selling her cloth under another name. He'd done the one thing she could never forgive; he had stolen Scotland's most precious treasure, the *Maide dalbh*. He must have been desperate for the recognition.

Suddenly Suisan was dizzy from the circling path their

lives had taken. She hated him; she didn't. She loved him; she shouldn't. She wanted to spend the rest of her life with him; she couldn't.

Her palms went dry as she turned the knob and entered Ollie's room. A wall of indifference began to surround her aching heart. Never again would she allow herself to be deceived by either Myles Cunningham or Uncle Rabby. Soon she would take back the last of the beloved pattern sticks and return to the safety of Scotland.

Emboldened by her strong sense of duty, Suisan retrieved the ledger. On lighter feet, she retraced her steps to the study. Ollie looked as if he'd been set down a notch, but Myles's expression had not changed. His appreciative smile was warm and his eyes danced with what she believed was anticipation. She managed a shy smile, handed the book to Myles, then took her leave.

Once in the kitchen, she went immediately to the back door. Her hands began to shake. Fear set her heart to pounding. What would she say if Myles came upon her now? What would she do if Will'am came home early? Growing less courageous with each possibility, Suisan knew she must put the alarming thoughts aside. She would do what had to be done. She'd made it all the way to England, hadn't she? A little more courage, a little more time. Only then she would go home. And only then she could relax.

Casting a quick glance over her shoulder, she begged the hinges to be silent and prayed Nelly would be there. She eased open the door. Nellie was there.

Suisan shot another glance toward the hall doorway and listened carefully. Silence. Holding her breath, she pulled Nelly into the kitchen and toward the cellar door.

With her first glimpse of Nelly's face, Suisan realized her maid was terrified. Nelly's ruddy complexion was pasty white and her shoulders were tucked to her neck.

"What's that awful smell?" Nelly asked.

Shooting her a wilting look, Suisan said, "Shush!"

"'Tis enough to make me sick." Nelly stuck out her tongue. "Weeds and dead birds and rotten little fish."

Ignoring her, Suisan reached for the knob on the cellar

door and turned. It was locked! She muttered one of Nelly's favorite obscenities.

"Where's the key?" Nelly's voice wavered and her eyes shifted nervously toward the hallway.

Suisan suspected Nelly's chatter was merely a mask for her fear. "In the pantry. Stay here and don't make a sound."

Nelly nodded, her braids jiggling, her body stiff as a soldier's.

Suisan found the key. The lock tumbled. The sound seemed loud enough to raise St. Ninian.

"You should oil this thing. 'Tis the mark of a poor housekeeper."

"You should keep silent!"

"What's that you've prepared?" Nelly jerked her head to the large bowl on the table.

"Nelly . . ." Suisan groaned as she swung the door open.

"Well, it smells bad. Only a Sassenach would eat that slop."

Deciding her maid would not be silent until she had her answer, Suisan said, "'Tis salmagundi."

Nelly put a hand to her stomach and pretended to vomit. "Sassenach garbage, not fit for MacIver's grubbiest sheepdog."

"Please, Nelly. I only know how to cook three things. This is a new one."

Nelly stuck out her chin. "You got no place cookin' an' curtsyin' for the likes of them."

"*Haud yer wheesht!*" Seething, Suisan pushed Nelly through the cellar door. "The twelfth step squeaks."

"Then put some of that chicken fat the English call food on it."

"I'll pinch off your head if you don't march quietly down those stairs and wait for me," Suisan ground out. "Do you want us to get caught?"

Nelly's eyes grew wide with fear. She sneezed. "Sorry. This cold I'm catching is fogging my head. How long must I wait?"

"Not long. I'm about to set the table. Do you remember where the box is?"

Nelly nodded but her braids did not quiver. "Under the stairs."

"Where's the cart?"

"In the stable, well out of sight."

Suisan began to relax; Nelly had done her part well. "You can light the lamp, but stay in the shadows so anyone passing won't see you. I'll be down when I can."

"How will you get away?"

"I left the wine off the table."

"Good." Nelly's warm hand gripped Suisan's arm. "Don't be afraid, milady. 'Twill be as easy as settin' up the looms."

Suisan exhaled loudly, the sound a whisper compared to the fear pounding in her head. With a shaking hand, she pulled the door closed. Tucking the small key into her apron pocket, she went about setting the table.

She was lighting the last of the candles on the dining room table when she heard Myles and Ollie approach. Trying very hard to appear impassive, she blew out the taper and turned to face them.

Myles, dressed in gray pants, a white shirt and double breasted waistcoat, had slowed his steps to match Ollie's cane-hampered gait. One of the steward's trouser legs had been split to accommodate the cast, and the fabric flapped as he walked. She wondered how someone so persnickety as Ollie dealt with the changes his broken leg had wrought.

"Lass?"

Myles pulled a chair away from the table and the inviting look on his face left no doubt as to who the chair was meant for.

She hadn't wanted to set a place for herself; she'd barely managed to prepare the meal. Why hadn't she thought he would expect her to sit at the table? She needed to go in and out of the room in case Nelly needed help. "I thought you and Ollie had business to discuss. I've already supped—but would enjoy serving you," was all she could think of.

Myles's expression grew curious, but before he could reply, Ollie plopped down in the proffered chair, laughing as he did. "You always did have good manners, Myles, my boy, and respect for your elders."

"No thanks to my teachers," Myles said sarcastically, pushing the chair too close to the table. Ollie grunted. Myles didn't seem to notice. Holding out his hand to her, he said, "You'll sit with us. Fetch another setting."

Mutinously Suisan complied. She dared not cross him tonight. When she put her plate next to his, he took her elbow and guided her into the chair. She glanced up at him and tried to smile, but her mind was firmly fixed on Nelly and the remaining patterns. The plan to smuggle them all out tonight suddenly seemed foolish.

Myles sent her an assessing look. Could he see her fear? He strolled gracefully to the head of the table and took his chair. "What have you cooked?"

She tapped her feet on the rug. "Salmagundi."

His expression told her he had more on his mind than food.

Stilling her jittery feet, she tossed the saladlike dish, consisting mainly of chicken, sorrel and eggs. The candle flames wavered, and she was struck by the silly notion that the candles were as nervous as she. Pushing the ridiculous thought aside, she served Myles first. He said nothing, but continued to watch her closely as she filled Ollie's plate and her own.

"I knew you hadn't supped," Myles said matter-of-factly. "And it wouldn't have been the first meal you've missed since Mackie's been gone. You're too thin, Maura."

Suisan licked her suddenly dry lips. His constant attention was disturbing enough, but she didn't know how she would get through the night if she continued to trip herself up.

Unable to reply and unable to hold his gaze, Suisan looked away. She willed herself to be calm. Oddly the candles now seemed to burn more steadily.

When Ollie had tasted the dish, he carefully wiped his moustache. "Splendid, Maura, girl. But how did a Scotswoman learn such distinctly English fare?"

"Mackie's recipe," she answered, feeling suddenly shy. "She said it was your favorite." She glanced at Myles, "And yours."

He picked up his fork and speared a mouthful. After he'd swallowed, he reached for the wine glass which wasn't there.

"Oh, my. I've forgotten the wine," she lied with ease.

"It'll wait." He drank water from a goblet instead. "You haven't touched your meal," he said, the candlelight flickering over his handsome face.

"Good as Mackie's," Ollie put in. "But don't tell her I said so." A wistful look appeared in his eyes; he began nudging the food around on his plate. "She'd just go on and on about it."

"Ollie's right," Myles said, grinning crookedly, and obviously aware of Ollie's pensive mood. "And by the time she gets back, she'll have plenty to chatter about. No need encouraging her."

Ollie turned to Myles now. "You're still set on buying that place in Cornwall?"

Suisan tried to hide her shock. Cornwall? Myles was moving to Cornwall? A low, keening pain formed in her breast.

"Aye," Myles answered. "I've had enough of London, the smell, the politics, the—"

She ceased to hear him. The candle flames on the table were again fluttering wildly. Nelly must have just opened the back door. Suisan's spirits soared, then fell. What if Myles or Ollie noticed? How could they not? She glanced surreptitiously at both men. Neither had noticed the flames, but they might before the meal was over.

The flames stilled.

". . . wasn't what I expected you to do." Ollie was saying. "I thought you might go to—"

"My decision is final."

She pulled her eyes away from the tell-tale candles. Myles absently reached again for his wine. Her eyes kept darting back to the candelabra. The flames began to flutter again.

She dropped her fork; it clattered loudly.

Myles looked curiously at her.

"I must get the wine," she blurted out, rising. Why hadn't she closed the blasted hall door? She must do it, and quickly, or she would give Nelly away.

Before either of them could comment, she left the table. Once in the kitchen, she closed the door and leaned against it. When her breathing had slowed, she hurried down the cellar stairs.

"Nelly?" she whispered.

"Here, milady." Nelly stepped out of the shadows holding one of the cumbersome *Maide dalbh* like a baby.

Suisan ran to her.

"What's amiss?" Nelly asked, glancing toward the stairs.

"Oh, Nelly. You must be more careful bringing them upstairs; each time you—"

"An' how could I be more careful?" Nelly's voice rose and her cheeks darkened. "I'm sneaking around like a fat field mouse scurryin' through a valley of hungry snakes."

"I know you are, but—"

"We was better off the other way," Nelly jerked her head toward the high windows, "passin' them through, one by one. I told you so."

Suisan explained about the candles.

"Oh." Nelly dropped her chin. "I hope the door stops the draught."

"We're both frightened," Suisan said softly, 'but 'tis almost done, thanks to you."

Nelly shrugged and shifted the burden in her arms. "I've been playin' a little game—bettin' each time I pick one up that it's the Royal Stewart."

Suisan hadn't thought of the individual clans represented by the *Maide dalbh*, not since passing the Lochiel Cameron pattern to safety. Bonny Prince Charlie's plaid was the best known and most dangerous. She should be elated at returning the Stewart's colors to Scotland. She tried to be, but all she could think of was the danger they faced, the hangman . . . and never returning to Perwickshire.

Nelly sneezed again. "Don't fret, milady," she whispered, sniffling. "Eight more trips and we're done."

Nelly's confidence wasn't enough for Suisan. "Nay," she said. "'Tis too dangerous. Take that pattern, but no more tonight. We'll use the window again."

Nelly looked at the pattern in her arms, then glanced into the darkness. "I thought you were anxious to be away from him."

"Of course I'm anxious to escape him," Suisan said much too quickly.

"Hmm. I was afraid of that. You love him."

"You're mistaken, for he means nothing to me," Suisan lied vehemently, still stung by the news that Myles was moving to Cornwall.

"So you say. Has he given you another bruise?"

"He's given me nothing," Suisan hissed. "And just where are your loyalties, Nelly Burke?"

"With these," she hefted the pattern in her arms, "and you, Lady Sui—"

"Oh, God," Suisan gasped and looked toward the landing. A long shadow darkened the steps. She turned back, but Nelly wasn't there anymore.

Then came the whispered words, "Just keep Himself over there. I'll be at the window tomorrow night."

Suisan moved to the wine rack and pretended to study the dusty labels. Myles started down the stairs. By the time his boots touched the earthen floor, Suisan felt a sense of doom settle over her. When his hands touched her shoulders, she almost jumped. What had made her think she could pull off such a trick?

"Lass?" he said softly, sounding concerned.

Knowing she had no choice, Suisan turned to face him. "Did I not bring the wine quickly enough?"

"I don't give a tinker's damn about the wine." He stroked her cheek, and she shivered. His touch evoked feelings very different from fear.

"Tell me," he insisted, lifting her chin, "what has upset you so?"

"Upset? I don't know what you mean." She slid a glance toward the spot where Nelly was hiding. The corner was dark.

"You're lying." His eyes bored into hers. "I had hoped we were past the point of deceiving each other."

With half her faculties rooted on Nelly Burke, Suisan didn't understand. Most likely he was deceiving her and all of Scotland. "I truly don't know what you mean."

"Then I'll refresh your memory." His arms surrounded her and pulled her to his chest. Then his lips sought hers. He kissed her gently, persuasively, and before she noticed the change, her mind was awash with only Myles. She found succor in his arms, a place of safety from the jumble her life had become.

His hands roamed her back, easing the tension from her muscles. His mouth played eagerly with her own, nipping, tracing and enticing, until she could think of naught else but the welcome shelter of his embrace.

He broke the kiss. "Was it Ollie's presence at the table that discomfited you so? 'Twas your idea, you know."

She blinked, bewildered by his innocent query. Knowing how important her answer was, yet hard-pressed to form a cohesive thought, Suisan forced her mind to the present. "'Twas that in part," she managed.

"Was it what Robert Harper did to Lady Suisan?"

Why did he have to bring that up? "Nay."

His teeth toyed with the inside of his upper lip. "You're upset because I came down to the kitchen naked and threatened to remain so in front of Ollie."

Suisan blushed, wishing Nelly wasn't hearing this conversation.

"I wouldn't have embarrassed you," he moved so their lips almost touched, "not for any price."

Pleased by his confession and mesmerized by his piercing gaze, Suisan softly said, "I didn't think you truly would, but—"

"But what?" he breathed across her lips.

She ached to close the slight distance between them, to feel his lips on hers. But Nelly was watching.

Myles moved back and raised his brows in question. "Tell me and I'll kiss you."

Her breath caught in her throat. Damn his arrogant hide! Spurred to retaliate, Suisan said, "Keep your kisses."

His brow creased and his teeth now toyed with his lower lip—the lip she had desperately wanted to kiss just seconds before. "Say it, lass."

Suisan searched her brain for some answer that would not come back to haunt her, for some scrap of truth. If Nelly sneezed now, they'd be caught. "The news of Robert Harper's visit."

"Ahah! I wish you had told me."

"'Twas not my place to object to your house guest."

"Your place is with me." he declared. "Robert is harmless, but I, my dear, am not."

Suisan remembered the estate in Cornwall. Knowing if she mentioned his moving to the country he would think her jealous, she chose a safer place to put the blame for her discomfiture. "And when your guest arrives? I won't have him witness you scurrying from my bed to yours—" What on earth had she said? Nelly was listening.

Myles grew still. Suisan grew frightened.

He tilted his head to the side and studied her. "He's not my friend, but Suisan's uncle. We exchange letters through him, though she doesn't write to me often." Myles paused and Suisan thought he looked hurt. But why would he be unhappy? She had always answered his correspondence. True, her letters had grown less personal over the years, but so had his. Hadn't he wanted it that way?

More confused and less confident, Suisan placed her hands on his shoulders. "When does Robert Harper arrive?"

Myles seemed to shake himself. "Before the end of the month."

Relief ran through her; if she and Nelly were quick, they'd have time to get the patterns out.

Myles's hands moved to her hips, then slowly began to lift her dress.

"Nay." She braved a glance to the corner where Nelly hid. "You mustn't."

"Oh, but I must." He bunched the skirt around her waist, pushed her legs apart, then rubbed himself against her. "Feel how I need you, lass."

He was hard and ready and insistent against her. The cool air on her legs contrasted with the heat building inside her. The cool air also reminded her that Nelly was watching them.

"Please . . ." Begging seemed to be her only option; he had to stop!

His nostrils flared. "So be it, lass," he unbuttoned his vest, "but I hadn't thought to take you standing here in the basement."

Dear God, he'd gotten it all wrong. "Nay, not that," she blurted out.

His eyebrows shot up but his hand moved down to the placket on his breeches. "The table?"

She couldn't answer.

"Will you unfasten these buttons?" He replaced his hand with hers.

Nelly could hear every damning word. Suisan knew she would never live down this moment. Hot with embarrassment, she said, "You misunderstood me." She ducked her head. "I did not mean to have you think I wanted to . . . well, the basement is not the place I would have chosen to—" She stopped, thoroughly disgusted with her stupid tongue.

"To what?" A playful glimmer lighted his eyes. His hand slipped between her legs.

She tried to jerk away, but his grip was too strong. Completely flustered, she stammered, "You know what I meant when I—Oh!"

He found the point of her greatest weakness. She gasped, then kissed goodbye any hope of ever controlling Nelly Burke again.

He groaned, leaning his forehead against hers. "You're so warm, lass, that I've changed my mind. Free me from these breeches. I would have you now."

She groaned too, but not wholly from the pleasure he aroused. Breathlessly, she said, "Change it back."

His hand moved up to her waist, then down her bare belly to resume his play. He slipped a finger inside her.

Suisan tried again to wiggle away. She succeeded in opening herself to him completely. "Myles!"

He sucked in his breath. "Let me fill you with something else, love."

She had to stop him! Grasping his shoulders, she wrenched away from him. Her skirts fell back into place. "Not here, Myles. Please not here. We must go back. Ollie will suspect."

She spared a glance at the dark corner under the stairs, but did not see Nelly. What difference did that make? Nelly had heard everything. Disgusted, Suisan looked back at Myles.

"I didn't mean to frighten you. I thought 'twas what you wanted." He smiled crookedly. "I forget sometimes that you came to me a virgin, and know naught of such things. You always respond so passionately."

"Please," she hissed. "We must go back."

"Not as I am, sweetheart," he said, fastening the buttons of his vest. "Ollie would make great sport of me."

The honest look in Myles's eyes gave Suisan pause. But to her way of thinking, Ollie Cookson was a mere amateur in the fine art of sharp words when compared to Nelly Burke, and Suisan would not give Nelly more fodder for bawdy jokes.

"We could choose the wine," she offered, relaxed now that he had put his clothing to rights. "'Tis why we came."

He smiled warmly. "'Tisn't why I came, and you still haven't told me why you seem so distant tonight."

"I did," she insisted and glanced again toward the corner.

Drat! Nelly was peeking around the wall of brandy cases. Suisan felt her temper rise. How would she ever live down this mess? Worse, how would she end it gracefully? She looked to Myles and the answer was written on his face. He wanted her to admit that she cared, that nothing had changed between them. Well, damn it all, she would.

Wrapping her arms about his neck, she seductively said, "I want you, Myles, but the meal will be cold if we dally."

He smiled fully, and in the soft glow of the lamplight Suisan thought he had never looked so handsome, so maddeningly desirable.

"The meal was cold to begin with, but this dallying sounds promising to me."

"Nay, not here." She slid a glance to the corner. And saw Nelly, arms empty and crossed over her breasts, a very satisfied—nay, smug—look on her traitorous face. She shook her head, braids twirling like ribbons on the maypole.

"I'll agree," Myles relented at last. "But only if you promise to serve my dessert later—much later."

Suisan would have promised to serve comfits to King

George himself in order to flee Nelly's knowing gaze. Though aware that her remark would be repeated by the maid for years to come, Suisan said, "Aye, but no crumbs in the bed."

His eyebrows shot up. "That's my girl. We've a bargain then."

Reaching around her, he splayed his fingers and pulled out two bottles of wine. "One for now," he kissed her cheek, "and one for later, my love."

∿ *Chapter 11* ∿

Suisan stared at Myles sleeping soundly beside her. In the rosy glow of dawn, his tanned skin seemed gilded and his golden hair sparkled like freshly mown wheat. She ached to touch him one last time, to run her hands over the smooth planes of his face, to lay her head against his chest and be enfolded in his arms.

But not this morning. She was leaving him today.

Her chest ached with grief as she continued to watch him sleep, and no power on Earth could have made her turn away. She recalled the moments they'd spent in this room during the past weeks; happy times, quiet times, lusty afternoons and lustier nights.

He had been thoughtful and attentive, and since Mackie's return he had become protective. If the housekeeper harbored any resentment toward Suisan for becoming Myles's mistress, she kept it to herself. And more, the household had taken on a family atmosphere. During meals which they all shared unless Myles was attending to business, Mackie entertained them with stories of her new grandson or Cookson told tales of the Colonies. Suisan had relaxed during those times, and occasionally volunteered a story about Perwickshire. At the mention of Suisan Harper, Mackie grew silent, Ollie usually sighed, but Myles always listened intently, as if hungry for news of Scotland.

Involuntarily, Suisan's hand touched his cheek. He turned his face into her palm, cradling and cuddling his cheek until he was satisfied with the fit. Then he hummed a contented sound and drifted deeper into sleep.

Tears welled in her eyes, and for a brief time she put aside the wrongs he had dealt her and thought of how their lives might have been. The pain of that tender reflection became too great. Although no words of love had passed between them she knew he cared for her; he'd shown her in a hundred ways. Would he too be distressed by her leaving? Was Myles still capable of sorrow or had the years hardened his heart? What if his next letter to Suisan came from Cornwall and bore no mention of a black-haired servant girl named Maura?

Misery ran rampant through her tortured soul and her future yawned before her, more lonely than ever before. She had her memories and perhaps she had something else. Perhaps Myles had given her a child—a strong, healthy son or daughter to ease her aging years and fill her heart with gladness.

A daughter like Aunt Ailis?

No! Suisan cringed at the cruel thought, then pushed it firmly aside. She must concentrate on the reality of what this day would bring, on what she must do, on what was to come.

Nelly's bout with the ague couldn't have come at a worse time. Suisan had managed to slip away when she could to nurse her maid, and even now felt guilty at not being able to stay beside her night and day. Brave, stubborn Nelly had never complained, but cursed London for bringing a good Scottish lassie so low.

Not until last night had they finally smuggled out the last of the Highland patterns. Now all that remained was booking their passage home.

Home. A vision of Ferwickshire and the turreted stone peaks of Roward Castle rose in her mind. Although the vision was clear and familiar, she did not feel the same old longing . . . because she had fallen in love with the man beside her, not even the prospect of returning to her beloved home could warm her heart, for home was in his arms.

Aware that she was foolishly prolonging her agony, she pulled her hand away from Myles. Those expressive golden brows, which had so often been raised imperiously or cocked in surprise at some jest she'd made, were now drawn in a frown. Would he miss her so much when he awoke?

She studied his face, committing to memory each feature: the finely honed lines of his jaw and chin, the high bridge and perfect slope of his nose, the gentle flare of his nostrils as he breathed in the sweet smell of morning. Lips that had once teased and taunted her were now parted the same as they did just before he kissed her. She longed to kiss him now, to seal her farewell, to tell him in a single gesture that she didn't truly wish to go, that she wanted circumstances to be different. But she couldn't; she was Lady Suisan Harper from Scotland, a passerby in his London life.

All her treasures were safe with Nelly. Now it was time to go home.

On legs weary and weak, she moved from the bed. Quietly she dressed, then walked to the fireplace. With shaking hands she grasped the carp-handled hourglass and set the timepiece in motion. Fighting the urge to look at Myles once more, she left the room.

Like a gust of cold wind, loneliness seeped into her bones. Instead of crumbling beneath the crush of emotion, she bowed her head and leaned against the wall. Gritting her teeth, she stared through the dark curtain of her hair but saw nothing.

She would never forget her sojourn in London, but how much time would pass before she could recall the splendor without the pain?

"Lassie?"

Glancing up, she saw Ollie Cookson standing just outside Mackie's room. The housekeeper's door was closed, and Suisan wondered if Ollie were coming or going. Either way, she had no time to spare for the steward.

"You brought it on yourself, girl," he said gently. "You've no one else to blame."

"Aye, Ollie," she whispered thickly, "that I did."

He smiled in a fatherly way. Bracing both hands on the head of his cane, he leaned forward and said, "You're different from the other women he's had."

Ironic laughter bubbled up inside her. She pushed her hair away from her face and walked toward the stairs. "You've no idea how different."

He frowned. "He cares for you, lass, but don't expect him to give you his heart. Had a rough go of it, he has. 'Twould take a miracle for him to fall in love."

And certainly not with a servant, she thought. Hiding the hurt, she said, "I expect nothing from him. Certainly not a miracle."

Ollie shook his head. "Don't do anything you'll regret."

Instantly alert, Suisan cursed herself for being so maudlin. If Ollie suspected she was leaving he'd surely tell Myles.

Gathering her wits and her courage, she put on a smile. "Thank you for warning me, Ollie, and if I don't get at the scones, I'll certainly regret that."

He looked surprised, a state completely unsuited to his tidy features. "Myles's bark is worse than his bite."

"I know. Thank you again."

Ollie wielded his cane with ease and entered his own room.

Feeling mentally bruised and emotionally battered, Suisan climbed the stairs to her chamber.

The valise was packed and fresh underclothes lay on the bed. When she'd washed her face and changed her dress, Suisan stoically walked out of Myles's house and back into her own life.

Street vendors were beginning their routes but Suisan paid little heed to their hawking rhymes. Tins of milk rattled to the rhythm of creaking wheels; pigeons cooed and fluttered in the early morning din. A thick fog, like billowy summer clouds, filled the air. A yawning lamplighter veered neither left nor right as he retraced his evening's path and methodically extinguished the night lamps of London.

Choosing a circuitous route, she wended her way through the mews behind London's finer addresses. Here and there she heard the swish-swishing of a birch broom or the pop-popping of linens being aired. Speaking in sharp, clipped words so different from her own Highland brogue, the servant class of London set about their daily chores.

As she trudged along the first leg of her journey home, Suisan tried to put her life back in order. She needed to gather the bits and pieces of herself she'd put away on arriving in London. She'd drilled herself to speak just so, to receive orders instead of giving them, to keep her opinions to herself. Now she needed the skills of a noblewoman again, for Perwickshire awaited and no doubt a bundle of troubles and long-standing feuds would welcome her at Roward Castle.

She sighed and shifted the valise from one hand to the other. The gesture brought a wistful thought to mind. Wouldn't it be fine if only she could switch back to her old self again so easily? A depressing notion occurred to her then. What if she were never the same? What if her sojourn in Myles's London life had forever changed her?

"Impossible," she quietly scoffed. She was a Lochiel Cameron, by God; a descendant of one of Scotland's most ancient and loyal Highland clans. Camerons had fought and died in every major battle of Scotland; her own conflict seemed petty by comparison.

When Suisan walked into the house on Beacon Row, Nelly was pacing a roundabout path through stacks of trunks and boxes.

"Oh, milady," she squealed, bumping into a crate in her haste to reach Suisan. "I thought you'd come last night."

"I couldn't get away." That was almost the truth.

Nelly looked inquisitive. "Are you well? You look drawn out."

Suisan felt lifeless. "I couldn't sleep last night." That was very true; the prospect of leaving Myles had troubled her sleep.

Nelly's color rose. "Too bad for that. 'Twas all for naught. The damned ship won't sail today."

Confused, Suisan looked at the piles of luggage. "Why ever not?"

"This bletherin fog."

"The captain said that? You went to the docks this morn?"

"Captain?" Nelly spat. "He's a damned English coward who calls himself a sea captain. More like a twisted son of a sailor's knot—to my way of thinking."

Suisan's spirits plummeted. "When will the ship sail?"

In a voice exaggerated and much too courtly, Nelly said, "Not 'til this inclement weather has passed, m'dear."

"How long will that be?"

Nelly reached for Suisan's bag. "God don't even know. I'll wager He gave up on this wretched hell hole years ago."

Suisan hid her disappointment. "We'll be fine."

Nelly looked very serious. "How did Himself take your leavin'?"

"I didn't tell him."

Blinking in disbelief, Nelly asked, "What if he comes lookin' for you?"

"He won't. He doesn't care enough." Suisan's voice was firm, decisive.

"That's drivel of the worst kind." Nelly argued. "You can't possibly believe he don't care."

"Nelly . . ."

Unaffected, Nelly drew herself up and stuck out her chin. "I saw you two in the cellar, don't be forgettin'. Myles Cunningham loves you. And he's got a temper I don't care to see again, especially since you'll be the one to set him off, once he finds out you're gone."

"He won't find us."

Nelly raised her eyes heavenward. "Let's pray he don't."

Anxious to be off the subject of Myles Cunningham, Suisan waved an arm around the cluttered room. "What's left to be done?"

A look of impatience flashed on Nelly's face. Suisan knew her maid wanted to continue the discussion about Myles. Tight-lipped and obviously resigned, Nelly said, "Everything's here—except the big trunks upstairs."

"We'll need a cab when the time comes," Suisan said, removing her mobcap. "You've seen to the rest, and admirably so."

"I've arranged for a dray," Nelly said proudly.

Suisan relaxed. Nelly seemed herself again, a good sign; perhaps things were returning to normal.

"Where are the *Maide dalbh*?"

Nelly grinned and planted her hands on her hips. "I scattered 'em out in four separate trunks with clothes mixed in to hide 'em."

"Very clever. And the other things?"

Nelly began counting on her fingers. "The MacKenzie's spy glass is packed with the linens. Gifts for the children are tucked away in them baskets. The other things are packed in boxes—a bit here, a bit there."

"You've thought of everyone? Of Flora, of Rowena?"

"Aye," Nelly said confidently. "I even bought Spanish spirits for the men in Aberdeen, but don't tell 'em 'til we're home. They'd spend a bloody year gettin' us back to Perwickshire if they know there's liquor to be had. If they ain't drunk themselves to death already."

"They always speak well of you, too," Suisan said wryly.

Nelly frowned. "We'll even get that dye off your hair."

Suisan hadn't thought of her hair; the prospect of looking like herself again was uplifting. Still she was doubtful Nelly could remove the dye. "With what?"

"Fresh eggs and some other things a lady don't have no business knowin' about."

"That would be wonderful," Suisan said. Chuckling confidently, she added, "If Myles does come after me, which I don't foresee, he'll never recognize me with red hair."

"But your Uncle Robert will."

"He's here?" Suisan gasped. "In London? Now?"

"Aye, 'twas the captain of the Aberdeen ship your uncle sailed on convinced the damned English coward the fog was too thick."

"You were careful? Rabby didn't see you?"

"Didn't see nobody. He was so sick they had to carry him off the boat and cart him to a nearby inn. Some pasty lookin' odd lot was chirpin' around Robert and orderin' the others about like your uncle was nigh to dyin'."

"Was it serious—his illness?"

"Likely sick from the sea was all," the maid said lightly, flipping one of her braids.

Suisan glanced toward the window. "The fog's thicker than the mists on Comyn's Moor."

"Aye. Smells like a storm's brewing, too."

"Did you book a cabin?"

Their eyes met. "I didn't know what name to give 'em."

Suisan smile was crooked. "'Tis a riddle to be sure, but I'll find a name *he* won't recognize, *if* he looks for me."

Nelly smiled knowingly.

Suisan bit back a reprimand. "We'll just be careful and make the best of it, and I would like to go home a redhead."

"Don't be fashin' yourself over that, milady; you're smarter than the lot of these Sassenachs. As soon as the dye's off your hair and the weather's cleared, we'll be on our way home."

The inclement weather outside was nothing compared to the storm going on inside Myles. A blanket of thick fog clouded the windows but he had long since ceased to notice. London was shrouded for the second day but he didn't care. Foremost in his mind was a black-haired wench who'd wriggled her way into his heart then scurried off without so much as a "by your leave."

Disgusted by another surge of self-pity, Myles tossed his empty glass into the cold fireplace. The crystal shattered on the marble, then fell amid the sparkling heap that had once been dozens of glasses. The pile of broken glass was climbing, keeping pace with his temper.

When he'd awakened alone in his bed two days ago, he'd thought the Scottish lass was merely testing him. Feeling blissfully sated from their hours of lovemaking, Myles had chuckled at her defiance in leaving the bed without first telling him. The hourglass she'd set in motion told him she had left just moments before and he assumed she was downstairs preparing his scones. By the time the sand had ceased to fall, Myles knew he must go after her. That had sparked his anger. Two futile days of searching the fog-draped docks and streets of London had fanned his temper to a full blown state of rage.

"I think I'll change my bet," Ollie said, entering the room and surveying the damage. "Looks like you'll outlast our store of glasses."

Myles scowled. "Have they found her?"

Ollie walked to the sideboard and poured two glasses of brandy. "Here," he said, handing one to Myles. "'Twill make the news more palatable."

"Cease your doting and tell me what you know!" Myles bellowed, then tossed down the brandy in one swallow.

"The tidings are good and ill, I fear."

Myles fell back in the chair that had been his post for the last few hours. Drilling Ollie with a cold stare, he waited.

Seemingly unperturbed, Ollie sipped his drink. By the time he set the glass down, Myles was ready to tear the news from his steward's throat.

"No one's seen her but—"

"Damn!" Myles rose and began pacing. "A score of seasoned seamen, at home in ports 'round the globe, and not one of them can find that black-haired wench."

"Some of the news is good," Ollie said reasonably.

Myles halted and spun around. Cocking an eyebrow, he waited again.

Ollie was quick to reply, "The harbor's still closed. No ships have departed for Scottish ports, and the lookouts we posted on the roads haven't seen her."

"And I'm to be encouraged by that?" Myles thundered.

Ollie shrugged. "Not especially, unless you consider it timely that a certain *femme seule* booked passage on an Aberdeen ship about an hour ago."

The angry countenance Myles had maintained for the last two days suddenly fell away. "And why," he began, his voice deceptively calm, "should I give a tinker's damn about the comings and goings of some withered old hag?"

"Nothing, I suppose," Ollie replied, just as casually, "*if* she was old, and *if* she didn't—" he paused. "Let me get it straight." Pointing an index finger in the air, he said, "Ah, I have it now. They say Miss MacKenzie, the lady who booked, speaks with the brogue of a Highlander—and she's not old.''

"What does she look like?"

Ollie shrugged. "The captain said she was wearing a bonnet and kept her head bowed."

Like a prowling beast who at last has his prey in sight, Myles grinned, but the expression boded danger. "No other *femme seule* has booked passage on a ship bound for Scotland?"

"Nor any other port of call; at least no Scottish lassies. The harbormaster was quite certain and I saw the passenger lists."

Myles's grin now became vengeful; the hunt was coming to a close.

"Mayhap you should go a round or two at the club with big Tory Watkins before you approach her."

"Oh, no," Myles growled. "'Tis the lass I'll go a round with. And she won't soon forget the match."

Ollie moved to refill their glasses. When he was safely across the room, he said, "Suppose it is the lass calling herself Miss MacKenzie—and we've no guarantee that's the case, but for the sake of discussion, let's assume the *femme seule* is in fact our Maura. Could it be that you're more than angry at her?" Ollie toyed with his beard. "Perhaps you've deeper feelings for her than you'd like to admit. Perhaps you've met your match."

"Shut up, Ollie. And fetch the carriage. You'll see how strong my feelings are for the deceiving chit."

"Spare me the confrontation. 'Tis serious or you wouldn't be acting like the caged beast she's made of you."

"I will not tolerate disobedience in my own house!" Myles roared. "Not yours nor hers."

"But she's not here," Ollie said logically, waving his free hand to include the house. "She's obviously decided to return to Scotland. Why not let her go?"

Myles knew the answer, but he wasn't about to share the information. Reaching for the brimming glass, he walked to the window and stared broodingly into the fog.

The girl had gotten under his skin all right, but his feelings for her went deeper than he wanted to admit. For the first time in his life he'd opened his heart to a woman, and instead of accepting him, she'd tossed the whole thing in his face and left without a word. Rejected him. Abandoned him. The words stung like cruel blows, blows aimed at a small and defenseless boy, alone on the streets of London.

The deep seated pain he'd long ago buried in his heart was suddenly free, but the hurt had grown, multiplied during the dormant years. Myles reeled beneath the onslaught, for it was of his own making. Why had he thought her special? What was it about her that made him think in terms of forever? Why did he care that she wasn't the woman for him? The answer was simple; the girl loved him. Why else would she have yielded her innocence and become his mistress? No doubt some little thing he'd said had upset her, or perhaps a catastrophe had called her home. But damn her for not telling him. They'd come too far for silly misunderstandings.

"There's other news," Ollie said quietly.

Myles sighed, at once tired and elated. He had no idea what he'd say to Maura, or what he'd do when he had her back, but one thing was certain; no woman had yet walked away from his bed, and Maura Forbes damned well wouldn't be the first.

"I saw Robert Harper on my way home," Ollie continued. "'Twould seem he was the victor in his bout with *mal de mer*."

"I'm delighted," Myles drawled sarcastically. "A lengthy illness would no doubt spoil his delicate complexion."

Ollie chuckled. "He's also on his way here."

Myles groaned. "'Tis just what I need after two sleepless nights." He paused. When he began speaking again, his voice took on a decidedly feminine tone, "No doubt sweet Robert and his companion will expect to stay for dinner."

Ollie laughed. "Perhaps we'll be lucky and Robert and Geoffrey will have another engagement." Then seriously, he added, "Mackie'll do her part in the kitchen as always, but she still refuses to step foot in the same room with Harper. In truth, we've little to offer them, without the lassie to—"

"Has she boarded?" Myles interrupted.

"No. And I inquired at every inn nearby but she's not listed. I've posted an extra guard near the ship. When she does board, we'll know."

"Who's her skipper?"

Ollie smiled confidently. "A fellow named Clarence Hocker."

Myles seated himself in the chair again. "Have Will'am take a case of brandy to this Hocker, along with a request that he keep his ship in port until he hears from me. Let her think she's made good her escape."

"Very well. Shall I call a halt to the search?"

"Aye, and give them extra pay. They've more than earned a bonus."

Ollie looked affronted. "But *I* found the ship."

"That's why you're the steward."

"One of the minor pitfalls in my rewarding life, no doubt," Ollie lamented.

"Just so," said Myles, unmoved. Ollie did very well for himself. His silence confirmed the opinion.

"'Tis all settled then." Myles held up his glass. "To an evening with Robert Harper, tart that he is," he toasted. "And to breakfast with the mysterious *femme seule* who thinks she's bound for Aberdeen."

~ *Chapter 12* ~

As he waited for Robert Harper to arrive, Myles sat in his study trying diligently to concentrate on the evening ahead. Of all the meetings he'd had with Robert, tonight's would be the least offensive, the most rewarding. Myles wondered how Robert would defend himself when faced with hard evidence of his crime against Lady Suisan and the people of Roward.

Thinking of that confrontation, Myles reached for the wooden rod stamped with the arrows of Lochiel. He chuckled, imagining Sibeal Harper's reaction to her daughter's daring. Somehow Myles didn't think of Suisan as being clever or proud like her mother. After years of disappointing letters and obvious lack of interest in him, he'd buried his hurt and regretfully ceased to think of Suisan in personal terms. But Maura's arrival had changed all that. During the course of one afternoon the lassie could tell him more about Lady Suisan Harper than all her insipid letters combined.

Like a compass adhering to a northward path, his mind stubbornly strayed to Maura. He squeezed the rod until his knuckles turned white and his fingers were numb. The painful effort went for naught; against his will, a vision of the lass, warm and yielding, rose in his mind.

The rod snapped in his hand; the vision remained in his mind. Still cursing, he fought back the urge to hurl the pieces of wood against the wall. Instead, with a sigh of disgust, he crossed the room and yanked open a desk drawer. And laughed aloud.

Nestled in the drawer were dozens of leather bags of money, the proceeds from the sale of the crippled *Highland Star*, the funds to purchase Suisan's cloth. But that was not how it would be spent this year.

Grinning vindictively, Myles placed the broken rod into the drawer and picked up one of the bags.

"Might as well pay Mackie her wages," Ollie said as he entered the room, "while you've the money out and all."

Still preoccupied, Myles said, "You do it. You always have."

Ollie limped toward the desk. "That brings something else to mind. I don't suppose you thought to give Maura her wages, did you? Some time back, Mackie gave the lass a few coins from the housekeeping fund, but not enough to pay her in full. You know how Scots are about money, and her work load doubled."

Knowing Ollie was referring to where Maura had been sleeping, Myles drilled him with a cold stare. "The lassie's my concern."

Ollie did not flinch. "And before this—" he tapped his

injured leg with his cane, "paying wages was my job. I was referring to the lassie's duties during Mackie's absence, not your arrangement with her."

Embarrassed, Myles said, "I assumed you saw to her wages. 'Tis still the steward's job, if I'm not behind the times."

Ollie cleared his throat. "You've never lived by convention, but you've always kept your women at the house on Partridge Street."

"She's different from the others."

"Aye, 'tis what she said."

"When?" Myles bolted to his feet. "When did you see her?"

"Often enough," Ollie said casually. "A proud one, she is. Perhaps money was the problem between you two. You might have hurt her pride by not paying her."

The possibility glared like a beacon on a stormy night, but in his heart Myles knew that wasn't true. Something else had driven the lass away, something he was both afraid yet bound to face. At least now he had a valid excuse to see her. Satisfied that he had a logical reason to comb London for the maid-servant, he put the bag into the drawer and sat down.

"Do you have a tally on the cloth Robert brought from Suisan?"

"Aye, the clerk at the warehouse delivered the figures yesterday," Ollie answered. "But I can't reckon them without the accounting from Madame LeBlanc." Chuckling, he added, "I'm guessin' Robert won't be too pleased, since he'll be owin' *you* money."

Myles retrieved the dressmaker's accounting from the desk. "I think you can safely wager your clappers on that. Still, it's a paltry sum considering the risk."

"I wonder why he did it?"

Ollie fingered his moustache. "He's been after that post in the Exchange Ministry for years. Maybe he's given up getting it."

"No. Ainsbury says Robert's making headway. You can be sure his days as a cloth merchant are over, once he has the job."

Mackie bustled into the room, a tray of cakes and pastries in her hands. Ollie grinned. Mackie flushed. Myles watched, wondering when the two would bring their affair into the open. He still remembered when Ollie had finally gotten Mackie into his bed. The persistent steward had strutted about the house for days afterward. Now that cockiness had mellowed into something warm and sweet . . . and enviable.

Myles pushed the sentimental thought aside. "What have you there, Mackie?"

She put the tray on a low table, then stood, fussing with her apron. "Food for the devil's spawn."

Myles chuckled but regretted it immediately.

Eyes blazing, she said, "'Tis a sin against God is what it is, and I'll not be a party to it. I told Mr. Cookson as much. Dismiss me if you will, but I ain't lookin' upon him or that prissy sweetmeat he always brings along."

Unwisely, Ollie put in, "Robert and Geoffrey won't turn you to salt, Mackie, dear."

Myles thought Ollie's bed would be cold tonight, but when Mackie marched from the room without a reply, he reconsidered. Ollie's bed might be cold for some nights to come.

"Another drink?" Myles offered.

Ollie nodded and grumbled a naughty proverb about God-fearing women on Earth and women-fearing gods in heaven. Myles didn't laugh; he had women problems of his own.

"Uh . . . Myles," Ollie drawled, "about that extra pay you allotted the men for what they've done the last few days. Under the circumstances, I do think I should buy Mackie a trinket. Nothing too grand, though."

Myles hooted, slapping his thigh. "You'd best be thinking on a bigger scale, Ollie. She won't come 'round easy, not after what you said. Buy her what you will; you deserve the bonus and she's worth it."

The steward looked like a love-struck youth, eyes twinkling and his mouth twisted in a wry grin. "Aye, she is," he said softly.

Ollie was putting the ledger away when Will'am announced their guests. Myles rose and as he passed Ollie, he said, "Keep your seat, Cookie. I'll do the honors."

Myles smelled the sticky sweet odor of pomatum—and Robert Harper.

Turning to face his guests, Myles fought back the urge to laugh. Behind him, Ollie wasn't so successful and the choked sounds of muffled laughter were almost Myles's undoing. Robert Harper had truly outdone himself.

Dressed in a frock coat of re-embroidered yellow satin and knee pants of orange brocade, Robert minced into the study. The outfit was trimmed with what Myles conservatively estimated to be a furlong of Brussels lace. But Robert wasn't the entire show, for on his jewel-studded heels sashayed the pinched-faced little popper, Geoffrey. Wearing a considerably smaller and pale blue version of Robert's own costume, Geoffrey was lecturing poor Will'am on the proper way to fold their cloaks.

The incongruous sight of Will'am, a boy lusting after his first willing wench, trying to comprehend Geoffrey, a grown man emulating a woman and tittering nervously about wrinkled satin, was enough to make Myles want to roar with laughter. Beneath the humor lay condemnation, but not just for Robert and Geoffrey. Silently Myles castigated the society which allowed Robert to flaunt his personal preferences while publicly seeking a government post. Privately Myles hoped Robert would again be refused the position.

Clearing his throat and scratching his nose with one hand to hide his mirth, Myles extended the other to Suisan's uncle.

"You're looking your usual self, Robert."

With a pained expression, Robert let out a tremulous sigh as he placed a velvet-gloved hand in Myles's.

"So kind of you to say," Robert began much too earnestly. "When I've all but been on my deathbed." Over his shoulder and around his monstrous powdered wig, Robert said, "Do come along, Geoffrey."

Myles indicated two chairs and found his own while Robert and Geoffrey greeted Cookson. Watching Robert, Myles remembered his benefactor, Edward Harper. Although brothers and truly alike physically, Robert had with his outlandish lifestyle effectively disguised any resemblance to the late Edward. Even those unmistakable Harper-blue eyes seemed pale on Robert.

Blue eyes. Myles thought of another pair of blue eyes, but they were alternately bright with laughter and deliriously dark with passion. Damn that chit! He couldn't get her out of his mind, even when faced with the upcoming confrontation.

When his guests were seated, Myles said, "Brandy?"

"By all means," Robert answered, taking an inordinate amount of time to remove his gloves. "The Madeira for Geoffrey. Can't hold his spirits, you know." Robert glanced affectionately at his companion.

"I can't," Geoffrey moued.

When Ollie started to rise, Myles said, "Keep your seat, I'll see to it."

Robert looked momentarily shocked at the breach of etiquette but then he noticed Ollie's cast. "Whatever have you done to your leg, Cookson?" he asked, flapping his wrist and setting the waterfall of lace to fluttering.

"Broke it, unloading the *Dream*," Ollie answered, his voice unnaturally deep and gruff.

"I've been near death myself," Robert said sympathetically, "and I'll tell you, it was enough to make me think twice about sailing on to France."

"It was," Geoffrey chirped, crossing silk-stockinged legs.

"I trust you're better now." Myles handed Robert his drink.

"Oh, I'm on the mend, Myles, since the physician bled me."

Geoffrey twitched his painted nose in distaste. "He did."

Fighting another bout of laughter at Geoffrey's whining voice, Myles turned to Cookson. "Where's the Madeira?"

"The basement," Ollie drawled, in sarcastic, if overdone, imitation of Geoffrey.

Myles leaned close to his steward and said, "Don't push your luck, Ollie. And keep your remarks to yourself."

"I will," came Cookson's lilting whisper.

Sending his steward a warning look, Myles turned to Geoffrey, who seemed fascinated by the cut of Myles's breeches. Hiding his distaste at both the man and his manners, Myles said, "I'll have to fetch the Madeira from the basement."

"Oh, no!" Geoffrey gasped.

"The basement?" Robert said. "Too much bother, my

dear boy.'' He waved a glove, sending a sickening gush of apple fragrance throughout the room. ''Geoffrey will have a spot of watered brandy. What man of quality would willingly frequent his basement? Leave the lower floors to the servants, I always say.''

''You do.'' Geoffrey took the watered-down snifter in his manicured hands.

''Have you seen the cloth?'' Robert asked.

Myles was immediately attentive, and grateful; Robert had broached the subject himself. ''The cloth from Strath or the cloth from Roward?''

''Either or both,'' Robert said with a dismissive wave of the hand. ''But the shipment from Roward is short this year. Suisan's too easy on her people.'' He sighed dramatically. ''I understand that look on your face, Myles, but don't blame me. Suisan's as stubborn as her mother—Cameron blood, you know.''

''She is,'' Geoffrey chirped, nodding his bewigged head.

Robert smiled indulgently at his paramour. ''She has no desire to regain the reputation the Camerons earned at Roward. She wouldn't use the new looms you bought; put them away in a tower room. Said she wouldn't have the contraptions in her weaving shed.''

''Really?'' Myles drawled.

''Yes,'' Robert said. ''What she needs is a husband, someone to tame that stubborn streak. But,'' he sighed, ''not much chance of that, as homely as she is. I even tried to buy her a beau but no one would have her.''

''He did.'' Geoffrey toyed smugly with his sapphire ring.

''Perhaps I should bring her to London for the high season,'' Myles offered. '''Tis the logical solution.''

Geoffrey fidgeted. Robert absently patted the fop's satin-clad knee. ''Not just yet. She's only nineteen.'' His tone was kind, yet apologetic. ''What decent man of breeding would accept Roward the way it is? Sorely outdated, wouldn't you say?''

Myles pictured the ancient Highland stronghold. Outdated was a gross understatement. ''Yes, and I wonder why, Robert?''

"I'll tell you why," Robert grumbled. "She ain't spent a farthing of her allowance on repairs. Were it not for me the place would look as tumbledown as it did the day after Cumberland came through. Thank God Sibeal had left by then to marry my dear brother, Edward, God rest his soul."

Myles was certain he detected a trace of sarcasm in Robert's tone, and felt a surge of anger. "Rest his soul, indeed," Myles said with conviction.

Ollie held up his glass. "To Edward Harper."

Robert cleared his throat. "My brother should have made better provisions for the girl. Had he left the business to me, I certainly wouldn't have agreed to Sibeal's deathbed wish, and bought that castle and moved Suisan there. Not that I mind the annual journey to see my niece and bring the cloth to market. Even though the separation is hard on Geoffrey."

"Then why don't you take him along?" Ollie blurted out.

"Geoffrey can't ride," Robert explained, glancing tenderly at his companion.

Geoffrey preened and shyly said, "I can't."

Myles wondered what the Highlanders thought of Robert Harper. And stranger still, how did Robert manage to ride all that distance dressed in pastel satin?

"If only she'd gotten Sibeal's good looks," Robert went on, "we wouldn't be in such a pinch over finding her a husband. I even bribed her neighbor, Lachlan MacKenzie, to court her. But my plan failed; MacKenzie'd never saddle himself with such a plain bride."

Myles couldn't dispute the point. Thinking of the little oval bearing Suisan's likeness, he swore to find his homely sister a suitable husband, just as soon as this business with the cloth was out of the way and the trouble with Maura was settled. He'd have to tell Suisan of Robert's deception and prevent it from happening again. How would she take the news? Myles cursed the fact that he'd been too young at Sibeal's death to have been appointed Suisan's guardian. Had she been in his charge none of this would ever have happened.

Opening the desk drawer, he pulled out the pieces of the rod and set them on the desk.

Robert glanced at them, then at Myles. "What have you there?"

"Oh, naught," Myles began, revenge pounding in his veins, "but the rolling rod from Suisan's cloth."

"Oh?" Idly Robert picked one up and examined it.

"See anything unusual?" Myles asked.

Robert's eyes narrowed. "Only that she insists on using valuable hardwood, when she needn't use a rod at all."

What a cheap bastard he is, thought Myles. Deep inside he felt pride for Suisan's presentation of her cloth. "Look closely, Robert. What do you see at the end of the rod."

When he spied the Cameron arrows, his expression grew serious. "That damned chit! I told her to cease this nonsense. She promised me years ago she had."

Myles was confused. "Why do you call the Cameron clan badge nonsense?"

"More than nonsense," Robert said angrily, "'tis a reason to hang. The Crown won't tolerate any references to those Cameron ancestors of hers. It's been all I could do to hide my ties with that family. If the truth were known, the ministers at the Exchange would pass me up like a poxed whore in Whitechapel. I want that post, and I intend to have it this time."

His calloused attitude disgusted Myles. He was also attentive to the reasons. Any association with those exiled Scottish clans was dangerous, but Myles had not seen the slender wooden rod for the treasonous symbol it was; he had been too concerned about Robert's cheating. Still, their arguing over what the Crown would do was getting away from the point.

"Robert," Myles began seriously, "This rod came from Madame LeBlanc. You sold Suisan's cloth under the name of Strath."

"Oh, no," Geoffrey gasped.

Alarm flickered in Robert's eyes but was quickly gone. "I had to or risk her being hanged for her stubborn ways." He picked up one of the broken rods. "The King does not like having Scotland's defiance waved in his face! And that's what I'd be doing—flaunting the Camerons of Lochiel. Think of it, Myles, and you'll see I had no choice.''

"But Suisan's cloth was on this rod!'' Myles yelled. "You cheated her out of the price difference between the cloth I send to the Colonies and the cloth I assumed came from Strath.''

"I will not admit to an act of treason,'' Robert growled, all traces of effeminate behavior gone. "She received all of the money—except what I had to pay MacKenzie to court her. I simply thought it was better to lead the Dragoons to Strath rather than to my niece.

"Mark my words, Myles, if the authorities get wind of this, they'll go after her quicker than the Irish after spirits. The English hate the Lochiel Camerons.''

Myles realized he had been willing to believe the worst of Robert. What if he were wrong? "But those arrows on the clan badge would lead them to Roward Castle.''

"No, they wouldn't,'' Robert insisted. "Cameron clans, including those devil Lochiels, scattered after Culloden. They married into other families, like Sibeal did. Had the Crown questioned the symbol, I planned to blame it on the Brodie clan. 'Tis much like theirs.''

Myles seethed; did Robert think him an idiot? "The Brodies live nowhere near Strathclyde.''

Robert's eyes narrowed, but his voice was smooth when he said, "Forgive me for questioning your knowledge of the clans of Scotland. Since you're so well informed, I'm certain you've forgotten that a Brodie lass married into the Galbraiths of Strath.''

Myles recognized the roundabout explanation for the diversionary tactic it was. "You're exaggerating. Argyle flaunts his clan badge and the Kennedys aren't shy about stamping their whiskey kegs with a swan.''

"Exaggerating? You believe this.'' Robert shook the rod. "It was Suisan's mischiefmaking. If you think you can control Sibeal's daughter any better than I have, you're welcome to petition the courts to take her off my hands. I didn't ask to be her guardian.''

Myles felt a familiar stab of regret. "I wanted to be Suisan's guardian."

"I know, I know," Robert said, all sympathy. "But you were too young when Edward died, and Sibeal didn't bother with a will."

Before Myles could comment, he added, "I'll send you an accounting of the money Suisan's been paid over the years."

Without Suisan's testimony, Myles couldn't argue the point, but he was still angry. The discussion was not going as he'd planned. "Why didn't you replace the rods instead of the cloth? You've led people to believe her weaving is inferior."

Looking decidedly uneasy, Robert fished out his pocket watch. "I forgot. Can't a man have a lapse in memory? In truth there's little difference in the cloth. A bit of salesmanship was all it took to convince Madame that she was buying something superior."

Myles didn't for a minute believe Robert. But what good would it do to continue the argument? Robert would never admit to the crime. And Myles was no expert on weaving; he could hardly tell one bolt from another. "I'll see that she ceases using the Cameron clan badge as her symbol. It's time I took a greater interest in my sister's future."

Robert's smile came too quickly. "By all means. And be angry if you choose, but I did what I thought was right."

Geoffrey bristled. "He did."

Cookson leaned forward, a piece of parchment in his hand. "I've tallied the figures."

Robert shot Ollie a look reminiscent of Edward Harper ready to scold a careless seaman. Myles felt a remnant of suspicion. Something was amiss; Robert was far too agreeable.

He took the paper, glanced at the figures, then shrugged. "This is hardly enough to cover the repairs I've commissioned for the castle. I'll call the fellow back, then, since you'll probably want your own man to oversee the work."

"You sent someone to repair the castle?" Myles asked, feeling both disbelief and guilt. "Who is he?"

"Weeks is his name," Robert said lightly. "Bartholomew Weeks, a stone mason." He pulled a letter from his pocket and placed it on Myles's desk. Smiling, he said, "Suisan sent you this."

In the turmoil his life had become, Myles had completely forgotten to write to Suisan. Since her letters were always boringly general, his replies had always been the same. Yet he'd never felt so tender toward another human being until . . . he pushed a sudden thought of Maura aside and took the letter. But seeing the handwriting, which was so reminiscent of Maura's, a vision of her rose in his mind. He held his breath and blinked the image away.

"You'll be replying to her directly from now on, I assume."

Myles nodded, too tired and too preoccupied to speak. And if that sniveling Geoffrey made one more sound, Myles promised to slam a fist into his puckered and painted mouth. That would bring the evening to a quick close.

Robert scanned the room. "Where did that boy Will'am get off to with our cloaks?"

"To his chores, I suspect," Myles said, distracted by Robert's amiable attitude. He was taking the accusations rather well.

"How odd," Robert drawled, "I just noticed the lack of females tonight." Turning to his companion, Robert made an exaggerated smirk. "Fathom that, will you, Geoffrey? No women in Myles Cunningham's household."

"None a'tall," Geoffrey warbled.

"And with your wealth," Robert chided. "'Tis a shame."

"Our maid left unexpectedly," Myles said, "I'm afraid I'm not able to accommodate guests at this time. You do understand, of course."

Robert seemed to be searching for words, which was odd, when he did speak, his voice was surprisingly pleasant. "Completely," he drawled. "And I'm rather enjoying the quaintness of the inn. Something different, you know, a bold adventure of sorts. Even though the food is deplorable." He glanced knowingly at Ollie, who had reclined in his chair. "Not up to Mackie's standards by any means."

"Sounds novel," Myles quickly put in, afraid Ollie would challenge Robert.

"Novel, indeed," Geoffrey said.

Robert checked his timepiece again. Hurriedly, he said, "Geoffrey and I will just be off then." He glanced at his companion. "He's been dying to visit the clubs, while I've been dying in bed."

"You tease," Geoffrey chided, giggling.

Myles showed them out. When he returned to the study, Ollie was topping off their glasses.

"Well, Ollie, that wasn't so bad," Myles said, accepting the drink. "You have to give him credit, though. He was caught dead to rights, and managed to come out of it with his dignity intact."

The steward pretended to spit on the rug. "He's a lace-edged bore, and God bless the sea for running him down a bit." He held up his glass in salute. "You put him in his place."

Myles touched his glass to Ollie's. "No kind words for Geoffrey?"

Ollie choked. "'Tis enough to shrivel a man's better parts, the sight of those two pansies is."

"They were rather subdued, though," Myles said thoughtfully. "I thought 'twas me."

Ollie shook his head. "Nay. Robert was off his tricks tonight, but I suspect he'll regroup and give us a good taste of his gibberish before he leaves for the Continent."

Using his thumb and forefinger, Myles marked a distance. "A small dose, I pray."

"I'm agreeable to that," Ollie declared. "Then he can take that pinched-nose little Geoffrey and his parrot replies off to France. The froggies deserve them."

"Hear, hear," Myles agreed, but his mind was full of questions. Much about the meeting with Robert seemed unfinished. He had seemed eager to relinquish responsibility for Suisan, and willing to pay back the money he'd taken from her. Perhaps she was, indeed, more trouble than she was worth to Robert. But all the same, hadn't Robert been a little too agreeable?

* * *

Myles yawned and kicked the blanket to the foot of the bed. He had been so tired earlier in the day. Why, then, couldn't he sleep? Too many things were happening in his life, too many things he couldn't control. He was exhausted, he was distracted, he was lonely.

A vision of Maura came to his mind, and he felt a spark of the remembered contentment she'd introduced into his life, and then heartlessly yanked away.

"Damn!" He flipped onto his back and stared at the ceiling.

A faint bumping noise came from the hall. Assuming the sound was from Ollie's cane, Myles closed his eyes. He was plagued once more by a vision of blue eyes, eyes so dark and lustrous a man could spend his life looking at them and never grow weary of the sight.

The thumping came again, louder and obviously from downstairs. Someone was at the door. Grunting, he slipped on his pants, lighted the lamp and walked into the hall. Ollie's door opened.

The steward looked befuddled. "Who could that be so late at night?"

"Probably Robert," Myles said impatiently, "come back to fetch a wayward glove."

Ollie shook his head in disgust. "I'll get my cane."

"Don't bother. I'm becoming a competent steward of late."

Ollie's laughter followed Myles down the stairs. The knocking grew louder, making him wonder how a fop like Robert Harper managed to pound so forcefully on the door. Or for that matter, sit a horse for the long journey to Perwickshire. An amusing picture came to mind, of Robert bedecked in lavender brocade while sitting astride one of those massive horses from the dales of the Clyde.

The pounding slowed. "Did you hurt your hand, ducks?" Myles murmured into the dark foyer. Prepared for an outrageous excuse from Robert and a tittering agreement from Geoffrey, Myles threw open the door.

And stared in shock.

A uniformed officer, his chin tilted high and his hand raised to resume the knocking, stepped back and barked a command. Before Myles could do more than frown in bewilderment, a troop of the King's Light Dragoons, dressed in a blaze of brass and braid, pushed their way into his home.

A gloved hand ripped the lamp from his hand. Two burly Dragoons shoved him roughly toward the stairs.

Outrage boiled up inside Myles. "What the devil?" he yelled.

Cocking his elbows, he shouldered his way through the guards until he reached the officer in charge. Gripping the officer's epaulets, Myles lifted the man off the floor and slammed him against the wall.

"Who are you? And what the devil is the meaning of this?" Myles struggled to keep his temper in check.

Eyes wide, his helmet askew, the officer sputtered, "Colonel Christopher Fletcher, and 'tis the King's business we're about."

Behind Myles, boots shuffled and sabers rattled, but his eyes were trained on the officer, who darted anxious glances at his men.

Myles shook the officer. The plumed helmet clanged to the floor. "What business does the King have that would cause you to invade my privacy so?"

Just as the man opened his mouth to answer, Myles felt the points of at least two swords at his back.

"Stand aside!"

Casting a quick glance over his shoulder, Myles saw Ollie approaching, his cane in one hand, a primed pistol in the other. The soldiers looked hesitantly at their commander, who nodded. The men made way for Ollie.

Myles released the officer, who slid to the floor. Scrambling, he regained his footing.

"State your business," Myles demanded.

Drawing himself up, the officer tried calmly to put his uniform to rights. He cleared his throat. "Are you Myles Cunningham?"

"Aye, and if you value your commission you'll apologize and be on your way."

The Colonel picked up his helmet, clicked his heels and announced, ''Then I arrest you in the name of His Majesty, King George.''

''On what charge?'' Myles scoffed.

''High treason!''

Myles fought back an annoyed laugh; he had always been too busy to involve himself in politics. Members of his club had often criticized his lack of participation in government matters. ''And what,'' he began in a carefully modulated voice, ''have I done to offend the Crown?''

Three more sabers touched his chest.

''You're harboring traitorous goods.''

''Impossible,'' bellowed Ollie. ''Who put you up to this prank?''

''Prank?'' sputtered the commander. ''I assure you 'tis no prank. We've proof of the charge. Proof that Myles Cunningham possesses the patterns for the traitorous and outlawed tartans of Scotland. We've a Royal warrant to search the premises and arrest you, sir.''

He whipped out his hand. A subaltern produced a rolled parchment and placed it in the officer's gauntleted palm. The officer unfurled the paper. In a halting, military cadence, he said, ''By order of His Royal Highness . . .''

Myles listened with half an ear. His mind was awash with possibilities, with questions, with confusion. Why would anyone accuse him of harboring the *Maide dalbh*, Sibeal Harper's treasures, the unmistakable hallmarks of the Highland clans?

Suddenly, he recalled Robert as he'd been on the day Edward Harper's will had been read. When Myles was named heir of Edward's estate, Robert flew into a rage. His familiar face, so like Edward's, had taken on a vicious sneer and his long forgotten words now echoed in Myles's ears: *The Harpers and the Camerons will rue this day. And Edward will squirm in his watery grave before I'm done.*

But how had Robert managed to resurrect the Highland patterns? He'd said he'd burned them. Were they indeed in Myles's house? The possibility was glaringly real. Someone must have aided Robert. A name flashed into Myles's mind with the force of a blow.

Maura Forbes.

His earlier anger at the girl was but a trifle compared to the feelings now brewing within him.

As the Colonel continued to recite the government's displeasure, Myles looked passively at the scene before him. He smiled wolfishly, envisioning the confrontations to come. He had too many close friends in high places, who, in turn, had closer friends in higher places. The charges would never hold; his connections with British nobility were solid and persuasive. His friends would see him exonerated.

The knowledge was a balm to Myles. When the reading of the warrant was done, the officer rolled up the parchment and held it out to Myles.

Glancing disdainfully at the array of blades still pressed to his chest, Myles made no move to accept the paper.

"Have your man turn over the gun," the officer said, "if you value your life and his."

Myles smiled grimly. He'd be out of this fix by teatime tomorrow and then, by God, heads would roll. And this vaunty Colonel might be the first to take a tumble.

Confidently Myles nodded to Ollie, who relinquished the weapon. The guards stepped away from Myles.

"We have it on the best authority that said Highland patterns are in your possession."

Raising an eyebrow, Myles sent the Colonel a challenging look. When the soldier did not flinch, Myles made an exaggerated affair of looking down the length of his near naked body. "And how many of the cumbersome relics am I thought to be possessing?"

"One's enough to hang for," the Colonel retorted. "But we've reason to believe considerably more are hidden in this house."

Myles laughed louder. "If every pattern for every Highland tartan were in this house, we'd scarcely have room for the furniture."

"What gibberish is this?" Ollie demanded angrily. "You'll find no patterns here."

"We shall see about that." The Colonel said, then turned to his men. "Bell! Wiggs!" he called. "Begin the search."

His heels clicking, the officer then pivoted smartly to his left. "Dawson! Smith! Take the prisoner away."

Myles was immediately flanked by the two soldiers. Turning to Ollie, he said, "Get Ainsbury out of bed if you must." Meaningfully, he added, "And keep my morning appointment with the *femme seule*. She'll be particularly interested in my fate, and I'm anxious to know her . . . thoughts on the matter."

"Aye, aye," Ollie said, complete understanding written on his face. "I'm certain she'll be most concerned about your welfare."

"I'm not so sure," Myles muttered.

~ *Chapter 13* ~

Myles squinted against the bright afternoon sunlight streaming through the barred and deeply recessed window. He leaned his head against the cold stone wall and closed his eyes, shutting out the reality of where he was and why. As he had done so many times during a week of long nights and endless days, he concentrated on freedom.

What if his connections were not as good as he thought?

Keys rattled in the distance; a female voice pleaded in soft, pitiful tones. Desperate sounds, prison sounds, sounds to terrify a lesser man.

Rolling his forehead over the hard surface, he stifled an agonized groan and tried to block out the murky world around him. But he couldn't battle the insidious images that snaked through his tortured mind. Terrifying times waited there—waited to be resurrected. Fearsome childhood experiences, overcome only by the grace of God and the innocence of youth, roared like demons in the dark night of a small boy.

How had that child ever survived alone on the streets of London?

Exhaustion made way for the memories to surge forth. Garbage-strewn mews had been his home during the early years. Shadows moving here, shadows moving there, and each one determined to capture a small boy before he could become a man. Cowering in the dark alleys, he had waited, for maturity meant safety and when he grew tall enough the devils would surely pass him by.

His stomach growled with remembered hunger. His imagination skittered from one danger to the next. Like a phantom beacon, safety eluded him. His throat ached with unspoken pleas for mercy, yet begging he could not abide. Never again.

He blew out his breath and turned his back to the stone wall. The boy had survived danger and deprivation. The man would face this new horror. How many others had suffered in this cold fortress called the Tower of London? He glanced around the cell. Evidence of past unfortunates was carved into the walls of Beauchamp Tower.

A part of the outer wall surrounding the infamous White Tower, Beauchamp had imprisoned citizens of rank for hundreds of years. The notorious Dudley brothers had been incarcerated here, and each had left his mark on the brick walls. Roses for Melrose, Earl of Warwick; oak leaves for Robert, Earl of Leicester; gillyflowers for Guildford, and honeysuckle for Henry.

The family mural was a sad epitaph; flowers and plants carved on the rugged stone wall seemed incongruous to Myles. Beauchamp Tower was a terrifyingly chill and lonely place, one completely unsuited as a canvas for living things.

Yet he found comfort in one of the carvings. When thoughts of his own dubious position became overwhelming, he sought the simple message authored by the ill-fated Guildford Dudley, beheaded two centuries before. Near the west window, four letters were carved into the wall, four letters spelling the name of Guildford's beloved wife, Jane, girl-Queen of England for nine days. If their tragic deaths were a true indication of English justice, Myles faced a long stay in the Tower and a longer walk to Executioner's Square.

Treason was treason in Britain; the crime was manifest, the penalty a foregone conclusion. Dudley and Jane had been guilty of worshiping their God in a fashion Bloody Mary could not abide. King George seemed an apron-tugging amateur when compared to her. But George would exact payment in his own way, and Myles's destiny hung on a single thread of proof.

Fighting the urge to howl with rage, he pounded his fists on the walls. How thorough had Robert and Maura been in their scheme? Myles tried to picture her carrying out her part of the scheme, tried to see her scurrying in the dark to hide the pattern sticks his house. But the image would not form. Still, she must have aided Robert.

Would the Light Dragoons, in fact, uncover Sibeal Harper's precious tartan patterns? If the *Maide dalbh* were found, Myles's fate could well be sealed. The oddity of it all was ironic to him, and he was struck by what a terrible roundabout course his life had taken. Edward had taken him in, Sibeal had treated him as her son, and now her treasures would send him to the grave.

"Those patterns'll be trouble, mark my words," Edward Harper had said years before. "Betimes I think she'd choose them over me. And by the saints, I haven't the courage to find out." The sad confession now seemed a warning, albeit a late one.

Where were the patterns now?

Myles splayed his fingers to still his trembling hands. Aye, the patterns were trouble, trouble brewed by a greedy sodomite and a devious black-haired wench. Myles ached to have her standing before him, so he could shake the truth from her. Truth, answers and reasons. Why, dear Christ, had she used him so?

The hurt went deeper each time he thought of Maura, but her treachery was not his only source of pain. His heart pined for the feel of hers beating next to his. His ears yearned to hear the sound of her voice. His eyes longed for the sight of her face, flushed with passion or sparkling with mirth. She had betrayed him beyond all betrayal, and by rights he should hate her. He tried, for to feel anything less than loathing would be to admit his own weakness. So why did he want her still? His broken heart knew the answer, but his pride had taken command.

"Pray you did your job well, beauty," he swore to the stone walls of Beauchamp Tower, "for when I'm free you'll rue the day you stepped into my life."

Thoughts of retribution momentarily blocked out reality. As Myles paced, he conjured the ways he could punish the blue-eyed temptress, and with each vengeful scenario, the compensation became more satisfying. She had foolishly played with the fire of his temper and knowingly kindled the flame until it had burst into a raging inferno. He pictured her smug and confident in her victory. He hoped she savored the moment well, for short-lived it would be; she had engaged herself in a battle she could not win.

But first he must obtain release from prison.

What if his influential friends failed? What if Ainsbury and his peers couldn't argue Myles's innocence? He might never have the chance to tell Suisan about Robert's deceit. She might be at the mercy of that bastard again. But would Suisan ever believe ill of her dear Uncle Rabby?

Myles ground his teeth and kicked at the wall. He felt helpless, a state he'd not encountered since his youth.

Footsteps and the rattling of keys drew him from his reverie. Muffled voices penetrated the thick wooden door; he leapt up to see who his guest could be. The answer came in the most pleasant and familiar of forms when the door swung open and Ollie Cookson stepped inside. His wide smile indicated that he bore good tidings.

Myles hurried to the door as Ollie turned to the jailer. The steward shifted the bundles he carried and withdrew a sack of gold from his waistcoat. The jailer licked his lips, grinned, then jerked the bag from Ollie's hand.

"An hour," the man said as if he were bestowing some great favor, "and not a tick o' the clock more."

Unaffected, Ollie said, "You promised a bath, and for the price you demanded, the water had better be hot and clean."

The jailer hissed through the gap between his front teeth. Jerking his head toward Myles, he said, "He ain't no Lord.

Time was he'd been took to Newgate where his kind belongs. Why he ain't even got no title, just a mister afore his name.''

"That may be true," Ollie said sharply, "but *Mister* Cunningham's gold is a color to your likin', is it not?"

Shrugging and pocketing the pouch, the man walked out. "At least the gentry knows their place," he grumbled, pulling the heavy door closed.

Ollie turned to Myles and handed him one of the bundles. "Mackie made you a cherry cake."

Clutching the sweet smelling gift, Myles felt a welcome semblance of normalcy. Nothing, not even having her employer in the Tower of London intimidated Mackie.

"How are you, sir?" The steward's gaze was searching, his voice laced with quiet concern.

Myles couldn't remember the last time Ollie had addressed him so formally. The caring gesture was a balm. "Well enough. Have you good news, then?"

"Aye," Ollie lowered his voice to a whisper. "They didn't find the *Maide dalbh* in the house."

A ray of hope shone in the shadows of Myles's mind. "Hallelujah! But did you find that black-haired wench?"

"Nay, I was too late; Hocker sailed to Aberdeen last night."

Myles balled his hands into fists. "Damn it all, Ollie. You should have stopped her."

"I couldn't hold back the tide, you know." Ollie walked to the table and wiped the surface clean before depositing the bundle of clothing. "I couldn't find Robert either. Seems he's sailed to France."

Immediately contrite, Myles considered Ollie's position in the dangerous affair and the many nights he'd likely gone without sleep. The steward had been all over London. Lowering his voice, Myles said, "Are you certain she was on Hocker's ship? She could have sailed with Robert."

"Not openly. The dockman went on and on about Geoffrey and Robert, but said nothing about the girl."

"Well, then, my friend," Myles kept his tone light, "since the Dragoons are done with the house, I should be released soon anyway. I can manage to put up with this place a little longer. Then I'll find her myself."

"And postpone your retirement to Cornwall?" Ollie asked, a twitch in his lips, a glitter in his eyes.

"Cornwall?" Myles waved off the notion. "Cornwall was merely an option. I've not thought seriously of it. And after this place, the stark landscape down there won't satisfy me at all."

Ollie cleared his throat. Staring at his shoes, he quietly said, "You may not be released straight away."

Myles's confidence wavered. "What do you mean?"

"They have orders to search your warehouses and any of your ships in port. They even plan to search the wreckage of the *Star*."

"My God," Myles swore. "They sound desperate. I don't even own what's left of her."

"No," Ollie spat, "they're not desperate. They're militia, and 'tis their God-given right to do as they please."

"The searching may take days."

"Or weeks, depending on how determined the Lord Chancellor is to convict you." Ollie walked to the bed. Pulling back the covers, he examined the threadbare linen and lumpy mattress. His nose twitched in distaste and he dropped the blanket. "Ghastly accommodations, considering the people who have stayed here."

Ollie's calmness reached Myles. "I'm sorry I yelled at you. I know you're doing your best."

"Bah! I've gotten used to that temper of yours."

"You're also getting sentimental," Myles accused, but his own voice was thicker than normal. At Ollie's embarrassed look, he added, "Must be Mackie's influence. Next you'll tell me you've proposed to her."

Ollie laughed. "Not while the Pope's Catholic. She won't marry a divorced man."

"Maybe she'll change her mind."

"Don't bet your topsails on that. George'll turn loose the Colonies before she changes her stubborn mind."

"I'm sorry about that too, Ollie."

"So am I, but apologizing to each other won't get Mackie down the aisle or you out of this mess."

Sympathy welled inside Myles. Once this was over he'd have a talk with Mackie. Maybe he could make her see the light. But that would have to wait; he had problems of his own. "Ollie, I want you to go to France and find Robert. He won't get away with this."

"Wait." Ollie held up a hand. "Let's talk about that wretched fopnose after you've had a bath and something to eat. Turns my stomach to think about him."

A pair of the King's Beefeaters delivered the tub. Soon, Myles languished in hot soapy water. "How is Mackie?"

Ollie expelled his breath in a rush. "About as mad as Briggs McCord was the time you dry-docked him for seducin' that Italian virgin." Chuckling, he added, "Bless our Mackie's heart, though. She coshed one of the guards on the head with my cane when he broke a jar of her berry jam. The lad howled like she'd knocked him in the other end."

"I can see they were thorough—and brave," Myles said goodnaturedly, "if they searched her pantry."

"Wasn't the pantry they were searchin' at the time. 'Twas the cellar. Went after it like gravediggers, they did."

Myles recalled the last time he'd been in the cellar. A flood of longing settled in his loins. He'd nearly taken Maura right there on the table. He remembered her maidenly objections. He'd been thinking of bringing her to pleasure. She'd been thinking of Highland relics. Had she resisted his seduction because she knew the patterns were nearby? Of course she had.

He sighed and rubbed his aching forehead. Maura had taken his heart and crushed it to rubble; those damned Dragoons had torn his household apart. "What about the Earl of Ainsbury?"

"You'd be proud of that one. He's been makin' the rounds and curryin' favor for you everywhere he can. He's meetin' opposition at the Exchange Ministry. They're a tight-knit lot, you know. But he keeps trying anyway."

"Good. If I don't get out of here soon, things will go badly for Maura when I find her and worse for Robert."

"Somehow I can't picture her rubbin' elbows in France with Robert and Geoffrey."

"Then she'd better be in Scotland," Myles shouted, slamming his hand into the tub and splashing soapy water in his face. "Damn!" He wiped his burning eyes.

"Have a care."

Myles chuckled grimly, thinking of how careful he'd be when he found her. Then another possibility lodged in his mind. "What if Robert plans some devilment for Suisan?"

Ollie held out a towel. "I wondered about that myself. Suisan must be told that Robert cheated her on the cloth. He could be cheating her on other things too, you know. If she's innocent."

Myles dropped the towel. "Of course, she's innocent. I'm surprised, though, that she didn't know what her cloth was worth."

"You and I didn't."

Myles sighed. "Neither of us are experts, but Maura knew."

"Aye, she knew a lot things, I think," Ollie said softly.

That was an understatement, thought Myles. She knew how to make his blood run hot and keep it boiling for hours. She knew how to trail her clever fingers across his belly and send shafts of longing to his loins. She knew how to make him smile and dream his dream again.

"She took Suisan's part in that nasty cloth business at Madame LeBlanc's," said Ollie.

"True." But to Myles, the worst of her crimes had nothing to do with counterfeited cloth or outlawed tartan patterns. "Perhaps Suisan was too timid to confront Robert herself, and sent Maura here to investigate the low price she was being paid for her cloth."

Ollie shook his grizzled head. "Timid don't sound like Sibeal and Edward's daughter to me."

"No, it doesn't."

"Unless Suisan aided Robert."

Myles slipped beneath the water to rinse himself. Doubts raced across his mind. Something wasn't right. "Why would Suisan help destroy the tartan patterns?"

"As I remember, Robert's the only one who said they were destroyed."

"He lied, I'm certain of it. They do exist, and I think his

plan was to use them against you. But somehow it went awry from the start.''

Ollie handed him a towel. "What do you mean?"

"Remember how different he was the last time we saw him?"

"Aye," grumbled Ollie. "He was as cocky as man who's beddin' a saucy wench.''

Myles laughed. "Let's assume Maura came to London to learn why Robert was paying Suisan so little for the cloth. Perhaps she stumbled onto the patterns and took them back to Scotland." His wounded heart wanted to believe that. His practical mind was not so weak.

"'Tis an attractive conclusion. I can't help wishin' Sibeal's daughter would value the *Maide dalbh* as much as she did.''

Was that why she'd she left without a word? She didn't trust him enough to confide in him? Pain needled its way into his guts. Damn her! He would have helped.

"What is it, Myles? What are you thinking?"

Images flashed in his mind. Maura defending Suisan. Maura praising Suisan. Maura buying that spyglass for Suisan's neighbor. "What if she *were* loyal to Suisan instead of Robert?"

Ollie frowned, his face a mask of confusion. "I don't follow you.''

Through the maze of suspicion and possibilities his mind had become, Myles suddenly saw a clear path. Sweat beaded his brow. "Consider this," he began, leaning forward. "Robert wanted me hanged for treason, so he stole the patterns from Suisan, brought them to London, and hid them in my house. She discovered they were gone, put two and two together, and sent Maura here to get them back.''

"Why not come herself? Why send Maura?"

"Because we'd recognize her. Not a day goes by that I don't look at that portrait.''

"Of course." Ollie toyed with his moustache. His lips puckered. "You're saying then, that Suisan and Robert were working at cross purposes.''

Myles wanted desperately to believe that. Now he needed to come up with a logical reason for Maura's abrupt departure.

"Yes, I am. It's the only explanation that makes sense." He snapped his fingers. "She knew Robert was coming; she saw his letter." She had opened it, too, and the contents had disturbed her, but Ollie didn't need to know about that.

"Sounds possible, and I'd rather believe that of the lass —both lassies. Imagine Maura being so loyal to Suisan, that she'd come all the way to London and risk so much. I wonder what else she did."

She tore my heart out and hung it on a pike, thought Myles. "She discovered that Robert cheated Suisan on the cloth."

"Aye, that she did. Plucky, lass, I'd say." Cautiously he added, "If indeed, that's what happened."

"Can you imagine her lugging those patterns about? As I recall, they weighed half a stone, and Sibeal had a passel of them."

"How can we be sure?"

"Robert's the key."

Ollie grimaced. "The key has fluttered off to France."

Another key rattled in the lock. The door opened. Myles watched in naked awe as the jailer admitted at least a dozen of the colorfully clad Beefeaters, ruffs bobbing, arms laden with household furnishings. In a matter of minutes, the stark room had been transformed into comfortable quarters.

"They'll be bringin' up your bed next."

"My bed?" Gratitude washed over Myles. With all the other things Ollie had on his mind, he'd still managed to consider Myles's comfort.

"Well," Ollie confessed, "not precisely *your* bed, but a decent mattress all the same. Here's your robe."

Shaking his head, Myles said, "You've thought of everything, I see."

Ollie stuffed his hands into the pockets of his waist coat and stared at the barred window. His voice was no more than a whisper laced with raw emotion when he said, "Nay, Myles. I forgot about Sibeal Harper and her tartan patterns. I never considered that Suisan could take after her mother, not until you brought it up. I also forgot what a greedy, vindictive bastard Robert Harper is."

"So did I."

The jailer sauntered in, his ham-like hands hitching up his belt as he walked. To Ollie, he said, "I brung the razor like you asked, and don't think I ain't risking my job by letting you shave him." Examining the blade, he added suspiciously, "Could be a weapon, ye know."

Ollie snatched up the razor. "Maybe I should use it on you."

"'Ave a go at it and I'll spread yer guts to the crows." Then he barked out an order to the Beefeaters and strolled out the door.

Myles said, "You could've held the blade to my throat, Ollie, used me as a hostage, and sworn vengeance upon the Highlanders who killed your English kin at Culloden Moor. Then you could've marched me out at knife point."

Eyes narrowed, mouth set in a grim line, Ollie said, "If I could get you out I would, but the killin' at Culloden Moor was naught compared to the massacre Cumberland staged after the battle. That bastard cut a bloody path through Scotland, butcherin' women and children, too. Confiscatin' property from clans who'd been in the Highlands since London was a Roman town. Now they're scattered across Scotland." He shook his head. "I'm glad I had no relatives on either side."

"My God, you *have* been thinking about Sibeal Harper, haven't you?"

"'Twas you who brought her up," Ollie admitted. "And 'tis time, by God." His voice broke. "She was a courageous and lovin' woman, and it ain't proper to let the memory of her bravery and devotion fade."

Myles felt a familiar twinge of sadness. How he'd grieved when Sibeal died. "It looks as though Suisan is more like her mother than we thought. Maura respected her, and the people of Perwickshire worship her."

"Aye, they do worship the lass," Ollie said sagely. "We saw that with our own eyes when we visited there last fall. All they could talk of was Lady Suisan this, Lady Suisan that."

"True. I'm anxious to see her and Maura. What are you doing?"

Ollie had his nose to the wall, the open razor in his hand. "I'm carving the Cameron arrows here—by Dudley's carvin' of Jane."

"You'll be arrested for defiling government property."

"They'll have to follow me to France to catch me," Ollie said, intent on his task. "I have an assignation with Robert Harper."

His mood lightened by both the warm bath and the good company, Myles said, "Right you are, Cookie. You'll be off cavorting with fairies while I'm trekking through the wilds of Scotland." Well aware of Ollie's aversion to traveling on land, Myles made a tisking sound and added, "'Tis a shame you'll not be going with me. Perhaps this time you'd fit in. Fergus MacKames might even let you win at arm wrestling."

When Ollie didn't reply, Myles said, "Will you stop that!"

"Very well." Ollie put the blade away and turned around. Suddenly serious and defensive, he retorted, "Let's be about that shave while the jailer is being generous."

"Nay." Myles waved him off. "I haven't grown a beard in years, and the prospect appeals to me."

Ollie shrugged. "Suit yourself. If you go to Scotland, you'll blend right in with the rest of those scruffy Highlanders."

"I intend to do just that," Myles said lightly, but he felt compelled to voice his worst fears. "Ollie, if things don't go as we planned—if I'm not released. . . ."

"Don't think on it, sir."

"But if the unthinkable happens, you'll look after Suisan?"

"Like she was my own."

Relieved of the heaviest burden, Myles was anxious to put his own plans into action. He smiled wickedly, thinking what he'd do to Maura when he found her and what he'd do to Robert. "Sit down, Ollie." He took the blade and whacked off a thick slice of cake. "Here's what you're to say to Robert. . . ."

"Ollie's here," Geoffrey hissed, excitement dancing in his eyes as he peered out the window. In his canary yellow frockcoat and murrey knee breeches, he looked like an over-grown boy, wriggling with glee. "Oh, Rabby! He's dressed in mourning black."

Robert's first impulse was to join Geoffrey, but after waiting for so many years for this moment, he tamped back the urge. He hadn't expected a personal visit. Still, the idea was immensely pleasing. His masterful plan had worked. Myles was dead. An unexpected pang of sadness settled in Robert's breast. Planning Myles's demise was one thing; facing it was another. He'd known Myles for years and now he was gone. None of this would have happened if he'd been willing to share the wealth.

"What's wrong?" demanded Geoffrey, his voice a nervous whisper.

"Nothing, love." Robert shoved away the sentimental thought of Myles. "Wait for Pierre to let Cookson in, dearie. Then you can escort him from the foyer."

"All right." Geoffrey raced for the door.

"Not so eagerly, dear. And wipe that smile off your face."

"*Oui, oui,*" Geoffrey said, plucking at the lace on his sleeves as he bounded down the stairs.

Unable to stay seated, Robert eased out of the chair and began pacing. Light and airy, the room provided an excellent view of the Seine, lined with bookstalls and flower stalls and spanned by stone bridges. The somber scholars of the *Rive Gauche* contrasted sharply to the high born shoppers on the fashionable *Rive Droite*. In the distance, the spires and steeples of Paris jutted to the heavens.

Although furnished with brocaded chairs and settees, and tables of polished oak, the decor was mediocre compared to the lush style of living he would soon enjoy. He would hire the finest craftsmen and decorators. One day very soon these walls would feature paintings by the grand masters; the floors would sport carpets from Persia. Someday very soon he'd have a splendid London residence too. He'd have Myles's mansion in Mayfair.

Until the day Edward had been lost at sea, Robert had lived in his formidable shadow. Always compared, always found wanting. He hated the sea, the water. Even the steaming waters at Bath made him ill. That aversion had made him the disfavored younger brother. By rights the shipping fortune should have passed to him.

He cringed, remembering the soul-wrenching embarrassment of being rejected by Edward and pitied by Sibeal.

And there had been Myles Cunningham. The callow youth had felt none of those things; he hadn't even mourned his benefactor properly. Oh, no. The brash Myles had transferred his possessions to Edward's discarded sea chest and sailed away, leaving Robert to comfort Sibeal and Suisan. A year later, when Sibeal died, he'd been forced to console Suisan again. But no more. He'd made sure Suisan wouldn't mourn her adolpted brother's passing. Still, Robert would make the attempt. What was another journey into the Highlands? Robert had dragged himself there once a year during the last decade.

At the tramp of footsteps, he turned his thoughts to the upcoming meeting. He almost laughed out loud at his first glimpse of Cookson.

Leaning heavily on a cane, his moustache drooping, his eyes grim, the steward looked as if he'd lost his best friend. Another twinge of remorse crept into Robert's mind, but he banished the feeling. He'd been ridiculed by Edward; he'd suffered in the shadow of his brother's success, but instead of coming into his own upon Edwards's death, he'd been rejected again. That pretentious upstart Myles Cunningham had wormed his way into Edward's heart and inherited the Harper wealth.

Robert had waited too long for this moment to let a maudlin bit of conscience dilute his exuberance. Now the Harper shipping fortune would fall into the pockets of its rightful owner.

"Welcome, Cookson," Robert said amiably, extending his hand. "This is a pleasant surprise."

"Thank you, Mr. Harper." His hand was as limp as Geoffrey's, his benign attitude a distinct departure from his normal surly mood. Even that ostentatious beard seemed bedraggled, dull.

"Please do sit, and rest your leg." Robert indicated a couch amid a grouping of furniture near the windows. Geoffrey scampered forth with a gout stool. "Pour the brandy, if you will, Geoffrey. Cookson looks as though he needs a nip."

Geoffrey scurried to the liquor cabinet and grasped the decanter with both hands. The tip of his tongue peeked out from between his crimson tinted lips. He seemed in deep concentration but his gaze was fixed on Cookson. Brandy sloshed over the rim of a glass as he poured. Robert held his breath. If Geoffrey botched his part, by God, he'd be playing the lute for shillings again in Drury Lane. Robert shot him a warning glance. By the time he served the drinks, Geoffrey was the picture of youthful deference.

Easing onto the sofa, Cookson glanced forlornly out the window. "It was Myles's wish that I come."

Jubilation bubbled up inside Robert. "I trust Myles is well."

"Myles is . . . well, he's feeling no pain."

The words were sweet music to Robert's ears. "No pain? Has something happened?"

"Aye," Cookson growled, his lower lip jutting out. "He was arrested for treason."

"Oh, no!" squealed Geoffrey.

Pretending outrage, Robert said, "But I've heard nothing of it. Why wasn't I informed?"

"I came as soon as the arrangements were made."

Robert leaned close to Cookson. "Why would Myles be arrested for treason? The man's a saint. My brother raised him as a loyal Englishman. Unless. . . ." He paused to inject a note of censure in his voice. "Unless he's done something seditious in the Colonies."

"Wasn't politics. Not Colonial politics, at least." Cookson sighed heavily. "The Lord Chancellor charged him with possessing the *Maide dalbh*."

"The tartan patterns? They arrested Myles because of Sibeal's old sticks? Impossible. They don't exist anymore."

"Tell that to the Dragoons who searched his house from top to bottom."

"Dragoons? Oh!" warbled Geoffrey.

Elation tingled inside Robert. "Well, I imagine they were embarrassed when they didn't find the wretched things."

Tears pooled in Cookson's eyes. Miserably, he said, "I told the Dragoons that the patterns weren't in the house. But would they believe me?" He shook his head.

"Don't worry," Robert said, imagining all that money at his disposal. "A few well placed bribes and Myles will be free."

"Oh, it's much too late for that, I'm afraid."

"Rascals!" Robert spat. He intended to reward those jolly fellows well. "Tell me everything that happened."

The steward dashed down the brandy in one swallow. Robert snapped his fingers at Geoffrey, who refilled the glass.

"'Twas the middle of the night when the soldiers came," Cookson began, staring into the glass. "Two of the bloody scourges hauled Myles off to the Tower while the others set upon the house. Scared the wits out of poor Mackie."

Robert wanted to say she didn't have any wits, but he kept his voice even, solemn. "When did the travesty occur?"

"A fortnight past. Such a terrible thing."

"So terrible," crooned Geoffrey, sipping his own brandy.

"I'm ashamed to call myself an Englishman," said Cookson, his sad gaze fixed on Geoffrey. "You know what they do to traitors?"

"No, what?"

Cookson brought his index finger to his shirt collar and made a cutting motion across his throat.

Geoffrey gasped: "How rude!"

"There, there," Robert said, all sympathy. Turning to Cookson, he said, "I'm sure you'll need my permission to carry on."

"You mean the ships, the warehouses, et cetera."

"Precisely. I'm prepared to be generous with you."

"How sweet," said Geoffrey, his manicured hands toying with the glass.

Cookson fairly oozed misery. "I hadn't thought to profit from this misfortune."

"But it's what poor Myles would have wanted."

"Poor Myles," crooned Geoffrey.

"Did he have any message for me?" Robert held his breath; any day now he'd wrap his fist around that Harper money.

"Message? Oh, he didn't say much . . . before he. . . ." Too overcome to continue, he focused bleary eyes on his cane.

"You can certainly count on me," Robert said. "I just wish I had known." Turning up a palm, he added, "Perhaps I could have done something to help."

"You might at that." Cookson slammed down his glass in sudden anger. "I know this is all the fault of that wench."

"A girl?" piped Geoffrey.

"Wench? What wench?" Robert asked.

"Maura Forbes," Cookson spat. "She was a servant from Roward Castle."

"I've never heard of her. What does she look like?"

"Black-haired vixen with blue eyes. She worked for us for a time."

Robert frowned. Could the woman in question be Jenny Keegan? But that tramp was supposed to be at Roward keeping an eye on the half-wit. No, it couldn't be Jenny; she had green eyes. But what did the wench matter? He hadn't even planned this convenient scapegoat in the form of a serving girl. Fate had simply chosen to smile on Robert Harper, and he had no intention of questioning his good luck. "I'm afraid I don't know any Maura Forbes. You say she was in your employ?"

"In Myles's employ." Cookson's voice held a tremor. "Odd thing is, she left the same day he was arrested. She returned to Scotland without notice."

"How do you know she returned to Scotland?"

"I checked with the harbormaster. She booked passage to Aberdeen."

Curious and wildly confident, Robert decided to play along; the servant was obviously very important to Cookson. "Blue eyes, you say? Black hair? And she's a servant?"

"*Said* she was a servant," Cookson scoffed. "But she acted more the lady of the manor. She brought a glowing letter of reference from Lady Suisan. That's why Mackie hired her, you know."

"You'd never seen her before? Not even when you visited Scotland last year?"

"No," Cookson grumbled. "She wasn't among the servants." He paused, fingering a tear in the upholstery. "Unless she was away with Lady Suisan."

Summoning an extra measure of vehemence, Robert said, "Damn Scots! You can't trust 'em no matter what. Suisan's always coddling those worthless people of hers. Did the Forbes woman steal from you?"

"Aye," he growled. "But the slut will be found and brought to justice. She played a dangerous game with those sticks."

With Myles Cunningham rotting in the ground, the wench posed no threat. "What sticks?" he asked out of curiosity.

"The *Maide dalbh*," Cookson growled

Robert felt as if a knife had been plunged between his shoulder blades. How could anyone refer to those dangerous patterns as mere sticks? But what did he care? They could call them holy relics for all the difference it made now.

Be bold, he told himself. He'd covered his tracks well, and no one in the Lord Chancellor's office could trace the matter to him. "I'll help you any way that I can. Boils a man's blood to think of her planting those Highland relics in the cellar and implicating an innocent man."

"Poor Myles," crooned Geoffrey.

Cookson leaned back and seemed to settle into the sofa. He arched a snowy eyebrow. "I never said the patterns were in the cellar."

The imaginary knife twisted, then worked a ragged path down Robert's spine. "But you said. . . ." He stopped; the conversation had taken a turn he didn't like. "It's just that the cellar would be a logical place—what with all that tosh and footle down there."

"The brandy's gone."

What the devil difference did that make? Confused, Robert got back to the subject at hand. "I'm certain Myles died honorably."

A speculative gleam shone in the steward's eyes. "I also never said Myles died . . . honorably, or not."

Immediately alert to the subtle change in Cookson's manner, Robert felt a shiver of trepidation. Something was wrong, but with Myles out of the way, the biggest hill had been scaled. "I'm sure he did, though."

Cookson's gaze narrowed to an angry leer. "I'm sure you would think so, since you and Maura Forbes put those pattern sticks in his house, then alerted the Dragoons."

"Nonsense," Robert hissed, grateful for the opportunity to let off steam. "I have no idea what you're taking about."

"Oh, I think you do," Cookson declared through his teeth.

Robert pretended to lose patience. "Cookson," he began as if talking to Geoffrey during a fit of stupidity, "you're upset at this travesty. We all are. I won't hold it against you."

"Upset?" Cookson chuckled. "Not anymore."

Why was Cookson so smug? Against his will, Robert stammered, "You would accuse me on a mere coincidence? I'm speechless."

"No," Cookson spat, "you're a liar."

Robert balled his fists to keep from battering Cookson's face. The steward was obviously distressed over Myles's death and striking out anywhere he could. "It must have been an enemy, someone Myles cheated over the years, someone he doesn't remember."

"Myles doesn't cheat, but he does remember your superiors. Knows them quite well, he does."

Robert was struck by the humor of the situation. He, who had managed to anonymously set the Dragoons on Myles was now to grovel before his superiors? He'd sooner stand before the King and call him the fumble brain he was. Besides, for all his wealth Myles couldn't possibly worm his way into the Exchange Ministry. Better men had tried and failed.

"Tell me something, Cookson."

"Certainly." A sly smile transformed his face. "Ask away."

"Why did you come here?"

The steward's expression turned bland. "Why, to bring Geoffrey dear that Madeira he likes so well. I had to search the cellar from top to bottom to find it—what with all the 'tosh and footle' down there. Myles hates being such a poor host, you know.'' Turning to Geoffrey, he said, ''You needn't feel slighted, ducks; I left a whole case of it with your Pierre.''

Geoffrey's eyes grew wide as dinner plates. ''Myles is. . . ?''

Cookson grinned like a hungry cat feasting on a plump mouse. ''On his way to Roward Castle to find the slut and give her her due. But rest assured, he won't forget you and your tastes in the future.'' He got to his feet and reached for his cane. Glancing at Robert, then Geoffrey, he said, ''Either of you. Good day.''

Numbly, Robert watched him hobble down the stairs. Myles had been set free! How? Why? Had he bribed the Dragoons? The notion was foolish; even Cumberland himself couldn't manipulate the Light Dragoons. Robert had done his work through a close friend at the Exchange Ministry—a close friend who had a dark secret to hide.

Suspicion tickled Robert's mind. He tried to tell himself all of it was absurd. His plan had been foolproof, and no women had been involved. So what was this nonsense about a serving wench in Myles's household being involved? Who was she? What had Cookson said? Blue eyes. Plenty of women had blue eyes. His blood ran cold, but his mind dashed through the possibilities. Had Suisan discovered the pattern sticks missing, and in a fit of loyalty to her mother tried to get them back? ''It can't be her,'' he mused.

Geoffrey plopped down on the sofa. ''Be who?''

Her hair was red and she was no servant. He couldn't picture the regal Suisan Harper passing herself off as a servant. No, the thought was ludicrous. He laughed out loud. ''I just had the most amusing idea.''

''Tell me.''

''The wench,'' Robert said, grateful for a place to target his anger. ''He was talking about a black-haired wench. For a moment I thought it might have been Suisan.''

''That's impossible.''

''Of course it is. And her hair's black.''

''But darling,'' purred Geoffrey. ''All my friends dye their hair. And who knows more about dye stuffs than Suisan Harper?''

Cookson's description of the girl came back. He had said she was a servant, but that she acted more the lady of the manor. She brought a glowing letter of reference from Lady Suisan. And left with the Highland tartan patterns. Only Suisan Harper knew of their existence; only Suisan Harper would want them back. And because of the miniature he had sent, Myles wouldn't know Suisan from Cicero.

Robert sat back and put up his feet. The facts rattled through his mind like pebbles off a cliff. Whatever the source of Myles's good luck, Robert still held the upper hand. As long as those patterns existed, he had the means to his end. He could be patient. He would simply reach into his bag of tricks again. "Whittle your quills, Geoffrey, and stir up your ink. It's time for you to play the scribe."

Geoffrey's boyish features, unaffected by two decades of debauchery, took on a sultry look. "I'd rather play the tardy schoolboy."

Robert felt his good humor return. "Later, love. We've work to do now."

Geoffrey minced out of the room. Robert picked up his glass and downed the brandy.

A soft, warm breeze fluttered the lace curtains. The Seine lapped gently at its banks. Paris had always been his retreat from the secret life he was forced to lead. But all that would soon change. If Suisan were responsible for Myles's freedom, she'd pay a stout price. And Myles Cunningham would dangle from a noose and gag on his own tongue.

Dark humor sprang up. Robert smiled. He'd devise a special punishment for Edward's daughter. Something wicked, something she wouldn't soon forget.

Ah, yes. He'd make her life miserable.

·~ *Chapter 14* ~·

Her stomach a roiling mass of misery, Suisan braced her hands on the cold stone wall of her room at Roward Castle. When the wave of sickness grew worse, she knelt over the chamber pot and gave herself up to the familiar nausea.

"Here, wipe your face and hands," Nelly said, holding out a damp cloth.

Suisan took a deep steadying breath and held the damp comforting cloth to her face.

"You'll have to tell everyone and bloody soon. No one's seen me emptying this 'til now, but 'twill happen, you can be sure.

Suisan braved a peek at her maid. Nelly's jaw was firmly set and her blue eyes cold.

"Hiding behind that cloth won't solve nothing." Her voice dropped and her expression softened. "How are you feeling?"

Suisan groaned. "Like I ate too much of the widow MacCormick's haggis."

Nelly laughed. "At least your humor's stayed with you. Some has the morning sickness worse than you."

Ruefully, Suisan said, "You'll pardon me if I find that hard to believe."

"Oh," Nelly challenged, "and what if you was Mrs. Peavey? A day don't pass without her moaning and groaning about the misery she suffered carrying that worthless lad of hers."

Suisan smiled in spite of her churning stomach. The cook, Mrs. Peavey, was over fifty years old. Her son Jamie was older than Suisan.

"See? You're feeling better already." Nelly reached for a glass. "Here, drink this, 'twill sweeten your mouth."

"Thank you, Nelly."

"'Tis nothin', but I do wish you'd tell everyone about the babe. 'Twould make the whole business easier."

Suisan walked to the window. "I'm thinking about it."

But she wasn't. Even as she looked at the wraith-like mist rising from Comyn's Moor, her thoughts spun back. During the long journey home to Perwickshire, she had hoped and prayed she was not carrying a child. In the weeks since her return, she had kept up the vigil. But nature had ignored her prayers.

A wave of despair lapped at the edge of her mind and threatened to engulf her. She was reminded of London, of the overwhelming odds she'd faced. And conquered. The positive thought offered some comfort and she clung to the idea of the success of her mission.

The patterns were hidden away deep in the castle dungeon. Roward cloth would henceforth be sold as Roward cloth. Outwardly, her life had returned to normal. Inwardly, she grew more miserable with each passing day.

Casting a glance over her shoulder, she was relieved to see Nelly straightening the bed linens. Suisan turned back to the window.

The massive wooden gates stood open, long since denuded of the Cameron coat of arms, by royal decree. Familiar forms passed through the portal. Mrs. MacIver, prim to the letter of feminine law and followed by a waddling gosling, traveled the well-worn path from the gate to the weaving shed in the southern corner of the inner bailey. Sorcha, Nelly's daughter, her golden hair braided and coiled crown-like on her head, skipped along behind the little goose. When Sorcha got too close, the gosling turned, ducking its head and hissing. Startled, Sorcha squealed and backed away. When the gosling scurried to catch Mrs. MacIver, Sorcha glanced about to see if anyone had witnessed her being set down by the small goose.

MacAdoo Dundas, Graeme's mischievous son, had noticed and as usual, proceeded to taunt little Sorcha. A predictable scuffle ensued, and by the time Graeme separated the two, Sorcha's braids dangled in disarray and MacAdoo was rubbing his shins, the objects of several well-placed kicks by Nelly's daughter.

The commonplace event lightened Suisan's spirits and she thought of the child she carried. Her imagination leapt to the future. She pictured a little girl with golden hair and warm brown eyes. She'd be a sprite. She'd romp through the white heather and make mischief as all children do.

Suisan thought of Ailis, and a crushing pain squeezed at her chest. Gritting her teeth, she pushed aside the happy vision of her child.

Turning to Nelly, she said, "Are you ready?"

"Aye," Nelly answered. "But you ain't answered. When will you tell everyone about the child?"

Suisan sighed, knowing Nelly was right. "Brownin' Day," she said, grasping a random date, "I'll tell them then."

"But that's a fortnight away."

"It will have to do," she said with finality.

"Very well. I've got my part of the tale thought out."

"No doubt you've embroidered the story well," Suisan said.

Looking affronted, Nelly tossed back her braids and said, "You're grumpy this morn. Must be the sickness."

"I'm not grumpy," Suisan hotly denied. "We've months of extra work to make up, for all the time lost in London, and I have my doubts we'll finish the cloth in time to find a decent market."

Nelly handed Suisan a dress. "But then again," the maid ventured in a knowing tone, "you could be pining away for the likes of a tall fellow with golden hair and brown eyes."

Suisan fought back a familiar pang of longing and took her time putting on the dress. If Nelly had any notion of how correct she was, Suisan would pay a dear price in endless lectures and "Didn't I say so's." Her nights were long and lonely. Only during the day when responsibilities weighed heavy on her mind was she able to forget Myles Cunningham, and then for only brief periods of time.

"You ain't asked for my story yet," Nelly said.

Grateful for the chance to get her mind off Myles, Suisan said, "I'm listening."

As if she'd rehearsed the speech, Nelly plunged in. "We were gone too long for them to believe we went from the Glasgow Fair to Strathclyde. Not even Aunt Ailis is daft enough to believe that story. But what's to keep us from admittin' we went to Londontown?"

Nelly looked so confident that Suisan wanted laugh. Instead, she said, "I don't think I'll bother sorting that out because you obviously have the answer."

"Of course. Nothin' is the answer, that's what."

"Very well. But that only covers part of it. Why are we admitting to going to London?"

Nelly stiffened her back and set her chin. "To find you a husband. That's why."

Suisan gasped. "That's nonsense. I've no need for, nor do I want, a husband."

Nelly held up her hand. "Just be hearin' me out, milady, for 'twould serve a double purpose."

Suisan looked away; the idea was preposterous.

"Milady?"

At the soft spoken address, Suisan slid a glance back to her maid.

Resting her hands on her knees, Nelly leaned forward. Her thick, blonde braids fell over her shoulders. "Some's been badgerin' you to find a mate—not that you ain't a fine and capable mistress, mind. But still there's a few who'd keep their waggin' tongues to themselves once Perwickshire had a laird. Ain't it so?"

"Aye," Suisan was forced to admit. "The older ones, especially."

"See?" Nelly's voice rose. "And since 'twould all be a fib from beginning to end, they'd be satisfied. But when the new laird, who they won't never see, of course, met with a sad but fatal accident on his way to Roward, they'd think you done your duty."

The story was simple enough to be true, but Suisan had reservations. "Why should I pretend to have a husband just to placate a few of our people?"

Nelly frowned and studied her hands. After a long silence, she said, "You need a husband because of that babe in yer belly."

Troubled to the point of depression, Suisan had skirted the issue. Hearing it now brought all the pain and misery she had expected. Dear God, what had she done?

"Don't let it get the better of you, milady," Nelly said calmly, "there's no certainty you'd birth a child like Ailis."

The possibility was too terrifying to face. Like a coward leaving the front lines, Suisan dashed the thought aside. "And who do you recommend we create for my dearly and newly departed laird?"

"Why, any name you please, milady, since the fellow don't exist," Nelly said, as calmly as if she were telling little Sorcha to wipe her face.

"And what if Myles comes to visit us again?"

"He won't dare," Nelly replied flippantly. "I'd sooner bet on MacIver and Seamus Hay settling their squabble over that mess your grandmother brewed up. Besides, you said yourself, Myles Cunningham don't favor you the tiniest bit. Unless you was only tellin' part of it."

At Nelly's curious expression, Suisan fought back the hurt gnawing at her vitals. "Myles is in love with someone else. The woman in that oval miniature he carries about."

"Then what's the harm in telling the tale?"

"None, I suppose." Rejecting her wayward emotions, Suisan fluffed out the skirt of her striped linen dress.

"I let out the seams." Nelly came to stand beside Suisan and tugged at the waist of the dress. "You should be thinkin' about some new frocks; you'll be needin' them soon."

In the face of her bleak future, the idea of worrying over a dress was suddenly humorous to Suisan. She turned away to hide her bitter mirth.

Behind her, she heard Nelly say, "You'd best get your cap—a blue one to match the stripes."

Suisan stopped. She remembered all the times Myles had taken issue with her caps. She also remembered the way his eyes had glittered with autumn light when she defied him.

"Well?" Nelly prompted. "Will you wear a cap or no?"

Suisan stiffened her back and fought the urge to tell Nelly what she could do with the suggestion.

"I'm wonderin'," Nelly ventured slyly as she folded Suisan's sleeping gown, "why the thought of wearing a serving cap upsets you so."

Breathing deeply, then putting on her best smile, Suisan spun around. "And hide my hair?" She shook her head, allowing the cascade of flaming Cameron tresses to fall over her shoulders. "Nay. I'm proud to be a redhead again."

Nelly frowned, disbelief written on her face. Suisan suspected her maid's inquisitive nature was battling with pride. Suisan knew she'd been correct when Nelly puffed up and replied, "Gettin' it back to red was only a matter of time, and didn't I say so?"

Suisan opened the door. "Aye, that you did, Nelly."

Suisan felt a slight chill as she stepped into the ancient hallway, but when she reached the spiral staircase leading from her personal quarters in the castle's southeast tower to the main hall, warmth from the fireplace drifted upwards.

As she descended, she pictured Roward Castle as it must have been, centuries before—before the Jacobites, before the accession of a Hanoverian King named George. At one time, the great hall had borne the likenesses of her Cameron ancestry. Mingled with the portraits had been battle shields and broadswords, banners and tartans of the related Cameron clans. But after Culloden, the marauding English army had swept through Perwickshire like a cold and killing north wind.

Although born too late to see the great hall as it once had been, Suisan often imagined the Camerons who had come before her. Lighter spots on the wall gave proof that many portraits had graced the walls of Roward, and deep in the cellar were rotted pieces of tarnished gilded wood she knew had once been massive frames. She touched a hand to the cold stone wall. Fancifully, she imagined which of her ancestors had done the same. Her great grandmother, Fiona Cameron, had passed this way. Fiona's daughter, Margaret, the heavy brace of keys rattling at her waist, had done the same.

But no likeness of dear Fiona or brave Margaret remained for Suisan to see.

Noise from below drew her from her reverie and reminded her of the task to come. To avoid repeating the story she and Nelly had concocted, Suisan would wait until Brownin' Day. The entire district would be here. She'd tell them as a group. Now she must find Graeme Dundas.

She reached the great hall, where several servants plied brooms and dusting cloths.

A young maid paused in her task of sweeping the thick rug before the fireplace. "Good morn, milady."

"Good morn, Rowena. Have you seen Dundas about?"

Giggling, her brown eyes twinkling with mirth, Rowena said, "Aye, he's out front givin' little Sorcha a spanking."

The maid's expression reminded Suisan of Myles. How many times had she basked in the glow of his golden gaze? And were those times enough to last the rest of her days? Knowing she would cry if she continued to lament over Myles, she breathed deeply and said, "From my window, I saw her fighting with MacAdoo. Did Dundas whip him as well?"

"Oh, aye," Rowena said, shifting the broom to her other hand, "he'd not show favor, even to his own bairn. And have you orders for the day, milady?"

Suisan looked around the hall. When her inspection was complete, she said, "Clean and polish the windows, and fetch those pots of gillyflowers Ailis has been tending. Put them on the window seat and put new torches in the hall sconces."

Rowena curtsied again. "Yes, milady. Gillyflowers'll brighten up the hall. Shall I be changin' the freshies?"

Suisan nodded and walked to the chairs facing the fireplace. On the floor were woven baskets containing herbs which disguised the musty smell prevalent in Roward Castle, no matter how often the rooms were swept and scrubbed. In ancient times, the aromatic herbs were scattered into the rush-strewn floor, but since the addition of rugs, the sweet smelling herbs were now stored in loosely woven baskets called freshies.

"Aye, change them today, then again before the celebration. Ailis made enough to last the winter."

When the maid curtsied and returned to her tasks, Suisan walked to the door. As she pulled it open, she spied Dundas, standing as tall as Murphy's sacred oak, his hands on his hips. He was staring after Sorcha who was running toward the weaving shed as if the demons of hell were after her.

"Dundas," Suisan called.

He turned around and began walking toward her. His craggy face, marred with a jagged scar earned on Culloden Moor, at the hand of Cumberland himself, showed through a thick red-gold beard. Massive shoulders were encased in a soft linen shirt, hand dyed and woven here at Roward. Muscular legs were sheathed in dark brown breeches of thick and nubby linen, also from the busy looms of Roward.

Graeme Dundas trained and commanded the soldiers of Perwickshire, saw to the castle's defense and the armory. A proponent of the old Highland ways, he considered himself Suisan's personal protector. He had led the small force of men accompanying Suisan to Aberdeen, then balked and stormed at her command that he stay behind. Finally, she had to threaten to turn him out unless he obeyed. On more occasions than she could count, Dundas had kept her safe from what he considered the only danger in Perwickshire: Lachlan MacKenzie and his pursuit of Suisan's heart.

When Dundas reached her, she said, "Good morn. Have you broken your fast?"

"Aye." His smile widened. "But 'twas quick; MacAdoo makes enough noise to give a man a pounding head."

The familiar longing crept up, and with joy in her heart she realized she'd have her own family soon. She didn't need Myles to help her raise their child. She didn't need anyone.

"I could have Mrs. MacCormick make you a posset," she ventured slyly.

His face twisted sourly. "I'd sooner spend the day with Nelly and her gossip."

Suisan laughed. "Send some of your men 'round the district today. We'll have Brownin' Day two weeks from Sunday." At his curious expression, she continued, "The dyeing will be done by then; we'll put away the vats and bring out the looms."

"A celebration's what the district needs," he said, "now that you're home to stay."

"I thought so myself. You're to go to the widow Mac-Cormick's and ask her for the fattest of her cattle. Slaughter it, then take it to Mrs. Peavey."

"Aye, milady. If the widow puts in the meat, perhaps she won't make haggis."

Suisan laughed again. "We're certain to be the only Highlanders who don't like haggis." The thought of spicy haggis made Suisan's stomach roil. She looked away until the nausea had passed. "Bring up enough whiskey and beer for the men, and berry wine for the—"

"Whiskey and beer?" he interjected. "They'll make merry, you can be sure."

"Since when do Highlanders need an occasion to celebrate?"

"Why, none at all, milady, and a bounty is what they need. Shall I send a man to the MacKenzie?"

Suisan felt distress at the mention of her neighbor and persistent suitor, Lachlan MacKenzie. "Aye, and have him deliver the spyglass I brought from London."

"I suspect," Graeme began, a sly look on his rugged face, "that His Grace will come without an invitation or a spyglass. Rumor has it he's still in high dudgeon over your leavin' without tellin' him. I'm surprised he ain't been 'round sooner."

Brownin' Day was soon enough to deal with Lachlan MacKenzie, Suisan thought. "Most likely his pride's hurt, or his mistress is jealous."

Dundas tactfully avoided comment on Lachlan's roguish ways. "Do you have a message for him?"

"Aye, I penned a letter yesterday. Nelly has it. Have your men tell all of our people that I've important news." At his curious expression, she added, "An announcement, you might say."

"Ah," he drawled. "'Tis best they know."

Immediately attentive to Graeme's grave tone, Suisan stiffened. "Best they know what?"

"About the babe," he said quietly.

Shocked and unnerved by his astuteness, she said sharply, "You've been gossiping with Nelly."

His arms fell to his sides and his mouth turned down. "I've no part of Nelly's gossip."

"Then how did you know?"

Smiling gently he said, "I overheard her mention it to Flora."

"Damn! You mustn't tell anyone."

"We wouldn't be having this conversation if you'd let me come to London with you."

Annoyed that he would give her a dressing down, she said. "You think you could have prevented it?"

"Of course I could have."

Picturing Dundas trying to keep her out of Myles's bed brought a secret chuckle of laughter to Suisan. "That's preposterous. You're just angry because you had to stay in Aberdeen."

"I should have gone with you."

The words prickled her ire. "You think so, do you? Next you'll be telling me you should be laird of this castle instead of me."

He opened his mouth, then closed it. Good, she thought.

"Will you tell them you went to London?" he asked.

She related the story she and Nelly had concocted.

Frowning, Dundas said, "Need I ask the name of the true father, milady?"

A dull ache drummed in the pit of her stomach at the thought of Myles Cunningham. Avoiding Graeme's searching gaze, she said, "I had hoped you wouldn't."

He stiffened. "Do you love him?"

"I did," she breathed, resigned to the heartache.

"'Tis as it should be, Lady Suisan," he said in that trusting, familiar tone. "I'll not question the tale, but what if he comes after you?"

"He won't." Tilting her head back, their eyes met. "I promise."

A muscle jumped in his jaw. "He's a fool then."

A knot of pride lodged in her throat. "Thank you."

He shrugged it off. "I'll ride to the widow's this morn. Was there something else?"

Some of the tension eased. Suisan searched the castle yard, now busy with activity. "Is Ailis about?"

"In her garden." Graeme's brow knitted in a frown. "I think 'tis best you see to her before going to the weaving shed."

"Is aught amiss?"

Dundas nodded. "Much. She's donned her winter coat and started diggin' up those new bulbs you brought her from London."

"But she just planted them."

"Aye, but she's convinced herself 'tis winter." He looked up at the sun drenched sky.

Suisan sighed. The day was windy, but warmer than most. "The poor thing. And she's been so well since we returned."

Dundas cleared his throat. "Not altogether."

Their eyes met. "What do you mean? Ailis was fine last evening."

"She had a spell while we were away—a bad one, they say. Some of it's still with her."

Anger churned inside Suisan. "Why wasn't I told?"

Dundas toyed with the dagger at his belt. "You had enough on your mind. I thought to spare you, and it did seem the spell had passed."

Suisan turned her steps toward the garden with Dundas at her heels. "What brought the spell on? Or should I ask Nelly?"

"You'll get nothing from Nelly on that," he said. "She don't know of the spell either."

Suisan was momentarily taken aback by his secretiveness. "But you do."

"Aye, 'twas that Bartholomew Weeks, your uncle's man. He's been courtin' the lorimer's daughter. Ailis was tending your mother's grave. Jenny and Weeks came upon her. The sight of Weeks scared Ailis into a fit."

"Jenny knows better than to let a strange man near Ailis —everyone does."

"Says it weren't her fault. Says she and him were walking in the woods near the cemetery."

"While Uncle Rabby's paying him good wages to repair the castle. I never understood why he sent us such a laggard."

"That's the right of it, milady."

Suisan envisioned poor Ailis, cowering as she often did when in the presence of a man. Damn men and their base schemes. "I'll go to her."

"Good, milady. If she don't get out of that coat she'll swoon in the heat." He waved goodbye, but stopped. "Will you be wantin' a fire on Brownin' Day?"

Suisan studied the sky, then scanned the horizon. "'Tis too dry this year, I think, for any but a wee blaze. The old vats will have to do." She patted his arm and said, "You've a long ride ahead of you to Mrs. MacCormick's."

He nodded. "I thought to take MacAdoo and Fergus along."

"And Sorcha?"

Graeme's mouth fell open. When Suisan laughed, he said, "That little hellion'll get her due—and her nosey mother, too—just you wait and see."

Suisan smiled. Of all the men she knew, Dundas was the best of the lot. He would never fail her.

As she rounded the south turret of the castle and passed the kitchen, she waved to Flora MacIver, who tended the herb garden. Moving onward, Suisan stopped beneath the arbor to admire the lush berry vines, now denuded of fruit. Upon entering Ailis's magnificent garden, she saw her aunt, bundled in a heavy coat and fussing with a row of seedlings.

Suisan's smile faded.

Frail and childlike, Ailis glanced nervously from the spot where Dundas had been to the place where Suisan was. Gloved hands worried a tulip bulb, picking at the layers of dirt and peeling the thin brown skin away. By the time Suisan reached her aunt, the saffron-colored bulb lay exposed. Suisan knew Ailis often felt as vulnerable and naked as the bulb.

"Good morn, Aunt Ailis," Suisan said and held out her hand for the bulb.

Pale blue eyes seemed to focus and a moment later Ailis relinquished the bulb. "The poor things'll freeze, don't I get 'em up before the snow."

"Don't you listen to that Mrs. Peavey, dear." Suisan lifted the shawl from Ailis's shoulders. "Nelly says 'twill be warm today."

"Nelly did?" Ailis asked, hope shining in her eyes.

"Aye, she did," Suisan answered, keeping her voice even. "I'd swear 'tis warmer already."

Beads of perspiration dotted the older woman's forehead. She glanced at the rows of maize, their golden tassels rustling in the breeze. "They told me 'twould freeze soon."

"Who did?"

Ailis's eyes shifted nervously. Suisan wondered at the trowie voices only Ailis seemed to hear. As the silence stretched out, she knew she would get no answer. Life's cruelties had found shelter in befuddled, sweet Ailis.

"Now who will you believe? Some would-be soothsayer on our own Nelly Burke?"

"She's very smart," Ailis said solemnly.

"Aye, that she is." Suisan made her voice light. "And today's washing day. She said if you wanted your coat fresh for winter I was to bring it to her."

Ailis hesitated for so long Suisan thought she might refuse. Then slowly she surrendered the heavy woolen garment. Her dress, of bright red cotton, was already wet with perspiration.

"We'll be having the brownin' soon. Will you gather some flowers for the hall?"

The breeze picked up and Ailis held her hand to her temple to keep the silver strands of her hair from her face. "And haven't I been nursing those red gillyflowers you favor?" she asked, sounding as normal as anyone in Perwickshire. "Two big barrels of them are blooming like you've never seen before. I'm certain it was the shade of the Rowans what did it."

Suisan chuckled. "Aye, I favor your gillyflowers and Rowena will see they're brought inside. But I wanted more flowers to set about the hall."

Ailis put a finger to her mouth and surveyed the large garden. "Bell flowers'd be nice 'n perky, with white heather and mustard for luck and Rowan boughs to keep the evil ones away. Thank St. George it's warm."

The small garden was ringed by Rowan trees, a living talisman against mischievous spirits. Every home in Perwickshire sported Rowans; seedlings were given as gifts, and jelly from the berries was highly prized. Ailis's garden, however, seemed an exaggerated example in the belief of the power of Rowans. Suisan thought of the unwanted spirits and thoughts plaguing her of late. She would have gladly filled her own tower chamber with the talismans, but not even the sacred Rowans could keep thoughts of Myles away.

"That would be lovely," Suisan said, certain Ailis had temporarily chased her own demons away. "We'll be bringin' out the looms soon."

Ailis nodded. Perspiration dripped down her nose. "When the browns are done."

"Aye. I've invited all of Perwickshire to share in the burning of the vats."

"'Tis late in the year for the brownin'," Ailis chided in a suddenly adult voice.

"A wee bit, but we'll manage."

"But why are we having a gathering this year?"

Suisan studied her aunt closely, trying to discern if Ailis were lucid enough today to understand. Deciding to test Nelly's scheme on Ailis, Suisan took her aunt's hand and said, "I've found a husband, but you mustn't tell anyone yet."

"No!" Ailis wailed and clasped Suisan's hand in a death grip. Beseeching blue eyes filled with tears and her paperlike skin faded to a pasty white. "You'll not like a man nor the things he'll do to you. Tell him no." Her eyes darted to the Rowans. "Tell him you've thought on it and—oh, sweet St. George, Suisan," she continued to wail, "tell him you won't—you can't. . . ."

Momentarily shocked at Ailis's vehemence, Suisan could but stare as the pleading continued. During a spell, Ailis reacted strongly to any change in the daily routine, but never had she been so agitated. Yet how would Ailis, a spinster, know of men? Dundas's accusation that a man had caused

Ailis's misery echoed in Suisan's ears. As she had done so many times during the years Ailis had been at Roward, Suisan wished she could see into her aunt's troubled mind.

". . . dreadful and vile and hurtful," Ailis swore. "Tell him you can't marry him. You're good and strong. Everyone listens to you. You don't need a man." Ailis's fretful expression suddenly vanished. She pulled her hands away and scurried to one of the Rowans ringing the garden. With jerky motions, she reached up and yanked a handful of waxy leaves from the tree, then rushed back to Suisan.

"These'll protect you from him," she said, stuffing the crisp leaves into Suisan's pockets.

Keeping her voice even, her tone determined, Suisan said, "And what of children, Ailis? Wouldn't you love a bonny wee lassie to cuddle in your arms and sing your pretty songs to?"

Ailis crossed her arms and began to sway as if rocking a baby.

"Ailis?" Suisan called softly.

Looking up, her eyes still wide with some unseen terror, Ailis said, "A lassie? Oh, yes. I'd like a lassie."

As the sun peeps through a dark storm cloud, joy and sweet but temporary sanity shone in Ailis Harper's eyes. Suisan's heart leapt at the sight. Frail and delicate Ailis had chased her goblins away—at least for now.

Steam rose in swirling wisps from the bubbling dye vat. Suisan wiped her brow and arched her tired back, but continued to stir the crimson-colored water. The sour smell of wet wool permeated the weaving shed and assaulted her nose. The next two weeks would be sheer torture.

She swallowed and gripped the paddle harder. When the nausea persisted, she tried to think of something else. She had long since given up wondering why the familiar smell now turned her stomach, because she knew why.

Thoughts of the babe she carried triggered thoughts of Myles Cunningham. Sadness settled rock-like in her queasy stomach. She imagined him in Cornwall, walking arm in arm with the woman he loved. Tears clouded her eyes; she paused to wipe them away.

"Give me that," Nelly demanded, reaching for the long wooden paddle. "You're fair exhausted, you know."

Suisan sighed but did not allow her eyes to meet Nelly's. Staring into the vat she said, "Let's have a look."

Nelly deftly laid the handle against the iron rim and levered the spade end of the paddle to the surface of the boiling cauldron.

"Damn!" she cursed when the paddle came up empty. She dipped it again and again. Each unsuccessful try was punctuated with a colorful word.

"Mind yer tongue, Nelly Burke, or I'll shut it with this." Mrs. MacIver shook her own paddle at Nelly. "There's innocent bairns about. No need sullyin' their minds with yer dicey tongue." She jerked her head toward the corner of the shed where the children were tended.

Stubborn to the core, Nelly continued the expletives but in a softer tone. Mrs. MacIver grumbled something under her breath and turned her attention to the vat before her.

Suisan looked down the row of bubbling cauldrons, the wood discolored from the harsh dyes and after today fit only to dye the browns. Once that was done they'd drain the four vats and burn them. Then the looms would be brought out and the weaving shed would come alive with the clickety-clack of a dozen shuttles. She imagined the bright reds, the jaunty stripes and the lively checks they would weave. Some bolts would be embroidered, some decorated with beads or appliques.

Nelly cursed again and Suisan focused her eyes on the vat. The soft wool and cotton they were dyeing would bring a fine price at market. But no longer would any of the cloth form the sweet symbols of the Highlander's culture: the tartan plaid.

"There! You dung-hearted son of a stinkin' ram," Nelly declared, balancing the paddle. Perched on the scoop was a lump of wool, lightly pink and steaming.

"Not quite dark enough," Suisan corrected sternly. "I want a red."

Nelly frowned and Suisan suspected the maid would argue the opinion. Nelly glanced around as if seeking support. With a disdainful lift of her head she passed by Mrs. MacIver. None of the other women acknowledged Nelly, for they were looking toward the door. When Nelly did the same, her mouth fell open and the paddle slipped from her hand and splashed into the vat.

"Sweet St. Ninian, protect us," Nelly hissed.

Curious, Suisan followed Nelly's line of vision. Her gaze riveted to the open door and her heart lurched into her throat.

For there in the door of the weaving shed, his handsome face bearded, his brown eyes blazing with anger, his booted feet firmly planted on Roward soil . . . stood Myles Cunningham.

~ *Chapter 15* ~

His eyes were gritty with Highland dirt and he was stiff from days in the saddle, but Myles ignored his discomfort and concentrated on his goal: finding Suisan Harper and then finding that black-hearted Maura Forbes. Squinting, he tried to adjust his weary eyes to the dim light in the weaving shed. Where was Suisan?

He'd asked the men in the stables and had been sent here. As a safeguard, he'd left Will'am there to keep watch for Maura, in case she learned of their arrival and tried to flee while he paid his respects to Suisan.

Toward the back of the room, Myles made out the vague outlines of several large vats, steam rising above, fires lapping beneath. Shadowy shapes tended the vats and he wondered if Suisan was among them. A flash of red hair drew his attention and he shook his head to focus his eyes. Then a woman was walking toward him, slim and poised, the bold blue and white stripes of her dress sashaying. Not Suisan, of course; this woman was nothing like the girl in the oval. He felt a stab of anger that once again someone other than Suisan would welcome him to Roward Castle.

Drawn by the fiery glow of her hair, he tried to focus his bleary eyes on her face. The name Sibeal Harper flashed in his mind. Thinking exhaustion the cause for dredging up the past, Myles flexed his shoulders and arched his aching back.

Intrigued, he took a step toward the woman.

She walked in a particularly appealing way, but her carriage also bespoke confidence and dignity. With that flaming Cameron hair she could be a cousin. Myles frowned, unable to see her features clearly in the dim light. He rubbed his eyes and was immediately sorry, for the dirt and dust ground like needles.

Hoping to spy Suisan Harper's plain-featured face, he scanned the room's other occupants. The people closest to him were all looking toward the redhaired woman in the striped dress. They smiled proudly, respectfully, and even though he couldn't see her well, Myles could discern her progress merely by watching the others. Who was she?

He took another step, but stopped.

She had turned to speak to a fair-haired child and as she did, a yard of flaming red hair cascaded over her shoulder, effectively hiding her face from his view. The child giggled, nodded her head vigorously, then dashed off, blonde braids flying.

Apprehension tickled at his brain, but Myles was too exhausted to decipher the source. He had one purpose in mind and he would not allow himself the luxury of rest or the distraction of a comely woman—not until he had found that black-haired vixen, Maura. Fury rose in him. When he did find her, by God, he'd find out exactly why she'd come to London and left without a word. He cursed himself for labeling her motives honorable; there was nothing honorable in what she'd done to him.

With a quick toss of her head, the woman swept the blanket of thick hair over her shoulder. In profile, she reminded Myles of a classically lovely face on a Greek coin. He wished she would face him, for his eyes had adjusted to the light, and the moment she did turn, he would be able see her clearly.

She squared her shoulders, lifted her chin and turned.

"Sweet mother Mary," he hissed, unable to move his feet, unable to draw breath into his lungs. Like hunters keen for the prey, his eyes searched her from head to toe. Red hair, Sibeal's hair. Expressive blue eyes, Edward's eyes . . . and Maura's eyes. Maura? It couldn't be. Where was her black hair? Suisan? It couldn't be. What had happened to that plain country mouse?

The woman before Myles was a blending of the only four people he had ever loved. She was a Harper. She was a Cameron. She was a blue-eyed vixen. With stunning clarity and a sinking heart, Myles realized he was looking at Suisan Harper. And Maura Forbes. *The two women were one and the same.*

His head began to pound and his limbs grew weak, yet his mind worked feverishly to find some logic in the discovery. The significance of her true identity lead to myriad questions, but his inquisitive mind ran a distant second when pitted against his manly pride. All his tender memories of Suisan, the child, faded.

For the first time since waking alone in his bed over two months ago, Myles felt the tension ease from his weary limbs. Now that she was within reach, he knew the upper hand was his, and he intended to interrogate her at his leisure.

"You don't seem the least bit afraid of me," he growled.

"Why should I fear you?" Her gaze encompassed the crowd of people nearby. "'Tis my home, Myles. You brought me here, then abandoned me. I've grown to love Roward."

On closer examination, he decided her words and her smile were pure bravado, for within the depths of her familiar blue eyes Myles saw fear. Her anxious expression was small comfort to a man who had spent long weeks plodding across the rugged Highlands of Scotland and longer weeks in the bloody Tower of London.

He forced himself to look away from her, for no matter how angry he was, he found himself drawn to her beauty.

She'd inherited Sibeal's lovely features, but those Cameron good looks had multiplied tenfold in Suisan. But why had Robert always said she was plain, then sent that fraudulent miniature likeness as proof? Was she a part of that deception, too? She was without doubt the most strikingly beautiful woman he had ever seen. The admission stirred his ire and his curiosity. But beauty or not, Harper or not, by God, she had some explaining to do.

In a voice loud enough for all in the room to hear, she said, "Welcome, Myles Cunningham. Welcome to Roward Castle." The musical quality of her Highland brogue took Myles by surprise, and before he could reply, she threaded an arm through his and added, "You must be exhausted from your journey. Let us see to your comfort."

The physical contact stirred a longing deep within him, a longing he could not afford. Leaning close, he whispered, "You'll see to my comfort, right enough, Lady Suisan. My comfort and all else of my choosing."

Her lush mouth turned up at the corners and her head tilted at just the proper angle to enhance her allure. "Aye, we will; 'tis our duty as Highlanders."

Boiling mad at her blasé attitude and desperate to get her alone, he narrowed his eyes and threatened, "Your duties will soon be redefined."

"My duties," she retorted, "were defined centuries ago, as you would know—had you bothered to inquire. Think you to change my position on a moment's notice?"

At her offended look, Myles said, "Why are you resentful? Our association was your doing. So was our separation."

"Aye," she whispered, "and I'll see us separated again —permanently."

Her words cut deeply and he sucked in his breath—a breath scented by the sweet smell of heather and Suisan. He was perched on the edge of emotions he knew he couldn't control. Not now. He was besieged by anger and confusion, he was assaulted by his attraction to this red-haired vixen. He was weary from days in the saddle. Yet deep inside he felt a grudging respect for Suisan's forthright manner; she could have easily barred the castle gates and called her men to arms.

He and Will'am would have been easy prey for the dozen archers on the battlements of Roward Castle. What was her ploy?

When they reached the door, she turned to several lads who stood at attention. "MacAdoo, Jimmie, do you remember Myles Cunningham?"

"Oh, aye, Lady Suisan," MacAdoo replied. "He was here for the harvest last year, but you was away."

Pulling her close, Myles whispered, "There'll be a harvest this time, to be sure. And you, my dear, shall be the crop." He took great pleasure in feeling her tense beneath his grasp. "By God, Suisan, I'll see you humbled and more."

"Aye, he was, MacAdoo," she said evenly, causing Myles to wonder where she found the courage. "You're to take his things to the north tower." She turned to Myles. "Have you come alone?"

Myles blinked, completely baffled by her polite manner. Didn't she see he was raging mad? When he found his voice, he said curtly, "Nay. I brought Will'am. He's in the stables."

She nodded regally and turned back to the lads. "Go to the stables and fetch Will'am to the north tower. Then you're to care for their horses."

"Aye, milady," they chirped in unison, then darted off to their appointed tasks.

"Are you hungry?" Her blue eyes were wide.

Myles felt his control slipping. "By God, woman, yes! I'm hungry enough to beat you where you stand! If you don't bridle that civil tongue, I'll see to it now!"

A smile tugged at the corners of her mouth. "Bridle my civil tongue," she mused, shaking her head and setting the blanket of fiery hair to dancing in the sunlight. "'Tis a novel request, and one I confess the need to ponder."

Myles gripped her arm and headed for the main door of the castle. "You'll be pondering more than confessions before I'm done with you, Suisan Harper."

"Confessions?" she asked. "I should think you're the one to make confessions, not I. 'Twas your greed that brought us to this."

Myles blinked in confusion, but his anger still overrode any other emotion.

"I don't know why you're so surprised at what I've become," she said in that maddeningly even tone. "Or why it took you so long to get here. You had but to visit more than once in ten years to know what I look like. That, or spare a glance at the painting Uncle Rabby sent you. 'Tis you who were fooled by a bit of black dye."

"Fooled?" he barked, covering his surprise with rage. "Perhaps I played your fool once, but mark my words, Lady Suisan Harper, I'll not be fooled again." That said, he began walking faster. Much to his surprise, he saw that she had no trouble adjusting her stride to his. Angered anew, he leaned close and growled, "You've no place else to run, Suisan."

"'Tis true," she said pensively, not the least bit winded. "But am I to be granted a last request . . . before the inquisition?"

"You push me too far," he warned, tempted to shake the indifference from her.

"Only as far as your bath—" She paused and twitched her perfectly sculptured nose. "One could faint from the smell."

"One could suffer for her insolence, as well," he growled and pulled open the castle door.

"We'll see," she said on a sigh as she preceded him into the hall. "Once you've eaten and bathed, you'll be in more agreeable humor. You always are."

"Enough," he bellowed and stopped. Gripping her arms, he lifted her off the ground. When they were nose to nose, he held her there and said, "A last warning, woman. Mind your tongue."

Fear flickered in her eyes and he was pleased he'd finally had some effect on her. Nervously, she glanced around the large room. "Put me down," she whispered.

"You'll cease this silly banter?" he asked, and was again assaulted by the sweet fragrance of heather.

"They're watching." Her eyes darted to the servants in the hall.

Frustrated and more confused than he'd ever been in his life, Myles fought back his violent urges. "King George himself could be watching for all I care. Will you stop this ridiculous wordplay?"

"Aye," she breathed, "I swear. Please set me down."

Scanning her flushed face, he was both awed and perplexed, for how could she look so different and yet so familiar? He blamed her hair for the quandary—her hair and what the fiery color did to her skin. He remembered how fair her complexion had seemed against that jet black hair of Maura Forbes. Now her skin appeared softer, more radiant and the Harper-blue eyes shone like sapphires.

"Please, Myles," she repeated, "set me down."

Shaking himself, which he seemed to be doing often, Myles lowered her to the floor but did not release her. "Rest assured, my dear, your set-down will come soon enough."

She cleared her throat and looked away. Myles took the gesture to mean she was afraid. Momentarily placated, he turned toward the main stairway, drawing her with him. The servants in the great hall had paused in their work, brooms and feather dusters gone still. Nervous eyes darted from her to Myles. One particularly young maid dropped a woven basket, spilling dried flower petals and herbs on the hand woven rug. He scowled, and she gasped and ran from the room, the spilled petals forgotten.

"You needn't drag me," Suisan said as if they were discussing blends of tea. "Nor upset the servants."

They had reached the stone staircase which led to the gallery. Myles released her arm but grasped her hand. "Then consider yourself and your household in jeopardy, for I've just begun."

She sighed and her expression spoke maddeningly of patience. Turning to the servants, she said, "Rowena, have Mrs. Peavey prepare a repast for our guest and bring it to the north tower." The girl bobbed a curtsy and disappeared behind a tapestry that depicted a hunt.

Placing a slippered foot on the first step of the staircase, Suisan said, "I'll show you to your rooms."

Male pride surged to the fore. How dare she seduce him in London and reject him out of hand in Scotland? "You'll show me to *your* room," he corrected as they ascended the stairs. He kept pace with her small steps, but in truth his legs were weary from sitting a saddle for weeks.

"'Tis impossible," she snapped, "and you'll be far more comfortable—"

"I'll be far angrier if you don't," he warned, cut to the core by her high-handed refusal. "You enjoyed sharing a bed with me in London, didn't you?"

Standing on the carpeted floor of the gallery, she turned to face him. Her eyes were wide and her gaze searching.

He cocked an eyebrow in response to her perusal. "We'll share a bed, Suisan. Do you doubt it?"

Her teeth toyed with her lush lips—lips he had kissed, lips he longed to kiss again. She opened her mouth to speak but must have decided against it. Sighing heavily, she closed her eyes. Her thick lashes, as dark as her hair had once been, fanned her flushed cheeks. Her shoulders drooped. She glanced down the hall then turned to one of the passageways leading from the gallery.

"This way."

Small torches mounted in decorative iron sconces flickered as they passed. The pungent smell of burning pitch assaulted his nose. Had she used all the candles he sent her regularly? Surely not. But Robert Harper had said she squandered her gifts, that she supported the district with her allowance instead of using the modern looms to produce better cloth and increase her income. Then again, Robert had often lied. Still, Myles pictured every thatched hovel in Perwickshire lighted with the expensive bayberry and cinnamon candles he purchased abroad and shipped to Robert for Suisan's personal use. "You're much too generous," he grumbled.

"I am?" she asked, tilting her face, an inquisitive look in her eyes. "Why would you say such a thing?"

"Because 'tis the truth."

"Oh, I see," she drawled, her words flavored with that Highland brogue.

How had she managed to speak so properly in London? Obviously she was a woman of many talents. No doubt she had employed every device she knew when she'd worked herself into his bed, then slithered away without a word when her purpose was served.

"I want candles to light the halls," he said petulantly, distracted by the enchanting sway of her hips.

"By all means," she said.

"And you to warm my bed."

She gasped, and Myles felt exceedingly pleased. Let her try and deny what they'd shared.

"Here we are." She pushed open the door to the spacious chamber. A massive bed covered with an elaborately embroidered spread and a grouping of high back chairs carved of Black Forest oak dominated the room. Woolen rugs of a shade not quite crimson, but darker than red, covered the stone floor. Where was the lovely Turkey carpet he'd rummaged through Constantinople for days to find? She'd probably given the expensive rug away or sold it in a flight of fancy.

Disgruntled by her insensitivity and weary beyond coherence, he folded his body into one of the chairs. She obviously hadn't given a tinker's damn for the treasures he'd sent her over the years. She obviously didn't give a tinker's damn about him either. A weak part of him wanted to believe she'd put the gifts away or displayed them in a guest chamber. He snorted aloud at the noble thought. She didn't seem to notice, but busied herself about the room, touching this and straightening that . . . and ignoring him completely.

"My boots," he demanded, hurt by her denial, "if you please."

Anger flashed in her eyes, and he felt he'd won a small victory. "Defy me," he growled, praying she would, begging she would; her benign attitude was driving him mad.

Much to his chagrin, she held her head high, crossed the room and knelt at this feet. Light from the window caught her blazing Cameron hair and turned it to flame. He ached to thread his hands through the thick and wavy mass, to pull her up on his lap and—

"Christ!" he spat, angry at the thought and angrier at his body's reaction to her nearness.

She glanced up, her gaze steady and searching, but her hands never paused in their task. When her fingers slid under the cuff of his high-topped boots, a jolt of desire shot through him. Good lord, would he never stop wanting this beguiling woman? He scowled again, and was pleased when she looked away.

"Why have you come back to Roward?" she asked when both boots were removed. "Surely you know 'tis futile, for I'll not let you get away with it again."

He was completely taken off guard by her direct question and puzzled beyond belief at the finality of her accusing statement. Here he was, thinking of naught but how wonderful she would feel beneath him, and there she was, blithely feigning ignorance of the whole affair. Hurt barrelled through him, effectively stifling his desire.

She drew back but did not rise. "I asked you why you've come to Scotland."

A thousand bitter answers came to mind and each one would taste, oh, so sweet on his lips. Just when he'd decided on a particularly nasty reply, a loud knock sounded at the door.

"Myles?" she prompted, obviously unconcerned about the person on the other side of the wooden door.

Still vexed by her question, he said, "You know precisely why I've come to Scotland. Don't pretend otherwise."

"Oh, I did pretend—for a time." She sighed and did her best to look offended.

"Lady Suisan?" a muffled voice called.

Gracefully, she rose and walked to the door. Will'am entered, his arms loaded with bags.

"Hello, Will'am," she said, clasping her hands in a nun-like pose. "Welcome to Roward Castle."

Slack-jawed, the boy stared in disbelief; he too realized who she was. Myles took pity on the boy. "Come in, Will'am."

Behind Will'am and obviously ignorant of the complex situation, the lads Jimmie and MacAdoo struggled with a large wooden tub. With the skill of a field general on maneuvers, Suisan took command, and sooner than Myles expected the tub was filled with steaming water. Fresh clothing was laid upon the bed, and Will'am was taken away to his quarters. Once again, to Myles's dark delight, they were alone.

Female voices drifted through the opened door. He cursed

under his breath when they were joined by three aproned women, two of whom looked very familiar.

"Come in, ladies," Suisan said and motioned them forward. "Mrs. MacIver, Rowena, you remember Mr. Cunningham."

They curtsied, holding out their skirts and bobbing their cap-covered heads. The stranger Rowena was flushed but Mrs. MacIver stood with her hands at her sides, her attention focused on her mistress. He knew where he'd seen the elder lady before; she'd been the one to welcome him last year during Suisan's absence.

"And this is Nelly Burke," Suisan added, drilling him with a cold stare. "You might remember her from our childhood days in Aberdeen. Before you brought me here."

"Nelly," he said smoothly, thinking she hadn't changed much over the years. "Of course," he drawled. "How could I forget the girl who taught me my first colorful Gaelic words?" In spite of the situation and his anger at Suisan, he found himself smiling at the remembrance of Nelly and her caustic tongue.

She didn't curtsy, but tipped her haughty nose in the air. "We was told to welcome you to Roward Castle," she said stubbornly, "and to give you a bath. I'll be the one to shave that beard off your nasty—"

"And Mrs. Peavey will bring you a tray," Suisan interrupted. "If there's nothing more," she continued politely, but shooting Nelly a warning glare, "I'll see what's keeping her."

If she thought to escape him or to shield herself with these women, she would have to think again. "Oh, there's much more, Suisan," he said meaningfully, "that I request of you."

Her face was inscrutable, but Nelly Burke huffed up and declared, "We'll see he gets cleaned, milady."

Angered by her insolence and well aware of her loyalty to Suisan, he decided to find out how much Nelly knew. "Nelly Burke," he said, scratching his beard. "I do remember you." Smiling confidently he turned to Suisan. "Ah, yes. I'll wager Nelly's a friend of Maura Forbes."

"Aye, she is." Suisan said haltingly.

He took perverse pleasure in her discomfiture. "And dear, dear, Maura said Nelly had married."

"I'm widowed." Nelly flipped a long blonde braid over her shoulder and added, "A fine lass, Maura, and too bonny for a hellhole like London."

"But you still carry your father's name?" he said doubtfully.

"'Tis the Highland way," she answered stiffly. "A custom you crawlin' Sassenachs wouldn't ken."

But Myles did ken. He remembered how proud Edward Harper had been each time he told the story of how Sibeal Cameron had taken his name. Depressed at the thought of Suisan's parents and grateful they could not see what had come to pass, he said, "Send your women away. You'll see to my bath yourself."

"She will not!" Nelly proclaimed. "'Twill take more 'n one pair of hands to get the grimy likes of you clean. You smell worse than MacIver's sheepdogs."

"Nelly . . ." Suisan warned.

But Nelly continued to glower at Myles, her fair face gone red with anger. "You've got no call to treat her so, you lame-witted excuse for a man."

"Nelly!" Suisan commanded, "*Haud yer wheesht!*"

The maid muttered a vulgar phrase under her breath. Rowena gasped and Mrs. MacIver shook her greying head in reproof. He fought back the urge to laugh out loud, because Nelly Burke hadn't changed at all in ten years. Oddly enough, he clung to the thought, for everything else in his life had changed drastically since his visit to Roward Castle last fall.

"That will be all, ladies," Suisan stated. "Nelly, you're to see what's keeping Mrs. Peavey and the meal."

The three marched from the room, but Nelly quickly returned, a tray in her hands. "Here's Lord Rodent's food," she spat. "Mrs. Peavey took pity on him—gave him extra cheese."

Without reply to Nelly's sarcasm, Suisan accepted the heavy tray. The dishes rattled when Nelly slammed the door shut. Shaking her head, Suisan crossed the room and put down the tray. "Beer?" she offered, holding up a tankard.

"Aye, and bring it here," he demanded crossly.

As she approached, he detected a smile hovering at the corners of her mouth.

He accepted the tankard and drank deeply of the yeasty beer. Scotland might be famous for its whiskey, but the Highlanders brewed beer to best any he'd ever had. They also bred the most willful and deceiving women in the world. When the mug was empty, he set it on the floor.

"Would you be liking another?" she asked.

"Several," he answered, rising. "But first my bath."

She turned to the tub, but not before Myles saw her frown. He was elated at the expression. He could deal with any emotion from her . . . except that infuriating indifference.

Holding back her hair, she leaned over to test the water. She paused a moment, then stood and waited.

"Well?" he prompted.

"The water's hot and the soap's rightly scented for a man. Towels are here and—"

"'Tis not what I was waiting for." Crossing his arms over his chest, he added, "Don't be coy, Suisan. You undressed me often and willingly enough in London. You may put your clever hands to work again."

"Nay!" she said hotly, stiffening her back. "'Tis not the same here."

He chuckled. "Oh, but you're wrong, lassie. Merely because you used the name Maura Forbes when you seduced me in London. . . ."

"Seduced?" she gasped, her eyes wide with indignation.

"Aye, seduced," he said, silently applauding his choice of words.

"'Tis lying prattle of the worst sort, Myles Cunningham," she said, pacing the room. "I was a virgin, unless you've twisted that bit of truth, too. *You* seduced *me*. And don't call me Maura," she insisted through clenched teeth. "'Tis a time and a name I'd sooner forget."

He cocked an eyebrow, but inside he was raging mad. How dare she reject him so easily? Knowing if she did not soon concede, he'd not be responsible for his actions, he said, "You will do as I say, or—" He paused and in three strides was beside her, "I'll make certain you are extremely sorry."

She stared him down. She was all defiance, all Cameron pride, all lush and beautiful woman. By God, she was his woman. And she was Suisan Harper, his childhood friend, and mistress of Roward. And she had probably known every nuance of Robert's plan before it occurred. The knowledge twisted his gut. "Do you doubt me?" he demanded.

Suddenly she looked bewildered. "What else under heaven could you possibly do to me . . . that you haven't managed already?"

His patience dwindled. "I'll show you." Reaching out, he wound his hand into her hair and slowly, with insistent pressure, he pulled her toward him.

"Let me be!" Her eyes blazed with defiance, and if the tales about redheaded women and tempers were true, he suspected she was as angry as he—at last. The knowledge roused primitive emotions within him. He longed to conquer this woman, to make her confess to what she'd done and why. He ached to have her as warm and willing as she had once been. His loins swelled at the prospect.

Unable to fight his desire, and anxious to appease his wounded pride, he tightened his grip and drew her to his chest. Small hands pushed against him. She turned her face away. Quickly, he seized her chin and forced her to look at him again. He read denial on her lovely features, and her eyes shouted "no" so loudly the sound rang in his ears. He would change that no to yes, a yes draped with sweet smelling garlands and poetic sighs of love.

He ground his lips on hers, determined to force her to yield. She tried to pull away but he held her fast, one hand in her hair, the other wrapped securely around her slender back. When he slanted his mouth across hers and plunged his tongue past her lips, she began fighting in earnest. He'd been too long without her, too lonely and too confused to accept defeat now.

Much to his delight, the battle was short-lived. With an anguished groan, she dug her nails into his chest. She went soft and subtle, then willingly returned the kiss.

Elated, he crushed her tighter against him. Time and place spun away, and like a dreamer too long without sleep, he plunged into fantasy. They were anywhere else, they were everywhere else, they were the only two people in the world.

She swayed and he felt himself do the same. Drawing back, he studied her face. She was a tormenting keepsake of his past; she was an essential part of his present. And she would be there in his future, he determined suddenly.

"If I weren't so tired and filthy," he rasped, cupping her beloved face in his hands, "I'd take you where you stand."

Her eyes fluttered open and filled with tears. His heart wrenched. "The people here view you as my brother." She looked away. "'Twould seem unnatural to them."

"Nonsense." But even as he voiced the denial, a doubt formed in his mind. Still, they could never go back. "I always thought of you as my sister, but that was long ago. Now too much passion burns between us. You will never again be like a sister to me."

"I hated being your sister and loathed being your mistress." She twisted out of his arms and retreated to the door. "Enjoy your bath, Myles," she said, her voice thick, "and your meal." With a proud lift to her chin, she added, "MacAdoo's close by."

"And you, Suisan?" he queried softly, suddenly aware of a deep sense of sorrow within her. "Where will you be?"

She swallowed visibly. With more bravado than he expected, she declared, "I'm off to my room to fetch my favorite mobcap."

Uneasiness crept over him. "Your room?"

"Aye," she snapped, her head held high, her shoulders squared, "to my room. This tower," she waved a hand about the circular room, "can be loosely termed a guest chamber. At least during your brief stay."

In a swirl of pride and flaming red hair, she exited the room. Myles blew out his breath and rubbed his weary eyes. Damn! Why had he assumed she would obey him? Nothing was the same. Almost nothing.

His desire for her had not dwindled in the least. Neither the Tower of London, nor the threat of death had changed his feelings for her. Even the knowledge of her true identity could not bank the fire within him.

Suisan Harper, the beloved daughter of Sibeal and Edward. Suisan Harper, the precocious, six-year-old child whose greatest ambition had been to equal her mother's talent at baking scones. Suisan Harper, who, upon her mother's death, had become Robert's ward. Thoughts of foppish Robert spawned questions Myles was too weary to pursue. Suisan had come to London and taken back the patterns. Why had she let them go in the first place? And why did she view Myles as the thief?

Something was dreadfully rotten in Perwickshire—and it had been allowed to ferment for a decade.

Suisan Harper was not the woman in the oval. Suisan Harper was no homely lass pining away for a beau. She didn't know about the miniature; Myles was certain of that. Robert had tricked them both. But ignorance did not exonerate her, not by any means.

"Oh, no, my sweet," he growled and began removing his clothes. "You are mine." He chuckled devilishly. "Kiss your lonely bed adieu, Suisan Harper, for you'll not be sleeping alone."

✧ Chapter 16 ✧

With a loud thwack, Suisan slammed the cupboard doors. Several hours had passed since her confrontation with Myles but she was still burning mad. How could she concentrate on the important work ahead when her mind kept dwelling on him? How could she make the important decisions affecting her people if she couldn't manage the simple task of setting out the salt for the evening meal?

"Damn his miserable hide."

"And nail it to the privy door!" Nelly spat, putting down

a basket brimming with freshly cut mustard flowers. "'Tis what the scurvy rat deserves."

Suisan sighed. How could she ever hope to manage Myles during his stay if she couldn't even control her own tongue? Or her disturbing thoughts. What would her people say if they knew Myles Cunningham was the father of her child? Would the superstitious Highlanders view it as a sin? Would they reject her child?

"Imagine him bein' nettled at you," Nelly snapped, as she placed the flowers in a vase, "and all for stealin' back what belongs to Scotland. He's a nervy one, he is."

"He's also more than 'nettled'," Suisan said ruefully.

Nelly bristled like a mother cat protecting her kitten. "Did he hurt you?"

Suisan sighed, thinking how inadequate the word sounded when compared to the deep pain she felt. Myles Cunningham had done more than hurt her. He'd deceived her in the oldest way known to man. Distracted by his seductive words and skillful hands, she had allowed herself to become his victim. Part of the blame lay with her, she knew, but self-recrimination only added to her pain. He had gotten her with child—the one situation she had feared since becoming a true woman.

"Did he?"

Valiantly Suisan shook herself. "Nay, but he promised to 'humble me for my treachery'."

Nelly's mouth dropped open. "He's a bletherin boxhead. With the likes of him around, even them odd-lots you got as guests won't seem so peculiar."

"I'm not afraid of Myles, Nelly."

"Of course you ain't. You ain't ever been afraid of no one." Nelly pointed toward the castle door. "An' what's the filthy creature to do? Fight Dundas and all your men-at-arms?" Her smile turned wicked. "That'd be a story to put to song—the day that Sassenach Myles Cunningham learns the purpose and the point of a Highland blade."

"The situation won't come to that," Suisan said. "I won't allow it, and he probably won't stay."

"You've kept better men than Myles Cunningham out of

your bed," Nelly said proudly. "But . . ." she drawled, a twinkle in her pale blue eyes, "it ain't like I didn't warn you. I said he'd come after you."

"But you were woefully wrong about his purpose," Suisan retorted, angered anew. In spite of Nelly's prideful tone, Suisan had to admit she felt flattered that he had come. But had he truly come for her or to salve his pride? Either way, she had to be rid of him today.

"What did he say?"

Wanting nothing more than to forget her confrontation with Myles, and knowing Nelly was fair dying for gossip, Suisan cast her maid a cold stare. "I do not intend to recount our conversation to you, Nelly Burke. I'd sooner shout it from the highest turret."

Nelly's face fell, except for her bottom lip, which jutted out. "I only told Flora. I swear. 'Twouldn't be proper—everyone knowin' your business."

Suisan rubbed her aching temples. "Dundas knows."

"He should know, if you asked me."

"Oh, Nelly. 'Tis a mix, to be sure. And there's so much else to do."

Nelly's hand was warm and comforting on Suisan's arm. "Don't fret, milady. We can start the weaving tomorrow. Ailis'll stay in her room tonight and—"

"St. Ninian, help me," Suisan whispered. She had completely forgotten about Ailis. The reminder of her eccentric aunt only added to her problems. Once her life had been a comfortable routine. She knew whom to trust and whom to doubt. No more; Myles Cunningham and Uncle Rabby had seen to that.

"It ain't so bad as that," Nelly objected. "The tinker'll be on his way back to Glasgow tomorrow. According to Lady Buchanan, she and her lord will be leavin' for Inverness within a few days."

The other visitors were insignificant to Suisan, but she was deeply concerned about her aunt. "You bring Ailis down to the table and seat her next to me."

Nelly shook her head. "And what if Lord Rodent makes a scene? Don't take a soothsayer to know he'll want the place next to you. Since he did come after you and all.'' She paused, as if struck. "Or he might even want to sit at the head himself. If he goes that far it won't do to have Ailis get away from herself at the table.''

Nelly was right. Ailis had had time to warm to the visiting tinker and the Buchanans, but she would be wary of Myles. "Very well. Seat her beside you and put Dundas to my right. Leave a space for Myles next to Mrs. MacIver.''

Nelly chuckled. "Flora deserves it. And the others will be in the middle. If that don't send a message to Himself, nothing will.''

Relief washed over Suisan; relief tinged with a faint measure of satisfaction. "I'll dress myself tonight. You're to attend Ailis; be sure she's dressed properly.''

"Aye, milady. I'll see to her now,'' Nelly said and headed for the stairs.

Angrier than she'd ever been in her life, Suisan tried with all her might to accomplish the simple task she performed every day. With a still shaking hand, she scooped out another portion of precious salt then transferred it to a crystal dish.

Servants dashed about the hall, the men bringing in kegs of beer and placing additional benches around the table, while the women set out pewter plates and mugs, butter and jams. More than a dozen people would dine at the castle tonight, and most of them would be seated between Suisan and Myles Cunningham. Whatever his scheme, she intended to thwart him from the outset, no matter how angry he became. She would not do his bidding; she was mistress of her own castle.

She fought back the urge to yell and scream, to call him the bastard he was, to order him out of her castle and away from Perwickshire. But in the same breath, a part of her welcomed him. No matter that his clothes were soiled with dirt, no matter that he hadn't shaved nor cut his hair, no matter that the light of the devil shone in his eyes, her woman's heart still ached for him. She longed for circumstances to be different; she yearned to have him smile at her with affection. She wanted nothing more than to fling herself into his arms and confess that she hadn't truly wanted to leave him in London. What would he say if she explained how precious the *Maide dalbh* were to her? To the people of Perwickshire? To all of Scotland? Would he beg her forgiveness and promise not to steal them again?

Why had he stolen them in the first place?

The query puzzled her. Granted, King George offered a sizeable reward for the patterns, but the amount was paltry when compared to Myles's wealth. He didn't seem to be the sort of man to garner favor or seek recognition, and both would come to the one who found the *Maide dalbh* and delivered them to King George. What then had been the purpose for stealing them?

She still did not know, but intended to find out.

Sadly Suisan accepted the fact that she loved Myles Cunningham. Wearily she gathered the scattered ends of her wounded pride and resumed the menial tasks at hand. Resolutely she promised herself to do all in her power to stave off her desire for him.

She failed—miserably so, for when he strolled into the noisy hall later that evening, her heart lurched with longing.

Handsome was an understatement when describing Myles Cunningham, for every woman in the great hall, servants and guests alike, stared in awe as he approached. Dressed in a tucked shirt of sleek blue silk and soft leather breeches, too snug from a recent cleaning, he looked unbearably attractive, and perfectly at home. A wide belt with a golden buckle, studded with light blue stones, accented his narrow hips and powerful flanks. He wore his long hair in cavalier fashion, falling to his shoulders in thick golden waves. His newly grown beard, rather than disguising his elegant features, accented his blade-like nose and high cheekbones. The golden moustache turned up a bit at the corners of his mouth, giving the appearance of a smile, an expression he would not bestow willingly on her. The knowledge was unsettling. She chose not to explore it.

He radiated confidence, he exuded male appeal, and completely against her will, Suisan went warm inside. She had lain with this man. She had fed him morsels from her own plate. She had undressed him. She had bathed with him. She had lolled away the afternoon in his arms. She had writhed beneath him in passion. She had cried broken-heartedly at leaving him. How could she love a thief? Desire withered into depression. Slowly, mustering her courage, she rose and cleared her throat.

"Good eventide, Myles Cunningham," she said. The room went deathly still. She waved a hand toward the empty seat, "Please join us."

Their eyes met, and much to Suisan's surprise, the edges of his moustache twitched, as if he were trying not to smile. Striding to her side, he captured her unoffered hand and made a courtly bow. The moustache tickled her palm. A wave of desire flooded her senses.

Yanking her hand from his, she stepped back, hoping he would simply sit down and embarrass her no more. When he merely stood, a rakish grin on his face, she was baffled. Where was his vengeful rage of only a few hours ago?

Then she looked past the grin and into his rich brown eyes, and saw a stranger—an angry and distant man determined to bend her to his will. Disappointment soured her stomach; Myles was only putting on a show for her people! Men, she fumed, were more trouble than they were worth.

She gasped when he gripped her about the waist and lifted her off the ground.

"Good eventide, my love," he declared, loudly enough for the Frasers in Aberdeenshire to hear.

Behind her, Nelly cursed. A tankard slammed to the table. Holding onto his shoulders and holding back a scathing retort, Suisan submitted to his foolish display of devotion. What devious male ploy was this?

Over the feminine titters and masculine murmurs, he whispered, "I'll make a scene beyond your wildest expectations if you don't call your lackeys off. After tonight no one will think of me as your brother." He set her down, but wrapped a tightly muscled arm about her waist to prevent her escape. Following his line of vision, she saw the reason for his threat. Dundas and three other men were marching toward them.

Dundas pushed the others aside, his complexion as red as his hair, his expression as stormy as the Great North Sea.

Taller than Myles by several inches, and loyal to the Camerons for several decades, Dundas would not hesitate to defend his mistress.

Myles pulled her closer, all but cutting off her wind. "Smile," he hissed through clenched teeth.

She groaned a tribute to his cleverness. He'd forced her into a corner and she had nowhere to run. He'd promised revenge earlier in the day, and if she had doubted him then, she was not doubting him now.

Forcing a smile, she held out a hand to the master of her guard. "Dundas, this is Myles Cunningham."

The big man stopped. He shot Myles a challenging look, but when he glanced at Suisan, she saw a question in his eyes.

Myles extended his free hand to Dundas, and in a voice smooth as woodsy pudding, said, "Ah, yes. We've both aged, Dundas, but I remember you from Lady Sibeal's funeral. 'Tis good to see you again—under happier circumstances." Smiling down at Suisan he added, "You were away from the Castle with my lady when last I visited, wasn't he, love?"

Warily Dundas gripped Myles's hand. Suisan wished he would wring Myles's deceitful neck.

She seethed in silent fury as he addressed the other men. To Fergus, he related an old story about Nelly; to the other men, he joked about the rugged Highland terrain and the painful effects of spending so many days in the saddle. As they talked congenially, Suisan scanned the table. Aunt Ailis had moved close to Nelly; Mrs. MacIver had moved close to Ailis. Suisan felt a measure of relief at the obviously protective gesture toward her befuddled aunt.

"See?" Myles said, his arm moving from Suisan's waist to her shoulder, "even Suisan's making sport of my travail." Their eyes met. His direct stare belied the smile on his lips. "Behind that lovely face is a smile you'd like to deny," he touched her nose, "and I believe 'tis at my expense." He turned back to Dundas. "What say you, Graeme? Is my lady hiding a smile?"

He was charming her people, winning them over with

smooth words and the magnetic spell of his personality. But Suisan wasn't fooled; she knew this man too well.

Neither was Dundas fooled, she suspected, for in answer, he gave a careless shrug but his eyes were seriously taking Myles's measure.

Breathing deeply and hoping for the best, she said, "Mrs. Peavey won't be smiling if we stand here talking while the meal gets cold. Take your seats, ladies, gentlemen, Myles."

Much to her dismay, Myles led her to her seat at the head of the table. "We'll share, my dear," he whispered, "just as we did in London." Then he sat down on the bench and patted the small space beside him.

The urge to slap his handsome face and see him rolling off the bench was nearly Suisan's undoing. Damn him! He had skillfully maneuvered her into a defenseless position. Oh, he'd pay for this trickery, and he'd pay dearly. Dredging up a smile, she curtsied, swung her gown to the side and seated herself next to him.

"A toast," Myles declared, picking up her mug and holding it high, "to Lady Suisan Harper, the fairest maid—" He paused. "Or rather, the fairest woman in all the Highlands."

Suisan gasped at the veiled insult and glanced quickly to the others to see if they had noticed. Nelly was speaking to Aunt Ailis, and Flora MacIver was examining the embroidery on her napkin. Lady Buchanan tittered and moued while her husband smiled indulgently. The tinker was holding his mug but his eyes were trained on Rowena. Dundas was speaking to Fergus. Suisan breathed a sigh of relief, for apparently no one else had caught the slight.

"To Lady Suisan Harper," the tinker seconded, even though his eyes were still riveted on the comely Rowena.

Hearty agreements resounded and the clink of tankards echoed through the hall. Rowena scurried around the table, refilling empty tankards and dodging the tinker. When the girl reached Suisan and offered to fetch another mug, Myles said, "Nay, Rowena. Suisan and I will share this one, won't we, my dear?" For Suisan's ears only, he whispered. "She reminds me of another serving maid I had once in London, a lass with jet-black hair and eyes as blue as the canopy over my bed."

At his pinchbeck grin, Suisan wanted to scratch his eyes out. She was keenly aware of his hard thigh pressing against hers, his masculine scent surrounding her. What would he do next?

"We will share, won't we?" he prompted smugly.

"Aye," she whispered, as impotent fury raged inside her.

He took a long pull, then held the mug to her lips. The imprint of his mouth was vivid. The blackguard intended for her to drink from the same spot! She did, and the memory of his lips on hers brought a dew of sweat to her brow.

Smugly, he turned his attention to the fare. He speared a leg of rabbit and waited patiently as Rowena filled the plate with savory vegetables. Spooning up a potato, he offered it to Suisan, saying, "Who are these people?"

"Visitors. *Invited* guests."

Cocking an eyebrow, he assumed the imperious expression she had come to know intimately. "And the woman sitting between Nelly and Mrs. MacIver?"

"A distant relative," Suisan answered, averting her eyes. Myles hadn't bothered to read her letters. Like everyone outside of Perwickshire, he believed Ailis Harper died when a child.

"She looks a bit tame to be a Cameron relative," he said, lifting the other brow.

Candlelight danced in his brown eyes; his golden hair and beard seemed to glow in the soft light. Suisan hated herself for thinking him handsome, and she loathed the way her body reacted to his nearness. "Nay. She does not use the Cameron name."

He looked to Ailis, who seemed engrossed in the meal and Nelly's conversation. Turning back, he said, "Open your mouth, Suisan."

Her name sounded like music on his lips. She opened her mouth and swallowed the bite of smoked salmon, but didn't taste it.

"Have I met her before?" Myles asked, watching her mouth. "When we lived in Aberdeen?"

Alarmed, Suisan swallowed and reached for the mug. Everyone outside the castle thought Ailis dead, but Robert had taken her from the asylum and sheltered her until after the death of Suisan's mother. Leery of strangers, Ailis had stayed in her room for the duration of Myles's earlier visit to Roward Castle.

"I doubt you've met her," Suisan said as blithely as she could. "She's only one Scotswoman. Why do you trouble yourself?"

A spark of anger flashed in his eyes. "Suisan," he began much too calmly, "I asked you a question. I expect an answer."

"You'll get no answers from me," she retorted, "not until you cease your play-acting."

"Play-acting?" A smile tucked the corners of his mouth.

"Aye," she seethed. "And I won't have it."

His gaze grew warm and with slow deliberation roamed her face, her shoulders and her breasts. She flushed, feeling as though his hands were caressing her.

"I think 'tis safe to say," he drawled seductively as his heated gaze continued to devour her, "that you *will* have *it*, my dear. And quite soon."

"You scoundrel!"

"Hmm. I must be making progress," he said cheerfully. "'Tis better than the last name you called me."

She wanted to toss her napkin on the table and run from the room, but Cameron pride would not allow a cowardly retreat. Haughtily she lifted her chin. Somehow, some way, she would banish him from her life before he could hurt her again. "I want nothing from you. Why don't you just scurry off to your dream home in Cornwall?"

For an instant he looked confused. "Cornwall?" Then he shrugged, grinning wickedly. "When I have you . . . and the Highlands to explore?"

"You bastard!" she hissed, discomfited as never before.

His sighed and closed his eyes. "Tell me something about myself I don't know, Suisan Harper."

She felt a twinge of regret, but refused to let it get the better of her. He might have dictated to her in London, but she was determined to have the upper hand in Scotland. She needed no man, least of all the smooth talking and crafty Myles Cunningham. Pride carried her through the meal.

Myles engaged everyone at the table in conversation, with the exception of Nelly, who ignored him, and Ailis, who fearfully bobbed her head aye or nay, but did not speak.

Fergus conversed freely with Myles, and Suisan suspected they had become fast friends during Myles's visit last fall. Somehow Suisan wasn't surprised by that; like most people in Perwickshire, Fergus was ignorant of Myles's evil deeds.

When the table was cleared, Suisan stood. "Thank you all for honoring us with your presence. Until the morrow, then." Before she had walked two steps, Myles was at her side.

"I'll go with you," he said and snared her arm.

She cast a worried glance over her shoulder, and was relieved to see Dundas headed toward them.

"Dundas always sees me to my chamber," she hissed. "'Tis his duty."

"Was his duty," Myles replied in a tone that brooked no argument.

"Are you challenging my sergeant-at-arms?" she asked, itching to slap that confident grin off his face. "He's twice your size."

Drawing her closer, Myles whispered, "But I've twice the reasons to want you alone, don't I?"

Suisan held her breath. Did he guess about the child she carried? Why else would he use the word 'twice'? She wondered how far he would venture in his bid to embarrass her. Very far, she decided as he pulled her along, completely ignoring Dundas, who walked several paces behind them.

When they reached her door, Myles started to follow her in. Dundas cleared his throat; Myles ignored him. But the scraping of steel against steel as Dundas drew his sword got Myles's attention.

"I'll show you to your room, sir," Dundas said mildly.

Myles stiffened his back, and in the dim candlelight of the hallway, his expression grew cold as the moors in winter. The new beard accentuated the stern set to his jaw. Suisan shivered, wondering which man would give ground first. She hoped Myles would, for Dundas stood ready to defend her. The sooner Myles learned that lesson, the better off he'd be. She only hoped he wouldn't force Dundas to violence.

Dundas took a step forward. Myles held his ground.

"Good night, Myles," Suisan quickly put in, "and sleep well."

He turned that rigid gaze on her, but instead of being frightened or angry, she once again thought of how handsome he was, of how giddy she felt at seeing him again.

He must have discerned her thoughts, for his beloved face broke into a dashing grin. Leaning close he kissed her ear and whispered, "The first battle to you, Suisan."

The warmth of his breath brought a weakness to her knees but the ominous statement, though softly whispered, raised her ire. She should hate him, but by all the saints in heaven, she could not. She didn't trust him, though.

The conflicting emotions were tearing her apart. Cameron pride took the fore—pride and the solid presence of Graeme Dundas.

She lifted her chin high. Her eyes met Myles's and what she saw completely discomfited her. Desire, thrilling and familiar, shone brightly in his eyes.

"Until the morrow, Myles." The words sounded breathless to her own ears. Confused and apprehensive, she sought the safety of her room.

Myles stared after her and stifled the urge to dash inside and bolt the door. Lust settled in his groin and simmered like a well-banked fire. Good God, he wanted her, and from the look in her eyes and the tone of her voice, she wanted him, too.

He thought of Dundas, the proud Highland warrior defending his mistress. Resolutely, Myles decided this war might be a long one. But he didn't care; he had all the time in the world to ferret out her motives. He'd done without her for months, and although his body protested, he could wait a little longer.

Turning, he faced Dundas. "Put your sword away, man, there'll be no weapons drawn in this contest." He smiled crookedly. "Unless perhaps 'tis the sting of a woman's tongue."

The sword disappeared into the scabbard but Dundas's expression did not change. "I'll defend her with my life," he pledged.

Myles chuckled and walked toward the stairs. "I don't think you can protect her this time."

It was the Highlander's turn to laugh. The deep sound echoed off the stone walls. "And who do you think has kept Lachlan MacKenzie and all her other suitors at bay since she became a woman?"

Myles stopped, completely taken off guard. Suisan wasn't plain and homely as he had been led to believe; she was a prize any man would treasure. Robert had obviously lied about paying MacKenzie to court her. Jealous rage erupted inside Myles when he thought she might love someone else. He remembered the gift she had purchased. Turning back to Dundas, he said, "Robert Harper swore he paid this MacKenzie to court her. Does she welcome his suit?"

"Harper lies." Dundas extinguished a candle. When he turned back his face lay in shadows. "She's welcomed no man's suit. Until now."

Mollified, Myles asked, "Tell me of this MacKenzie."

"He's our neighbor to the north," he said proudly. "His family hails from Cromarty, but after Culloden, his dukedom was forfeit."

"But he managed to get back Longmoor."

"Nay. The English refused him his estates but allowed him to buy Longmoor Castle—at a steep price. He's not so poor as to take money to court a woman. He can have, and generally gets, any woman he favors."

Myles's mind worked feverishly to overcome the jealousy and to think logically. Suisan had come to his bed a virgin, so she'd avoided MacKenzie's lust. But why then had she brought him a gift from London? And why had she yielded so easily to Myles? The answer echoed in his mind and soothed his pride: she loved him.

Dundas declared, "I wouldn't be smilin' too much, Cunningham. Lady Suisan's a bonny lassie. She could have had the MacKenzie for her laird—if she was wantin' a husband."

"Are you saying she does not want a husband?"

"Of course, she doesn't. But all that's changed—" Dundas

stopped suddenly. "Follow me," he grumbled, "I'll show you to the north tower."

Myles fell into step, but his mind was fixed on what Dundas had almost said. "What did you mean, about the changes? What's changed, Dundas?"

He said nothing until they reached the gallery. "I'll not be carrying tales like Nelly Burke. You'll get no more from me. 'Twill come from Lady Suisan or not at all."

Curiosity burned inside Myles. Was it the patterns, or Robert's counterfeiting of her cloth? "What, exactly, will come from Lady Suisan?"

"I've nothin' more to say," Dundas ground out, his angry words thick with the Highland brogue.

"Would this MacKenzie have anything to say?" Myles asked, his gaze drilling the soldier.

"Of course not, he wouldn't know about the—" He stopped again and Myles suspected the answer he wanted was only a breath away.

"Know about the what, Dundas?" Myles demanded.

Legendary Highland pride, immortalized by bards and scholars, shone fiercely in Dundas's eyes. How had these people fallen to the English, Myles wondered.

They stood side by side. The Highlander's large hands gripped the gallery railing and when he turned to Myles, his expression was grim. "Why do you claim Lady Suisan?"

"Because she's mine."

Dundas's expression changed to one of amused curiosity. "Ah, so that's the way of it," he murmured. "You love her, do you?"

Myles knew he should be silent, but God help him, he could not. "Love her?" he growled, staving off the pain of her rejection. "For ten years I had been tricked into believing she was a mush-faced twit. Then she slipped into my home, sent me to the bloody Tower of London and all but wound the hangman's noose around my neck." Myles, too, gripped the railing. "Be loyal to her if you will, Graeme Dundas, but by God, she is mine!"

The Highlander looked away. Pensively, he gazed out over the railing, then to the stuccoed ceiling. When he faced Myles again, his expression spoke of determination. Quietly, he said, "You'll get no more interference from me—not if you win her fairly."

A gasp sounded from the shadows. "Who goes there?" Dundas demanded.

A foot appeared in the pool of light, then the folds of a skirt.

"I shoulda known 'twas you, Nelly Burke," Dundas growled. "You'd brave a Highland storm for a scrap of gossip."

As Nelly approached, Myles was reminded of a dark night in London and a pistol-wielding maid. "It was you," he accused. "You were in London with her."

"Aye, 'twas me," she snapped, "and if I had that pistol now I'd blow yer bloody brains out, hard as they might be to find." She glanced pointedly and proudly at Dundas before adding, "You're a fool, Myles Cunningham, to stand on Roward soil and tell such lies about Lady Suisan and her uncle. *You* slithered into Scotland last fall and *you* played the thief. She had to go all the way to that rat trap you call London, and play the lowly servant to take back what rightfully belongs to—"

"Hold yer tongue, Nelly," Dundas interrupted, glancing about the empty hallway. Lowering his voice, he said, "And hie yerself to bed. You've said aplenty."

She gasped in anger. Leaning close to the soldier, she said, "If you were man enough you'd draw that sword and use it proper, instead of promisin' to aid this—" She shot a heated glance toward Myles. "This Sassenach. Then we'd all of us be safe again."

She spun around and disappeared through a dark doorway.

"The north tower's this way," Dundas said, pointing to a doorway.

Shaking himself, Myles fell into step beside the soldier. As they walked, he tried to sort out Nelly's words. Why would that sharp-tongued maid think he had stolen the *Maide dalbh*? Good God, the relics were the kiss of death. They were in the castle, he was certain of that. But where? He had to find the infernal things and destroy them.

When they reached the chamber, Dundas pushed the door open. "Don't judge Lady Suisan too harshly. She's relied on Robert Harper since her mother died. You've hardly spared her any time at all."

Their eyes met, and Myles gritted his teeth at the protective expression on the Scotsman's face. "You all believe Nelly's tale, don't you? You all believe I ignored Suisan all these years and that I stole the tartan patterns."

"Only Nelly and I know about the *Maide dalbh*, and what passed between you and Lady Suisan in London." His expression turned fierce. "I ask you, for the good of Scotland, to let the matter drop."

Myles was taken aback. "Listen, Dundas. This was all Robert Harper's doing. He stole those patterns and planted them in my house to prove me a traitor. He'll do it again, or perhaps Suisan will be his next target. Where are they?"

Dundas said nothing.

Myles felt a suspicious uneasiness. Had Suisan yielded the *Maide dalbh* in the first place? The idea was too dangerous to consider. "Robert Harper swore he destroyed the *Maide dalbh*."

"Aye. When milady was but a bairn—a lonely bairn, since you left her here."

Anger surged through Myles. "By God, Dundas, I'll not be raked over by you! I did what I thought was right."

"English right," Dundas snorted.

"Explain yourself."

"I'm a Highlander. You know naught of our kind, nor of our land." Softly, he added, "nor of Lady Suisan."

Myles was moved by the truth of Dundas's words. But more, he was encouraged. Dundas seemed more interested in Suisan's private life than any danger the pattern sticks or Robert could pose.

Myles saw his opening and took it. "I've a yen to see if everyone here is as concerned with Suisan's welfare as you are."

Dundas tilted his head to the side, "Think you to win Lady Suisan's favor by courtin' her people?"

A smile curled the edges of Myles's moustache. "Oh, I'll

have her again, Dundas. Any way I can. And you gave your word you wouldn't interfere.''

Myles gave a casual salute, entered his chamber and closed the heavy wooden door. He poured a noggin of beer from the pewter pitcher left on the table, then seated himself in one of the large chairs and considered his situation. He'd been wrong in his earlier dealings with Suisan. She was as stubborn as her mother, and if he had any intention of breaking through that Cameron pride, he'd have to be very clever. Bullying her hadn't worked; wooing her hadn't either. Not yet, at least. His pride stung a little at that. But then he remembered the feel of her maidenhead giving way beneath him. His manhood strained against the tight leather breeches. He stretched out his legs to ease the growing discomfort. Images flashed through his mind; Suisan, straddling him in his London bed, her voice a throaty whisper as she pleaded for release. Suisan, shocked and delighted, when he insisted on taking her on the floor in front of his fireplace. Suisan, swathed only in a cloak of jet-black hair, perched on his bed and feeding him buttered scones.

A wistful vision came to mind. Suisan, regal and proud as any Highland queen, her soft hand resting on his arm as she led him down the stairs of Roward Castle to present him to the people of Perwickshire. Suisan, calling him her laird, and giving him strong sons to rule this rugged land. Suisan, being tricked and used by Robert Harper. Suisan, falling into Myles's arms when she learned the truth.

He was thirsty as never before in his life. The cool beer eased his craving for liquid. But then he was hungry. Hungry for a red-haired lassie he would call his wife; hungry for a place to call home, a Scottish place called Perwickshire.

Determination ran strong in his blood. He would win Suisan Harper and protect her from Robert, but first he would win over her people.

~ *Chapter 17* ~

Myles stood in the rock-strewn road and gazed out over the countryside. To the south lay Glasgow; to the west, Inverness; to the north, Moray Firth; to the east, Roward Castle. And Suisan.

Since his arrival a fortnight ago, she had skillfully avoided his attempts to get her alone. She seemed ignorant of Robert's involvement in the theft of the pattern sticks, and each time Myles broached the matter, she changed the subject. In public, she was gracious to Myles. In private, he knew, she wouldn't trust him with a farthing, let alone her heart. He intended to change all that, but first he had to find the tartan patterns. Each night he silently scoured the castle, but to no avail. Perhaps she kept them in her chamber. He laughed at that, for if it were up to her, he'd never set foot there.

Behind him, Dundas barked orders to several men who had stopped to help clear the ancient road. Jagged rocks, recently fallen from the rain-soaked craggy hill, spilled over the thoroughfare and made passage impossible. One brave wagoneer, anxious to reach Roward and the upcoming celebration, had tried to negotiate the rocky way. His dray had been moved aside, the axle bent, the back wheels splintered. His wife and children waited under the shade of a nearby sycamore.

Sweat beaded Myles's brow. Using the sleeve of his borrowed tunic, he wiped the moisture away. The homespun fabric was soft to the touch, and although a size too large, the garment was comfortable beyond any he had ever worn. Of nubby cotton, dyed the color of sand and embroidered with tiny brown thistles, the tunic was beautifully woven and sewn.

"Wear it," Dundas had said, handing Myles the shirt. "'Tis fair enough, and more serviceable than your French-man's silk." Lowering his voice, he added, "But nothin' takes the place of a Highlander's plaid."

It always came back to that, Myles thought. In the High-lands of Scotland, the plaid and the tradition it represented were valued above all else. Sibeal Harper had spoken so. Neither the passage of time nor the bloody battlefields had changed the Highlands and her people. Was he wrong to want to see the *Maide dalbh* destroyed? Should they be guarded in spite of the danger?

Turning his face to the wind, Myles surveyed the land he had once thought rugged. Starlings and thrushes worked tire-lessly to bring food to nestlings in nearby birches and firs. Shaggy longhorned cattle, native to the Highlands, grazed on the sweet flowering clover that blanketed the open fields. Wild marigolds carpeted the meadow, the patch of golden-yellow flowers so odd-shaped Myles pictured some giant hand flinging the seeds to the wind. The hills beyond shimmered purple with ripened heather.

How, he pondered wistfully, could anyone term this land harsh? The Highlands of Scotland, notorious for fierce and stubborn clansmen, smelly sheep and ancient stone fortresses, were in reality a palette splashed with the finest color and beauty nature had to offer. Not the maple forests of the Col-onies, golden orange in fall, nor the valleys of Europe, lush and fertile in spring, could compare to the wild splendor of the land before him.

London had never been home, and his elegant house was no more than a place to stay between voyages, or an expensive setting where he garnered favor with influential noblemen. But Scotland was seeping into his soul, calling to him, chal-lenging him to find fault with her bounty. He simply could not. He wanted to plant his feet in this land, to join the legions of others who had called Scotland home. He wanted his children to be born here.

But first he must win Suisan Harper. And win her he would. She'd loved him in London, she'd love him here. With time and patience he'd revive her love, and pray God she relented soon. His body ached for her, his heart longed for her.

A horse nickered behind him, the high-pitched sound harmonizing with the low and musical tones of Gaelic, the language Dundas and the others were speaking. Sibeal had taught Myles the Highland tongue years ago, and although he didn't remember every phrase, he recalled enough to understand the gist of their conversation. Dundas wanted to use the man's horses to help clear the road. With one last look toward Roward, Myles picked his way through the fallen rocks and returned to the others.

He stifled a chuckle at the scene before him. The three men were busy rigging the horses for the task ahead, but the horses themselves were the cause of Myles's mirth. Legendary for their massive size and notorious for their gentle dispositions, the pair of Clydesdales dwarfed Dundas and the others.

Their coats glistened like roasted chestnuts; their long manes and tails fluttered like ripened wheat in a summer breeze. They might have been some storybook team wearing garlands of flowers and drawing Gulliver's own carriage. Only their massive hooves, the long hair muddied from a trek through some Highland stream, gave evidence of their role as working animals.

And work they did. Yokes, fashioned of wood and covered with cowhide, were draped about the Clydesdales' necks. Lengths of chain, wrought from precious and imported iron, were attached to the yokes. A large log, long denuded of limbs and bark, was chained to the horses and pulled rake-like across the cluttered road. The Clydesdales were led back and forth over the road, the wayward rocks pushed aside with each pass.

Someone called his name. Turning toward Roward, he saw MacAdoo approaching. The boy's mount seemed pony-like compared to the massive Clydesdales. Huffing, the lad jumped down, tripping over a rock in his haste to reach Myles.

"Steady there, lad," Myles said, chuckling.

Redfaced at his clumsiness, MacAdoo cleared his throat. "'Tis the mistress, sir. She sent me to fetch you to the castle—" he paused, gasping for breath. "Said she'd have your head on a pike if you dawdled."

Work behind Myles ceased. The men awaited his reply to the summons.

Masking his mirth at the regally worded and very familiar threat, Myles replied, "Tell Lady Suisan I'm engaged." He waved a hand toward the group of men and the Clydesdales. "Tell her I'll come in due time."

The boy's mouth dropped open. "But, sir," he stammered, glancing to his father for support. "She said to fetch you *now*."

Dundas let out a whistle; the other men exchanged quiet comments. Myles crossed his arms over his chest. With exaggerated patience, he said, "Tell her I can't come now, MacAdoo,"

"Aye, sir," The boy said. Frowning, he cast Myles a skeptical look before whipping the Highland pony into a gallop.

Doing all he could to hide his excitement at Suisan's desire to see him, Myles returned to the others.

"'Tis that damned, meddling Nelly, I trow," Dundas said, leading the Clydesdales again.

Myles merely grinned and again bent his back to the task of helping to clear the road. Sooner than he expected, MacAdoo returned, his mount lathered from the break-neck ride.

"Milady says," the boy began, as if reciting a lesson, "if you don't get your deceitful Sassenach hide to the castle, she'll boil Will'am in oil." A vigorous nod concluded the message.

Scratching his head, Myles pretended surprise. "Hmm." He rolled his eyes. "Methinks the lady is miffed."

Hearty laughter rang out behind him.

"Oh no, sir," MacAdoo quickly cut in, "she's madder'n MacIver's prize ewe on shearin' day."

"Well, in that case, I don't think I'll go at all."

The boy sucked in his breath, then let it out in a rush. "Oh, please come, sir. She'll have my hide, too, if'n you refuse."

"We're done here," Dundas said, coming to stand beside Myles. "Take one of the Clydesdales." He smiled and winked. "'Twill make the ride more interesting, an' don't forget to send back the smithy and a couple of wheels." To his son, he said, "Well done, lad."

Still feigning indifference, Myles mounted one of the horses and followed MacAdoo down the road to Roward. He was surprised at the speed of the massive horse, and although his legs ached a bit from the animal's wide girth, Myles soon adjusted and let his mind ponder the conversation to come.

He had only seen Suisan angry once. In London after she disobeyed him and left their bed without first waking him. Her Harper-blue eyes had flashed with defiance when he rebuked her.

Now her Harper eyes blazed with anger when he entered her solar. Her back was stiff, her glorious, unbound hair swishing as she paced back and forth giving orders to Nelly, who sat cross-legged on the Turkish carpet—the carpet he'd sent Suisan years before. Seeing the rug gave him pause. He'd accused her unjustly of selling the thing, but any guilt he felt was overshadowed by excited apprehension when she turned to face him.

The finely made dress she wore was cut low enough to tease another man with a hint of her wonderfully full breasts, but Myles remembered perfectly well what she looked like beneath the frock, every line, every contour. She was different, though, he had to admit, and the difference had little to do with her Cameron hair or her fine clothing. She was confident, she was regal, and much to his dismay she seemed completely in control of the situation. Still, he couldn't help but smile at the lovely picture she made.

Her color was high but her voice was low and carefully modulated when she looked straight at him and said, "Take the stripes to Mrs. MacIver, Nelly. We'll choose the other designs later."

Nelly cast Myles a venomous glance before gathering up the bundles of wooden sticks.

Remembering Sibeal Harper and her treasures, Myles couldn't help but ask, "Are those the *Maide dalbh*?"

Nelly laughed. Suisan looked at him scornfully. Myles congratulated himself for his earlier appraisal of Suisan's mood; her dudgeon was indeed as high as her color. His wish for an end to her indifference had obviously been granted. Still, he did not relish being laughed at by Nelly Burke. To Suisan, he said, "I asked if those are tartan patterns."

"Of course they ain't the *Maide dalbh*, you daft heathen Englishman," Nelly spat over the hollow rattle of wood as she gathered the sticks together. "Your English King'd hang us proper for keeping the tartan patterns, don't ye ken? These are Lady Suisan's patterns." She indicated a swatch of striped cloth attached to the end of one of the pattern sticks. "You of all people ought to know these ain't the *Maide dalbh*—"

"Nelly." Suisan cut in, her voice quietly commanding.

In a rustle of skirts, Suisan walked to Myles's side. He stared down at her, and the first word that came to mind was . . . lovely. He felt himself go soft inside. On the outside, however, the effect was completely opposite. His eager body, so long denied the pleasure of her own, responded with undisciplined quickness.

When Suisan's face flushed under his scrutiny, he cleared his mind of the lusty thoughts and forced his body into submission. "Send your maid away, lass," he said.

"Don't order me about!"

"Then let her stay," he said, exasperated. "Or throw open the castle doors so all can hear. I care not. But know this well, Suisan Harper. We will have this out and we will have it out now."

"I won't leave you alone with this heathen," Nelly said bravely.

Suisan was near the breaking point. She would not allow Myles a foothold at Roward. Not with Nelly, and certainly not with Dundas and her men-at-arms. Myles must leave the Highlands today.

Tomorrow was Brownin' Day. If Myles were here she couldn't tell the story about a dead husband. He must not learn of the babe she carried or locate the *Maide dalbh*. "You'll do as I say, Nelly Burke," Suisan spat. "Off with you."

Indignantly, the maid got to her feet and hoisted the patterns to her shoulder. Sample swatches of cloth, some striped, others checked, dangled from the end of each stick. Nelly's face was flushed from the weight. Myles was reminded of a Highlander carrying his forbidden bagpipes, a picture he'd not seen since his youth, a picture he would never see again, thanks to the King's edict.

After whispering something to Nelly, Suisan shooed her maid into the hall and closed the door. Then she turned and walked toward him, her hips swaying in that same, delectable way. She was smiling that delightful little smile, and Myles felt his eager body respond. She was more than meeting him halfway; she was coming to him. He could afford to be magnanimous with her. She obviously wanted to end the riff between them.

With a loud smack, her palm connected with his bearded cheek. Pain rang in his ears and tiny points of light flashed in his eyes. Hellfire, the lass packed a punch even big Tory Watkins would envy.

Grabbing her wrists, Myles held her at arm's length, for he could tell by the firm set of her lovely jaw she wanted to slap him again.

She tried to jerk away, her breasts heaving, her mouth taut with anger. "Let go of me, you miserable churl," she spat, her eyes blazing with anger. "And take your detestable self back to London where you belong. I don't want you here. I don't want—"

"Silence!" He cut short her hurtful words. She did want him. She loved him; he knew she did. Once he proved Robert was at fault, she'd welcome him with open arms.

"Stop it! Let me go," she hissed, deathly afraid he would charm her again. Even though she loved him, she could not expose her people to the devil he had become.

He held her fast, growling, "Nay."

Lovely eyes grew wide and Myles found himself fighting the urge to kiss her. She was a feisty one, as emotional in anger as she was in passion. His loins ached at the thought.

Her foot slammed into his shin; Myles stepped back, passion fleeing as pain darted up his leg.

She wrenched herself from his grasp, but did not move away. Her expression was smug, as if she were pleased with the blows she'd dealt him. "You may leave on your own," she began regally, "or I'll have my men escort you to the border. The choice is yours."

He had once suspected she was as stubborn as her mother; now he was certain. In an exaggeratedly reasonable tone, he said, "Are you afraid I'll cause trouble between you and Lachlan MacKenzie?"

Her eyes grew wide, then narrowed. "I had no troubles before you came into my life."

"That may be true, Suisan, but you never had Roward Castle, either. Did you?"

"You are daft," she said. "First you tell Dundas and my maid that I sent your worthless hide to the Tower of London, and now you speak this drivel about my family home."

"'Tis not precisely *your* home, Suisan," he said as reasonably as his emotions would allow.

She blinked, unable to discern his means or his motives for such a ridiculous statement. "Roward Castle has been home to the Lochiel Camerons since you Sassenachs were living in caves! You have no power here."

Smiling, he tilted his head to the side and said, "Oh, but I do. I can and will stay as long as I please."

Her back stiffened. "Are you threatening me?" She waved a hand about the room. "Here?" She looked indignant. "In *my* home?"

Deciding now was as good a time as any to reveal his promise to her mother, he said, "Roward Castle is mine, Suisan. Has been since your mother's death."

The color drained from her face. Had he the power to take her home? Dear God—he had taken her heart, gotten her with child. What more could he do? Bewildered, she opened her mouth, closed it, then opened it again, but no words came.

"Suisan . . ." he prompted.

"But the land . . . the castle is mine," she said in a distant voice. "Uncle Rabby spoke to the King himself and bought Roward back."

Aching to touch her, Myles took a step forward. "Robert has done many things, but acquiring the castle for you is not one of them," he said softly. "'Twas a promise I made to your mother, Suisan. I pawned my inheritance to buy back the Cameron land," he explained. She glanced up quickly, her eyes alert. "Upon my death," he continued, "or upon your marriage, the land passes to you."

Her eyes glittered at that. Smiling a little, he said, "I don't have to guess which option you prefer."

"You're a liar and a thief, Myles Cunningham. You stole my property," she said defensively, her heart breaking over girlish dreams that could never be. "Then you wove some fantastic tale about being imprisoned in the Tower of London. Now you expect me to believe you are my benefactor." Spinning around, she turned her back to him. "I will not believe it! You have no proof."

He grasped her shoulders and brought her back to where she belonged. Then he leaned forward so they were nose to nose. "I did not steal your precious tartan patterns," he swore, his eyes boring into hers.

"Ha!" she scoffed. "How can you deny it when I saw them in your house with my own eyes?"

"But I do deny it," he said firmly. "I know how those patterns got there."

"You stole them, that's how. I know you did." But her voice lacked conviction. "They were right there—in your cellar."

"And you took them, didn't you?"

Sliding a hand beneath her chin, he turned her face back to him. Seeing her stubborn expression, he sighed. He was losing ground with her again. "Suisan," he began patiently, only to feel her stiffen once more. "Use your wits, love. Why would I risk stealing them?"

"How should I know what makes that addled mind of yours work?" she challenged, the late afternoon sun turning her hair to fire. "Next you'll say some Scottish sprites spirited the *Maide dalbh* away on wings of gold."

"No, Suisan." He smiled crookedly. "I say but the truth. Robert Harper stole your patterns."

"Uncle Rabby?" she scoffed. "Why would he want them?"

Myles gazed steadily at her, knowing she needed time to

absorb the shock. "He wanted them in my basement so I'd be charged with the crime of possessing them. 'Tis the truth, I swear it."

He saw the utter disbelief in her wide eyes change to doubt. "Nay!" She took a step back. "He is my blood kin. I won't believe it. I can't believe it of him." In a swirl of brightly woven linen, she turned away again. Her back was rigid once more, the curves of her body outlined to perfection by the beautifully tailored dress.

Myles's empty hands fell to his side. Disappointment twisted in his chest. She still didn't trust him. She was loyal to Robert!

He searched for some gentle and tactful way to make her see the truth, but each idea was quickly discarded, until he remembered the miniature. "I had thought my word would be enough for you, my love," he said evenly. "I had no part in switching your cloth. Have you forgotten that?"

Slowly, she turned around, her hands folded as if in prayer. "Nay," she whispered. "I accused you wrongly, and for that I'm sorry."

"But. . . ."

She breathed deeply. Her breasts swelled above the neckline of her dress. "'Tis settled now. I'll market the cloth myself."

"But you won't forget, will you Suisan? And you won't trust me either."

Her silence cut him to the core. "Very well," he said, willing to put the matter of the cloth behind them. "I've tangible proof of Robert's guilt."

"Proof?" She waved him off. "Ha! 'Tis another of your lies."

Smarting from the cruel remark, he turned, walked to the door and opened it. His lips tightened in annoyance, for Nelly was still there.

"Go to my room and fetch the miniature painting," he ordered. "'Tis in my—"

"I know where the bleedin' picture is." Her eyes narrowed. "You cheatin' wretch. It ain't enough what you done to Lady Suisan in London, but now you—"

"Leave off, Nelly!" he bellowed, his patience pushed to

the limit. "Get it now or I swear by all the saints, you'll be sorry. And don't ever listen at my door again."

"*Your* door?" she jeered, then muttered a vulgar Gaelic phrase which put to rest the question of his parenthood. She flounced off and down the hall. Myles reentered Suisan's room, his mind wrestling with the problem of where to start and what to say and how to do both gently.

Thoughts of the upcoming explanation fled when he spied Suisan standing by the bed, a pensive expression on her lovely face. The finely made dress was a compliment to her in every way. On a background of white linen were windowpane plaids of indigo blue, and within each square was a delicately embroidered bouquet of flowers.

Pride and compassion welled up inside him, pride for Suisan's talent at the looms, and compassion for her when she finally accepted the truth about her uncle. He must tread lightly when he exposed Robert. Clearing the thickness from his throat, he asked, "Did you sew your dress, Suisan?"

She seemed to shake herself from some deep thought. "Nay." She seated herself on the bed. "I've no talent with a needle. 'Tis Nelly's work."

"But you wove the cloth."

She looked down at the dress and ran a slender finger over one of the narrow blue plaids. "Aye, the design is mine."

"'Tis lovely," he said, in absolute truth, "and finer, I think, than any your mother attempted. No wonder you were so angry when you learned Robert had counterfeited your cloth."

She faced him, her regal head tilted to the side, her blazing hair falling over her shoulders. But her courage wavered. How could she be strong enough to force him from her life if he continued to find her weaknesses? "Please don't bring up my uncle or mother," she managed. "Not now."

Her eyes were intently searching his own. He held her gaze and willed her to see his sincerity. Looking at Suisan Harper was the most enjoyable pastime he could imagine, and only through sheer determination did he keep his place. He wanted to pull her into his arms and hold her gently. He wanted to—

The door banged open and Nelly stalked into the room. "Here!" She thrust the ornately framed oval into his hands. "Ye bleedin' English bounder. May the devil take yer black soul and drag you down to hell." Then she curtsied to Suisan and said sweetly, "I'll be in the kitchen, milady, should you be needin' me."

Suisan nodded. Nelly flounced out.

Myles sat on the Turkish rug at Suisan's feet. "Stay." He touched her arm when she started to rise from the bed.

Her eyes darted to the miniature, then to some point over his shoulder. He held the gold frame in both hands and studied the woman pictured there. The whey-faced lady bore no resemblance to the vibrant Suisan Harper. But how would she react to the truth?

"Do you know who this is supposed to be?"

She straightened. Her teeth toyed with her bottom lip. "Aye," came the soft reply. "I know who she is."

"Who?"

She shot him a look he suspected was reserved for recalcitrant servants. Exuding the dignity of a queen, she said, "'Tis the woman you intend to marry—the woman of your favor."

Watching her closely, Myles said, "Aye, 'tis *supposed* to be the woman I love."

There it was. A slight tightening at the corners of her mouth, and a glittering of tears in her eyes. His heart soared; Suisan was disconsolate over the possibility that he might love someone else.

"Robert sent this to me—after I asked him for your likeness."

Suisan went still inside. "'Twas a portrait my uncle commissioned, not a miniature. And 'tis not me."

"I never saw the portrait. I commissioned a miniature of you, Suisan, to take with me on my ship. Robert wanted me to believe this is your likeness."

"What trick is this? I don't believe he sent you this. Why would he do such a thing?"

Smiling crookedly and hoping for the best, Myles said, "He did it so that I would think you homely." In a lighter tone, he added, ''As you can see, I had good cause to call you plain. 'Tis why I wrote so often about finding you a husband.''

Looking up, she said, ''I still don't believe you. You never mentioned a marriage, not in the brief notes you wrote.''

''Brief?'' His patience was strung tight as a Welsh bow. He closed his eyes, blew out his breath, and said, ''Then what of my letter about the oval, Suisan? I wrote you my thanks and told you of the new frame. Have you forgotten that as well?''

''You wrote me no such thing!''

''Do you still have the letter?''

''Aye. All of them.'' She sprang from the bed and marched to the writing desk. From one of the pigeon holes she pulled a neatly bound stack of letters.

Swinging her long hair over her shoulder, she shot him a challenging look, then tossed him the bundle. ''I'm not some dull-witted country lass to swallow up your lies,'' she said, crossing her arms and lifting her chin.

Somewhere in the distance a hammer slammed against an anvil. The pounding rang loudly in Myles's ears. Here he was, alone with Suisan at last, and trying desperately to show her the truth. In his hand was a bundle of letters he'd never seen before. The hammer sounded again, ringing out a death knell to all his good intentions. God, how naive he'd been.

Picking up the oval, he placed the likeness and the forged letters on the floor. ''This is no more my writing than that likeness is you.''

''An' why is it,'' she began, her voice musical with the Highland brogue, ''I knew you'd be sayin' something like that.''

She would be hurt when she believed the truth at last. Catching her gaze, he prayed she would see the answer in his own. ''My letters to you were both long and frequent at first, but when you answered with hastily written notes about the crops and the looms—well. . . .'' He sighed, disgusted with the obstacles between them, and frightened that he might lose her. ''I wanted us to be as brother and sister, as we were before the death of your parents, before you moved here.''

She blinked, then looked back at him. On a half laugh, she said, "Dear God, Myles, 'tis true I reacted like the child I was when you left me here, but I was only ten. I'm an adult now, and not so doiled as to be believin' that drivel about brother and sister. 'Tis hardly pertinent, I would say, considering—" She stopped, a blush creeping up her cheeks.

His mind worked hastily to find the words to convince her. "Robert sent me the likeness and forged those letters. I'll send for him today if I must. I'm innocent, Suisan." Hoping to ease the animosity, he smiled ruefully and added, "My Sassenach heart is not so black as you believe."

In the next moment, he witnessed a detailed and intimate tutorial on the subject of Suisan Harper. Myriad emotions, ranging from disbelief to outrage, from pleasure to pain, crossed her lovely face. Only the one emotion he wanted, acceptance, was omitted. Only the one reaction he hated, denial, was what he saw.

"You're daft if you expect me to believe you."

"Then what of us, Suisan?" he queried softly, thinking himself a fool to lay his heart open to more hurt, yet unable to stop the words. "And what we made in London? Will you deny that as well?"

She gasped and her deep sapphire eyes grew wide with alarm, a reaction he hadn't expected. "Made? What do you mean?" she demanded, her eyes searching his.

He was shocked at the accusing tone of her voice, and tired of the verbal battle. If passion was their only bond, he would use it, until she accepted the truth and admitted that she loved him, too.

Rising, he held out a hand to her. "Suisan, come here."

She stepped back. "Nay."

"Are you afraid?" he asked.

Apprehension clouded her lovely face. "The only thing I fear is losing my home."

Hurt knifed through him, but he kept his expression bland. He would have her any way he could. "You know the way to keep Perwickshire."

She sighed heavily. "Aye. I must play your whore again —or marry." Resigned, she added, "Lachlan will be here tomorrow. If you like, you may speak to him of the matter then.''

Myles spat a vulgar word and pulled her into his arms. ''You will not marry this Lachlan MacKenzie,'' he bellowed.

Suisan stood her ground. She had no choice now. The story of a deceased husband was no longer feasible, not with Myles here, and in spite of her slapping him and insulting him, he had no intention of leaving. ''But I must wed.''

''Then you will marry me,'' he ground out.

Her heart was pounding madly, and her mind was a jumble of unanswered questions. ''You think I'd marry a liar and a thief?''

Had she not been so confused about his motives, she might have felt guilty at his wounded expression.

''Very well,'' he said much too reasonably, ''I'll send Will'am for your proof.''

Immediately suspicious, she said, ''Why not go yourself?''

''*Moi?*'' Golden eyebrows arched, and his eyes grew innocently wide. ''But I'm just getting to know you again. And I like it here.''

''Tis foolery,'' she said, past the point of logical thinking. ''You may have borrowed clothes from Dundas, and dressed yourself up as a Scotsman, but you'll never be a Highlander, Myles Cunningham. And I'll not fall in love with you again.''

Suddenly the ambience in the room changed. A chill raced up her spine. Blessed St. Ninian, what had she said?

He smiled the smile she remembered, the smile that had made her grow weak while in a crowded London shop, the smile that had sent Ollie Cookson limping from the room to leave them alone, the smile she would remember when she was old and alone.

''Love me again, Suisan.''

Then his lips were on hers, and nothing else mattered, for she was under his spell once more. As sure as the rowans would bloom in spring, she loved this man. He had coddled her as a child, taught her things as is a brother's role. And now, with familiar hands and loving mouth, he was bringing her to the peak of rapture, as is a husband's part.

His mouth twisted upon hers and she felt the soft silk of his beard on her chin. She touched a hand to his cheek and threaded her fingers through the new growth of hair. Then her hands slipped lower—to his broad chest and lean waist. Through the haze of passion, her hands told her mind he was thinner than before. Her mind answered that he was hungrier than ever before. He wanted her with what she deemed desperation, and though his kisses were not rough, she sensed an expediency about him.

Wooed by him, and dizzy with the knowledge that he needed her so, laughter and happiness bubbled inside Suisan. His powerful hands caressed her waist and his lips moved over her neck and shoulders.

"Will you take me to bed?" she asked, her mind awash with the feel and the smell of him. In answer, he pulled her bodice down to her waist. "Myles!" she gasped, "will you up my skirts and have me where I stand?"

His voice vibrated against her aching nipple. "I almost did that, as I recall—one evening in the cellar in London." He left a trail of warm kisses as he moved to the other breast. "But not today, love, and not here, for as you can tell," he rubbed himself against her, "my need for you is beyond inventive bed sport."

Feeling him, long and hard and ready, made her own desire soar like a pheasant hawk on a summer wind. She was empty for him, she ached for him, and she would die if she didn't have him soon.

He had stolen from her; he was the worst of all thieves, the best of all liars, but, God help her, she no longer cared.

In the next instant her dress whooshed to the floor and the soft summer air caressed her where her chemise had been. Anticipation pounded drum-like in her ears and clouded her vision. She felt her feet leave the ground and then the softness of her bed against her back and the warmth and the weight of Myles above her. His nubby tunic rasped against her skin while his hand worked between their bellies. Then he lay full length upon her, his weight shifting to his elbows and his hands cradling her face. His eyes were bright, the soft gold of the sunset dancing within the warm brown color she loved so well. Then he was sliding into her and urging her to lift her hips and ease his hurried way. She did so, eager and delirious to be one with him again.

His muscles strained and he grew taut above her while he pushed closer to the goal they sought. Against her ear, he gasped, "By all the saints, Suisan, you feel like home to me."

The combined assault of his persuasive love words and his hard driving thrusts took her breath away. He seemed desperate to deliver them both to the rapturous plane they had experienced so many times before. She gave herself up to his loving, and when he grasped her hips and pulled her fiercely to him, claiming her, branding her, she found the sweet heaven of release.

Drifting aimlessly amid the aftermath of pure bliss, she heard him groan her name, call her his love and swear he could wait no longer. Then in a pounding furious explosion, he poured himself into her.

Not until her breathing slowed and her mind cleared did Suisan realize he had not taken the time to remove his clothes. Straining, she looked down the length of his body. "God in heaven, Myles," she laughed, "you even have on your boots."

Lifting himself up on strong arms, he craned his neck to follow her line of vision. His eyes turned back to hers, twinkling with mischief as he cleared his throat and said, "So I have, lassie, but I was sorely distracted." He placed a chaste kiss on her nose. "'Tis your fault, most probably."

She gasped, delirious with pleasure at the familiar banter. "'Twas no doing of mine," she said with mock severity and shifted, trying to dislodge his still firmly rooted manhood.

He chuckled. "Keep that up, lassie, and you'll double your crime and treble your penance."

~ *Chapter 18* ~

Suisan awakened to the delightful sounds of squealing children, rowdy in their early morning games of peevers and chase. Chickens squawked, and she suspected some fat hen or cocky rooster had become the object of a turn at tag.

She stretched, and her foot connected with a leg, a long leg, a muscled leg, a leg covered with silky hair.

Myles.

The yawn in her throat became a thick knot of apprehension. Heart pounding, her mind still dizzy with sleep, she listened carefully to his breathing. Steady and deep, and precisely what she'd hoped for. Cautiously, so as not to wake him, she moved her foot and tried to twist her body away, but his arm lay across her waist.

Besieged by conflicting emotions, and perched on the edge of a bout of morning sickness, she lay still, willing her mind and her stomach to do the same. But try as she would, her mind continued to picture the last day and night's events, while her stomach tossed and turned at nature's whim.

She scanned the familiar furnishings. Her eyes rested on the bundle of letters and the small oval, both discarded like the ill tidings they were. Swallowing hard, she momentarily kept the nausea at bay, then focused on the oft-read envelopes. The newer ones were white, but toward the bottom of the stack, the papers had yellowed with age. A progression of years flashed before her face and she saw herself, an elated and expectant young lass of sixteen, ripping open Myles's letter, eager to see what special greeting he'd sent for her.

Tears stung her eyes, as they'd done that important day when Myles hadn't bothered to acknowledge her passage into womanhood. Even amid the clamoring celebration and well wishes of her dearest friends, the pain of Myles's neglect had stayed with her. That day had marked the turning point in their relationship, for Suisan. Never again did she squeal with delight when Rabby delivered Myles's letters, nor did she seek the privacy of her room to read the missives over and over again.

Wisdom prevailed from that day forth.

Over her shoulder, she spied his golden head.

Wisdom was not prevailing now.

Blinking back the tears, she tried to wish away the sad memory of her sixteenth birthday.

I did not write those letters, Myles had said.

Her stomach cartwheeled and her throat grew thick with nausea. *Could Rabby have done so many wicked things?* Cold sweat beaded her brow. Knowing she would disgrace herself if she did not escape the bed, she clutched Myles's thick wrist and gently lifted his arm from about her waist. He shifted and wiggled closer. She held her breath for a moment, then could wait no longer. Slipping from under his arm, she raced for the chamberpot and dropped to the stone floor. Closing her eyes, she surrendered to the roiling storm in her belly.

After a few agonizing moments, her stomach listed to an even keel. She felt blindly for the towel Nelly always left on a small table nearby. The wooden surface was bare. Before she could open her eyes, a blanket fell about her shoulders.

Out of habit, she murmured weakly, "Thank you, Nelly."

Receiving no reply, she glanced to her left. And saw a pair of very masculine knees. Groaning, she buried her face in the blanket, sat back on her heels, and waited.

Apprehensive of his mood, she braved a glance his way. His expression was dark as a thundercloud, and his eyes appeared almost black. In his hand was a dampened cloth. Water droplets splashed onto the stone floor, the sound echoing as loudly as a cannon blast.

"Are you all right?" he asked gruffly.

Angered by his seeming insensitivity, and embarrassed by the fact that she'd been thoroughly sick, she mumbled, "Bonny as the heather in July."

"Take the damned cloth," he said, extending the wet towel. His eyes darted to her naked stomach.

Misery clutched at her insides and she thought she might be ill again. His accusing gaze pierced her with the force of a Highland halber.

He opened his hand; the cold, wet cloth plopped onto her bare thighs. Without a word or a softening in his expression, he pivoted on a heel and walked toward the bed. His back was rigid, his naked flanks taut, and his hands balled into fists. Bending, he snatched up the oval. He hurled the small painting against the wall. A dull crack broke the silence and the porcelain. Separated from the frame, the miniature fell in a dozen pieces upon the rug.

Her breath caught. Her father had warned her of Myles's temper. For the first time she was seeing the full force of his rage. She was certain it was because he knew she was with child, and that knowledge must displease him.

In angry motions, he gathered up his tunic and trousers and jerked them on. Stalking to the bed, he grabbed the coverlet and carelessly tossed it aside. Plump pillows flew through the air. With a low growl, he reached for the mattress.

"Nay!" she said, clutching the blanket and walking toward him.

His head jerked around. "Where the hell are my boots?"

She stopped. The look in his eyes was deadly. He radiated anger, pure and raw and awesome. Gathering every bit of strength she possessed, she took a step. Cold eyes raked her from head to toe, pausing at her stomach.

"Stay where you are, Suisan Harper," he growled, "or you'll wish you had. My patience has fled."

Her own temper flared at his angry command. Placing a hand to her stomach she said, "And what will you do to me, Myles Cunningham, that you haven't done already?"

"Don't act so self-righteous, you deceiving little witch."

"I suppose 'tis all my fault I conceived your child. You, of course, had no part in it—save your unbridled lust."

His eyes narrowed and his nostrils flared. Overcome by bitterness and hurt, she lost control. She marched across the cold floor and picked up his boots. Cocking an arm, she threw them at him. One thudded against his chest, the other he caught in mid-air. Still, his eyes were affixed to hers.

With his hair falling to his shoulders, his beard shining golden in the morning light, and his countenance as angry as the devil's own, Myles Cunningham did look like a Highlander, an Englishman's fearsome picture of a Highlander.

Through a haze of wretched despair, she heard the castle gates creak open, and the jangle of harnesses and the clip-clopping of shod hooves. The people of Roward were welcoming the people of Perwickshire. How could she face the day's activities when such a strain lay between her and Myles?

"Why didn't you tell me you carried my child?" he said, his voice strained, accusing . . . and hurt.

She felt a rush of regret. He was right, but how could she have told him without revealing the truth about Aunt Ailis? She couldn't, so she used her best line of defense. "An' what would ye hae done then? Jilted that poor woman in Cornwall?"

His anger returned. "There *is* no woman in Cornwall," he roared.

Afraid that in that instant he was angry enough to do her harm, Suisan abandoned her pride and retreated. He must have seen her fear, for he closed his eyes and slowly expelled his breath. He was counting to some unknown number, trying to get hold of himself. Her father had taught them both that trick when she was but a child.

At length he opened his eyes and looked at her, a long and measuring look. "We'll speak of this later," he said.

"I think not."

"Then think again, Suisan Harper," he said, stuffing the boots under an arm and marching from the room.

She swayed, fear and alarm coursing through her. With a shaking hand, she grasped the bedpost. His ominous words and the implied threat echoed dizzily in her ears. What would he do?

The castle was filling with people. If he made an issue of their problems today, everyone in Perwickshire would know.

She bowed her head. Out of the corner of her eye, she spotted a piece of the oval lying face down on the rug. She started to turn away, but stopped when she spied writing on the back of the horrid thing. Frowning, she picked up the palm-sized broken piece and studied the letters. Unable to make out what was written, she quickly sought out the other pieces and sat down on the floor. Trying first one combination, then another, she worked at the puzzle with growing consternation until the oval was whole again.

Her heart faltered when she deciphered the inscription. Written in her Uncle Rabby's familiar and looping hand were the words: *Lady Suisan Harper, for Myles Cunningham, 28 February, 1759.* . . . The ghastly lie ended with, *Robert Harper, Esq. Aberdeen.*

A tortured cry rose in her throat, and she tossed the pieces to the floor. They fell in disarray, some face up, some face down, but even scattered as they were, she could still see the awful words. So, she thought, as despair seeped into her soul, Myles had been telling the truth; Uncle Rabby had lied all along. Dear heaven, why would he do such a terrible thing? She had trusted him and loved him, and he had used her.

Through a haze of heartbreak and confusion, she heard a commotion in the castle yard. She raced to one of the embrasures. Leaning out, she scanned the busy castle yard below until she spotted Myles. His angry strides cut knife-like through the milling crowd. His boots were slung over his shoulder, and slapped against his back with each step he took.

She opened her mouth to call him back, but knew he couldn't hear her over the crowd. And what would she say? An apology seemed inadequate when compared to the guilt she felt. She had misjudged him in this, but what of the *Maide dalbh*? He couldn't pretend they hadn't been in his basement; she knew better. He had come to Scotland to fetch the patterns, and dally with her. Like a fool, she had fallen into his trap.

Just as her angry lover reached the stable, she leaned farther out the window. A smiling Dundas stepped in his path and extended a hand in greeting. Myles knocked it away and continued his angry strides. Dundas was bearing the brunt of a fury he didn't deserve.

The people in the courtyard grew silent and all eyes seemed

to be trained on the stable. Horses whinnied shrilly from within the darkened building. Dundas waved his arms and shouted for everyone to get back. The throng parted on either side of the door. A sleek black stallion burst through the dark opening and into the light. A collective gasp rose from the crowd. Suisan's eyes focused on the rider. Myles crouched low over the horse, his hands grasping the flowing black mane and his legs gripping the animal's bare back.

Once in the open courtyard, he jerked the stallion in the direction of the gate. The animal reared; its powerful front legs pawed the air. Suisan's heart lodged in her throat. He roared a command to the horse. The animal immediately dropped his fore legs. Murmurs swept the group like wind through heather. Oblivious to his rapt audience, he again turned the horse to the gate. Just as the animal moved, Myles looked up. His pain-filled gaze tore at her heart. Before she could call out his name, he urged the stallion into motion.

Staring at the open castle gates, she wondered where he'd gone, when he'd return. A part of her longed to apologize, but how could she ever hope to heal the wound when Myles did not want the child? How could she trust him enough to reveal the awful truth?

She was still asking herself the same question several hours later as she strolled through the castle yard, mingling with the people of Perwickshire and pretending to enjoy the small-talk.

Smoke drifted from the large cooking pit where Mrs. MacCormick's steer was spitted and basted, and turned slowly over the fire. Kegs of fresh beer were stacked in front of the lorimer's shop, where blind Jake Keegan and his daughter, Jenny, took turns tapping the kegs and pouring the yeasty brew. Beside them, Gibbon MacIver tended the brewhouse, serving up ale, cider and whiskey. Throughout the castle yard were brightly decorated tables and booths, some offering breads or cheeses or pastries, others containing Pretty Polls and whigmaleeries for the children, and poultice makings and tonics for the adults.

Nelly sat on a barrel in front of the smithy, holding court with the gossips. Between sips of ale, she told of her adventures in Londontown.

Near the old well, Aunt Ailis sat on a milking stool surrounded by dozens of children, each waiting for one of her beribboned flower garlands.

In years to come, Suisan thought wistfully, her own child would sit near the well and hold out chubby hands for one of Ailis's special favors. Later, her child would ride a Highland pony in one of the races held on celebration days. And everyone in Perwickshire would love her child, even if Myles did not. Suisan shook off the heart-wrenching thought and turned her attention to the celebration.

Yet again she looked toward the castle gates, both dreading and hoping for Myles to return.

Dundas came to stand beside her. "I can send a man up to keep a lookout."

"Did he say where he was going?" she asked.

"Nay, and I wasn't fool enough to ask him. Nelly said he had the devil's own temper. She didn't embroider that at least. He'll come back, though, when he's cooled out—or remembers where he left his boots."

"Maybe he won't come back," she said, voicing the fear that had nagged at her since morning.

Dundas laughed. "If ye believe that, milady, ye've had too much of blind Jake's beer."

She fought the doldrums clawing at her insides. Putting on a smile she didn't want and conjuring a laugh she didn't feel, she said, "An' how could I be drinkin' too much of Jake's ale? Your men are lined up two-score deep just to have Jenny fill their tankards."

Dundas frowned, then said, "She's a bonny one 'tis true. An' Jake's blind in more ways than one." He glanced at the lorimer's raven-haired daughter.

"Perhaps Jenny's growing up at last."

Dundas smiled knowingly. "She's grown enough to torment all my men."

That was true. At seventeen, green-eyed Jenny Keegan had her pick of the men in Perwickshire. She flirted outrageously. Wearing a peasant blouse pulled off her shoulders, she leaned forward just enough to give the men around her a peek at her ample charms.

"She's forgotten Bartholomew Weeks," Suisan said. "I'm

told he's gone to Aberdeen for supplies, and praise God, for he upset Aunt Ailis.''

Before Dundas could speak, someone yelled. ''The MacKenzie! The MacKenzie!''

Suisan rolled her eyes and smiled. ''He's making a grand entrance again.''

The clamor in the castle yard was deafening. The crowd continued to cheer as they awaited the arrival of Lachlan MacKenzie. He was their favorite, and well he knew it. Suisan laughed, wondering what he would do this time. Taking Dundas's arm, she walked toward the gates to greet her flamboyant guest.

Lachlan rode a blood bay Clydesdale and carried a hooded falcon on one leather-clad arm. The horse's black mane and tail were braided with green and red ribbons, dried holly and gillyflowers. Lachlan had chosen braids for himself as well. In Highland fashion, he'd plaited his own hair at the temples. He wore neither bonnet nor badge, but Lachlan MacKenzie needed no ornamentation to announce his heritage.

Regally he grinned for the crowd, showing perfect white teeth set in a mouth and face so typical of his Highland clan Suisan felt herself swell with pride for him. His nose was long and narrow, the same as every man in his line. His forehead was broad and marked with slashing eyebrows a shade lighter than his brown hair. But more than the other features of his handsome face, his flaming red beard stamped his heritage.

''The MacKenzie! The MacKenzie!'' the crowd continued to roar. To the people of Perwickshire, MacKenzie represented the old ways, and even if he couldn't wear a plaid and call up the bagpipers, they knew him as a laird, a clansman—the kind of man they wanted for their own.

With the noble bearing of a monarch and every aspect of a true Highland laird, Lachlan guided the massive Clydesdale closer. When he reached her, he tossed the reins aside and, drawing a leg over the saddle, leapt gracefully from the horse. Sweeping her a bow, he said, ''Good Brownin' Day to ye, Lady Suisan.''

He was her friend; he was her neighbor. He was determined to make her his wife. She had always viewed his attention with a practical eye. Their lands adjoined, and she was the only woman between Roward and Inverness worthy of his social ranking. Had the Crown not taken his heritage, he'd be the reigning Duke of Cromarty.

"You look fit, Your Grace, as always. Welcome to Roward Castle." Out of respect, she curtsied.

Dundas came to attention and offered to take the bird.

"But don't be feedin' her," Lachlan said, "I've a mind to send her acourtin' a fat pigeon or two before the day is out."

"Aye, sir." Dundas smiled, accepted the falcon and walked away.

Lachlan moved closer. "You're the bonniest lass in all the Highlands, Suisan Harper." His lusty blue eyes examined her from head to toe. "'Tis good to hae you hame again."

Ignoring his intimate tone, she regarded him with amused tolerance. "An' did you miss me now?"

"Aye, as I miss Cromarty," he said.

"'Tis a pretty sentiment, Lachlan, but a bit dreepy, even coming from you." She patted his arm in a sisterly fashion. "I was hardly gone that long."

He covered her hand with his own, his expression endearingly earnest. "Seemed forever, me lovely. Did you truly go to London?"

"Aye, I did."

"Why?"

How could she answer him? Certainly not with the truth, for if Lachlan knew she possessed the pattern for the tartan of the MacKenzies, he'd hound her to weave one for him. He'd probably wear the garment, too, and get himself hanged in the doing.

Teasingly, she pointed to his belt and said, "To bring you back that spyglass."

He raised his brows at that. "'Tis a bonny gift, Suisan, and I treasure it. But I'd rather have you."

Accustomed to his bold declarations, she pulled her hand from his, and changed the subject. "'Twas quiet here, I'm told. With the exception of Seamus Hay fashing MacIver again naught happened while I was away.''

Lachlan chuckled. '''Tis a tradition, MacIver surrendering that ol' sheepdog to Seamus. At least Seamus and Gibbon don't go after each other with claymores the way their grandfathers did.''

"I'm lucky their feud has become less fierce," she put in, feeling comfortable with Lachlan MacKenzie, as she always did. "But if the dog's not returned by the harvest I'll have to step in.''

He reached for her hand again but she evaded him. He frowned and looked into the milling crowd. Even in profile, he possessed a face to turn women's heads and command men's loyalties.

Comfortable now that Lachlan's eye was roving, Suisan teased, "Have ye a thirst then, MacKenzie?"

"Aye, 'twas dusty on the road.'' The roving eye avoided her as he began walking toward the lorimer's shop. "Blind Jake's got the hang of brewin' beer.''

Suisan stifled a laugh. "He's also got a lovely daughter. Perhaps you should use your spyglass?''

"Aye," Lachlan said too quickly. He turned, gazing purposefully into her eyes. "If you'd agree to wed with me, I'd nae be lookin' at the lassie. And I'd nae use my spyglass on any woman but you.''

She felt herself redden, as he grinned and let out a lusty chuckle. Gossip said Lachlan kept a mistress at Longmoor Castle, and she believed the rumor. Others said more than a few children in his district bore a striking resemblance to him, but she'd never believed they were his, for he would have claimed them.

"With or without your spyglass, Jenny'll expect you to notice her," she said suggestively. Suddenly she saw him differently. She saw him through eyes that had witnessed a man's cruelty.

Lachlan had more than noticed Jenny Keegan, and if he didn't flirt outright with the lorimer's daughter, the silent message he conveyed was obvious to all—except blind Jake.

Lachlan was downing his second tankard of ale and gazing

at Jenny's breasts, when Dundas walked up. "'Tis time to bring out the vats, milady. If we wait the men'll be too drunk to do it up right."

She turned to Lachlan. "You will excuse me?"

He did, with the good manners of a man of his social standing. Suisan and Dundas started for the weaving shed. Unconsciously, she glanced toward the castle gates.

Damn Myles Cunningham! she swore to herself. *Damn his miserable hide to hell!* Even as she cursed him, she wondered if he would come back and give her a chance to apologize. But deep in her heart she knew that making amends wouldn't heal the wound. Nay, it would merely delay the inevitable. He had come to resume his affair with her and to steal the tartan patterns. He must go before he was sure of the child.

"Milady?"

At the sound of Dundas's voice, she vowed not to think of Myles again. She broke the vow at least twenty times in the next hour. Dundas and the soldiers rolled out the enormous dye vats and pounded off the iron bands. With axes, they chopped the wood into small pieces. With help from the children, they piled the wood in the center of the castle yard.

Once the weaving shed was swept clean, Suisan and Flora MacIver supervised the setting up of the looms. From the hundreds of commercial patterns, she picked several favorites. While fitting a floral pattern into the body of a loom, Suisan looked up and saw Dundas approach.

"He's back."

Her heart began to race and her palms went damp, but she kept her face calm. "Did you speak with him?"

"Nay, 'twas Nelly gave me the news," he said wryly. "He's ordered a bath."

Knowing she had a little time yet, Suisan took herself in hand. By the time the looms were set, she felt much more confident. By the time she left the weaving shed and walked into the noisy yard, she had herself under control. Having Lachlan and Dundas nearby added to her feeling of security. They stood near the small playing field, watching the sporting games. Some men tossed horseshoes; others arm wrestled for prizes.

"'Tis a good match," Lachlan said, indicating the table where two men were arm wrestling.

Both contenders were soldiers; one from Roward, the other from Longmoor. Their knuckles were stark white, their wrists coiled like snakes, their faces poppy red from the strain of the contest. The spectators cheered their favorites and upped their bets when their man gained the advantage.

"Aye, 'tis a fair match," Suisan agreed, "but my man will win."

Lachlan assumed a look of superiority. "If 'twere Dundas on your side, I'd be agreein'."

Suisan glanced up at Dundas to ask his opinion, but he was looking toward the castle doors. Following his gaze, she saw Myles strolling down the steps as if he were the laird of Roward Castle. Despite her efforts to remain cool, she felt her blood heat. But where was his anger?

His hair was still damp from the bath, and he'd donned another tunic of a better fit. She knew where he'd gotten the crimson garment, for she'd recognize Nelly's fine stitches anywhere. She was immediately upset with Nelly for showing him such generosity, and for choosing a color so complimentary to his dashing good looks. He wore the tight fitting leather breeches and bucket top boots; both accentuated his long legs and lean flanks. The other women were noticing, too, their whispers floating over the low drone of male musings.

Why shouldn't they be curious? Suisan thought. The scene he caused in the castle yard this morning had become the gossip of the day.

"I say there's Highland blood in him," she overheard someone say.

"Aye. He has the look of a Brodie. An' who else could handle a mount the way he done?" came the reply.

She felt a wellspring of pride; they were impressed with Myles Cunningham. They wanted a laird.

Much to her chagrin, he didn't even acknowledge her when he joined them, but addressed Dundas, "May I have a word with you?"

She was annoyed by his lack of manners, even if she did

feel ashamed of her earlier behavior toward him. Her uncle had lied and deceived them both, but that didn't give Myles the right to be rude—unless he no longer cared for her.

When they were out of her hearing range, Myles began to speak. His earlier anger appeared to be gone, and if she didn't know better, she might have only imagined his heated exit this morning. Perplexed, she wondered what he was talking to Dundas about.

"So that's him," Lachlan said bitterly, appearing at her side. "I've been hearin' tales today—tales about you and him."

"He's visiting from London."

"Rumor says Myles Cunningham's more than visitin' with ye. Hardly a Brodie, nor a man deservin' of their respect." Lachlan raised his voice. "Considerin' how he's treated ye o'er the years. If they knew what a bastard he is they'd be ashamed of themselves."

"Lower your voice," she hissed. "My uncle lied about him." At Lachlan's raised brows, she added, "In much, Myles is not the scoundrel I thought him to be."

"My grandfather had a sayin' about that," he mused, that charming air in full force. " 'Time will tell. Dung will smell. And water will seek its own level.' We'll see about this Myles Cunningham. I would be sure if he's a man of his word."

Suisan didn't reply; her attention was focused on Myles and Dundas. Myles seemed to be making some sort of speech. When he was done, he extended a hand to Dundas, who accepted the friendly gesture.

Once the traitorous pact was made, Dundas said not a word to her but walked purposefully toward the castle, yelling for Fergus MacKames as he went. Myles walked toward Suisan.

The spit over the cooking fire stopped turning. Horseshoes ceased to clang against the iron posts. A loud grunt followed by a hollow thud against the table ended the arm wrestling match. No one applauded the winner, nor chided the loser. Only the children seemed unaffected by the tension in the air.

Myles took her hand. Bowing from the waist, he turned her hand over and kissed the satin-like palm. "My apologies,

Suisan," he intentionally used the intimate address, "for storming away earlier."

Expecting her to try and pull her hand away, Myles held her tighter than necessary. He was shocked by the jealous rage he felt at the sight of her standing so close to the other man, the man Dundas had identified as Lachlan MacKenzie.

"You had a right, Myles," she said as if the admission were painful. "May I present Lachlan MacKenzie of Longmoor Castle?"

Myles bristled at the sight of the spyglass dangling from Lachlan's belt, but extended his hand. "'Tis a pleasure, MacKenzie."

The Highlander grinned confidently and grasped Myles's hand much too tightly. "Our Suisan's mentioned you . . . a time or two over the years, I trow."

More than anything else in the world, Myles wanted to slam his fist into MacKenzie's smug face and yank those braids out by the roots. Instead, he tightened his grip and said, "You have me at the disadvantage then, for she's never bothered to mention you."

MacKenzie's face turned red and he released Myles's hand abruptly. Suisan stepped between them. "Will you have some ale?" she asked glancing nervously from one to the other.

"Aye," Lachlan growled, "an' a turn on the boards." He jerked his head to the table where the men had been arm wrestling. "If the Sassenach's game."

Myles cocked his eyebrows in mock surprise at the boastful challenge, but he had to establish his position with regard to Suisan and the people of Perwickshire. Lachlan MacKenzie seemed the place to start. Wrapping his arm around her shoulder, he pulled her to his side. She gasped and tried to pull away, but he held her fast. "You're welcome to try my arm, MacKenzie, but understand the lady's favor is not in the balance."

The Highlander looked curiously at Suisan, then spun on a booted heel and marched to the table, his supporters gathering around him.

In a loud, clear voice, she said, "The winner lights the

fire." In the roar of the crowd, she hissed, "You're a dishonorable bastard, Myles Cunningham."

He bent his head and whispered, "But I did not lie. Your letters bore no mention of Lachlan MacKenzie."

A frown now worried her perfect brow. "Oh—and I saw the writing on the back of the oval." She bowed her head. "I never dreamed Rabby would do such a terrible thing. I was wrong and foolish to trust him."

Myles lifted her chin and gazed into her lovely blue eyes. He saw pain, wariness. He fought back the urge to pick her up, swing her around, and shout that she needn't worry, that he'd take care of her and their child. He felt a warming in the pit of his gut at the thought of being a father. A good father. A loving father.

Looking down at the mother of his child, he felt the tension ease. "'Tis in the past and better forgotten, love. Will you stand beside me now, and give me your support while I best the MacKenzie?"

"Do I have a choice?"

He wanted to say he'd take whatever she was willing to give until she learned to trust him again, but he could not. "Actually, no."

"You had no right to embarrass Lachlan," she said solemnly. "He'll make you pay for that. Even Dundas cannot match him on the boards."

Her grave expression gave Myles pause, and he smiled down at her. "Then you think I'll lose?"

"Aye," she whispered, smiling tremulously. "The MacKenzie's a braw Highlander."

"And what," he began, touching her nose, "my bonny, bonny lassie, do you suppose rugged sailors do to pass the time at sea?"

Her eyes grew wide with understanding. "They arm wrestle?" she whispered.

A blanket of pure contentment settled over Myles. "Aye," he breathed, "sailors arm wrestle, when they're not riding the whales or looking for mermaids."

"You're mocking me."

"*Moi*?" he asked, feigning surprise.

"'Twill serve you right to lose," she scolded prettily.

"What's so important about lighting a fire?"

She purred like a cat just come from the creamery. "Only a Highlander would understand."

He smiled to disguise the hurt her words had caused. "We'll see."

He released her, but felt her hand on his arm. "You can't shame him further, Myles. He's a proud man, laird of his people. He's different from you. You don't ken our ways."

"Then why don't you explain."

"He can't lose face."

"And I can?"

"Oh, Myles." Her voice held a patient appeal. "Lachlan's my neighbor, and will be for the rest of my life. I would have peace between our people. Do you ken?"

"Aye, and I'll still light that fire." *And win your heart*, he added to himself.

He had second thoughts about his boastful words once the match began. Lachlan might be the shorter man, but he was strong and skilled in the art of arm wrestling. And he tried his best to goad Myles into making a mistake.

"You'll dance at our wedding," he hissed through his teeth as he gained a slight advantage. His blue eyes glittering with anticipated success, he whispered. "An' I'll toss ye the bloody sheets, Cunningham, after I've made her mine."

Rage pumped through Myles. Scowling into his opponent's eyes, he rasped, "Difficult, MacKenzie, since I've beaten you to her bed and planted my child in her belly."

The Scotsman's jaw went slack; his grip wavered. Growling a feral roar of victory, Myles drove MacKenzie's arm to the boards.

"The Sassenach cheated!" someone in the crowd yelled.

Myles leaned close until their noses almost touched. Over the din, he said, "I love her, MacKenzie. And I'll kill any man who stands in my way. But she wants peace between our peoples." In Gaelic, he added, "So do I. Do ye ken?"

Eyes narrowed and doubtful, Lachlan said, "For a man

who talks of not wantin' trouble, ye've a boxy way of showin' it.''

Myles released him abruptly and turned to Suisan. He pulled her onto his lap. "Tell the MacKenzie we're getting married, love.''

Lachlan sat up straight and began rubbing his wrist. Those around him continued to complain of foul play. In a move more diplomatic than she expected of him, Lachlan Mac-Kenzie, deposed Duke of Cromarty and laird of Longmoor Castle, raised his arms and smiled to the crowd. "Settle down, lads. He played by English rules.''

The grumbling ceased.

"Tell him we're going to be married, Suisan," Myles prompted.

She ached to know what had passed between them. Lachlan looked every inch the jilted knight, nobly keeping his head high and jesting with those around him. Myles looked confident as he held her, yet she suspected his confidence came from something other than besting Lachlan at arm wrestling or shamelessly holding her on his lap. Men, she thought in disgust, will go to any ends to preserve their pride.

"Suisan. . . .'' Myles nudged her arm.

How could she agree? There had been so much deceit; so many lies lay between them. She could not wed Myles without first explaining her fears for the child and the truth about Ailis. Nay, she would have to tell him, if she became his wife. He might deal unfairly with her, but that didn't mean she would stoop to deceit as well. Most important, her people would have their laird for a while and her child would always have his name.

Sighing heavily and anticipating the worst of consequences, she said, "Aye, I'll marry Myles Cunningham.''

Lachlan drew a thumb and forefinger to his lips and let out an ear-piercing whistle. "Grab yer tankards, lads and lassies,'' he said, "and be quick about it. The Sassenach won the only way he knows how, and he's saved his English pride.''

"Englishmen got no pride!''

Lachlan roared with laughter. "Aye, Gibbon, there's some

truth to that. But he got milady. Nelly Burke!'' he yelled out, effectively putting an end to the squabbling. ''Fetch the Agreement Cup. Our own Lady Suisan has found herself a mate, an' we'll be givin' them a proper Highland salute.''

The hearty declaration brought the crowd to life. En masse, they cheered and called out for beer. A keg was tossed high, then seemed to dance on air as it was passed overhead from one pair of hands to the other. Jenny Keegan appeared with an overflowing mug of ale which she presented to MacKenzie, along with an inviting view of her cleavage.

''Oh ho, laddies!'' he roared, ''look at the bounty we have here.''

He accepted the mug, held it high, then downed the contents in one long swallow. Foam coated his thick red moustache. Tossing the mug aside, he grasped Jenny's waist and lifted her into the air. She squealed like a virgin, bringing a host of declarations to the contrary.

Taking hold of her blouse with his teeth, Lachlan yanked the flimsy garment down to her waist. While the men cheered him on with bawdy encouragements, he hefted her higher, setting her exposed breasts to bouncing.

''Ride 'er like the stallion ye be, MacKenzie. She's well-broke, an' hotter'n MacIver's randiest ewe in season.''

''Aye,'' Lachlan agreed, looking up into Jenny's smiling face. So saying, he buried his bearded face in her cleavage, shaking his head and growling like a lion on the prowl. His braids swung back and forth, slapping her puckered nipples.

Embarrassed by the bawdy display, and crushed that he seemed to forget her so quickly, Suisan despaired. For years, Lachlan had sworn his devotion and pledged his love. Even though she never planned to marry, she had expected resistance today. Now she faced the bitter truth: she meant no more to him than a score of other women. Men, she seethed, men couldn't be trusted nor counted on.

''What are you thinking?'' Myles whispered in her ear.

''I'm thinking I've just made a bargain I'll regret.''

''Don't say that.''

Tilting her head back until their eyes met, she studied his face. Lord help her if she trusted him again. ''I'm also thinkin' you've the luck o' the Irish, Myles Cunningham. An' that you should be thankin' Lachlan for being such a gentleman." Remembering the mention of bloody sheets, she added, "Well, except for that one wee slip of his nasty tongue."

"Oh, I do feel grateful," he drawled innocently. "And I'd love to slip *my* nasty tongue into your wee—"

"Myles Cunningham!" she gasped.

A fortnight later, in the great hall of Roward Castle, Suisan and Myles were wed. When asked if she would change her name from Harper to Cunningham, Suisan agreed. Deep in her heart she expected him to return to London some day, but until that time she would give the people of Perwickshire what they wanted: a laird. Taking his name seemed the simplest way. It also eased her guilty conscience for not telling him about Ailis.

They were toasted and wished well by everyone in Perwickshire. Even timid Aunt Ailis, wearing a dark green gown of embroidered satin, her silver hair hidden beneath a snood, came forward to say her simple words of congratulation.

Suisan's heart catapulted into her throat when Myles said, "Ailis. 'Tis a lovely name, and one I've heard before. But that lady is long dead." Leaning down, he took the small hand in his. "And from where do you come, Ailis?"

Her face a mask of bewilderment, Ailis blinked and said, "Why, from over there." Withdrawing her hand, she pointed to the empty chair next to Nelly. Suisan let out a shaky breath as Ailis returned to her seat. It wasn't fair, keeping the truth from Myles. He should know that Ailis Harper hadn't died of a childhood illness. He had a right to know that the Harpers had put her away to keep the family strain of madness a secret.

But Myles kept secrets from her, too. In the dark of night, he scoured the castle for her treasures.

"Why are you frowning?" he asked. "What's amiss?"

She shook her head. "Nothing."

Yet the spectre of his lies and the truth about Ailis's affliction hung unspoken in the balmy air.

·~ *Chapter 19* ~·

Myles arched his back and plopped down on the worn plank floor of the weaving shed. He blew out an exhausted breath and closed his mind to the noise and activity around him. A chilling breeze seeped through the shuttered window above his head, cooling his damp brow and reminding him the Highland summer had passed. Since his wedding six weeks ago, the days had gradually grown frostier, and the weaving had begun in earnest.

But not on the ancient looms as he'd been led to believe. The weavers of Roward used the modern looms he'd sent to Suisan three years ago—the same looms Robert swore she had stubbornly locked away in a tower. Myles hadn't bothered to explain to Suisan, for the matter of the looms was small when compared to the other trouble Robert had caused. Soon the truth about his other deceptions would be revealed, and his schemes would topple like ninepins.

Myles felt little satisfaction at the prospect, for when faced with the proof of her uncle's forgeries of her letters she would be hurt again. Even now she did not fully trust Myles. Would he lose ground by revealing the truth?

On the surface their marriage appeared sound and amiable, and she deferred to him from time to time in matters of running the castle. But he detected a reservation each time she did. In the privacy of their tower chamber, she was always the passionate, loving sweetheart. But he felt a desperation about her each time they made love. What would she do when Will'am returned from London with her letters? Myles knew he would be exonerated, but the necessity of providing evidence wounded him deeply. That she was often troubled and held herself aloof wounded him deeper still. Why couldn't she simply believe him, confide in him, love him?

He loved her intensely, completely, and he had never thought himself capable of loving anyone. He loved Scotland and the Highland people, too. He felt at home here, especially in this room that was the heart of Roward. He wanted to tell her that he'd sold his ships and his London house. He wanted to tell her he was here to stay. He knew she wouldn't believe him, but sooner or later he'd find a way to show her.

The weaving shed came alive with the clackety-clack of shuttles, the thump-thumping of pedal bars, and the melodious brogue of the Highlands. Nelly chatted incessantly. Mrs. MacIver whistled a droning tune Myles suspected had once been played on bagpipes. Suisan moved gracefully from one loom to the next, alternately complimenting the weaver or making some tactful suggestion. Only one member of the closeknit Roward family was missing: Ailis.

Skittish and flighty one movement, thoughtful and lucid the next, Aunt Ailis, as everyone called her, did not work in the weaving shed. Recently she'd had what Nelly termed a "bad spell," and since then had withdrawn. Who was she? he wondered.

Of everyone at Roward, Suisan was the most protective of Ailis and her peculiar ways. When he asked Suisan why, she invariably changed the subject. When he'd asked Nelly, she huffed up and accused him of meddling into things better left alone. Since that day, he'd ceased to ask questions about Ailis; he vowed to make friends with her, and he knew the way. He would build a hothouse for the flowers she loved.

He closed his mind and his eyes to the temporary problems in his life and let the familiar and pleasant sounds wash over him. Perhaps Suisan had been correct, perhaps he did possess an extra measure of luck. But Irish? He didn't know, of course, for his parentage was a mystery. But his child wouldn't suffer as he had. Oh no. Every day he thought of the things he would share with his child.

A soft hand touched his brow, brushing the hair away from his face. He smiled, breathing in the delightful fragrance of heather and woman. His woman.

"I thought you were sleeping," she said, bending over him.

He opened his eyes. "Not with you touching me, love." Angling his head, he kissed her palm. "Your hands are so soft."

"'Tis from the wool." She smiled the smile that made his groin grow tight.

"Sit with me." He patted the space beside him.

She did, but in public she always acted the trusting bride. He draped an arm over her shoulder and threaded his hand in hers. With his free hand he touched the rounded curve of her belly.

"Sibeal's hands were soft . . . like yours," he mused. "I'll always remember the times she was nursemaid to me."

"When you fell from the rigging of Papa's ship and hurt your shoulder?"

"Aye, that was one." Long-buried memories flooded him. "She cared for me like I was her own son."

"You were," she said quietly.

Tenderness welled up inside Myles. Tenderness for a kind and loving woman dead before her time, and tenderness for a gangly youth who'd never expected to know a mother's love.

"Myles. . . ." She stared at the rocking pedals of a loom, her teeth worrying her bottom lip. Something weighed on her mind. From her expression he knew that it was something serious.

"What is it, love?"

"When is Fergus coming back?"

Myles had wondered how long it would take her to ask about the absence of Fergus and Will'am. "As soon as Will'am has finished his errands. Are you angry because I didn't discuss it with you?"

"Your errands?"

"Aye."

She tilted her head back and studied the ceiling. "Will'am went for the letters Uncle Rabby forged, didn't he?"

"Aye. And to arrange some business matters that Ollie's conducting on my behalf." *Tell her that you sold all of your ships but one. Tell her you've sold the house in Mayfair.* He couldn't. Not until she confessed her love.

Clearing the sudden tightness from his throat, he asked. "How do you feel?"

Her pensive expression blossomed into laughter. "Like I swallowed a tumchie, whole."

"Hmm." He pretended to seriously consider the statement while rubbing her belly and thanking God for his good fortune. "A small tumchie, to be sure, hardly enough for one of Mrs. Peavey's puddings. Or perhaps 'tis a clootie dumpling."

She sucked in her breath and her smile vanished. "What is it?" he asked, immediately alert to her distress.

"'Tis nothing," she began in a shaky tone, "but speaking of puddings . . ." She sat up straight, suddenly all business again. "I'd better check with Mrs. Peavey about the evening meal."

Myles frowned and tightened his hold on her shoulders. "You work too hard."

Her dark blue eyes went round with surprise, and her head tilted inquisitively. "An' what of you, Myles Cunningham?" she chided softly. "You've done naught but work since we were wed." She nodded toward the back of the room as her Cameron hair cascaded over his hands. "Two new fireplaces, and enough firewood and peat to last the winter through. And new glass for the broken windows."

Myles ached to know what she was really thinking, but he knew she wouldn't confide in him; she never did. He hated the gap between them. "Dundas laid the bricks. And I've only sent for the windowmaker." He didn't tell her about the hothouse for Ailis; if his wife insisted on keeping secrets, he would keep some too.

She twitched her nose and tossed back her hair. "Insignificant details. The fact remains that you've worked as hard as anyone."

She'd said that before, and always with the same underlying tone of surprise. Always before, though, Myles thought the remark was meant to tease; today he wasn't sure. He looked her straight in the eyes and asked, "What do you mean by that? Why are you surprised that I think of Roward as my home?''

There it was, a familiar and painful flicker of doubt in her eyes. Sadder to Myles than her lack of trust was the fact that she didn't even suspect he knew. An instant later, the expression was gone.

''Of course 'tis your home.'' Giggling, she added, ''Even though you gave it to me.''

Ownership of Roward Castle and the surrounding Cameron lands had been his wedding gift to Suisan. ''Seems I'm forever buying or giving the place away,'' he said, trying to lighten his own spirits and ease his hurt feelings. ''I'd see it passed on to our child.''

She kissed him on the cheek, but she was generally free with her attention now that they were wed. He wanted more, though. He felt better when she said, ''And a generous laird you are, Myles. No one in Perwickshire can fault you. Even Lachlan says so.''

''An accolade I positively yearn for.''

''Then I'll be certain to have him mention it again when he gets here.''

Suisan had called a meeting to plan the upcoming harvest. Representatives from Perwickshire and Longshire would attend and combine their forces. In doing so, the crops would be delivered to market before the other districts, and would draw a better price. The tatties, as potatoes were called, onions, neeps, barley, nuts and berries would be shared among both districts.

Suisan had engineered the entire process herself, Myles had learned. She had been fifteen at the time. The plan was brilliant, efficient, and at a time when other Highland districts scraped and struggled to survive, the people of Perwickshire and Longshire prospered. Side by side. That was the key, for seldom in the history of the clan-governed Highlands had any two districts existed in peace for any length of time, let alone worked together in things so basic as putting food in their bellies and coin in their pockets. How different would Scotland be today, Myles wondered with pride, if she had had more leaders like Suisan?

* * *

Seated at the head of the long trestle table, Suisan glanced at her notes in the leather bound book before her. When she was satisfied that every detail of the upcoming harvest had been planned, discussed and documented, she closed the cover.

She leaned close to Myles, who sat on her right. "'Tis time," she whispered, "to see to the business of MacIver's sheepdog."

"What can I do?"

She fought the malaise that always assaulted her when he involved himself in the affairs of Perwickshire. Surely he would leave someday, but she couldn't think about that now; she had a kingdom to govern. "Stand by me?" she asked.

His expression softened. "You're doing that again," he said plaintively. "You're looking at me as if I were a stranger instead of your husband and the father of your child."

Oh, God, she yearned to unburden herself, but she'd been hurt too many times.

His gaze did not falter. "I love you. And if you shed those tears Seamus will have the advantage."

With every breath she wanted to beg him to understand about their child. But where could she find the courage to tell him his son or daughter might well be afflicted like Ailis? What if she did not survive the birth? How could she put her trust and the responsibility of Perwickshire in his hands?

Beneath the table, her hand sought his. She felt callouses and tried to remember if they'd been there before. She couldn't, but then again, she couldn't remember much of anything when he looked at her with love in his eyes.

"Now you're blushing, Suisan." His eyes, oak brown and warm with concern, crinkled at the corners.

She squeezed his hand. "Hardly the proper countenance when there's such serious work to be done."

"I could have old Seamus kidnapped and put aboard the *Highland Dream* before her next voyage. That would temporarily solve your problem."

"That or wash the dog," she whispered, her spirits lifted by his thoughtfulness.

"What?" he bellowed. Several people looked their way.

She stifled a laugh. "Ruins the dog for the sheep, washing does," she whispered. "'Tis also bad luck."

"I see." He didn't look as though he did.

"You do?" she asked.

Tossing his head back, he laughed. "Not in the least—and you'd better wait 'til later to explain; everyone's watching."

She was immediately attentive. Although she wanted nothing more than to sit at his side and speak of things that would never be, she knew better. He'd hate her when he found out about Ailis. What man wanted children like—

Suisan stopped. Dwelling on it served no purpose. Besides, the trouble with Hay and MacIver must be settled. She wondered how her grandmother had managed to create such a mess. She also wondered if her own mother had felt the same way. Steepling her fingers against her chin, she scanned the men and women at the table until she located Seamus Hay, who sat next to Lachlan.

An elaborately carved scrimshaw pipe was clenched between Hay's yellowed teeth. His eyes squinted against the blue-gray smoke that hung about his weathered face. He was a stubborn man who clung to the old ways as staunchly as Dundas clung to his claymore. This year Seamus was clinging as never before. The harvest was upon them, and he had yet to return MacIver's dog. Now she must force him to do so.

She looked at MacIver. He sat near the end of the long table, a mug of beer in one hand, his chin in the other. Throughout the meal and the meeting, he'd continued to glower at his perennial adversary. Studying him, she was reminded of Myles's housekeeper, Mrs. Mackie. MacIver's nose was button-like, and always a shade of red, but with the coming of winter his nose rivaled a beet at harvest. He was a pleasant man, and the cousin of Flora MacIver, who worked the looms. Each year, in payment for an insult his grandfather had dealt Hay's grandfather, MacIver forfeited his dog for the traditional restitution period of seven weeks.

But this year Seamus Hay had taken unfair advantage. Since her grandmother had been the object of the original dispute, Suisan was responsible for resolving the situation.

She dropped her hands to the table. "There's but one thing more to settle."

Hay took the pipe from his mouth. MacIver set down his mug and folded his hands over his chest.

"You'll return MacIver's sheepdog on the morrow, Seamus. The debt is more than paid."

Hay scowled. "What would a MacIver be knowin' about payin' debts? The whole reeky lot of 'em, from the time of the Bruce on down, hae been a sore on the bonny face of the Highlands."

"*Haud yer wheesht*!" she demanded.

"Nay," Hay growled. "I'll have me say."

Myles bolted to his feet. "Measure your words with care, Seamus."

Lachlan pounded his mug on the table. "Do as Cunningham says, or ye'll be gummin' neeps 'n tatties the rest of your days. You'll show Lady Suisan the respect she deserves."

"I shoulda known ye'd turn on your own man," Seamus accused. "An' for what? For her connivin' grandmother and the likes o' that scunner? Bah! MacIver's no better'n the worthless cur he passes off for a shepherd's dog."

Suisan slammed her hands on the table. "Seamus!"

MacIver shot to his feet. So did Lachlan. Myles started toward Seamus. Ailis wailed and rocked from side to side.

Suisan's patience snapped. Leaning forward she said, "Sit down! All of you! Please, Myles." When he did as she asked, she turned to her maid. "Nelly, take Ailis to her room."

Lachlan was the last to remain standing.

"Mind your place, MacKenzie," she warned. "The matter is between Seamus, the MacIver, and the Camerons." Turning to Seamus, she said, "You will return the dog by sunset tomorrow, or forfeit your share of the harvest."

At the magnitude of her threat, several people gasped. Seamus dropped his pipe. Frowning, he grumbled something under his breath.

She clenched her fists; she could not back down now. "Would you care to repeat that remark, Seamus?"

When he said nothing, Myles started to rise again. She uncoiled her hand and, splaying her fingers, motioned him to stay seated.

"Nay," Seamus spat, casting a hateful look at MacIver, who grinned triumphantly.

"'Tis settled, then. For another year." Breathing a sigh of relief, she sat down and turned to Myles.

He wrapped an arm around her shoulders and gave her an encouraging hug. She wanted to fling herself into his arms and bask in the warmth he offered. But was he the laird she had always dreamed of? For how long would he be willing to stand beside her and share her life? He seemed concerned about the Highlanders, and for that she was grateful, but he was also the scoundrel who had stolen the *Maide dalbh*. Had he discovered yet where she'd hidden them?

Clearing her throat, she announced, "Mrs. Peavey, you may now serve dessert and bring me the Agreement Cup."

As was his habit most mornings, Myles awakened before Suisan. Easing from their bed, he walked quietly to the wardrobe and donned his clothing. He searched through Suisan's toiletries until he found what he needed. Looking at her private possessions reminded him of the day he'd painstakingly explored this room in search of the *Maide dalbh*. He'd felt embarrassed and dishonest at the end of the fruitless search. Where the hell were they?

He tiptoed to the bed and leaned over to kiss her satiny forehead. She murmured contentedly and burrowed deeper into the down-filled mattress. She was naked beneath the covers, a direct result of their long and heated lovemaking the night before. His loins tightened at the memory, and he wanted to climb back in bed and love her 'til she cried out his name. But not today, for he had an important task to perform. Judiciously he pulled the blanket up to her adorably stubborn chin.

God, how he loved her. Seeing her last night standing up

to Seamus Hay and Lachlan MacKenzie had excited Myles beyond belief. She was a woman with strength of character, a woman to be proud of, but she was not yet his friend. Myles was saddened by that.

"Someday, Suisan," he vowed softly, "someday you'll trust me."

He reached the hall and found Dundas seated at the table and devouring a mountainous plate of scones. Nelly stood over him, scowling.

"Could ye hae spoken up for her?" Nelly jeered. "Nay. Why she put you in charge of the castle's defense is a stumper. You can't even defend your mistress against those reeky old sheep howkers."

Dundas continued to eat, seemingly oblivious to Nelly's tirade. "Morning, sir," he said between bites.

"Ye bletherin coward!"

Dundas stared at the wall hanging over the sideboard. Myles stifled a laugh.

"Get the master his tea, Nelly," Dundas said, still staring at the woven mural depicting St. Columba leading the men of Connaught into battle against King Diarmaid.

Nelly looked as if she would explode. She spat a blue insult in Gaelic, then marched from the room, braids flying, dudgeon high, eyebrows low.

Myles sat down. "You know what will happen to Suisan if she's caught with the *Maide dalbh*."

Dundas shot him a withering glare. "Ye've said that a dozen times since ye come here. My answer's the same: I ain't seen the bletherin patterns since you brought Lady Suisan here years ago."

"Then why didn't you tell me Robert lied when he swore he destroyed them?"

"Ye didn't ask."

"Very well." Myles signed, resigned. He'd get no more out of Dundas today then he had before. Damn these stubborn Highlanders! He knew, though, that he couldn't afford to alienate Dundas.

"If something happened to MacIver's dog, wouldn't Seamus just demand another?" Myles asked.

"Nay," Dundas said around a mouthful of scone. "Gibbon quit breeding the border collies. The bitch is last of her line."

"Then why doesn't someone just kill the beast?"

Dundas glanced at Myles, at St. Columba, then back at Myles again. "Ye don't ken our ways. Until the breed's gone, only a Cameron can settle the feud."

Myles didn't understand, but that wouldn't stop him. "Am I a Cameron yet?"

Dundas looked suspicious. "Aye, ye are now—in a manner of speaking."

Myles relaxed. "Will you go with me to Seamus Hay's?"

Dundas stopped eating. "Today? What have ye planned?"

"I intend to personally return the dog to MacIver."

"Good. Lady Suisan's in no condition to travel so far, and she would, if Seamus defies her. She won't be disobeyed."

"Then let's be off before she wakes." Myles placed the item he'd taken from Suisan's wardrobe on the table.

Dundas's mouth dropped open. "Good God, sir, You don't mean to use that for what I think you're thinkin'—" He stopped, shaking his head in confusion.

"Indeed I do." Myles picked up the bar of soap and sniffed it. "Heather. Quite a nice scent, don't you think?"

Dundas choked and his eyes went wide. "Yer truly goin' to bathe the beast?"

Holding back a laugh, Myles pounded Dundas on the back. "That I am. With your help, of course. I'll see an end to this ridiculous squabble, and if the soap doesn't work, I'm prepared for stronger measures."

Dundas looked awed. "Why didn't someone think of that before?" he said. "Wash the beast."

Myles wasn't about to confess that the idea had been Suisan's. Not yet, at least, for he was still confused about the whole thing.

"By all the saints, they'll write a song about ye for this, Myles Cunningham."

"For washing and returning a sheepdog?"

"That's what ye thought?" Dundas looked aghast. "Sweet St. Ninian. The dog's naught but the top of a deep well. Margaret Cameron, Lady Suisan's grandmother, caused the feud."

"Perhaps you'd better explain what Lady Margaret did."

Dundas glanced around the hall, then leaned toward Myles. "'Twas back when Callum Hay, Seamus's grandfather, and the old MacIver were both wealthy landholders—before Culloden, ye ken. Callum had a passion for Lady Mar—" Dundas stopped when the door swung open. Myles snatched the soap from the table.

"I'll tell ye the rest later," Dundas whispered.

Nelly entered the room, her nose in the air and a suspicious look on her face. Myles drank the spiced tea quickly, avoiding her steely gaze. Curiosity tormented him, but he composed himself until he and Dundas were on the northern road. "Finish the story of Margaret Cameron."

Dundas drew his horse alongside Myles's black stallion. "She was a bonny lass, they say, with that flamin' Cameron hair and eyes as black and mysterious as Loch Eil in winter. Like Lady Suisan, Margaret, too, was an only child, and destined, some say, to rule Perwickshire alone. . . ."

A sense of foreboding hung mist-like around Suisan as she took the leather folder from an exhausted Will'am. By rote, she commanded the servants to see to the lad and her soldiers who had accompanied him to London. Part of her wanted to rush upstairs and view the packet's contents before Myles and Dundas returned from their mysterious errand. Another part of her was afraid.

The anxiety had trebled by the time she reached the tower room she shared with Myles, the tower room that had always been her sanctuary. At ten, frightened and alone, she'd huddled against the wall, alternately crying for her mother and cursing Myles for leaving her here. After a time, she'd become awed by the room and by the Camerons who had gone before her. In later years, she'd taken strength from their memories and pride in the family name that was as vital to Scottish history as heather is to the face of the Highlands. Generations of Lochiel Camerons had been born in this tower room. Soon she would birth another.

She stifled a sob and pressed a hand to her stomach. The child moved, as if in response. Would this babe be strong and able? Or would her child drift through life as Ailis did, and in the process, doom into obscurity a great clan of Scotland? What if Suisan died in childbirth? Who would see to the looms, to the people, or keep the memories alive. Myles? She wasn't sure.

She felt a jarring kick to her ribs, then the child did a rolling flip, only to kick her again.

Suisan leaned back against the wall of her beloved tower room, taking great joy in the frolicking of her babe.

When the child had settled once more, she dabbed at her tears and turned her attention to the leather pouch. The contents would exonerate Myles Cunningham and implicate Uncle Rabby. Even as she loosened the tie and withdrew the small stack of letters, she knew what she would find. Penned in a style she now recognized as a variation of Rabby's hand were dozens of pages, each filled with trite prose and empty sentiments. Each letter was signed with her name. No wonder Myles hadn't found her out that morning in London. He'd never seen her handwriting before.

As she pictured the person Myles had come to know through these meaningless missives, she wondered why he'd even bothered with her at all. Was he living out some sense of duty? Then she remembered the letters she'd received. Silently, she compared them one to the other; one spoke in apples, the other in oranges.

What terrible damage had Uncle Rabby done! Hurt clutched at her heart like an enemy determined to tear it from her breast. To a Lochiel Cameron, one whose lineage was steeped in tradition, loyalty and clanship, Rabby's betrayal was devastating. Scots had been betrayed for centuries, but she never thought to experience such a deception from one of her own. She felt more the Scot today than ever before in her life. Yet she was no mighty clan chieftain, like William Douglas or David Lindsay. She was not brave and resourceful like Black Agnes, defending her home from the Earl of Salisbury. She was Suisan Harper Cunningham, a woman deeply in love with the man she'd wronged, a woman horribly betrayed by the uncle she'd loved. A woman who might be carrying a child like Ailis.

As if burned, Suisan tossed the awful letters aside. Her pride, her determination, fled. Pain and heartache became her only companions. Moaning, she drew up her knees, bowed her head, and cried.

Trapped in a miserable web of sorrow, she lost all track of time and place. At the sound of the door opening, she raised her tear-stained face and saw Myles. His smile faded and the greeting died on his lips. He glanced to the discarded letters, then walked slowly toward her. Their eyes locked; his full of understanding, hers full of pain. Boot leather creaked as he knelt beside her.

"I thought Uncle Rabby loved me," she murmured. "I trusted him. He's the only family I've had." Her voice caught and she lowered her head.

Myles reached for her, clutching her to his chest and crooning, "I'm so sorry, Suisan, my own. I know you loved him."

"He told me terrible things about you," she sobbed. "He told me you'd squandered everything . . . that you wanted Roward for your own. That I should never, never trust you."

"Shush, sweetheart." His voice was soothing and wonderful. His arms were strong and comforting. "'Tis over now."

"That's why I knew you stole the patterns. They're all I have of my mother's people."

"You have much more of the Lochiel Camerons than a box of tartan patterns."

She sniffled, her whole being anchored to his voice. She raised her head. "I do?"

He smiled and she thought her heart would melt. "Aye, you do." He kissed her nose. "You've this magnificent hair even the great Bruce would have envied." He wrapped a long strand about his wrist. "You've the strength of that countess who kept her Scottish castle safe from siege."

"Black Agnes."

"Aye, that one."

"I was just thinking of her."

"As well you should, love. You've much in common with her."

"Nay, I'm weak and stupid."

He placed his hand on her swollen stomach. The child stirred. Hoping to drive the last of her demons away, he said, "No weak woman could grow such a strong child. A feisty little Cameron, to be sure. We'll have to get him a pony."

Myles was shocked by her renewed fit of crying. Great sobs shook her slender frame and tore at his heart. Words failed him, and he responded to her the only way he could. Pulling her tightly into his arms, he rocked her as he would a child and murmured every soothing phrase Sibeal Harper had crooned to him. When she quieted, he carried her to the bed and tucked her in.

He picked up the ghastly letters, and put them away for safekeeping; they would be evidence against Robert Harper. Then he walked to the great hall and plopped down in a chair. He stared broodingly into the fireplace, searching for some way to ease Suisan's pain. He pounded his fists on the hardened muscles of his thighs, then tossed back his head and expelled his breath.

"Sir?" Flora MacIver stood over him, an understanding look on her face, a mug of beer in her hand. They were alone in the hall.

"Betimes the Highlands can be harsh, and the people cruel. This'll wash the bitter taste away."

She was speaking of the feud. Myles wanted to laugh, for the trouble with Hay and MacIver was paltry compared to the damage Robert Harper had done. "My thanks, Flora." He said and drank deeply.

"Ye've proved yerself a fittin' laird today." Shyly, she added, "Not that all of us needed convincin', ye ken."

He was moved by the simple declaration of trust. "I ken, but if I don't get a bath soon, my sterling reputation will suffer."

"You do smell a bit like the beast—even though Dundas said 'twas milady's soap you used. 'Tis a clever lot ye are, Myles Cunningham."

He laughed, and as his shoulders shook, he felt some of the tension drain away. Flora blushed.

"Pay me no mind," he said, trying to ease her embarrassment. "But I would ask you a question."

She stood straighter. "Aye, sir."

"Why is milady so protective of Ailis?"

Flora's expression became thoughtful. "Like the trouble with my cousin and Hay, Ailis is a family matter."

Perhaps Ailis was a Cameron bastard. Perhaps—

"Lady Suisan's a fine and capable leader; nothing against you, sir. But she's a woman at the mercy of nature. The coming of the babe will ease her mind."

Myles had never considered that her emotions might be affected by the babe. But how often had he heard that breeding women were moody? Often. "Of course."

"Will that be all?"

One other question had been niggling at Myles's mind for years. "How does Robert Harper dress when he comes to Roward?"

Flora laughed. "'Tis funny you should be askin' that. He wears the same frock coat and tight breeches—" She paused, looking embarrassed again. "Tight breeches ain't the same on an older man, ye ken?"

"Leather *is* better for riding," Myles said solemnly, but he was complimented all the same.

"We've been mendin' and alterin' those same clothes for years." She made a tisking sound. "Ye'd think he'd have more respect for Lady Suisan. That or accept the new ones she offers him."

So that was how he hid his French vice, thought Myles. Feeling comfortable with Flora, he asked, "Does he ever wear satin?"

"Harper?" A frown creased her brow. "Nay, he don't. An' from what he says, he don't have the coin to buy it."

He had found out what he wanted to know about Robert. How long would it be before he learned the true identity of the woman they called Ailis Harper?

∼ *Chapter 20* ∼

Myles had just settled into the steaming tub when Will'am entered the room. "You relayed my message to Cookson?"

"Aye, aye, sir, I did."

"And his reply?"

Will'am stood at attention. "Mr. Cookson sent some papers for you to sign, and he said to tell you that the fairies have fluttered home to Aberdeen."

"What else?"

His eyes brimming with laughter and self-confidence, Will'am said, "You should have seen Cookson when I told him who Maura was."

Myles conjured a picture of Ollie, baffled, his mouth hanging open, his arsenal of cutting ripostes lying belly up in his brain. "How long did it take him to find his tongue?"

Will'am shook his head. "About as long as it took Mackie to swoon. He caught her before she hit the floor, though. She moped around for days sayin' how her tongue oughta be cut out and fed to the devils." He lowered his voice. "When Cookson told her what Robert had done with the letters, she said she'd go to her grave bein' ashamed of the things she'd said about Lady Suisan. Cookson must have changed her mind, 'cause the next morning she breezed around the house, either hummin' a tune or declarin' a Bible verse about the devil's spawn corruptin' good Christians."

Myles felt the familiar tug of friendship.

"Sir?"

Will'am placed the satchel of papers on the bed. He looked uncomfortable. "As I was leaving', Mr. Cookson said to tell you that Sibeal and Edward would be pleased. I think he had tears in his eyes. Ain't that surprisin'?''

It was and it wasn't. Myles sighed, thinking how lucky he'd been in his life. Who would have thought that scruffy, foul-mouthed gutter child would someday be lounging in his own Highland kingdom, basking in the warm glow of friendship, with the woman he loved for his wife? Utter peace settled over him.

Will'am cleared his throat. ''Mr. Cookson also said 'twas more important than ever that you 'rid your house of a set of problems.' '' Myles's tranquil mood shattered like a main sail struck by lighting.

''He was insistent on that, sir. Then he said you should find the traitor at Roward before he finds that set of problems.''

His mind still reeling, Myles sat straight up in the tub. ''What traitor?''

''Cookson didn't know his name—he just learned of the bastard, too.''

A sense of foreboding crept up Myles's spine. ''How?''

''From Robert. Her uncle found out Lady Suisan come to London and fetched her property back. That's what Cookson said.''

''Damn!'' Myles swore, realizing he'd underestimated Robert Harper. What would the boy-loving bastard do next? What could Myles do to prevent it? Destroying the tartan patterns was the answer; they were Robert's only weapon. Suisan must yield the bloody things. Would she? Myles didn't think so, but if he could find them himself he wouldn't have to ask. Blessed saints, she'd been through enough hurt already. Asking her to be disloyal to Sibeal was simply asking too much; Suisan would never do it.

His only option was to take the decision out her hands. He'd have to start searching again. He should never have stopped, but he'd been overwhelmed by the task. The castle was a rabbit warren of centuries-old nooks and crannies.

Frustrated, Myles pounded his fists on the rim of the wooden tub. Suisan still didn't trust him. If he found the pattern sticks and destroyed them, what would she do? Curse him to bloody hell most likely. He didn't like the options, but what choice did he have? Unless he found the traitor first. But who could it be? How many people knew of the *Maide dalbh*? Did Will'am?

Studying the boy, Myles detected a change, a maturing. Will'am would be loyal, of that Myles was certain, and Dundas could be counted on especially if Suisan was in danger.

Myles leaned back in the tub. Once the first snow set in the roads would be impassable, and he'd have the long, bitter winter to find both the traitor and the patterns.

Comforted, he sought a pleasant subject. "How was the journey, lad? Did you have any trouble?"

Will'am stood taller. "Nay, sir. Me and the soldiers didn't have a wink o' trouble," he declared. "An' I'm broke into a saddle fer good. Me crackers didn't swell up nor get sore on the way home."

"Crackers?" Myles asked, fighting back a grin at the lad's newfound confidence.

"Ain't right, Fergus says, to call a man's better parts some silly name like nobs or seedin' sacks," he said with great conviction.

Myles cleared his throat. Fergus MacKames, one of Dundas's officers, had done more than lead Will'am to London; he'd taken the boy under his wing. "Well, now that we've settled that, tell me what I've missed."

Will'am explained that Robert hadn't returned from France straightaway, so Ollie left a man over there to keep an eye on him and the popper. "But when Robert did come back, dressed up in red satin an' feathers, an' smellin' like a Liverpool whore, Mrs. Mackie ran off to church." Will'am shook his head in weighty appraisal of the image. "The hired man said he'd had enough of watchin' painted-up perverts and wasn't followin' Robert to Aberdeen, so Cookson had to find someone else."

A knock sounded at the door. Wiping away the tears of laughter Myles said, "See who it is."

Suisan stepped hesitantly into the room, a tray of food in her hands. "Oh, I'm disturbing you." A blush tinted her cheeks. She took a step back.

"Impossible, my love," Myles said, warmed from his racing heart to his naked toes. She had survived the ordeal of Robert's letters, and she was getting on with living. "Come sit by me. Will'am's telling tales of Mackie and Cookson."

She wore a yellow velvet gown, the full skirt embroidered with curling vines and spring flowers. The design cloaked her blooming figure, and the color enhanced her lovely skin and eyes. Her hair was loose, in the style he liked, and hung in rippling waves.

"Come give me a kiss, my lovely wife," he said.

"Wife?" Will'am gasped, looking from one to the other.

"Aye," Myles said, grinning like the lucky man he was. "And we've a child on the way."

"My congratulations, sir . . . milady. Wait'll I tell Cookson and Mackie."

Suisan put the tray on the table and approached the tub. Smiling shyly, she held back her hair and leaned over to kiss his cheek. Myles turned at the last moment so their lips met. Warm water sloshed in the tub; hot desire pounded in his head. Were they alone, he'd pull her into the tub and love her 'til she'd forgotten her uncle's betrayal.

When she drew back, Myles whispered, "I love you." Tears pooled in her eyes, but he knew they were tears of pleasure, not sadness. "None of that, my sweet," he declared. "The past is behind us now. Sit down, and hear how our London friends are getting on."

When she was seated on a small stool, Myles turned to Will'am.

The lad frowned and put a finger to his lips. His eyes darted back and forth as he tried to remember his place.

Myles picked up the soap and began washing himself. "Mackie was about to address Geoffrey, I believe," he prompted.

"Oh, yes, sir. I remember now. She'd come back from church, properly cleansed, she said." Will'am licked his lips. "She didn't like Robert's red satin, and said as much. Geoffrey upped his painted nose an' asked where you was. Mackie told the little strutter 'twas none of his affair." Will'am put his hands on his hips and wiggled in imitation of Geoffrey.

"Then Geoffrey said Mackie wouldn't know an affair if it crawled up her skirts."

Myles laughed and was pleased when Suisan did, too.

"Who is Geoffrey?" she asked. "He sounds like a merry fellow to go on with Mackie so."

Will'am's eyes grew wide, and he blinked in confusion.

"I'll explain later, love." Myles didn't relish the idea of telling Suisan about Robert's proclivity. Perhaps she would forget; she had been through enough already because of Robert.

"What did Cookson do?" Myles asked.

Will'am folded his arms over his chest. "He asked Mackie for a glass of brandy, an' told Geoffrey they'd have to stay at the inn again."

"I'll wager Mackie liked that."

"Right you are, sir. She settled herself down, straightened her cap, and poured another brandy."

Myles was lathering his hair. He paused, his elbows jutting awkwardly. "She poured a brandy for herself? In mixed company?"

Suisan smothered her laughter.

"Nay," Will'am declared. "For Lord Ainsbury. Downed it in one helpin' he did, too."

Dropping his hands to the side of the tub, Myles said, "How did Ainsbury get there?"

"His carriage, I suppose."

"What was he doing there?"

A frown wrinkled Will'am's brow. "He came to get the persuasion and a wagon load of satin for his mistress. Cookson said he must've been desperate or in Dutch to come himself."

Suisan giggled. "Or perhaps he came to see if Myles had hired a new maid."

"When I think of the way he pawed you—damn," Myles cursed as the soap burned his eyes.

"Let me," Suisan said.

Then she was kneeling beside him, offering a towel. He wiped his eyes, but his senses were attuned to her hands as she began washing his hair.

"Will'am, you're to rest up a few days, then take the papers back to London." At the lad's hesitant look, Myles added, "Fergus and the others will be going along, too."

The light of adventure shone in his eyes. "Aye, sir."

Suisan's hands were drawing lazy circles at Myles's temples. His breathing grew strained. "That will be all, Will'am."

When the door closed, Myles leaned back against her.

"Myles! You're soaking my dress."

"Then take it off . . . and join me." He was prepared to pull her into the tub, to have his wife, dressed or not.

She drew her hands away and came to stand in front of him. Her inquisitive gaze searched his face, then traveled down his chest and lower. "Oh, my," she breathed, having seen the extent of his desire.

His hands gripped the side of the tub and his need throbbed uncontrollably. "The dress," he rasped, "and quickly."

Desire sang a siren song in her ears, and Suisan barely heard the lusty command. He was rigid and ready for her; she was weak and wet with wanting him. Of their own accord, her hands found the fastenings of her dress. He quickened as she moved, and her breathing became labored, her mouth hungry for the taste of his own, her body aching for the rapture he offered.

"The petticoats, Suisan."

She looked up, and went weaker still at the intense desire smoldering in his eyes. The muscles of his neck and arms and chest were taut, as taut as his. . . . On the edge of a swoon, she kicked off her slippers and made quick work of discarding her undergarments. Bending over, she started to roll down her stockings.

"Good God, woman," he growled, "you'll drive me to ravishment if you dawdle at your hose. Just take them off!"

Her head went light at the urgency in his tone, and her hands moved to comply. He had comforted her in her darkest moment; he had forgiven her for believing the worst of him. He had ended the oldest feud in Perwickshire, and salvaged the pride of two stubborn Highlanders in the doing.

She should tell him about Ailis now. She should be as honest with him as he'd been with her. But as her stockings fell to the floor and her eyes locked with his, Suisan could not find the courage to begin. He might hate her for a coward someday, and he might be ashamed of the child she bore him, but none of that mattered now. He was here and he was hers, and she wanted him with such desperation she thought her heart would burst.

He held out his hand, the calloused palm ridged deep from clutching the wooden rim of the tub. Then he was pulling her to him and placing her feet on either side of his hips. On a wave of desire and wanting, she drifted down until the tepid water lapped at her naked skin and the heat of his desire tortured her aching emptiness.

She expected him to take her immediately, but when he'd settled her to his satisfaction, he grasped her about the waist and held himself back.

He must have read her thoughts. "I want you as a thirsty man wants drink," he pledged, his voice no more than a husky murmur, "but I might harm the babe."

Enchanted by his hearty declaration and moved by his concern for their child, she closed her eyes and leaned back against his bended knees. "Worry not about the babe. Not now."

Her breath caught in her throat when his lips and teeth teased and tugged at her sensitive nipples. He tended each of her breasts thusly and, as he did, he uttered lusty phrases of how wild and wonderful she made him feel. "Your breasts are fuller," he rasped.

"'Tis the babe," she managed weakly.

His hands roamed her swollen belly; he whispered that her body had never felt so enchanting. At last he opened wide his mouth and suckled eagerly, hungrily at her breasts. When she moaned and clasped his head, he suckled harder, murmuring naughty promises of what he'd do when he'd taken his fill at her breasts.

She felt totally wanton, yet still she tumbled headlong toward that magical moment of fulfillment. Unable to control the pleasure spiraling through her and unwilling to postpone the moment of euphoria, she raised up and slowly guided him into her. He groaned deep in his throat then expelled his breath in a searing rush against her breast.

His hips surged upward, then withdrew, only to rise again with greater force and need. Water sloshed to the floor in time with his rhythmic thrusts, and she found herself clinging to him for balance, for sanity, for some anchor against the pulsating pleasure racing from her head to her toes.

Then she was one with the pleasure, and the siren song of rapture was pouring from her lips in joyful cries and delirious whispers. She floated, feather-like, on the trailing tendrils of bliss until her mind cleared and her wits returned. Grasping his shoulders, she raised her head and leaned back. His hands gripped her tighter.

"Stay still awhile, lassie." His voice was tight and strained; his eyes were lustrous and dreamy. "I'll not end this loving yet."

She felt him then, stiff and long and magnificently primed within her. She went weak again, a victim of the tingling sensations marching over her skin, but when he drew her to his chest, she took the lead. "Aye, you will end it," she breathed the threat into his ear, "I'm going to turn your brain to pudding, I'm going to make you cry out my name when you take your pleasure of me."

He grasped her thickened waist to hold her still. "Don't move," he rasped.

She paid him no mind. She would hear his cries of contentment and she would hear them now. Confidence raged through her as she ground her hips upon his, clutching at him with hands and legs and hidden muscles, urging him to set free the lusty beast clawing at his loins. "You can't wait, Myles. You know you can't. You're bursting inside and you can't hold back."

With a feral roar that would echo in her mind for a long time to come, he pushed upward, almost propelling her out of the water on the sheer strength of his hammering, pounding release.

She felt cleansed and free, and selfishly, naively, she felt forgiven for deceiving him so.

"I'm delighted, but baffled," he said, gasping for breath, "at where you learned such brazen things to say."

She giggled. "'Twas you who inspired me with your wicked ways. I only changed the wording here and there."

"Ah, love," he sighed, hugging her fiercely, "I shall endeavor to keep up my wickedness. But now I need food."

She shifted to lift her body from his.

"Gently, my dear," he said, sliding free of her silken warmth, "and have a care for my crackers."

"Your what?"

He explained Will'am's new name for parts of the male anatomy.

Standing beside the tub, she looked him over. "Crackers hardly fits you, milord. I suspect a grander term would better befit such a considerable subject."

"And you, milady, flatter me well."

She gave him a naked curtsy, dripping water on the floor. "Gather up your manly pride then, and dry yourself, Laird Cunningham. Word of your brilliant win over Seamus Hay is spreading through the district. And even as we dally, the hall is filling with subjects eager to pay you homage."

Wearing only a crooked grin, Myles stepped out of the tub. "Dundas told me the story of Margaret Cameron and the sheepdog. You should have seen the expression on MacIver's face when I returned the perfumed bitch."

She laughed. "I'll wager it rivaled the expression on Callum Hay's face the night he climbed into a carriage thinking my grandmother was eagerly awaiting him, and all he found was a smelly sheepdog wearing MacIver's colors."

Myles grew serious. "I intend to tell them 'twas your idea, Suisan."

"Oh, nay." She rushed to his side and clasped his arm. "You must not. Promise me, Myles. Swear you'll let them think as they do."

"Why?" He was shocked at her vehemence.

How could she explain a Highlander's pride? "Even though they've considered me their laird for many years, some still think of me as a Harper, a Lowlander. They have no tartans to show their allegiance. They have no bagpipes to play their songs, and the great men of their time are dead or gone to exile. Pride is all they have left, and to lose to me—to a woman not yet twenty, would bring them to their knees.''

"And you won't do that."

"Nay."

"But you're a Cameron."

"Aye, but they are a dying part of Scotland."

"You're wonderful." He reached for her.

She spun away, even though her spirit soared at the warmth of his words. Over her shoulder, she immodestly declared, "True."

He made no move to chase her. Folding his arms over his bare chest and cocking one golden brow, he examined her from head to toe. "You've a tartness about you, wench."

She went warm inside. He was superbly handsome in his nakedness; he looked like a bold and braw Scotsman. Holding her petticoat up she swept him a courtly bow. "And I shall sit at your feet tonight, milord, and when the beer's passed 'round I shall fill your cup. And when the story's told I shall sing hosannas at the mention of your name. I love you."

He lifted his eyes and held his arms up to the ceiling. "I *am* Irish. I *must* be."

He could be Irish, he could be English; Suisan didn't care. He had done the impossible. Myles Cunningham had come to the Highlands a stranger, an outsider, and now her people were praising his name.

"You're everything," she cried, launching herself at him.

She hugged him fiercely. Silently she vowed to explain about Ailis and the child before Will'am left again for London. Myles could take his leave of her then, and no one would suspect the true reason for his departure.

A gaggle of fat geese, led by a stately, black-dappled gander, waddled and cooed on their morning promenade through the castle yard. At Myles's approach, the leader extended his head and hissed, setting his devoted female followers to honking and flapping their wings. With loud complaints, the flock parted and made way for Myles as he continued toward the stables.

The smell of smoke, rich from dried peat, scented the crisp

October air. From the smithy's shop came the sound of metal clanging against metal, and from the nearby stables, horses blew noisily over the rustling of hay and the bantering of stableboys. The lads were arguing over who would saddle Fergus MacKames's mount, and who would accompany Will'am and the soldiers to England.

Myles rubbed his belly, recently stuffed with Scotched eggs, porridge, smoked fish, and steaming spiced tea. He'd eaten too quickly, but he wanted to speak to Will'am.

Nelly's daughter, Sorcha, sat atop a barrel in front of the stables. Flapping her elbows, she pretended the barrel was a horse.

"Hello, lass. Have you seen Will'am about?"

She dropped her hands and screwed up her freckled face. "He's back of the lorimer's shop, kissin' that slut Jenny Keegan. Mama says 'tis a blessing ol' Jake's blind and can't see her for what she is."

Myles knew Will'am was courting Jenny, and considered the association educational but harmless. Sorcha's language, however, was not. Even though he was secretly amused by the precocious lass, he felt bound to correct her. "You've a foul mouth, Sorcha. I'm tempted to tell your mother."

Pursing her lips, Sorcha stubbornly replied, "'Tis the truth about Jenny—even if you are the laird now."

He could see the anxiety in Sorcha's eyes. "Will you promise not to call Jenny a slut again?"

She relaxed visibly. "I promise."

"When Will'am and Jenny have said their goodbyes, you're to tell him I want to see him. I'll be in the garden."

Sorcha wiggled her nose. "Why are you goin' *there*, sir?"

"Because it pleases me to do so."

"But today ain't a celebratin' day, and Mama says 'tis best to leave Aunt Ailis be."

Ailis was having another "bad spell." She hadn't been down for meals, and left her room only to tend her garden. Myles was frustrated by the situation. For the last month, he'd thought of ways to approach the troubled woman, to make friends with her.

"Don't question your elders, Sorcha," he scolded. "Just tell Will'am what I said."

Sorcha shot him a defiant look that was pure Nelly Burke. "Sorcha . . ." he warned.

"Aye, sir."

Stifling a laugh, he turned away and as he passed through the arbor, the garden came into view. The noise receded. Ailis's domain was always quiet, for few ventured among her tulips and tansy.

Even with winter approaching, the garden was alive with color. Rowan berries hung from the trees in bright red clusters, their vivid color a glorious complement to the gold and yellow of the few remaining leaves. Within the circle of rowans, one or two hearty rose bushes offered up a last blossom. But most of the bushes sported only roseships, the orange balls clinging like decorations on the stark and thorny bushes.

Geometrically boxed and carefully orchestrated, the garden was typically English, and Myles wondered why. Perhaps he would ask Ailis today why she had designed such a garden. He intended to tell her about the hothouse, to ask her preference on size and placement. Myles wanted to get to know the woman who had created this little piece of England. Something special existed between Suisan and the poor, addled woman, but he had no idea what the something was. Suisan was always vague on the subject, and her silence wounded him deeply. Perhaps Ailis would be lucid enough today to supply the answers. But he had to find her first, and she was nowhere in sight.

Piles of trimmed foliage dotted the hay-strewn paths that meandered between maze-like rows of cabbage roses, squares of gillyflowers, and diamond-shaped patches of red sage and white heather. He stepped over a pile of uprooted rain lilies, their pink blossoms not yet wilted, their white roots bare of soil. Obviously Ailis had recently weeded the unwanted rogues from a patch of fragrant basil. No doubt some other task had intruded upon her malleable mind and diverted her from disposing of the wayward wildflowers. But what task?

He searched in earnest for her, but to no avail. A bulb spade and dirt-stained gloves lay on one of the half dozen benches that formed a cloverleaf in the center of garden.

"Morning, sir. Sorcha said you wanted to see me."

Myles turned to see Will'am carefully threading his way between a fleur-de-lis shaped patch of prickly holly and a six pointed star of junipers. Dressed for the journey to London, Will'am wore riding boots and leather pants, a crisp linen shirt, and a jaunty bonnet. He carried a heavy woolen tunic over one arm, under the other he clutched a leather pouch containing instructions and correspondence for Cookson.

Will'am had adjusted to the Highlands as easily as a poor man adjusts to wealth. Myles knew why. The Highlands had a way of calling to a man, of seeping into his dreams of home and hearth, and planting her bonny roots into his soul until he was powerless to embrace any other land.

"Morning, lad."

Will'am shifted the packet and extended his hand in greeting. The lad's grip was sure and steady.

"I take it you've concluded your—um—goodbyes."

Will'am flushed. "Aye, sir."

"Have you everything then?"

Will'am stood straighter. "Everything, sir, exceptin' the list of things you wanted from the London house. Maybe Cookson's left Mackie alone long enough to sell the mansion."

Myles fought back a grin at the new look of knowing in Will'am's eyes, a tribute to Jenny Keegan's talents, no doubt. "I'm certain he has." Myles intended to surprise Suisan by having the rugs and furniture sent to Roward. From his pocket he withdrew a piece of paper and passed it to Will'am.

"And be sure to have Mackie pack the hourglasses and supervise the crating of the downstairs clock . . . I don't want them damaged."

"Aye, sir. She'll have a merry time fussin' over—"

A piercing scream rent the air.

Myles jerked around and scanned the immediate area, but saw nothing different, except the postern gate. The small wooden door was slightly ajar. A second scream sounded. Myles took off running. Behind him, he heard the packet hit the ground. Will'am was running, too.

Cursing at the dead end paths, Myles hurdled over the maze. Had Suisan fallen? Was she losing the babe? Besieged by fear, Myles ran faster. Just as he reached the opening in the wall, the woman screamed again. The high-pitched wail was laced with terror and desperation. The sound beat at Myles's chest and rang in his ears.

With both hands, he grasped the postern gate. The hinges squealed loudly. Myles jerked with all his strength. Finally the door pulled free. Pushing it wide, he ducked through the opening.

He paused and listened, seeing no one but still hearing vivid screams. He ran toward the sounds. Over the pounding of his heart, he heard Will'am's labored breathing a few paces behind. Dried leaves crackled beneath his boots. Limbs of cedar and camphor trees slapped against his chest and face. The pungent smells assaulted his nostrils and mixed with the raw taste of fear in his mouth.

The path spilled into the open expanse of the cemetery. Ailis's pink dress shone like a beacon among the sea of grey headstones. But Myles attention was riveted to the man who was dragging her toward the mausoleum. Like a rag doll, frail Ailis dangled in his beefy grasp. Her hair hung loose, the silvered strands whipping against a face gone white with fear.

"Release her!" Myles yelled.

The man turned. His arms fell away from Ailis; she crumpled to the ground. He darted off. Surging after him, Myles dodged the taller gravestones and leapt the shorter ones. Will'am was beside him, his gangly legs pumping to stay abreast.

"It's Bartholomew Weeks isn't it?" Will'am shouted. "Robert Harper's lackey."

Myles ran faster, his hands knotted into fists he would use to pound the bastard to pulp.

God! How could any man be beast enough to torment poor Ailis?

The gap between them closed. Seeing his chance to end the chase, Myles dove at the man. Wrapping his arms around the bastard's knees, he pulled him down. Grunting and cursing, they tumbled on the rocky ground. The man tried to kick free but Myles held him.

Fighting the urge to kill the worthless piece of garbage, Myles used his superior strength to subdue the man, whose frightened eyes darted here and there, looking for some means of escape.

Staring down into the scarred face, Myles said, "Resist me, and you're a dead man."

The man fell still.

Myles breathed deeply, and became aware of his surroundings. Behind him, Ailis was sobbing, and Will'am was awkwardly trying to comfort her. Footsteps pounded the earth. Or was it the hammering of his heart? He heard Dundas shouting orders. A sword blade appeared at the downed man's throat. Fearful eyes went wide.

Myles glanced up. Dundas stood holding the claymore and regarding Myles with grave approval. He extended his free hand. "We'll take the bounder now, sir."

His tone was solemn, yet laced with respect. Satisfaction swelled within Myles. He put his hand in Dundas's and as he was pulled to his feet, something passed between them. Myles felt a closeness, a camaraderie with the Highland soldier.

"Now we know how Robert got his information," Myles said.

Dundas nodded. "Weeks won't be tellin' Harper naught else."

Myles turned to Will'am. The lad's jaw was clenched tight and his eyes bored into the fallen man. Ailis keened softly, her face buried in her hands.

"No. Keep him away," she wailed, child-like. "He'll hurt me again. He'll lock me up in there. He'll make me tell him things about Suisan." She stopped and began shaking.

Rage pumped through Myles. Robert Harper would pay dearly for all his crimes.

"What else do you know of him, lad?"

Will'am drilled a hateful gaze at Weeks. "He ain't a stone mason. I shared a beer and a game of dice with him in the stables when Robert was visitin' Cookson. The scurvy lot cheated me out of half a crown."

So, Myles thought, this weasel who'd done minor repairs to the castle, courted Jenny Keegan and assaulted poor Ailis, was supplying Robert Harper with information. That explained Weeks's absences from Roward. The credentials seemed oddly fitting; a pervert like Robert would choose such slime to do his bidding.

"See that Will'am gets his money back, Dundas," Myles said. Meaningfully, he added, "And Weeks knows some things I'd be interested in."

Dundas smiled. "Aye, sir. I'm certain he does at that. And I know just the way to be convincin' him. He'll be sorry for what he done to Ailis Harper."

At the sound of her name, Ailis flung herself at Myles, clutching him around the waist and sobbing against his chest. "He made me tell him. He hu-hurt me."

Over her head, Myles eyes met Dundas's. The soldier looked surprised, but not nearly as surprised as Myles.

"There, there, Ailis. 'Tis over and you're safe," he soothed, though his mind was fixed on what Dundas had said.

Ailis Harper. Dundas had called her Harper. But that was impossible. Robert and Edward's younger sister had died of a stomach ailment when she was five years old. She was buried in the family plot in St. Machar's cemetery in Aberdeen.

"Why do you call her Harper?" Myles asked.

The Highlander stared at Myles as if he were addled. "She's milady's aunt, of course—Robert's sister. He brought her here—" Dundas paused as if searching his memory. "The spring of milady's twelfth birthday."

Abruptly Bartholomew Weeks tried to scoot away. "Seize the rotter," Dundas growled to his men. Boots scuffled as the men surrounded Ailis's attacker, but Myles's senses were still attuned to Dundas's words.

His knees went weak, his stomach sour, and he found himself clutching Ailis fiercely. Rather than balk at his hold, she seemed to quiet. Dear God, Robert Harper had done some filthy things in his life, but this deception about Ailis was beyond even the bounds of Robert's perverted mind. The poor soul had obviously been used as an unwitting spy in Robert's scheme.

Speaking in Gaelic, Myles said, "'Tis a lie, Dundas, for Edward's sister died years ago. This woman is no Harper."

A protective gleam shone in the Highlander's eyes. "Aye, she is."

"What's happened here? Why are they holding Mr. Weeks?"

Myles turned at the sound of Suisan's voice. Then she was running toward them, graceful as a gazelle and pretty as a spring poppy. Her pregnancy was obvious now, and Myles found himself smiling with pride. The other men came to attention as she approached.

When she stood beside Myles, he said, "Weeks, here, tried to drag Ailis into the mausoleum, but Will'am and I stopped him."

"Why? What would he want with Ailis?" she demanded.

"Robert Harper paid him to ask questions about you." He paused and added, "That's how your uncle managed to get your—things—to London. Weeks here took them."

Her eyes went wide with understanding and her lovely face was flushed with anger. "Sweet St. Ninian, I'll kill him myself." Her fists balled into knots, and her back rigid with anger, she turned to Ailis's attacker. "You rotten wretch," she spat, "you'll rue the day you stepped foot on Roward soil." She tossed back her flaming hair. "Take him away, Dundas. The sight of him makes me sick." Then she reached for Ailis, who cringed and buried her face in Myles's shirt.

"What's he done to you, Aunt Ailis?" Suisan pleaded, her gaze shifting from Myles to Ailis.

Myles ground his teeth in frustration at the worried expression in Suisan's eyes. She truly believed this woman was her aunt! Despite the deception, he felt only pity for the frightened woman in his arms, whoever she was. He made a promise then, he would learn her true identity. Then he would broach the subject with Suisan.

"Myles . . ." Suisan implored. "Has he hurt her?"

The woman in his arms began to tremble violently. Knowing that she needed another woman's comfort, Myles tried to dislodge her.

She shrieked, "I told him nothin' this time. I swear on St. George's sword I didn't. Even when he said he'd lock me up again I didn't tell him where they are."

"Let Suisan help you," Myles encouraged. Ailis whimpered and dug her fingernails into his back.

"Sir?" Dundas said. "What shall we do with him?"

"Take him to the dungeon," Myles growled, "where he belongs."

"Nay!" Suisan gasped.

"Leave this to me, love," Myles said softly.

Suisan turned to Dundas. "Take him to the stables. Have the smithy put him in irons."

Why was she countermanding his order? Myles wondered. More forcefully, he said, "I'll see to it, Suisan. The dungeon's the place for him."

"Not the dungeon," she said, wringing her hands and glancing from Dundas to Myles. "Take him to . . . to the scullery or the east tower. Aye, the east tower. Take him there, Dundas."

Why was she so nervous? "Why not the dungeon?" Myles persisted.

"Because . . ." She paused to expel a breath. "The torches haven't been oiled in years, and 'tis black as pitch down there. Someone could fall and break a leg—or be bitten by rats."

Her tone was too flippant. "You're upset about Ailis, sweet," Myles said. "See to her now, and think of the bastard no more." He managed to pull Ailis's arms from his waist, and gently handed the quaking woman over to Suisan. Smiling, he said, "She needs you, Suisan. Take her now and comfort her. Leave Weeks to me."

Suisan's eyes went wide, then filled with tears. Thinking she was concerned for his safety, Myles murmured, "I'll be careful in the dungeon, love."

Clutching Ailis closely, Suisan said in a rush, "You mustn't. He'll only catch the ague down there . . . then he'll be of no use to us." She glanced at Dundas again. "You'll have to carry wood down and food and—and there's no furniture or blankets, and the well's likely frozen—"

"Don't trouble yourself," Myles ground out, his patience hanging by a thread. "See to her." He glanced pointedly at the gray-haired woman in Suisan's arms.

"Oh, for the love of God!" Suisan snapped. "This castle belongs to me, Myles Cunningham! And I order you to put him anywhere but the dungeon."

Myles studied her closely. She was angry, but something else was on her mind. In her eyes he saw the old doubts, the painful misgivings. And if he hadn't loved her so much, he might have hated her for that look and the pain it dealt him. Defensively, he drawled, "Are you commanding me, Lady Suisan?"

Her expression softened. "Myles . . ." she pleaded, "do not take him to the dungeon."

"Milady's right," Dundas said. "The dungeon cells are dangerous."

Like the blaring of a foghorn on a soup-thick night, Myles saw the truth. *The pattern sticks were hidden in the dungeon cells*. He'd scoured those dank and ancient corridors, but he hadn't looked in the right place. He hadn't seen the cells. He hadn't seen a well.

Outwardly resigned, inwardly relieved, he nodded. "Take him to the smithy."

~ *Chapter 21* ~

Holding Aunt Ailis's frail form, Suisan took a deep breath and tried to stave off the misery clutching at her heart. Once again, the *Maide dalbh* had come between her and Myles, but this time she was to blame. Oh, why couldn't she have held her tongue? The dungeon was a maze of dark chambers, and the odds were against Myles taking Bartholomew Weeks to the particular cell where she'd hidden the chest of pattern sticks. Thanks to her thoughtless outburst Myles now knew her secret. She'd seen it in his eyes. She'd seen the hurt there, too.

Wretchedly, she realized he would never understand about the patterns, nor would he condone her keeping them. She would be forced to lie again to preserve her mother's legacy. Regret settled like a rock in her throat, and she felt she would choke on her own dishonesty.

Holding her head high and struggling to do the same with her foundering spirits, she grasped Ailis's hand and began walking to the castle. By the time they reached the garden, Ailis had quieted. When she withdrew her hand from Suisan's and began twisting up her hair, Suisan insisted her aunt should rest a while.

"I've no time for a nap today, my dear," Ailis said, retrieving her discarded gloves. "You know how these rain lilies are. They'll breed like London churchmice over the winter if I don't get them out now." She turned away, plunging the spade into the soil.

The episode in the cemetery was forgotten; Ailis was herself again. Suisan breathed a sigh of relief for Ailis, but she had her own troubles to bear and her own problems to solve.

Tears pooled in her eyes and she raised her face to the blue Highland sky. A gust of chill wind crackled through the trees. Ripe rowan berries rattled like tiny drums against one another. A wayward leaf drifted on the wind, a leaf as golden as Myles's hair. The Highland breeze seemed to wrap around her like an old and comforting cloak. She would hide her treasures again so that one day, when the English came to their senses and rescinded the ban on Highland tartans, she would weave a plaid for her child.

But as penance for her silence about the *Maide dalbh* Suisan promised to be honest with her husband about the other matter between them. Knowing Myles Cunningham deserved better than she'd given him, and painfully aware of the obstacles between them, Suisan vowed to tell him the truth about Ailis.

She repeated that pledge as she lifted the pattern sticks that would someday yield the tartan of the Lochiel Camerons. Oblivious to the dampness and the cold, but keenly aware of Nelly standing guard nearby, Suisan began moving the *Maide dalbh* to a new hiding place. At last the deed was done; the patterns were safe once more. She ordered Nelly to fetch forty ordinary patterns from the hundreds on hand in the weaving shed.

Suisan knew what she must do.

By the time she'd washed her hands and prepared her speech to Myles, she had made peace with herself. Soon she must do the same with the man she loved, even if she lost him in the balance. But she never got the chance, for Myles was sleeping when she entered their chamber, and the next morning she awakened to shocking news. Bartholomew Weeks had escaped. Myles had gone after him.

A fortnight later, Weeks stood in the study of Robert's elegant Aberdeen house. A fire crackled in the hearth; enmity flamed in Robert's mind. The half-wit Weeks had no reason to come to Aberdeen, unless there was trouble in Perwickshire. But what more could be going on there? Suisan had the patterns back, and somehow married Myles. Robert had been livid until Geoffrey pointed out that the situation was indeed a blessing. When the tartan patterns were found, both Myles and Suisan would be hanged. Isolated and ignorant of the hunter's next move, the prey had fallen into the trap.

The High Commission of the Foreign Exchange Ministry was a hair's breath from granting Robert the post he had long sought. If Weeks botched his part, he'd regret it the rest of his life—if he lived.

"Who is this?" Robert demanded, eyeing the woman with Weeks.

"She's Jenny, the lorimer's daughter," Weeks answered, drawing her forward. "She's the one's been helpin' me."

Robert eyed the buxom girl suspiciously. Much to his cha-grin, she glared back insolently. That she aided Weeks in Perwickshire was one thing; that he was fool enough to bring to her to Aberdeen was something else altogether. She looked like a crafty wench; Robert credited her with that. No doubt she was behind the success that idiot Weeks had achieved in Perwickshire. "What's your price this time, girl?"

"Yes, what?" asked Geoffrey.

She drew her disbelieving gaze from Geoffrey, who sat near the fireplace daintily brushing powder from one of his many elaborate wigs. "Two hundred pounds," she said with-out blinking, "and passage to the Colonies."

Geoffrey gasped and dropped the wig. Robert laughed; this country slut was a bold one, indeed. Still, he would never part with such a princely sum—even if he gleaned the in-formation he desired. "Did you find the pattern sticks, then?"

"Did you?" Geoffrey reiterated.

"I was just about to, sir, but Cunningham caught me with the half-wit and—"

"Hold your tongue!" Jenny cut him short. She took a step forward. "Weeks here don't see the whole of it, ye ken? The patterns are at the castle; Lady Suisan'd never part with the mouldy old things. And the addled one's no threat, you can be sure of that."

Robert was immediately attentive. "You know where the patterns are hidden?"

"Do you?" demanded Geoffrey.

Jenny smiled confidently. Placing her hands on her hips, she said, "Maybe I do, and maybe I don't."

"I see," Robert rubbed his chin. "And for two hundred pounds you could be certain."

"Very certain," Geoffrey spat.

She sauntered closer. "That . . . and passage to the Col-onies."

"How silly of me to have overlooked that part of the bargain," he said. But his mild words were a mask for the rage building inside him. How dare this Highland doxy try to coerce him? He would get what he wanted from her, but she and Weeks would pay, and pay dearly. They'd both be going to the Colonies, but as indentured servants, not paying passengers. Still, he wondered just how greedy the tart was. "I agree to your terms then. And will you be traveling alone?"

"Will you?" Geoffrey echoed.

She glanced at Weeks, then turned back to Robert. Winking, she said, "And lose my Barty boy? I wouldn't think of it."

So, Robert thought, the tart was cutting Weeks out of his share. Well, let her think she had won. Perhaps the prospect of victory would further loosen her tongue.

"Now that we've settled the matter of your reward, tell me one more thing—for my gold." Robert hated mentioning Myles's name, but he needed to know the situation. The bastard should have been hanged for treason months ago. "How fares the happy couple in Perwickshire?"

Geoffrey put down the wig. "Yes, how?"

She chuckled in a tone Robert assumed was meant to be seductive.

Eyeing her jealously, Geoffrey came to sit at Robert's feet.

"They call him laird, and treat him like he was born o' the Highlands," she said, obviously pleased at supplying the information. "Even milady defers to him. But that's expected, since she's breedin' and all."

"She is?" Geoffrey gasped.

Robert went cold inside. How could Myles have planted a babe in her belly so fast? She was never to have married, let alone produce heirs to share in the profits from Roward. He thought he'd seen to that. "Did the half-wit tell you Suisan carries a child?"

"Bah!" Jenny scoffed. "Most times the loonie wouldn't know a babe from a bannock. Lady Suisan's out to here already." She held a hand in front of her stomach. "And what's the half-wit got to do with it all anyway?"

Robert relaxed somewhat. Jenny didn't know the truth either; her confused expression and her question proved as much. Vindictively, he chuckled inside at the prospect of Suisan's mental state while carrying a child. Sibeal and Edward's disloyal bitch would pay for her crimes—and the babe would pay, too. A simple fall could be arranged, or a potion to strip her womb. She should have stayed in Perwickshire where she belonged; she should have given up on those damned tartan patterns.

In spite of his influence, she had turned out like her mother. Bile rose in his throat at the thought of Sibeal Harper. That red-haired witch had captivated Edward with her feminine wiles and turned him away from his own kin. Robert hated them both for that. Now he would see that their daughter paid the price. Myles would pay, too. Bitterness filled Robert's mouth at the thought of Edward's stepson. Myles, the orphan? Bah! From the day Myles entered the family, Robert became the orphan.

He rose from the chair. "Come 'round tomorrow. I'll have your gold and my steward will have made your traveling arrangements."

"Then 'tis a bargain. We'll be back at four o'clock tomorrow." She moved close to Robert, and extending her hand, whispered. "*I'll* be here at *one* o'clock, an' the devil take Barty boy."

When they were alone, Geoffrey seated himself on Robert's lap. Leaning close he whispered, "A copper for your thoughts, my love."

Sweet, fragrant honeysuckle drifted to Robert's nose. With an effort, he told Geoffrey of his plans for Jenny and Weeks.

"You are the sly one," Geoffrey moued, squirming in a way that set Robert's groin to burning.

Robert chuckled, thinking how modest his lover was. "Name your reward, sweet. It will be my first duty as Minister of Exchange."

A long lacquered nail traced a path from Robert's ear to his collar bone. "I want that lovely mansion in London."

"Easy enough." Robert gave himself up to the magic of Geoffrey's touch.

"But what about Lady Suisan? The law's lenient with breeding women."

Robert's biggest concern now was haste, for surely Myles would try and convince Suisan to destroy the pattern sticks. The Dragoons must be sent to the castle before that came to pass.

Exceedingly pleased with himself, Robert grinned. "I won't tell them she's breeding. Perhaps the shock of our arrival will be too much for her. Perhaps she'll lose the babe."

Geoffrey put a hand on Robert's thigh. "You're such a smart man." His fingers playfully crept closer to Robert's swelling groin. "You know what I'm thinking of?" Geoffrey asked.

Robert's thoughts of Suisan Harper grew hazy as Geoffrey continued his wickedly wonderful caresses. "Earning a copper?"

"A shilling. Nothing less than a shilling."

"Then you'd best consider a change of venue, love; you can't earn a shilling where you are."

"Oh, I think I can."

Robert's last coherent thought before he succumbed to the delicious lust inflamed by Geoffrey's considerable expertise was that he would accompany the soldiers to Roward. He would witness for himself the long-awaited demise of Myles and Suisan Cunningham.

After a week of scouring the rugged terrain in search of Bartholomew Weeks, Dundas had convinced Myles that the man could not be found. Angry and frustrated, Myles marched into their tower room to confront Suisan.

"Where are the *Maide dalbh*?"

Her shoulders slumped, and she folded her hands over her belly. She seemed resigned, but the raw emotion in her eyes spoke of regret. He supposed she was thinking of her mother, but Myles was thinking of Sibeal, too. He hated Sibeal Harper at that moment, hated her for her Highland pride, hated her for burdening the life of the woman he loved.

Tension replaced his anger. "Where are they, Suisan?"

She sniffled, then raised tear-filled eyes to his. His heart wrenched at the misery reflected there. "I threw them in the dungeon well the day Ailis was attacked."

Like a stiff and welcome breeze after a long and deadly calm, relief roared through him. "Suisan—"

She held up her hand. "I'm sorry for putting you in such danger." Her voice broke. After a moment, she continued, "I promise they'll trouble you no more."

He wondered why she had excluded herself from the danger. He supposed that after living with the secret of the *Maide dalbh* for so long, she had lost sight of the risk involved. She was safe now, and he intended to keep her that way.

"I'm also sorry for gainsaying you in front of Dundas and the soldiers. 'Twas your place to deal with Bartholomew Weeks."

She seemed so submissive, so defeated, so unlike the woman who had come to London, so unlike the woman who had stolen his heart. He went to her, enfolded her in his arms.

Several hours later, when all in the castle had retired, Myles eased from their bed and made his way to the dungeons. A lighted torch in his hand, a mountain of grief in his heart, he scoured the ancient corridors until the found the well. Hating himself for doubting her, he raised the light and peered into the well.

He drew in a breath, but the cool air turned to fire and burned a path to his chest. He began to tremble. The light wavered, casting eerie shadows over the pitiful carnage below. Half-submerged in the ink-black water and covered with dirt and rubble, lay the Highland tartan patterns.

He ached to rip out the hearts of his own countrymen.

A rat squealed and scurried for cover. Myles dragged himself back to bed, pulled the woman he loved into his arms, and vowed he'd never mention the *Maide dalbh* again.

A fortnight later, Suisan stepped into the partially completed hothouse and looked around. The air was fragrant with the pungent aroma of freshly cut cedar and the first bite of snow. Ailis was in the back cleaning the windows installed earlier that day. Myles stood near a workbench, one booted foot braced on a stool, an arm resting on his knee. In his hand he held a hammer. He seemed to be studying the tool, but Suisan doubted that. His broad shoulders drooped the slightest bit, as if he carried some dreadful weight.

I want to talk to you about Ailis.

He'd said those words this morning while they were still lying abed, and Nelly had interrupted with tea. Suisan's heart twisted and she fought with all her might not to cry. He'd asked her to meet him here. It would all end now, all those little girl hopes and foolish, foolish dreams would stop here, for now she would tell him the truth.

He looked so vulnerable she was reminded of that morning in London when she'd silently said her farewells. She was reminded of the pain, too, but saying goodbye to him that first time seemed easy in retrospect.

He raised his head then, and in his beloved face, Suisan saw apprehension, doubt, and something else she could not name. Only his eyes moved, raking her from head to toe, and resting as they often did on the swollen mound of her belly.

I want to talk to you about Ailis.

Suisan had known this day would come and moments ago she'd been prepared to deal with it, but now the reality of what she had to do seemed overwhelming. She tried to smile, but failed. She searched for some distracting thought, but beneath his intense gaze, she could think of naught but losing him.

Her feet moved, though how she did not know, for her eyes, her senses, were locked with his. With shocking clarity Suisan realized Myles Cunningham had become her life. In a matter of months her singularly unremarkable existence had become hopelessly tied with his. Those calloused fingers had performed the simple tasks of threading her needle and adjusting her loom. Those powerful hands had brushed her hair and felt the life within her move. He was a part of everything she did; he was a friend to everyone she knew. Oh, they loved him here in Perwickshire. He was their laird, their leader, their confidante. Even poor Ailis had succumbed to Myles Cunningham, and since the attack, she had been as normal as anyone at Roward.

As she did most days since the arrival of the glazier, Ailis worked side by side with Myles during the construction of the hothouse. From sunrise to sunset, they could be found here. Often laughing, always talking, they had become the fastest of friends. In a matter of weeks, Myles had drawn Ailis out and sent her demons away.

The demons will soon be mine, Suisan's breaking heart said.

A coward rose within her, a weak and wilting creature able to deny the truth and skirt the unpleasant task ahead.

I want to talk to you about Ailis.

With each step Suisan tried to bolster her courage. She would have her dreams to remember, wouldn't she? She would have her treasures to cherish and pass on to their child. Uncertainty rose within her. Would her child be clever enough to understand the importance of the *Maide dalbh*?

I want to talk to you about Ailis.

Aye, you will, my love, she pledged, you will hear the truth from my lips. She owed Myles Cunningham that much—that much and more.

He straightened as she neared, but his grave expression did not change. Her knees threatened to buckle. She sat down on the bench and folded her hands over the roundness of her belly. Forcing a smile, she glanced up. "Join me?"

She waited, her heart knocking in her breast, her confession hovering on her lips.

She glanced at her aunt, who was working industriously a safe distance away.

Myles cleared his throat. "'Tis time we talked about Ailis. You were told a wicked lie—"

"Nay, Myles," she interrupted, keeping her voice low. "'Tis I who should speak of my Aunt Ailis—" Her voice faltered. Her courage wavered.

Myles dropped the hammer. "She's not your aunt," he said simply.

Suisan smiled sadly, thinking how innocent he was now, how disappointed he would be later. Leaning down, she picked up the tool. Toying with the clawed end, she said, "That's what the Harpers wanted you to believe."

"'Tis the truth," he said adamantly. "She's no relative of yours."

He sounded so certain Suisan wished she could look at

him. But she was not brave enough, for his expression would surely be her undoing. "She is, Myles," Suisan began softly. "She's also the reason I vowed never to marry."

Myles took the hammer from her hand and pulled her close. "Why would Ailis make difference? Did you think I would send her away?"

The words sat perched on the tip of her tongue, but God help her, she couldn't voice them yet. Cowardly, she admitted, "Nay; I wanted no husband."

"But you have one who loves you very much," he said kindly, touching her stomach.

Her throat went tight and her vision blurred. "I have no place as your wife; I could fail you . . . and the Cameron name."

"How?"

The words she had so carefully phrased refused to come. On the verge of tears, she blurted out, "Our child may be as Ailis is. You'll want strong sons and—and I know I should have warned you before but—"

"What?" He grasped her shoulders and turned her toward him. "Look at me, Suisan."

She couldn't. The muscles in his neck were taut and his strong hands bit into her skin. Oh, God, he would hate her now.

"Suisan . . ."

She gathered her courage and lifted her face. His brown eyes drilled into hers. "Your uncle lied," he said gently. "Ailis Harper is buried in St. Machar's Cemetery. She—" He jerked his head toward the rear of the hothouse, "is no relation of yours. Do you understand? She is part of Robert's scheme."

Tears rolled down her cheeks. He didn't understand. "Please hear me out, Myles."

"Nay. Robert had done this awful thing to you. Why, I do not know. But know this, my love—" His voice dropped. "Edward Harper was the kindest man I've ever known. He wouldn't have lied about his sister. He spoke often of Ailis, and always with fondness and love. Do you remember?"

"Aye. But it matters not. He was doing as his parents

wished, and he was only a lad when it all happened. Perhaps he didn't even know the truth.''

"And yet Robert did? Doesn't that strike you as odd?''

"Nay. He was the son who stayed on land. Rabby hated the sea, and his father couldn't abide that. He called him weak. He disinherited Rabby.''

"That's a lie,'' Myles spat. "Robert received a generous share of the Harper wealth, and he squandered it away before his parents were cold in their graves. Think, Suisan, of his other lies, and remember the wrongs he's done to you—to us.''

She sighed; he would never accept the truth. "You're influenced by what my father told you. You weren't there. You want to believe him.''

"Do you remember the stories your father told us about his sister Ailis?''

She had, years before, but with the passage of time and the presence of her aunt, the stories had grown dim.

Mimicking Edward's fatherly voice, Myles said, "That one was a Harper, through and through, from her bonny blue eyes to her sturdy frame.'' In his own voice, Myles added, "This Ailis has light blue eyes—and look at her, Suisan. She's hardly sturdy.''

"But she's old.''

"She is not your aunt.''

He seemed so positive that Suisan felt the convictions of a lifetime begin to waver. Watching Ailis fussing over a pot of pansies and humming a cheery tune. Suisan tried to recall the other stories her father had told about her aunt. Brave Ailis running away from home because she had been denied a puppy. Little Ailis, up before dawn and tagging behind the old lamplighter. Sweet Ailis, the delight of every sailor in the crew.

Myles sighed and looked at some distant point. "That's why you always think I'll leave here—you think I'll be disappointed with you and our child.''

"Aye.''

"I'm saddened you know so little of me. I will love this child and all the others to come.''

"There will be no more children.''

"Because of Ailis."

"Aye."

He gave a growl of frustration. "She's English, Suisan. I'll wager my life on it. Listen to the tune she hums. 'Tis an English ditty about Queen Bess and Lord Dudley. Would a Scotswoman sing that song?"

"Oh, Myles, my father was a Lowlander. Mama was the one from the Highlands. People from the border lands act more English than Scots."

"And Ailis always swears by St. George's sword. What Scotswoman, even a Lowlander, would take that saint? What of her garden? 'Tis not Scottish, but English from start to finish."

"Perhaps the asylum where her parents sent her had such a garden. She could have learned her English ways there."

"Then you admit she seems more English than Scots?"

Now that Suisan considered her aunt's little nuances, she had to agree. "Aye, Myles, but it means naught. You must understand—"

Myles shot to his feet. "Stay here," he ordered. He walked to Ailis, took her hand. Smiling and eager, she followed.

Suisan's heart plunged into her stomach as she stared at her aunt. Dressed in dark blue wool, and bundled in a heavy shawl, she seemed more fragile than ever. Her silver hair was braided and wrapped in coronet fashion at the crown of her head. She seemed so very small besides Myles. A phrase came back to Suisan, *she's sturdy*. But Ailis wasn't; she was frail and childlike. Pain clutched at Suisan's heart and robbed her of breath. Did she want so badly to believe Myles that she was beginning to see Ailis through his eyes?

Myles seated Ailis next to Suisan and then crouched before them, taking Ailis's gaunt hands in his.

"Suisan and I were just speaking of your garden," he said to Ailis. "I told her I had seen none finer, not anywhere in England."

"Oh, there's some finer, to be sure," Ailis said, blushing.

"That's where you saw the gardens—in England?"

"Sometimes I get confused about that. But I think I copied the hedgerows from Shepton, you see." Frowning, she added, "But it's been so long . . . I might have forgotten some of the things to grow. I don't remember well, and I get nervous, you see. They wouldn't all of them do here anyway. 'Tis too cold."

Myles's eyes met Suisan's. He was willing her to open her mind, to believe.

"You told me where that other garden was, but I've forgotten," Myles said.

Ailis stared at her garden, now dormant except for the evergreen shrubs. "In Shepton Mallet, Somerset, as I recall."

"What's your name?" Myles asked.

Ailis blinked, and Suisan expected her to bolt from bench. At last she said, "Lucy. Lucy Saunders."

Suisan felt herself go weak. She stared at the woman who was supposed to be her aunt.

"You're English."

"Yes, now that you say I am, I seem to remember being English." She looked up at Suisan and smiled that naive, trusting smile Suisan knew so well. "But now I'm Scottish, aren't I? I'm part of your family. I always wanted a family and he promised if I was good you wouldn't send me away."

"Who made you that promise?" Myles asked.

Suisan couldn't speak, couldn't draw breath into her lungs. Her ears began to ring and dark spots appeared on the fringes of her vision.

"We'd never send you away, Ailis," Myles said kindly, but his worried gaze was fixed on Suisan. "Tell us the man's name."

"Why, it was Robert Harper."

The last coherent thought Suisan could manage was a name, a gloriously sweet and blessedly welcome English name. Lucy Saunders.

~ *Chapter 22* ~

The frosty night wind soughed a familiar lullaby to Suisan, and the song sounded sweeter than ever before. From her vantage point on the southern battlement, she could look down upon the castle yard or out onto the moors. She'd come to this place often, but tonight was different, for Myles stood beside her.

The yard below stirred with activity as the people of Roward Castle celebrated Hogmanay. The New Year. It was the most important day in Scotland; it was a day to sweep aside the old times, to toss out the bad luck. It was a time for counting blessings, for starting anew.

She reflected on her own good fortune. Wrapped in Myles's loving arms and gazing out over the snow-covered hills of Perwickshire, a healthy babe growing in her belly, Suisan had every reason to celebrate—except one.

"'Tis a lovely sight, a Highland winter," he whispered, distracting her. "Look there." He pointed over the castle wall to Comyn's Moor. "The snow glistens like an ocean of silver."

She was warmed to her toes and contented beyond her heart's imaginings by his fondness for the land she loved. Still, a faint fear made her wonder at the source of his words. Turning in his arms, she asked, "Do you miss the sea?"

"Honestly?"

"Honestly."

Lowering his head, he rubbed his beard across her temple. "With my kingdom all around me? With the woman I love here in my arms? With our firstborn between us?" He caressed her belly.

"I'm as big as Mrs. Peavey's milch cow," she murmured. "And you haven't answered me."

"You're as luscious as a ripe pear, and nay, I don't miss the sea."

The finality of his tone surprised her. "I remember a time when you talked of naught else."

"Only because *you* were too shy to talk at all."

"I never was," she protested, even though he spoke the truth. From the moment her father had brought Myles home, she had been in awe of him.

He hummed a sentimental tune, then pressed his lips to her forehead. "We've a wonderful life ahead of us, Suisan, and a wonderful past."

"Except for my uncle."

"Robert Harper can't hurt us, love, for you destroyed the patterns. I never even thanked you. I know you wanted to keep them, for Sibeal and for Scotland."

She clenched her teeth against an onslaught of guilt and shivered with apprehension. He was being truthful; he was opening his heart to her.

She was lying to him—again.

"Are you cold? Shall we go in?"

"Nay." Subduing her wretched guilt, she tilted her head back. "I love this place. On clear nights you can almost see the lights of Longmoor Castle. Later tonight we'll see Lachlan's fire."

"What do you see in the sky?"

"I see a cloth of bluest black with shimmering silver threads running through."

"Will you weave such a cloth?"

"Oh, perhaps." She sighed, preoccupied with her good fortune. How many times had she stood before this very merlon and wished for the things she now called her own? Guilt tugged at her heart—guilt and suspicion. What if Uncle Rabby tried again to take this all away?

"You should be proud of your craft. When we market the bolts this spring, everyone will know how fine Roward cloth is."

His words of praise brought tears of joy to her eyes. She sniffled. "Thank you."

"You *are* cold, love." He cuddled her closer and she felt the soothing pressure of his fingers on her lower back.

"Nay, I was just remembering."

Softly, he asked, "Remembering what?"

She thought of the old days, the lonely days. She couldn't be honest with him about the patterns, but she could be honest about other things in her past. "After you left me here, I would come to this spot and make up dreadfully childish poems about you."

"I'm sorry I left you." He hugged her fiercely. "I was so lost in my own grief after Sibeal died that I gave little thought to you. When the court decreed me too young to be your guardian and appointed Robert, I naively agreed 'twas best." With a note of bitterness, he added, "Robert assured me you were happy here."

She had never considered Myles's feelings, nor remembered how deeply he'd loved her mother. Youth and her uncle's wicked tales had influenced her, too. She should tell Myles about the patterns now, for surely he would understand. But what of that long ago pledge uttered by a frightened, lonely little girl to her dying mother? What of the clans of Scotland? The memory hardened her resolve to keep silent.

"I'd like to hear one of the poems you wrote about me."

Her guilty mind welcomed the change in topic. She shook her head. "They were silly, childish words, but they came from the heart."

"Then you must recite them later, when your turn comes."

Everyone wrote poems at Hogmanay. Later tonight, when the bonfire was lighted, some would stand in front of the crowd and recite a piece. "It's been too long now. I can't even recall the words," she replied honestly.

Running footsteps sounded behind them. "Sir! Milady!" Sorcha Burke called out breathlessly. "Mama says 'tis time."

Myles chuckled. "I'm thinking Dundas and the troops are demanding whiskey. Shall we go?"

A short time later, she stood on the steps at the castle entrance, a long-handled broom in her hands. Like sentinels bound to drive the evil spirits away, garlands of dried white heather and rowan boughs decorated the massive doors of

Roward. When the case clock in the great hall chimed the hour of midnight, Suisan began the ritual of sweeping her doorstep. Throughout the district of Perwickshire and all across Scotland, others were doing the same.

With each stroke of the clock, she plied the broom. When the timepiece fell silent, her doorstep was clean, her life ready to begin anew.

She straightened, arching her back and rubbing the hard swell of her stomach. Before the winter was out, she would bring her child into the world. A healthy child, a normal child, a child with the blood of the Camerons, a child with the soul of Myles Cunningham. Her heart took flight at the thought. Yet beneath her joy, she felt hatred for her uncle and the vicious lies he'd told. A gust of cold wind whistled through the yard. She shivered. When her spirits began to plummet, she wished the destructive thoughts away. Today was Hogmanay, a time to rejoice, a time to build.

She plied the broom one last time. "Be away, foul man, and take your evil deeds elsewhere."

Then she smiled and walked into the great hall.

The women of the castle were gathered around the stone fireplace. The Widow MacCormick dozed. Nelly served ale. Mrs. Peavey handed out sweet cakes. The younger girls were huddled to the side, giggling. Rowena separated herself from the others and approached Suisan.

"Will the laird come soon, milady? 'Tis midnight and past."

Suisan had asked herself that question. Had Myles truly become a Highlander? Would he act out the most romantic ritual of Hogmanay?

Nelly said, "When Himself does come, he'll change the tradition. He's no dark and handsome suitor, like the legend says."

"He's already a legend—since the day he ended the feud between MacIver and Seamus Hay." Rowena defended. "But will he come to you?"

A loud knocking came at the door. The young girls squealed with joy. The older women nodded their approval.

Suisan's heart fluttered wildly in her breast as she took the first step toward the door. How many times over the years had she, like the other girls, longed for such a visitor? But she had always wished her wishes in silence, for until now, she had no hope of opening her door and her life to the man of her dreams.

She went weak at the sight of him. She vaguely heard the sounds of admiration from the women behind her.

He filled the doorway with his presence, his golden hair and beard glistening in the torchlight, his brown eyes full of love and expectation. He wore the trappings of a Highland laird: a sheepskin about his shoulders, sturdy homespun breeches tucked into thick woolen socks criss-crossed with leather wrappings. He smiled, and Suisan felt like the luckiest, most beautiful woman in the world.

"For you, milady," he said solemnly.

He offered her a piece of coal. ". . . to warm our home."

He offered her a bottle of wine. ". . . to quench our thirst."

He offered her a salted fish bound with a bright ribbon. ". . . to fill our bellies."

Through a blur of tears for dreams fulfilled, she accepted his gifts. Bowing her head, she curtsied. "My laird does greatly honor his lady and his household."

He grasped her arms and drew her up, his touch gentle, his eyes aglow with pleasure.

They ate with the others, they drank, they talked of the future, until Dundas summoned everyone to the castle yard.

Myles had brought in wagonloads of precious wood for the largest bonfire in the history of Perwickshire. When lighted, the blaze would be seen for miles around.

He held her close, keeping the chill of the night from her. The whiskey barrels were tapped, gladsad songs were sung. Bad times were forgotten. Arm in arm, Seamus Hay and the MacIver drunkenly recited a tribute to Margaret Cameron's beauty. Ailis—Lucy Saunders—sat nearby surrounded by the younger children. A new look of contentment and security shone in her eyes.

Sorcha Burke curtsied before Myles. "Can I say my poem, sir?"

He smiled indulgently. "Aye, lassie, let's hear what tale you've brewed."

She straightened her shoulders, stuck out her chin and flipped back her braids. In a musical voice laced with pride, she said, "The Hogmanay Fish, by Sorcha Margaret Burke."

A round of boisterous applause rang through the frosty yard.

She cleared her throat.

"'Twas harvestime in Perwickshire, but our laird weren't in the fields.

"He was over to Loch Eil, thinking of our lady fair,

"And watchin' Mr. Fish.

"He seen our laird acomin' but didn't swim away.

"Too braw he was for any hook no matter what the day.

"He washed his face and used the pot, then swam his mornin' stroll.

"Our laird began to hum a tune and he sang Mr. Fish to sleep.

"Then like he charmed our fair Lady Suisan, Myles Cun—"

Sorcha tripped over the English name. Wide—eyed with embarrassment, she glanced at Nelly, who mouthed the last two syllables.

Young MacAdoo Dundas popped up, his flaxen hair glowing white in the light of the bonfire. "Hoots! Sorcha don't even ken the laird's name!"

Sorcha's face went red. "*Haud yer wheesht*! you foosty scunner. I ken the words." Drawing herself up and turning to Myles, she said,

"Myles Cun . . . Cunningham charmed Mr. Fish to sleep.

"Then he scooped him from the stream,

"And put him in a barrel and piled it full of salt.

"When Hogmanay came, he took Mr. Fish, and gave him to Lady Suisan."

The poem over, Sorcha curtsied, then went to MacAdoo. Drawing back one foot, she kicked the laughing boy in the shin. Hoots of mirth turned to howls of pain.

"I'll get you for that," he gasped out.

Sorcha spun around and raced to the stairs leading to the battlements. MacAdoo hobbled after her as fast as he could.

Myles started to rise, but Suisan stopped him. "He won't hurt her. They've always squabbled."

"But he's bigger."

Suisan smiled, but her mind was fixed on the meaning of Sorcha's poem. Absently, she said, "Aye, but he's younger. Sorcha can put MacAdoo in his place."

Myles grinned. "'Tis a trait of Scottish lassies, I think, keeping men in their places."

"Did you go fishing last fall?" she asked and held her breath.

He studied the tips of his woolen socks. "Aye," he said quietly. "Sibeal told me about the legend years ago, about how lassies expect a visitor—"

"Oh, Myles!" She clasped her arms about his neck. Her heart filled with joy. He had never intended to leave her.

"I swear," he breathed near her ear. "I would've caught a dozen fish, had I known what my reward would be."

"You're wonderful," she declared, knowing to the depths of her soul that she was right.

"I'm glad you think so, my love, but if you don't unhand me, Fergus will never get to say his piece."

Suisan lifted her head and scanned the crowd. And saw a sea of knowing smiles. She had naught to fear anymore. Myles loved her; she loved him. The past lay behind them.

He draped an arm over her shoulders and pulled her close again. She felt protected; she felt cherished. The babe squirmed in her belly as if he, too, felt the comfort of Myles's presence.

Fergus MacKames began his poem, a boastful rhyme about Bonny Prince Charlie's daring escape to France after the battle of Culloden. The crowd shouted encouragement and spiced up the tale. Each and every face was aglow with the light of the fire—and something more—Hope. Suisan knew the source: Myles Cunningham.

In profile, his beloved face seemed dusted with gold and bathed in kindness. Beneath that handsome visage was a good man, an honest man, a man who'd sworn his allegiance to the people of Perwickshire. She knew why they had accepted him as their laird: they had come to depend on his fair and solid leadership; they had come to expect his hearty jests and easy laughter.

"Hmm," he drawled contentedly, his eyes crinkling at the corners, "I love it when you look at me so."

She felt an overwhelming sense of security. When he looked down at her, she breathed the words, "I love you."

A mischievous light glimmered in his eyes. "Say that again and you'll forego the end of MacKames's poem."

She grew soft inside. "That would be rude."

He chuckled, "Not half so rude as what I'm thinking, love."

"Oh?" she taunted, "and what naughty thoughts are you brewing, husband mine?"

He leaned closer and jiggled his flaring brows suggestively. "I'm thinking how much I'd like to carry you inside, sit you before a fire, peel those clothes away, garment by garment, then lay you down and kiss and taste—"

"The MacKenzie! The MacKenzie!" MacAdoo's voice sliced through the cold night air.

"Perhaps our neighbor ran out of beer," said Myles. "Or women."

Suisan leaned her head on her husband's shoulder, her blood still pounding from his seductive words. "It must be beer, for the MacKenzie will never run out of women. Look, he's making an entrance."

"Again."

Lachlan jumped from his horse. His chest heaving, his breath forming thick white puffs, he raced toward them. "English soldiers are on their way here." He lowered his voice. "Robert Harper's with them."

Fear rattled a path up Suisan's spine. "Sweet Jesus," she hissed.

"Don't worry, love, we've nothing to hide."

Dundas joined them. "My money says it's a batch of grubby Redcoats who've lost their way in the snow."

"Put 'em back on the path," someone yelled. "To Cambria!" Hearty laughter sounded throughout the yard.

Myles grasped Lachlan's arm. "How many?"

Melting snow dripped from MacKenzie's braids. Highland pride sparkled in his eyes. "I don't know. They were comin' down the Inverness Road, just roundin' the blind turn at Cameron's Mount. I counted twenty before I spied Robert Harper," he said distastefully. "I'm sure there's more, but I didn't stay to count."

Concern raced through Myles, but he tamped it back. "Will you ride out with me, MacKenzie?"

"Aye, but I'll need a fresh mount."

Myles ordered MacAdoo to saddle two horses.

"Nay," Suisan gasped. "Stay here. We'll call out the archers and man the battlements." Her nervous gaze darted to Dundas.

"Suisan." Myles grasped her shoulders. "Calm yourself. We won't open fire on them. Lachlan and I will see what they want."

Her eyes widened in fear. She clutched his coat. "You can't trust them, Myles. They're English. They might kill you. Imprison you."

"For what? I've committed no crime."

Holding her, he glanced at the other Scots. From Flora MacIver to Sorcha Burke, their expressions revealed the same distrust.

Myles kissed his wife roughly. "Stay here. Stay warm. We'll see what they want." When she opened her mouth to protest, he released her and placed a finger to her lips. "I'll be back before the last log burns."

"But Myles—"

"They won't kill me. I'm English, remember? And who knows? Perhaps MacKenzie wound up in the wrong bed and 'tis some angry husband seeking satisfaction."

Once mounted, Myles didn't spare a backward glance, but charged through the gates, MacKenzie at his side.

Only when they'd crossed Comyn's Moor and started up a hill did Myles draw rein. The horses blew hard. Under the nervous prancing of hooves, ice crackled. Myles steadied his mount. In the distance, harnesses creaked and hooves thudded.

He turned to MacKenzie. "They're over the next rise."

"Aye," he said softly. "Why would Robert come with a military escort?"

Myles would have gladly forfeited his remaining ship, the *Highland Dream*, to know the answer to that. "Robert's up to no good, I'm certain of that." But what? The answer blazed into his mind.

The *Maide dalbh*.

Without his spies, Robert had probably assumed that Suisan still harbored the tartan patterns. He breathed a sigh of relief. "You're absolutely certain it was Harper you saw?"

"Oh, aye," Lachlan spat. "I'd know that bottom rutter in a Highland fog."

Looking at his brash neighbor, Myles felt respect. They were friends, allied in their protection of the woman and the people they both loved and admired. But did Lachlan know that Suisan had once harbored the *Maide dalbh*? Myles didn't think so, and he wasn't about to reveal that information. It would serve no purpose now, for after weeks in the well, the patterns would be rotted beyond recognition.

"We shouldn't go lookin' for trouble, Cunningham. Ye ken?"

Caution was the last thing he expected from MacKenzie, and Myles found himself rethinking his opinion of the deposed Duke of Cromarty. "Aye, Your Grace, I ken."

Lachlan grinned, then started forward. "We won't be havin' them think we're weaklings, either."

Myles urged his mount onward. "I'd battle every Dragoon in England to keep Suisan safe."

MacKenzie faced ahead. His eyes glittered and tension tightened his jaw. He raised his arm and pointed to the west. "You may get your chance."

Myles looked up. His breath caught. Charging toward them, plain as day in the bright moonlight were five hundred Light Dragoons swords drawn, banners flying.

In spite of the heat from the bonfire, Suisan's hands felt cold. Why had Myles ridden out with only Lachlan? Why had Uncle Rabby brought the soldiers? She knew the answers to both. Myles was unaware of the danger and too proud to show distress. Rabby had come for the *Maide dalbh* again. But this time he'd brought the Dragoons. Damn his black soul to hell. Dear God, what would she do?

Instinctively, she wrapped her arms around her belly. The child stirred. Dread seeped into her soul. If the *Maide dalbh* were found and she were charged what would become of this child? They wouldn't hang her until after she'd delivered the babe; even the English had rules about that. Myles would raise their babe. Myles would take care of her people. Her mind conjured a grisly scene. She would be shackled and dragged to London. Before a jeering crowd, they'd drop a noose around her neck. In the end, her head would be jammed on a pike and displayed for all to see.

Fear knotted in her throat. Her people had fallen silent. All eyes were fixed on her. The hiss and roar of the fire rose higher. She must have swayed, for Dundas grabbed her arm.

"You're a Cameron, my lady," he whispered, "and brave enough to face the King himself."

The words, the meaning seeped into Suisan's mind. A *Cameron*. A *Lochiel Cameron*. The legacy of her mother's conviction drummed through her. Yet foremost in her mind was the lie she'd told to Myles and the promise she'd made to her mother.

She swallowed back her torment and studied her subjects. Familiar faces which had been alight with the joy of Hogmanay now flashed with Scottish pride; fists were knotted, shoulders squared. They were remembering Culloden, and they would all die rather than yield to the English again. The normally peaceful group of bonnet farmers were rounding up clubs and claymores, and discussing battle strategy. They would fight; she knew they would. These good, honest people would lay down their lives for her, for Myles Cunningham, for the *Maide dalbh*.

She couldn't let it come to that.

The solution to the awful impasse came with stunning clarity. A sob tore from her throat. "Nelly!" she called, before her courage deserted her.

When the maid stood before her, Suisan said, "Show Dundas where the patterns are. Bring them here."

"Blessed St. Ninian," Nelly spat, her face paling.. "You can't mean to hand them over to the English."

If she thought too long on the decision, Suisan knew she might relent. "I'll hand them over to no one." She turned to Dundas. "You'll need help."

He made no reply, but the determination and loyalty shining in his eyes spoke volumes. He called for MacKames. Looking neither left nor right, they followed Nelly through the door of the keep.

Suisan turned to the crowd. Tankards of whiskey lay discarded, Hogmanay gifts cast aside. When Seamus Hay and several others headed for the battlement steps, she knew she must act.

"Do you trust me to do what's right?"

Seamus Hay turned and approached. "Aye, milady. Better than those English swine."

Scottish curses and waving fists filled the air. "What do the Sassenachs want?" someone asked.

"The same thing they always want," shouted another. "Scottish blood."

Suisan held up her hands. "Hear me out."

Just when the crowd quieted, Nelly and the soldiers emerged, the men struggling beneath the weight of the coffin-like chest.

"Set it down here," Suisan commanded.

Dundas stared defiantly, but she repeated, "Set it down!"

From the depths of the roaring fire, a log popped, sending a volcano of sparks shooting into the night. The crowd stepped back. Grunting, MacKames and Dundas did as they were told.

She waited, her eyes fixed on the chest, her hands folded over her swollen belly. Firelight danced on the satiny surface of the large box, illuminating the ancient symbols and figures carved into the aged and darkened Balticwood.

With infinite sadness eating away at her heart, she trailed a hand over the chest. Her hand seemed detached; her fingers might have been touching the downy head of a gosling, or admiring some new design Nelly had artfully stitched.

Calm swept the fire-gilt castle yard. All the raging emotions and fierce pride seemed to be held in abeyance. Every eye stayed trained on the mistress of Roward Castle.

Heat from the fire brought a sheen of perspiration to her knitted brow. With a flick of her wrist she freed the worn brass latch. Using both hands she lifted the lid.

As she always did, Suisan stared in awe at the neatly stacked contents of the chest, the tartan patterns of Scotland.

Sibeal's treasures. Suisan's sacrifice.

Bending, she reached into the chest and withdrew one of the patterns. The four ancient sticks, dotted with colored pegs and bound together with ragged twine, were worn smooth at the edges. Margaret and Fiona Cameron had touched these patterns. Sibeal had, too. Suisan's heart plummeted at the thought, for she would be the last Cameron to hold the *Maide dalbh.*

A bleak silence reigned. As she lifted the heavy pattern and held it to the fire, she turned slowly, studying every face in the crowd.

"Nay," Nelly cried. "Sweet God in heaven, nay!"

The collective gasp was deafening, drowning out the hiss and whir of the hungry fire.

"St. Ninian preserve us," Flora MacIver wailed and fell to her knees. Others followed her lead.

Suisan hoisted the pattern higher. The wind caught the square of cloth which identified the pattern of clan Cameron. Taking a deep breath, she said, "Ten years ago, as she lay dying, my mother begged me to hide these patterns. I have done so. If any of you remember Sibeal Harper, you will recall her loyalty to the outlawed clans. She believed Scotland would rise again and defeat the English." Her arms aching, Suisan lowered the pattern to her breast.

Seamus Hay took a step forward. "Keepin' them's a hangin' offense, milady."

Murmurs ran like a brush fire through the throng.

"Aye. By harboring these patterns I have risked all your lives. But no more, for my uncle knows they exist. The demon is at our door. I will not give to the English what belongs to

Scotland alone. The tartans will live in our hearts where no Sassenach may tread.''

She brought the bundle to her lips, and as she placed a kiss of farewell on the symbol of one of Scotland's great clans, her eyes filled with tears which rolled down her cheeks. Sighs of regret and choked sobs of sorrow echoed through the awestruck crowd.

''Forgive me, Mother,'' she breathed. ''Let no—'' Her voice broke. Gathering her resolve, she closed her eyes for an instant and breathed deeply. ''Let no blood be shed this night,'' she declared, ''Scottish or English. *Mo righ's mo dhuthaich!*''

She flung the pattern onto the blaze. The fire roared, lapping at the offering, hungrily devouring the ancient wood. A giant hand seemed to rip the heart from her breast. Tortured moans rose from Scottish throats and hung in the frosty Highland night. Hats were doffed, heads were bowed as a wave of respectful murmurs rippled through the crowd.

''For God and King,'' someone cried, echoing Suisan's last words, the motto of the Camerons of Lochiel. An ironic motto, she thought, for the king who declared himself ruler of Scotland despised the *Maide dalbh* and all they stood for.

She felt a hand on her arm, and turned to see a sad-faced Flora MacIver. ''You've carried the burden too long, milady,'' she said. Then she plucked a pattern from the chest and cast a challenging look to the crowd. ''We're still Scots, and farin' better than most. Where's your courage, lads? Lassies?'' She tossed the pattern on the fire.

Nelly came next. Oddly silent, she, too, retrieved a pattern and threw it on the fire.

A line formed. Like mourners casting a last look at a loved one, they paused before the chest. Some touched the box and moved on; others cried as they gazed at the contents; a few followed Suisan's lead and threw a pattern into the fire. Dundas reached in and when he stood he cradled the last of the *Maide dalbh*, the pattern for the Royal Stewart plaid. Suisan's resolve faltered. A Cameron she might be, but the gaily woven plaid of Clan Stewart held a special place in the hearts of the Highlanders.

"*Virescit vulnere virtus*," His voice boomed across the yard. As if it were a caber, he held the sticks in the cup of his hands. With a mighty heave, he tossed the pattern onto the fire.

The crowd wailed and keened. Now that all of the tartan patterns were cast into oblivion, Suisan closed the lid on the empty box. The fire crackled and popped.

"They're coming, my lady," MacAdoo shouted from his lookout post.

All heads turned toward the gates.

The Dragoons had arrived.

Flanked by Dundas and Fergus, Suisan clutched the fringe of her shawl and walked to the gates. Crowded around the box, Flora MacIver comforted a nervous Lucy Saunders. Suisan held her breath and prayed to St. Margaret.

Frozen hinges groaned in protest as Dundas slid back the draw bars. The massive gates swung open. A gust of icy wind poured into the castle yard and fanned the roaring fire. Suisan stopped at the ominous sound of clinking harnesses and marching horses.

Out of the cold moonlit night marched an endless parade of red-caped Dragoons. A restless murmur spread through the crowd. Shawls were pulled tight; children were drawn close. Suisan longed for a glimpse of Myles's beloved face, for reassurance to still her quaking fears. She scanned the intruders and saw a civilian, but it wasn't Myles— it was Uncle Rabby. His eyes pierced hers. His face seemed a malevolent caricature of the man she'd once respected.

Unable to hold his hostile gaze, she searched beyond him and found Myles and Lachlan. Her eyes scoured them both, looking for injury or distress. She saw neither. Their heads held high, they looked out of place among all that English might. Myles's face shone with love and confidence. Lachlan emanated Scottish pride.

Satisfied that Myles was unharmed, her gaze turned to the leader. As the soldier moved toward her, the black plume on his helmet dipped and danced. The once grand feather was stiff with cold and ruined beyond repair. The legs of his white mount were caked with sticky tar from plodding through a peat bog. The animal's head was bowed with fatigue. Steaming lather coated its heaving chest.

When the officer and several of his men dismounted before Suisan, Rabby did the same.

"What do you want?" she asked him.

His face pulled into a sneer. "Justice, my dear niece. Only justice."

As she gazed into those familiar Harper eyes, Suisan felt no triumph that she'd beaten him, only sadness. He emanated greed and hatred, as bitter and cold as the north wind. He knew her secret; he'd come to do his worst.

"Suisan, Suisan," he said with an exaggerated sigh. "How have you come to this?"

Myles dismounted and hastened to her side. "Don't listen to him, love," he whispered. "The bastard thinks to try one last trick. We've naught to fear."

But the fear Myles scoffed at was like an iron band about her chest.

A saber rattled. The officer bowed to her. "Colonel Fletcher, Ma'am," he said. "And you are Lady Suisan, daughter of Sibeal Cameron and Edward Harper?"

Drawing herself up and clutching her bulky shawl with shaking hands, Suisan said, "Aye."

"Then I arrest you in the name of King George."

✨ *Chapter 23* ✨

A collective gasp sounded behind Suisan.

Myles put a protective arm around his wife. "This is outrageous, Fletcher!" he said. "Did you learn nothing in London?"

"Of course, he did," Robert said. "We're here to see justice done."

Lucy Saunders wailed, then shouted, "Send that dreadful man away! I'll not go with him again!"

Myles glared at Robert. "What lies have you told this time?"

With great confidence Robert said, "Lies? I think not, Myles. I offer the truth, as any loyal subject of the King is bound to."

"You wouldn't know the truth if it were dressed up in satin and paraded down Fleet Street on Saturday afternoon."

"Why, you detestable. . . ." Robert quickly composed himself. Turning to the officer, he said, "I defer to your command, Colonel Fletcher. Read the King's warrant if you must, but mark my words: you'll find what you seek this time. She's a traitor, cut from the same rebel cloth as her Cameron mother. And he—" Robert pointed to Myles, "conspired with her. He's as guilty as she."

Suisan lifted her gaze to Myles. He detected an apology there, and a deep sense of regret. But why? She tried to smile, but the effort yielded naught but forlorn grief.

"My love, my love," he murmured close to her ear. "You mustn't fear."

With a haughty flourish, the Colonel unrolled a beribboned document. Holding it at arm's length, he shifted to gain the greatest light from the fire. He drilled her with a gaze as hard and cold as Peterhead granite, and began reading the devastating mandate.

"By order of His Majesty, the King of England, and in accordance with the will of Parliament, I charge you, Suisan Harper, with the willful violation of the Disarming Act. . . ."

Scarcely registering the words, Suisan looked at Uncle Rabby. Bile rose in her throat. He had never loved her. He'd only used her.

Clinging to her husband's loving arms, she forced herself to turn away from her uncle's hateful stare. She thought of Myles in London. Myles in Beauchamp Tower. As her lawful husband, he would suffer along with her. But there would be no more suffering.

The fire roared behind her. Water dripped from the melting feather on the soldier's helmet. Firelight glowed yellow on the parchment.

". . . taken to the Tower of London until such time as you may be punished for your treasonous crime."

"He's bluffing, sweet," Myles whispered. "Let them search the castle. You've nothing to hide. Remember that."

"I know," she murmured, wondering if he could read the guilt on her face.

Robert edged closer to the Colonel. "You'd best restrain Myles Cunningham and that MacKenzie with him." He scanned the crowd. "My niece has become Cunningham's whore. One word from him and these Highlanders," he gestured at the angry crowd, "will not stand by and see you haul off their traitorous lady." He looked at Myles with disdain, as he added, "Or their so-called laird."

The tattered black feather bobbed, as the Colonel summoned a subaltern. Before Myles could protest or Lachlan could move, a redcoat yanked Suisan from Myles's arms. Three more soldiers thrust a trio of sabers against his chest. Calloused hands gripped her shoulders. The shawl fell open.

"She's child, sir," stammered the man holding her.

"Take your hands off my wife!" Myles bellowed, his face taut with anger.

"Leave her be!" Lachlan yelled. "Or I'll slit you from guggle to nether thatch."

The Colonel rounded on Lachlan. "Enough, MacKenzie." Lachlan clamped his mouth shut but his eyes glowed with menace.

The Colonel glanced at Suisan's belly, then shot a reproving glare at Robert Harper.

"Why do you care, Fletcher, for another rebel brat?" Robert sneered. "She's still a traitor."

"She's no traitor," Lachlan roared, grasping the officer's arm.

"Move that hand or lose it," the Colonel barked.

"Go easy, Lachlan," Myles warned.

Grudgingly, Lachlan obeyed.

The Colonel addressed Suisan. "Are you wife to Myles Cunningham?"

Of all the questions he could have asked, it was easiest to answer. Head high, she said, "Aye, I'm his wife and proud to be."

"Then I charge you both with the crime of treason."

Myles must have sensed her anguish. Addressing the men of Perwickshire, he said, "Hold fast, friends."

"Nay," shouted Gibbon MacIver, "they're English dogs. What would they be knowin' about our laws, our ways? We've seen their justice—the moor at Culloden ran red with it."

Murmurs of assent swept the crowd.

The officer raised a gloved hand and sketched a circle in the air. The mounted troopers moved to surround the crowd. Outnumbered, the men of Perwickshire paused in uneasy silence. Widow MacCormick teetered and would have fallen, but Rowena caught her. Nelly and Sorcha huddled together, their fair round faces shadowed with fear. Lucy wrung her hands, her eyes darting from Robert to Suisan.

"My wife is a woman of honor," Myles swore, lunging at Fletcher.

"I told you to contain him," Robert yelled.

"O'Brien!" the Colonel barked. "Bring the irons."

Suisan watched in horror as one of the soldiers produced a heavy length of chain. "Nay," she pleaded. But the metal bands were clamped about Myles's wrists. When the soldier withdrew, Myles's arms drooped under the weight of the chains dangling from the manacles.

"Wiggs! Bell! Dawson-Smith!" the officer snapped. Amid a rattling of sabers and a creaking of leather, the travel-weary soldiers appeared. They saluted smartly.

The Colonel turned to Robert Harper. "You said we'd find the tartan patterns."

"She knows where they are," Robert growled.

Suisan held her head high. *Let them look. All they'd find was an empty chest and a pile of ashes.*

"His Majesty does not execute anyone without proof," the Colonel ground out.

"I have no tartan patterns," she declared. Once Flora and the other women moved aside, he would see that for himself.

Chains rattled. "She speaks the truth," Myles said. "The *Maide dalbh* no longer exist, Colonel. They were destroyed. You've been deceived again by Robert Harper."

And you, Suisan thought miserably, *have been deceived by me*.

"Cunningham lies!" Robert bellowed, marching toward Suisan. He looked deeply into her eyes and said viciously, "Yield them, Suisan. If Fletcher can't hang *you*, he'll hang my brother's heir, and the father of that puling babe in your belly. Aye, they'll hang him here and now."

Sickened by his cruelty, Suisan stared into the face she had once cherished—the face so like her father's, the eyes so like her own. Uncle Rabby had been her link to the family she'd lost at such a tender age. She had respected him, she had loved him, and all the while he had hated her, and stolen from her.

Struggling to keep her voice even, she said, "Why, Uncle Rabby? Why? First my cloth, and then—"

"And then what, dear niece?" He looked as cold and callous as a stranger. "My brother denied me all but a stipend. And would Sibeal share the legacy? No! The bitch was poisoned by Edward and his lies. I got nothing from them."

"But they did give you something, Rabby," she said, feeling very small and very frightened. "They gave you me."

He laughed, a scornful, hurting laugh. "They gave me a millstone around my neck."

Suisan was dumbstruck by his cruel words. All gentleness and longing for his love fled. "You cheated me!" she railed. "I saw my cloth in London, fine cloth you peddled under the Strathclyde name. And I saw the miniature! And the forged letters! It wasn't enough for you to thwart the reputation of my weavers, but you led me to believe Myles cared naught for me." Anger pounded through her veins, thinning the sorrow, fueling her courage.

"And Lucy Saunders! For the love of God, Rabby—how could you tell me she was my aunt?" Suisan drew back her arm and slapped him with all her might. The contact jarred her arm but she welcomed the pain as a balm to her numbing fury.

He staggered. Growling, he raised his arm to strike her back. Quick as a roe deer, Lachlan leapt forward and grabbed Robert's arm.

"I'll kill you!" Myles roared, rushing toward them, trying to raise his weighted arms.

"Seize Harper!" The clipped order of the English Colonel bit like steel.

Then she was free, free to fall into Myles's manacled arms, free to feel his steely strength, free to hear his familiar voice. "I've got you, love," he crooned. "I've got you."

"Interfere again, Harper," the Colonel growled, "and you'll face the same end as the traitors."

"Traitors to what?" Myles demanded. "There are no tartan patterns at Roward Castle. There were no tartan patterns in London. You've been manipulated again by Robert Harper."

The Colonel took in every aspect of the situation. "Step away from him, my lady." He said to Suisan.

Behind her, the people of Perwickshire were fast becoming an angry mob. Before her, the fire leapt and sizzled to mythical proportions. Sabers sliced from English scabbards. Horses whinnied and pranced nervously. The Colonel raised his arm again as if to order his men to battle. Rage enveloped her. Rage and helplessness. When the Colonel drilled her with a hard stare, she moved a step away from Myles.

Nelly rushed to her side. In her wake lay a direct path to the Balticwood chest.

"There's your proof!" yelled Rabby. "That's the Cameron chest." He struggled against his captors. Suddenly, he broke free and ran toward the fire. "I told you they were here, Fletcher." Laughing wickedly, he grasped the latch. "When I'm done reporting to your superior, you'll be shipped off to dodge arrows in the Colonies. You'll rue the day you doubted Robert Harper."

He flung open the lid. He stared. A howl of rage escaped his lips.

"Tell the Colonel what ye found, Harper," jeered Dundas.

"Your scheme has gone up in smoke," Suisan whispered.

Frantically, Rabby searched the crowd as if looking for the patterns. At last his fierce gaze rested on the fire. "You burned them!" he shouted as he swung around to Suisan. "You wretched bitch!"

She held herself proudly, until she saw Myles's shocked face. "What the devil—" he bit out.

Lachlan laughed at the top of his lungs. "Who's the fool now, Harper?"

"Quiet!" The Colonel's face was set in stern lines. Firelight glistened on the sweat trickling from beneath his plumed helmet. He hesitated. Then slowly, he raised a gloved hand and motioned his men back. The people of Perwickshire grew still as the soldiers retreated.

Myles made a move toward Suisan. The point of an English blade made a move toward his neck. He stopped, frustrated. She had lied about the sticks in the well, but when the Dragoons threatened, she'd done what needed to be done. *You do not ken our ways.* At last, he fully understood the meaning.

"You know the patterns were in that box," Robert raged at the Colonel.

"I know of no such thing," said Fletcher.

"You fool! Have you forgotten her forebears? She's a rebel, same as all the Lochiel Camerons."

"Silence!" the officer snapped.

Robert obeyed, but the baleful expression in his eyes as he glared at Suisan promised vengeance. A pang of regret assaulted Myles as he gazed into those familiar eyes. Wearing a somber black frock coat instead of his usual foppish attire, Robert bore a striking resemblance to Edward. Yet the resemblance went only skin deep. Inside Robert was corrupt, black as sin.

Myles flayed himself for being so naive about Robert.

"Damn you, Harper," he shouted, wishing the words could wound that perverted bastard. "Damn you for hurting her so."

"Enough, Cunningham!" the officer commanded.

Suisan turned and even from a distance Myles could see the desolate expression on her face. Her lovely eyes, normally alight with joyous and mischievous laughter, were now glassy with tears and haunted with sorrow.

He ached to console his wife, for surely she was feeling abandoned and betrayed by her once beloved uncle. Yet, as he watched her proudly facing her adversary, he was reminded of Sibeal. His throat grew tight.

Sibeal's treasures had not rotted in that dungeon well. Suisan had burned them tonight. *She had lied to him again.* Depression thundered through him.

He focused weary eyes on her slumped figure, big with his child, and a pang of guilt shot through him. Dear God, he thought, how miserable she must feel. His anger and disappointment fled under a rush of concern. He silently begged her to turn to him.

He forgot the lie she'd told about destroying the patterns, forgot the pain the lie had wrought; both meant nothing in the face of her sacrifice. She had bartered the devices of the outlawed clans of Scotland to save his life, the life of a London orphan.

An orphan who now bore allegiance to her and her people.

Kingdoms had been lost, entire clans had died to protect what Suisan had guarded. Standing with an English blade poised at his throat, Myles ached with love for her and these people.

"You're weak, Fletcher," shouted Robert. "They've made you look the fool."

The Colonel whirled around. "Detain him!"

Half a dozen soldiers surrounded and subdued Robert. "Have you lost your wits?" he bellowed, flailing his arms and trying to evade his guards. "You're a damned coward, Fletcher!" he called out, straining against the soldiers who held him. "You had orders to hang them. She's a criminal. He helped her flout the King's law!"

Rage pounded through Myles. "You dare call us cowards?" he bellowed. "After what you've done to Lucy Saunders?"

Robert's nervous gaze fell on the addled woman, who still clung to Flora MacIver.

Myles had had enough. His wife was near to collapsing, and his people were growing restless again. Addressing the Colonel, he said, "Even as we stand here, my solicitors have presented the Lord Chancellor with proof of Robert Harper's crimes of embezzlement and kidnapping. For years, he's swindled Lady Suisan and her weavers."

Clasping his hands, Myles lifted his manacled arms and made a sweep of the stunned crowd. Only the dull rattling of heavy chains and the low roar of the fire broke the silence. "Robert Harper has duped these good Scottish people, and defiled the last thread of their Highland culture.

"The scoundrel purchased Lucy Saunders from Axminster Infirmary, then presented her to my wife as aunt."

He turned to Suisan, and his heart ached at the desolate expression on her beloved face. "Lady Suisan was but a child at the time. She believed his stitched-up tale of lies, and took the poor woman into her home. But worse, Colonel Fletcher," Myles glanced at the officer, "because of Robert Harper's treachery, my wife believed she would bear me a simple-minded child."

"He lies!" Robert's voice rose into a hysterical scream. "That mad woman is my sister, Ailis Harper."

Timidly, Lucy approached the Colonel. "I'm not his sister, although betimes I am confused. They'll remember me at Axminster. I tended the gardens there."

Looking into her eyes, the Colonel's expression softened. "I'll silence the scoundrel for good. Excuse me, Ma'am." He marched to Robert. Doubling a gauntleted fist, he cocked his arm and landed a roundhouse punch to Robert's jaw. On wobbly knees, Robert slithered to the ground. Pivoting, the Colonel walked to Myles.

Squaring her shoulders, Suisan approached them. Her lovely blue eyes were glassy with grief. Her voice was hollow when she said, "I swear this before God. You've no cause to hang me or my husband, sir. You may search this castle if you choose."

The Colonel removed his helmet. He stared at the chest,

then at the fire. At last his gaze moved to her. "No, Lady Suisan, that won't be necessary," he replied. "His Majesty's justice is done in the matter of the tartan patterns."

He raised his hand. "Scotland has lost enough this night." Then he turned to the soldier guarding Myles. "Release him. And put those irons on Robert Harper."

The crowd cheered wildly. The soldiers relaxed.

The instant the manacles were removed, Myles held out his arms to Suisan. She hesitated, doubt and despair clouding her eyes.

"Come, my love."

With an anguished cry, she lunged into his arms. "Oh, Myles, if you knew what I've done. . . ."

She cried softly as he rocked her from side to side, whispering, "I know, my love. I know."

The Colonel coughed nervously. Myles looked up. Over the top of Suisan's head, their eyes met.

"My apologies to you and Lady Suisan. Harper will be tried for his crimes and convicted, I can promise you that, for I will testify on your behalf."

Suisan raised a tear-stained face to Fletcher. "Will he go to prison?"

"Aye, Lady Suisan, that or he'll be deported to Georgia Colony."

"You can't deport me to the Colonies!" Robert screamed, shaking his head and struggling to stand. "No! Suisan! You can't let them."

A guard stepped forward. Robert fell silent.

Colonel Fletcher smiled ruefully. "Have you a place," he began haltingly. "A cell—where we can put Robert Harper until the morrow? And I would ask a measure of your fine Highland hospitality, for my men are cold and weary, and our horses hungry and tired."

"Suisan?" Myles whispered, desperate to ease her pain.

She looked up. Love shone in her eyes and a tremulous smile curved her mouth.

Myles went warm and feathery inside. "Have we hospitality for these men, and a cell for Robert?"

Her soft palm touched his cheek. "'Tis for my husband, the laird of Roward Castle, to decide."

Boundless joy erupted within Myles. She was the answer to a prayer; she was the essence of everlasting happiness. Grinning, and blinking back the tears, he turned his head and kissed her hand.

"Aye, Colonel Fletcher, we welcome English visitors at Roward Castle."

⁓ *Epilogue* ⁓

Perwickshire, 1782

Feeling as taut as the strings of a Lowlander's lute, Suisan wrung her hands and glanced again at the open castle gates.

Empty. And waiting.

She surveyed the yard. Lining the walls and chattering excitedly stood the castle's weavers and bonnet farmers, their work temporarily abandoned. Lachlan, his demure American wife and their huge family stood with hands clasped.

Nervously Suisan glanced to her left. "Sibeal, be still. You'll rumple your father's frock coat."

Her ten-year-old daughter went rigid on Myles's lap. "I want Cameron to come," she complained.

A trumpet blared. The level of chatter rose sharply.

Sibeal squealed and clapped her hands. "They're coming!"

Myles raised his eyebrows expectantly, but the anxious expression could not mask the pride shining in his warm brown eyes. Suisan's own pulse leapt. Sitting forward, her heart pounding, she turned to the gates once more. Like the early morning fog on Loch Eil, anticipation hung heavy in the air.

Then she saw him. Her son. Cameron Cunningham.

Sitting proudly atop a magnificent blood-bay Clydesdale, the next laird of Roward Castle passed through the gates.

Feminine sighs and masculine murmurs cooed through the throng. Suisan smiled, for no better accolade suited her handsome son. His broad shoulders were covered by a massive sheepskin coat, his powerful legs swathed in fine leather boots.

"Mama, why isn't Cameron smiling?" asked Sibeal.

Suisan felt the first stab of disappointment. His mission had failed.

Cameron had gone to London to bargain with King George. In the past year, her son had spent every farthing of his portion. All in the name of Scotland. During the last months he had bargained with naught but that irresistible smile and winning manner.

As Suisan's spirits plummeted, the cheers of the Highland people rose. They didn't understand—yet.

Cameron guided the Clydesdale toward her. Suddenly, he stopped.

The crowd stirred fitfully.

Her throat grew thick at the courage he displayed. A tenacious optimist, Cameron had been certain he could convince the King to allow the Scots their tartans and bagpipes once again. She wanted to run to him, to hold out her arms and soothe his tattered pride. But she couldn't; Cameron was no longer the sensitive lad. Nay, he was a brave and independent man of one-and-twenty years.

Standing up in the stirrups, he raised both arms. He smiled that heart-stopping smile. Through teary eyes, Suisan watched him unfasten his cloak.

"Cameron, we've missed you," Sibeal called.

He blew his sister a kiss, then brought his hand to his neck. With a flick of his wrist, he cast aside his coat.

And revealed a tartan.

Suisan's heart surged, for Cameron was wearing the first Highland plaid seen in Scotland in thirty-six years.

"A Cameron, a Cameron, a Lochiel Cameron!" the people roared.

Pride, honed by the long years of repression and sharpened by a mother's love, pierced Suisan's heart.

For the first time in her life, she gave thanks to an English king. George III had rescinded the ban on Highland tartans.

"MacAdoo!" Cameron bellowed, signaling his sergeant-at-arms forward.

MacAdoo Dundas, his flaxen hair shining in the autumn sun, his grin as wide as Comyn's moor, guided his mount to Cameron's side and drew rein. He, too, tossed off his cloak. And revealed the bagpipes.

Soon the haunting skirl filled the castle yard—and the hearts and minds of the people of Perwickshire.

"And how," Myles demanded, putting Sibeal on her feet, "did you manage to weave that tartan? I know you burned the pattern over twenty years ago."

Holding his stern gaze, Suisan said. "Aye, I burned the *Maide dalbh*—all of them."

"You're sure this time?" he demanded, leaning closer.

Suisan took a deep breath. "Aye, I'm sure. I copied the sett of the patterns to parchment, but it's not the same as having the *Maide dalbh*." There. It was said.

His eyes locked with hers. "You saved all the designs and didn't tell me? All these years, you let me think the tartans lost to you?"

"Aye, my love," she confessed. "That I did."

"You lied to me."

Uneasiness crept up her spine. Hoping to distract him she cried, "Look! Oh, Myles, see how the red and black favor our Cameron." She turned to her son, who was drawing a buxom and ebullient Sorcha Burke up into the saddle. "He has your fair coloring, except for—"

"Suisan . . ." Myles growled, not fooled by her change in topics.

Ignoring his tone, she continued lightly, "Except for his eyes, you see. They're mine. But his volatile temper is another matter, of course. He's much like you in that."

"I do not have a temper!" Myles roared, bringing a giggle from Sibeal. "Go to your brother, Sibeal."

Brown eyes twinkling, she did not budge.

He turned to Suisan. "Where were we?"

"I was just saying, my darling, that you don't have a temper." Suisan kissed his bearded cheek and winked at their daughter. "You're as gentle as MacIver's spring lambs. 'Tis but one of the reasons I love you."

GET
LOVESTRUCK!

AND GET STRIKING ROMANCES FROM POPULAR LIBRARY'S BELOVED AUTHORS

Watch for these exciting romances in the months to come:

August 1990
THREADS OF DESTINY by Arnette Lamb

September 1990
BY INVITATION ONLY by Catherine Craco

October 1990
PASSION'S CHOICE by Gloria Dale Skinner

November 1990
EMERALD FIRE by Laurie Grant

December 1990
AND HEAVEN TOO by Julie Tetel

POPULAR LIBRARY